SOMETHING MIGHT BE GAINING ON YOU

By

George D. Schultz

*We at Trafford believe that it is the responsibility of us all, as both individuals and corporations,
to make choices that are environmentally and socially sound. You, in turn, are supporting this
responsible conduct each time you purchase a Trafford book, or make use of our publishing services.
To find out how you are helping, please visit www.trafford.com/responsiblepublishing.html*

*Our mission is to efficiently provide the world's finest, most comprehensive book publishing
service, enabling every author to experience success. To find out how to publish your book, your
way, and have it available worldwide, visit us online at www.trafford.com*

Trafford rev. 7/23/2009

 www.trafford.com

North America & international
toll-free: 1 888 232 4444 (USA & Canada)
phone: 250 383 6864 ♦ fax: 250 383 6804 ♦ email: info@trafford.com

The United Kingdom & Europe
phone: +44 (0)1865 487 395 ♦ local rate: 0845 230 9601
facsimile: +44 (0)1865 481 507 ♦ email: info.uk@trafford.com

ONE

The scene was almost out of a thirties melodrama:

Janet wiped at the perspiration, cascading down her forehead and temples. It was no help. The back of her hand and her forearm were just as sweaty. Trying to keep the salty fluids from searing her reddened eyes was proving virtually impossible. Literally impossible. The fact that her shoulder-length blond hair was matted down – and wringing wet, soaked in sweat – was not helping.

Why did it have to be so beastly hot?

Even in Detroit, the temperature had been known to reach into the nineties, from time to time. But, this was the eighth or ninth or tenth day in a row. Ridiculous!

Janet, of course, was not alone in her discomfort. Three other women also manned the brutal, steam-spewing, garment pressers – each machine operating at 80 pounds of pressure. Certainly, the never-ending gush of boiling steam had to be every bit as wearying to the other three.

The lone air-conditioned oasis, in the entire, massive, washing/drying/pressing area – which comprised three-fourths of the **Truesdale's Laundry & Dry Cleaning** building – was a small cubicle of an office, used by Horace Truesdale himself.

The prissy, balding, little man, in his mid-sixties, was also a throwback to a thirties melodrama. He was the diametrically-opposite image of what an employer was supposed to be, in the enlightened, union-conscious, Motor City of the seventies..

However, in 1979, Detroit was in the throes of a major recession.

Although they were seldom seen in "Motown", Toyotas, Nissans, Hondas, Audis and a plethora of other foreign cars had invaded the United States.

The cost in jobs to southeastern Michigan had been devastating. **Ford, General Motors** and **Chrysler** had closed many of their antiquated plants – and had laid-off workers by the thousands.

In such an economic wasteland, Horace Truesdale was king! He paid minimum wage to new employees. To all new employees. Even after six months, raises were exceptionally difficult to come by.

During the halcyon days of the fifties and sixties, Truesdale had operated a much smaller plant – using, for the most part, relatives as workers. Included among those "devoted" employees had been his wife and three sons.

As the bottom had begun to fall out of the local economy, Truesdale had been able to expand – hiring from the legions of the unemployed. He'd paid those people whose unemployment compensation benefits had been exhausted. Grudgingly paid them. Paid them what amounted to a starvation wage.

The tight labor costs allowed Truesdale to begin to bid on some of the larger industrial jobs – encouraging prospective clients to terminate existing arrangements with other laundries. Laundries which had suddenly found themselves incapable of competing in such an arena. The additional business, of course, enabled the penurious Truesdale to expand and to take on more workers – also, of course, at minimum wage.

The policy had worked like a charm.

His employees consistently referred to Truesdale as "Eb" – taken from the well-known "Scrooge" character in Dickens' *A Christmas Carol.*

Janet squinted through the blinding perspiration at her watch. It was almost impossible to see the hands. Moisture had collected under the crystal. It seemed to indicate that the time was just shy of 3:00PM.

"Two more lousy hours," she muttered aloud. "Thank God."

As she lifted the pale-blue skirt from the steam presser – to examine her handiwork – Janet saw Mr. Truesdale approaching. He was followed by two other men.

Wonderful. Just what I need. Now what did I do?

"Mrs. Bolton?" Truesdale's traditional nasal tone seemed especially irritating. "Mrs. Bolton, these men are here to talk to you."

Janet made a heroic attempt at forcing a smile. It didn't quite work.

The two visitors appeared to be police officers. One, obviously, from the West – as evidenced by the cowboy boots and *Stetson* five-gallon hat. Even in plain clothes, law enforcement people all seemed to have some sort of special "look" about them.

"Yes, gentlemen?" Janet's voice was awash with fatigue.

"Mister Truesdale," observed the red-headed man, without the boots and *Stetson*, "I had no idea it'd be anywhere near this crowded … or this hot … out here. Like we said before, it'd be much better if we could use your office to speak with Mrs. Bolton."

"He's got that right," agreed the other stranger, with an emphatic nod. The latter's dark-blue, western-cut, suit was in stark contrast to the light-grey business suit, worn by the red-headed man. "Out here," he continued, "is just plain no good."

"Very well," replied Truesdale, looking as though his best friend had just been murdered.

With obvious reluctance, he led Janet and the two men to the tiny enclosure in the far corner. The air-conditioned office was a panacea. By the time the quartet reached the cubicle, both strangers were perspiring profusely. Almost as much as was Janet.

Horace Truesdale forced as much of a smile as he was capable, and muttered, "I'll leave you people here to talk. When, you're done, please be sure to close the office door. Don't want to waste the coolness, y'know."

"Yes, Sir," answered the man in the *Stetson*. "Be a crime to let this cold air get out there … where those folks are. We'll be sure and closer 'er up tight. Thank y'all."

Once Truesdale had left, the westerner turned to Janet and drawled, "Miz Bolton, my name is Deputy Claiborne. Deputy Busch Claiborne." He produced a badge. "I'm from Tarrant County," he advised her. "Down in Texas, Ma'am."

"Fort Worth, Mrs. Bolton," explained the other man with a smile. A warm, reassuring smile. "I'm Detective Francis," he went on. "Steve Francis. Michigan State Police. Deputy Claiborne, here, is up from Fort Worth ... investigating a case. A case ... one we think you might be able to help us with. We'd like to ... "

"How would I know anything about something going on in Fort Worth?" she asked, impatiently. "I've never been there in my life. Nowhere even close."

"Well, Ma'am," drawled Claiborne, "a fella name of James Bolton has been there. Would that be your husband, Miz Bolton?"

The color drained from Janet's till-then-flushed face. Still reeling from the oppressive heat, that proved to be no simple accomplishment.

"Why ... why ... why, I ... I haven't seen my husband in something like seven years. Eight years, maybe. Uh ... well ... yes. His name was Jim. James." She sighed – and almost seemed to deflate. "Would you mind telling me what this is all about?" she asked, wearily.

"Well, Mrs. Bolton," began Detective Francis – in his most soothing voice, "I'm afraid we have some bad news for you."

"Bad ... bad news?"

Janet was aware that her voice was rising – in volume and pitch.

"Yes, Ma'am," nodded Claiborne. "There really isn't any easy way of tellin' you this, Miz Bolton. Your husband is dead."

Janet was astonished at her lack of response to the deputy's macabre, fateful, words. It was obvious that both officers had expected a more pronounced reaction. When none was forthcoming, both were visibly relieved.

"How ... how did Jim die?" Her words were slow. Deliberate.

"Well, Ma'am," answered Claiborne, "he was kinda involved in somethin' that wasn't quite legal."

"I assumed as much," responded Janet, her voice devoid of emotion. "I don't understand, though, what light I could shed on anything. I haven't seen Jim in seven ... maybe eight ... years. As I told you before. I've never been much further south than Toledo."

"Uh ... you see, Miz Bolton," drawled Claiborne, "Mister Bolton was mixed up in some kind of drug dealin's. He was kinda a front for the real drug people, down there."

Janet sighed deeply. Closing her soft blue/green eyes, she wished that the other officer would say something. She was certain that Deputy Claiborne was doing his best, in a most-difficult situation. However, Detective Francis seemed more sensitive. More attuned to her feelings – to her flood of emotions – at that point.

She ran her hands through her still-stringy hair – and wondered how she could know of the stranger's feelings! Especially when the man had said so little.

"When you say 'real drug people', Mister Claiborne," she asked, "do you mean that Jim was not actually involved with pushing the drugs themselves? What I guess you'd call 'drug dealing'?"

"Yes, Ma'am. That's correct. They set him up as a respectable businessman ... in a respectable business ... is what they did."

"I can ... I can see where that'd be possible. Jim always kind of presented himself as a respectable businessman," Janet observed, dryly. "Always came off that way."

"Now," continued Claiborne, "he didn't use the name James Bolton. Took a whole lot of lookin' and scratchin' ... for us to really come up with that name. And ... until a couple days ago ... we really weren't sure that the name meant anythin'. The name he used down there was 'James Arthur'."

"'James Arthur'?"

"Yes, Ma'am. Name mean anythin' to you?"

"No, Sir." Janet's voice was barely audible. "I've never heard the name before. Jim's middle name wasn't even Arthur. It was Richard."

"Well now, Miz Bolton," responded Claiborne, "we'd sure admire for you not to be coverin' up anything now. I mean, the man's dead ... and I'm sorry. Truly sorry. But, I got to tell you: We've had lots of problems already with this investigation. And we'd really admire not to have any more of 'em ... if you know what I mean."

"I doubt that Mrs. Bolton knows anything about this, Busch," interjected Detective Francis. "In fact, I'd bet the rent money that she hasn't the foggiest idea ... about any of this."

Janet was totally exasperated.

"Well, of course I don't," she snapped. "Of course I don't."

She pulled her slender body up to its five-feet, four-inch, height and – through clenched teeth – asked, "Would one of you gentlemen please tell me what the hell's going on? Because, I ... for one ... am damn sick of all this beating around the bush. Now what is it? What is it that you're trying to say? Or ask? Or accuse?" Tears began to trickle down her cheeks. "What do you want of me?" she rasped.

"I'm sorry, Ma'am," soothed Claiborne. "I'm awful sorry. Didn't mean to upset you none."

"What do you think you're doing?" Her voice seemed to have risen another pitch or two. "What is it you think that you're doing ... if not upsetting me?"

"Well, Miz Bolton," replied the man from Texas, "we seem to have discovered most of Arthur's ... Mister Bolton's ... connections down there, in Fort Worth."

"As well as in Dallas, Houston, Austin, San Antonio ... and, probably, Laredo," added Steve Francis.

Claiborne nodded.

"Most of the stuff," the deputy expanded, "the dope ... seemed to be comin' into the country through Laredo. That's down on the Mexican border, y'know. Now, Arthur ... your husband ... he seemed to be sendin' out money. All over the country. Some of it came to a fella up here. A fella at some bank ... here in Inkster. And some more money ... well, it came up to some other fella. Up in Pontiac. Now, Miz Bolton, you can't even imagine ... I don't guess ... just how much money's involved here."

"Deputy Claiborne's been up here for a couple days now," said Detective Francis. "Your name entered into the investigation just yesterday."

His voice was such a welcome – such a soothing – respite from grittiness of Busch Claiborne's drawl. Well-meaning – but, gritty.

"That's right," agreed the Texan. "Like he says ... just yesterday. Now, there's nothin' personal, Miz Bolton, but we did do a little checkin' around ... and we found out who you are and where you live and what you do for a livin'. And let me say right here and now, Miz Bolton, that we ain't never thought nothin' bad about you. We don't think you've been involved. Nothin' like that."

"Right," chimed in Steve Francis, with a reassuring nod. "For one thing, if you'd been caught up in the drug thing ... getting any kind of percentage of the massive amounts of money that were involved ... there's no way you'd be slaving away in a damnable sweatshop like this

God-awful firetrap. I don't know how you do it. I honestly don't. I doubt that I'd be able to cope … more than three or four minutes. The heat out there is … why, it must be almost debilitating!"

"Almost?" responded Janet, with a forced smile.

"And our friend, Mister Truesdale," continued Steve, "is certainly not J. Good-body Sweetpants." He was referring to a saintly cartoon character in the *L'il Abner* comic strip.

"No." Janet's smile became less artificial. More genuine. "He's most positively not."

"Anyway," said Steve, "Deputy Claiborne did want to talk to you. See if you'd ever heard the name 'James Arthur' … or if you might know either of the guys. The ones from Inkster or Pontiac."

The man from Fort Worth withdrew a small, Spiral, notebook.

"Now, lessee," he mumbled. "One of 'em's name is Pierce Hawkins. White male. About thirty-five-years-of-age. Blond hair. Slight build. He's the guy from Pontiac. The Inkster fella … his name is Willard Mallow Culp. Black male. Mid-twenties. Slight Afro hairstyle. Wears a moustache and goatee … so we understand."

"I've never heard of either one of them, Officer Claiborne." Fatigue was fast beginning to drain Janet. Even the cool of the little enclosure seemed to be losing its effect. "I've never heard the name 'James Arthur' either," she continued, sighing deeply. "The only thing I can tell you officers is that … about seven or eight years ago … my husband deserted! Left! Deserted me and my children."

"How many children?" Steve's voice indicated more than strictly official curiosity. More than a public servant's obligatory concern.

"Five," she answered wearily. "Five kids. The youngest two … my little boys … why, they were nothing more than babies! Infants! Literally! One was two-years-old. The other one was only ten months."

Busch Claiborne managed to stifle the epithet! It had been a monumental struggle.

"You mean," rasped Steve, "that you never heard from your husband again? That he just picked up … and … and … and left you? You just never heard from him? Ever again?"

"That depends," replied Janet, her voice much firmer than mere seconds before. "Depends on what you mean by 'not hearing' from him. He sent us money ... always in the form of money orders. Those kind of money orders ... the ones that look the same ... no matter where you buy 'em. They always came from different parts of the country. I never understood that. Especially, if he's been in Fort Worth for all those years. I don't know how he could've gotten around ... all over the country ... like that."

"Well now, Miz Bolton," advised Claiborne, "there's lotsa mail-forwarders out there. All across the U.S. of A. Wouldn't surprise me none ... if he didn't just use lotsa those people to mail his money orders from their different towns. That way, you don't never know which way they're gonna come from."

Once more, Janet sighed deeply.

"Yes," she answered. "Yes, I guess I never really thought of that. I imagine that it does make sense, though. But, the money did come. All those years, the money did come. Nothing really stupendous. I don't know how much money he could've been making ... from what you gentlemen say he was doing. But, I certainly ... "

"He was makin' plenty, Ma'am," interrupted the Texan. "He was damn well takin' in plenty. Puh-lenty."

"Well," muttered Janet, "he didn't really send me all that much. The amount increased ... somewhat ... through the years. Not much, but it increased. I always had the feeling that they were all cost of living adjustments. That'd be so like Jim. He was very meticulous."

"Yep," agreed Claiborne. "That he was. Fortunately for us, no one's infallible. If he'd-a been perfect, in what he was doin' ... why, we'd still be lookin' for him. In point of fact, if he'd-a been perfect, we still wouldn't know that he even existed. As it was, it turned out that he made one or two little slip-ups. And that kinda, y'know, it allowed us to get onto him, a little bitty. We started diggin' around ... nosin' around, y'know. One thing kinda led to another."

"How did my husband die, Mister Claiborne?"

"Well, now ... we don't exactly know, Miz Bolton. Well, that's not quite true, either. We do know that he got himself shot."

"That would seem to be sufficient to kill him," she observed, cryptically.

"Yes, Ma'am. That's not what I meant. What I meant was ... was that we don't know who it was who killed him. Hadda be people ...

ones, y'know, that he was dealin' with. Y'see, he was launderin' their money. Launderin' a good bit of their money. Had been launderin' it … over a good many number of years. Now, we found him one night … almost two weeks ago. Be two weeks … lessee … the day after tomorrow. He was sittin' in a car … in the parkin' lot of a bar. Out in the unincorporated area of Tarrant County. Three-fifty-seven magnum did the trick! Four bullets. Don't b'lieve the man ever knew what it was that hit him. I'm sure that he'd of known whoever it was that went ahead and did it, though."

"Why on earth would they want to kill him?" asked Janet. "Especially if he was doing such a wonderful job for them?"

"Well, to their way of thinkin', Ma'am, it got to where it wasn't such a wonderful job anymore. Your husband … he slipped and goofed up in a couple areas. And we kinda got on to him. Ever' body knew, I guess, that we were on to him. They must-a decided, I reckon, that they couldn't afford to have him go ahead and get himself caught. Have him face a grand jury, y'know. Go to trial … or whatever. So, they just went on ahead … and had him shot. Easiest thing in the world, for them … beggin' your pardon, Miz Bolton."

"He's right," added Steve. "Those people have no conscience. Absolutely no principles. None at all. None! Just as soon blow you away … as look at you. Totally amoral."

"We got a line on almost ever' one that 'Arthur' … uh, your husband … had any dealin's with," advised Claiborne. "Ain't gonna do 'em no good … what they did to your husband. They're still gonna get themselves had."

The very-practical, down-to-earth, impact – the obvious monetary reality – was just beginning to dawn on Janet.

"You say that Jim died about two weeks ago?" she asked the man from Texas.

"Yes, Ma'am. Be two weeks … in just a couple days."

Janet's sigh was louder than she'd intended.

"It's about a week-and-a-half ago that I got my last money order." Her voice was barely audible.

"I'm sorry, Miz Bolton," soothed the deputy. "I truly am. But, I don't really b'lieve that I'd be lookin' for any more money orders. From any part of the country."

A sinking feeling was rapidly engulfing Janet. The news of her husband's death, while a shock, was not nearly as devastating as she would've imagined. Jim had, after all, ceased to be a part of her family – a part of her life – years before. In a manner of speaking, he had "died" – the day that he'd deserted her and her children.

On a more pragmatic note, Janet had been barely "making it" – on her "four glorious dollars an hour" wage. One of the loftiest stipends paid by the sainted **Truesdale's Laundry & Dry Cleaning**. It was an ever-so-reluctant tribute to her length of – and devotion to – duty.

She'd been barely surviving on the money she was earning at the laundry – augmented by the semi-monthly money orders from Jim. There would, of course, be no more money orders.

Steve Francis – obviously moved by Janet's despair – put one of his large, craggy, hands on her shoulder. The gesture caught her by surprise. His touch – the suddenness of it – made her jump. Or was it merely the suddenness? As opposed to the touch? It was unlike any reaction she'd experienced – well, since she was a child, attending one of her favorite "spooky" movies.

"I ... I'm sorry, Mrs. Bolton," the bemused Steve was able to blurt. "I didn't mean anything ... anything bad. It's just that I ... "

"No," responded Janet, immediately. "No, it's all right. I didn't mean to jump out of my skin, like that either. I ... I just guess ... I guess that it's all of this coming out of the blue like it has ... "

"Tell me this, Miz Bolton," interrupted Claiborne. "Was it that y'all really expected Mister Bolton ... that he'd ever come back?"

"Yes. No!" Tears were welling up once more. "Oh ... I don't know! I guess I didn't. Well, there for a while, I suppose I did. At first, anyway. Then? After awhile? I ... I really don't know."

"You have five children, Mrs. Bolton," rasped Steve. "That's amazing!"

Janet tried to smile. It was a losing battle.

"Not really," she said, at length. "They just ... well, they all ... they just came."

The deputy from Fort Worth stifled a laugh.

"I don't think that's what Steve meant, Miz Bolton," he managed to advise. "I think he meant that it's amazin' that you were able to support 'em all. To support all those kids. Support 'em that well. And for that long a time."

"I don't know how well I've supported them, Mister Claiborne. There've been a lot of awfully austere meals around our house. Sometimes the kids had to wear second-hand clothes. Stuff that was out of style. I really didn't do all that well, you know."

"We went by your house, Mrs. Bolton," interjected Steve. "It's not as if your kids have been growing up in some kind of hovel. Some tarpaper shack or something. You have a really nice house. I mean that ... sincerely. A really nice house."

Janet shrugged. She was surprised that her eyes had dried once more.

"It's just a house," she answered. "I guess that ... yeah ... it's a nice house. We've been there ... gosh ... almost fifteen years now, I guess."

"Your kids, Miz Bolton," inquired Claiborne. "Your children. How old are they?"

"Well ... let me see. My oldest ... Barbara ... is seventeen. She just turned seventeen. Patti's fifteen ... and Joanie'll be fourteen. Next week in fact. The two boys ... Robbie and Rickie ... they're nine and eight."

"Good Lord!" exclaimed Steve. "I don't know how you did it."

"I didn't really do it, Mister Francis. I had lots of help."

"I'm sure that's true," replied Steve. "No one ... I don't care how rich or independent he or she is ... no one can do it all. Not on their own. Not completely. We all need a helping hand from time to time. In many areas."

"That's awful deep, Steve," laughed Claiborne. "When was it that you became a philosopher?"

"I'm no philosopher." Steve's answer was without a trace of humor. "It just happens to be true. No one ... but no one ... can make it alone. Not completely."

"Well," responded Janet, "I'd have to give most of the credit to my daughters. Especially Barb and Patti. Barb just simply took over. Almost as though she was the head of the house ... in some cases. She ... and then Patti ... they've practically raised the boys. And now that Joanie's old enough, she's getting into the act. Barb slings pizzas at a hole-in-the-wall pizza parlor. Patti baby sits every kid in the neighborhood, these days. So, it's really fallen to poor Joanie, nowadays, to wind up taking care of the boys, most of the time."

"I'm sure that they're remarkable kids, Mrs. Bolton," rasped Steve. "But, then, they've got a remarkable mother."

<u>Did he actually say that?</u>

Janet blushed. The more she struggled to come up with an answer – a halfway intelligent response – to Steve's totally-unexpected compliment, the more frustrated she became. Her face took on an even deeper shade of crimson. Independent of the fearsome heat, from which she'd so recently escaped.

"Now look what you went and did," observed Busch Claiborne – grinning at Steve. Turning to Janet, he smiled. "Miz Bolton," he said, "I can't remember when I've been quite so taken with a woman ... with any person. And I can't ... for the life of me ... remember the last time I ever saw a woman go ahead and blush.""

"I hate to blush," muttered Janet. "It's so embarrassing."

"It's also very refreshing," observed Steve. "Especially in this day and age."

"What're you gonna do now, Miz Bolton," asked the deputy.

"I guess that ... for the present ... I guess the main thing is that I'm going to have to tell my children. Tell them that their father is dead. That he'll never be back. I've thought about the possibility of having to do that ... from time to time, anyway. But, now that it's actually coming to that, why, I don't know if ... "

She began to cry, softly.

"Mrs. Bolton," began Steve, "is ... is there anything I can do?"

"No. No, Sir. No. Thank you very much. You and Mister Claiborne have been most ... most kind. Most understanding. I'm ... I'm sorry if I may have snapped at you."

"No, Ma'am," replied the Texan. "You were ... b'lieve me ... you were just fine. We're sorry ... both of us are real sorry ... that we had to be bearin' such bad news."

"This may sound insensitive, Mister Claiborne," said Janet, "but, in a way, it's been a help. At least I'll have some closure ... for whatever good that'll do. I'll, at long last, know what's going on. Or what's not going on. I won't have to go on wondering if every car that stops in front of the house is Jim's. When the phone rings, I won't have to worry … or hope … that it'll be Jim on the other end. At least that part's been resolved. For better or for worse."

"I … I think we understand, Mrs. Bolton," soothed Steve. "Look! If there's ever anything that I can do … "

Janet put her hand on Steve's forearm – surprising herself. Shocking herself.

"That's sweet of you … nice of you … Mister Francis." Her voice was a husky whisper. "But … right now … I think that I'll just go home. Try to find a way to tell my children the news. The news … that they have no father."

"Beggin' your pardon, Miz Bolton," observed Claiborne. "But, it don't seem to me as though they had much of a father in the first place."

TWO

It was fully one week later, before Janet could call a full-fledged family meeting – "At The Summit" (also known as the dining room table).

On the evening of Steve Francis' and Busch Claiborne's visit, she'd, of course, advised her children of their father's demise – but, on a piecemeal basis. She was only able to speak with her children whenever – and wherever – the opportunity would've presented itself.

She'd believed that the most difficult task would be to inform her young sons. But, that had turned out to be the "easiest" undertaking of all. The boys had absolutely no recollection of their father. He'd been just a form of reference to them. A nonentity.

The three daughters? It had been almost impossible to determine their reaction – despite a goodly amount of discussion. Well, difficult to gauge their reaction – with one exception. Barbara's response had been an out and out shocker. Certainly no one – none of the children – had been moved to tears. None of this was quite what Janet had expected. Well, in truth, she'd not known what to expect. Still, Barbara's "insensitive" response had been most disquieting.

It was always very difficult to assemble the entire family. Barbara and Patti seemed, always, to have so many commitments. To a point, so did Joan – who'd just observed a rather reserved 14th birthday. Despite the fact she'd not seen her father – in virtually half her lifetime – his death had still cast a bit of a pall over the anything-but-festive occasion.

On "Summit" Wednesday night, Janet had invoked "Marshall

Law". Attendance was mandatory. The six members of the Bolton clan convened at the huge, ponderous, antiquated, oak table.

Robbie and Rickie – nine and eight respectively – had badgered their mother, for the entire evening, in an effort to determine what was to be discussed. Their three older sisters, of course, already knew.

"Gang," Janet began, tentatively, "we've got a rather hairy situation to talk over. It has to do with your father's death."

Silence filled the room.

When she'd informed the kids of Jim's demise, a week before, the news had elicited a genuine rise from only one of the children. Barbara. The eldest.

"I'm glad," Barbara had stated flatly.

"Barbara! You don't mean that," responded a shocked Janet.

"You bet your fanny I mean it!"

"Barb! He is … he was … your father. As such, he's due a certain amount of respect. A certain amount of love."

"Not from me. Listen, Mother … what you say may be true. Probably is true. But, whatever respect or love … or anything else … that James Bolton was due from me, was, as far as I'm concerned, all used up! And then some! If he'd have come back to us … even a day or two before he died … and sincerely apologized for running out on us, why then, I'd probably have to agree with you. Not only would he be due some respect … some love … but, I probably would've forgiven him. Eventually, anyway. But, you know as well as I do, Mother, that he was never coming back. Like, ever. Never going to come back. As far as I'm concerned, he simply turned his back on his responsibilities. On his wife. On his children. Well, I'm one of his children. When he did that … as far as I'm concerned … he stopped being my father. It was his choice. It sure wasn't mine. He took the coward's way out. Go sneaking off … in the dead of night. Even a rattlesnake'll warn you before he strikes!"

At the "Summit", Janet's eldest had remained equally as vehement regarding her feelings toward her father. Neither her tone nor her scorching criticism of James Bolton had, in the slightest, abated.

The bitterness in Barbara's voice – even after a week's time had elapsed – probably should not have come as such a shock. She had become a most mature young woman! She'd had no choice. She'd been forced to grow up. Years before. And she had grown up – almost immediately. Matured far beyond her years.

The other four children had, as stated, taken the news much more stoically. It was almost as though they'd never heard of Jim Bolton. Of course, for Robbie and Rickie, it had not been an act.

Janet had advised her children, on the night when she'd informed them of Jim's death, that it would be possible to have their father's body flown from Texas to Detroit, for burial. Otherwise, the authorities in The Lone Star State would handle the interment.

"I think we should leave him down there," Barbara had volunteered – her words clipped. Brutally crisp. "He didn't want to be here in life. I can't think of one good reason for him to be here … in death."

Again, the venom had been a real shock!

Joan hadn't been quite so sure. "It might be nice to see Dad … one last time," she'd said, sighing deeply.

"Joanie," Barbara had responded, in the same brittle, staccato, manner, "he's been dead for almost two weeks now. Do you think that he's going to be anything like what you remember? It's best to just let it go! Let it be! Remember him whatever way you want to remember him. But, to see him now … " Her brown eyes had softened. "He's not going to be the same. Not look the same." Then, the granite in her voice had also lessened. "I don't care what kind of preservatives … or whatever it is they use … it'd be terribly, terribly, morbid. It'd be … well, it'd be God-awful macabre."

"I agree with Barb," Patti had offered, at length. Her voice was scarcely a whisper. "It's hard for me to say this, but I agree with Barb. I'm supposed to have been his favorite … but, still, I have no use for the man. I've … I've seen … seen what his leaving has done. What his sneaking out has done … done to you, Mom."

"That's right," Barbara had chimed in. "It's amazing that you don't look eighty-years-old, Mother. You know, when you dress up … and put on the right makeup and have your hair done … you look about thirty. But, that's no thanks to your husband."

The final two words – "your husband" – had been a bitter hiss!

A tear had trickled down Janet's cheek.

"That's because I love you … all of you," she rasped. "Most of it, though … most of the responsibility … has fallen on you, Barb. And on Patti and Joanie too. But, Barb? I can see now ... where you went from being a little girl to a grown woman! In about a day-and-a-half." She'd begun to cry. "I don't know what I'd have done without you! Without all of you! Each and every one of you!"

That had been a week before. The family, at that point, had agreed to let the State of Texas assume responsibility for the burial of James Bolton.

<<>>

Janet had called the "Summit" meeting for the express purpose of discussing the Bolton's precarious financial situation. James' demise had, by then, become past tense The money aspect hung heavily over the table. Barbara decided to take the offensive:

Before Janet could launch into the subject, she said, "Mother, I've been thinking. It's time ... long past time ... that you quit that damned sweat shop of a laundry. There've got to be other jobs. How long have you been there? Three years? That's long enough! Too long! Too damn long!"

"It has been quite a while," acknowledged her mother – sighing heavily. "Quite a while."

"You've got to get out of there, Mother,' pressed Barbara.. Just quit! Quit! Get out of there!"

"That's easier said than done." Janet's second sigh was even more pronounced.

"You'll find something else," assured her eldest daughter. "We'll be all right. I've got my job at **Galiano's** and so it's not like ... ". She forced a smile. "We'll be all right." The young woman's voice was filled with resolve.

"Oh, Barb! I couldn't do that! My God! Especially now that the money won't be coming anymore from your ... coming from Jim. I just couldn't ... "

"Yes, you could!" It was Joan. Her tone – the undiluted resolve in the 14-year-old's voice – was a big surprise.

"And another thing," injected Patti, "you're going to have to start dating more. It's time you started being able to let it hang out a little. The three of us ... Barb, Joanie and I ... we're just about grown, y'know. It's time that you … that you started thinking of … of yourself a little."

"Yes," agreed Barbara. "And if it were me, I'd sure look for someone new and wonderful … and different. Someone beside Fletcher Groome."

"I would too," resumed Patti. "Definitely different from Mister Groome. But, one way or another, you've got to start dating more. Getting out more. I realize that Barb has her job at the pizza place … and I baby-sit all over the place. But, that's no big deal. None of it's a big deal. If we're not around, Joanie can sit on Robbie and Rickie. Heck, they're no problem."

"That's not what you tell us," said Robbie, with a laugh.

"Shaddap, Kid," snapped Patti, in mock anger.

The "Summit" was taking on a dimension that Janet had not anticipated.

"Look, gang," she said. "I appreciate all this. But, who's going to take out a decrepit, old, thirty-six-year-old woman? Well, besides Fletcher Groome, I mean."

"A thirty-six-year-old beautiful woman," Barbara corrected. "Mother, you're really very pretty. Positively gorgeous, as a matter of fact. Really! You are! You've got a beautiful face and figure. I just wish I was as chesty as you are."

"Barbara! You … you're … you're … "

"When you dress up," Barbara persisted, "and do your hair and do your nails, you're probably the most beautiful woman I've ever seen."

"I'm the luckiest woman you've ever seen," responded Janet. "Lucky to have you guys. But, listen. I'm sure you know that … by the time I ever drag my fanny home from work and … "

"That's exactly why you've got to get away from that da … from that laundry," said Patti. "By the time you do drag your fanny in here at night … every night … you're too pooped to participate. You've got to get yourself an office job, Mom. Working your bottom off … over that stupid presser every day … well, that just doesn't cut it."

"Office?" responded Janet, "I don't have any office skills. I can't type. I can't take shorthand. I can't do any of that good stuff. I don't have the money … or the time, really … to go to school and learn it, either. Especially now with the thing that's happened to … ah … that's happened down in Texas."

"Mother," snapped Barbara, "you're going to have to improve your self image. You can go as far as you want to take yourself. And I'm not just quoting from some stupid self-help book. It's the God's-honest truth."

Janet smiled. "You know," she reflected, "there are times when I have a hard time … trying to figure out who's the mother and who's the daughter around here. I appreciate what you're saying, Barb. Appreciate what you're trying to do. But … "

"I'm not trying to do anything, Mother. It's got to be you. You're the one who's got to do something. Anything! Just as long as it's something you do … out of the damnable clutches of that damnable old reprobate at the damnable laundry!"

"Why don't you take Mister Groome up?" asked Patti. "Take him up on his offer? His offer to put you through secretarial school. Or accounting school. Something … anything … like that. That could be an answer. A really important answer. I'm sure you'd be able to pay him back … eventually."

"I don't like Mister Groome," said Rickie. "He's too nice."

"Yeah," agreed Robbie. "No one's that nice."

The girls, obviously, weren't the only ones mature beyond their years.

<<>>

On the Saturday following the "Summit", Janet parked her 10-year-old Maverick in her driveway. Wearily pulling herself up and out of the car, she made her way toward the side door of the house.

The weather had broken! Finally! After almost three weeks of inferno-like temperatures! The heat wave – cumulatively – had taken its toll. Despite the fact that the mercury had not risen above 70 degrees that day, Janet couldn't remember having been more exhausted. She fervently hoped that the next day – Sunday, her day off – would be sufficient to allow her to "recharge her batteries". Take a nice, relaxing, cool, bath. That usually helped.

She let herself in – and stood on the landing, halfway between the kitchen and the basement. The six steps up to the first floor seemed, at that point, insurmountable!

"Hi, Mom!"

She could hear Rickie – barreling through the dining room and into the kitchen. In a matter of seconds, he stood at the top of the steps – with his arms extended.

"Do I get a kiss tonight?" he asked.

"Hoo! Do you ever!"

With renewed vigor, Janet climbed the steps and lifted her youngest son into her arms.

"My goodness," she exclaimed. "You must've gained a hundred-and-fifty pounds since this morning, Ol' Boy."

"Nah. Maybe a hunnert."

She kissed him and put him down.

"A hunnert it is," she told him. "Where is everybody?"

"Oh, Robbie's across the street ... at Clark's house. Joanie's watching some mushy story on tee vee. Barb ... she went to work. I don't know where Patti is. I didn't see her in a long time. She could maybe be sitting ... probably over at Murphy's."

Janet leaned down and kissed him again – on his forehead.

"My gazette," she said, with a fatigued smile. "I'm sure glad that I've got someone around here ... someone who knows what's going on all the time."

"Aw, Mom. Everybody knows what's going on around here."

"Yeah. All except me, half the time. I swear ... there are times when ... "

She was interrupted by the doorbell.

"Wonder who that can be," she muttered.

"See?" observed the boy, brightly. "I don't know that."

Janet strode through the dining room, cut through one corner of the living room – and descended the one step into the tiny vestibule, just inside the front door.

As she attempted to focus her gaze through the tiny glass "peephole" in the ponderous wooden door, Joan said – almost as an afterthought, "Oh, hi Mom."

"Hi yourself, Baby."

Janet was still unable to identify the visitor – standing outside on the porch.

"Damn," she muttered. "I'm just going to have to break down, one of these days … and have my eyes examined."

She gave the through-the-door surveillance up as a bad job – and flung the portal open! Just as Detective Steve Francis was ringing the bell a second time.

"Oh! Mister Francis! Won't you come in?"

"Thank you, Mrs. Bolton. I hope you don't mind the intrusion."

"Why … uh … no. Not at all."

Janet invited the officer inside, closed the door and led him into the living room.

"This is my Number-Three Daughter, Joanie." Then, turning to her little boy, she said, "And this is one of the two loves of my life … Rickie."

Steve shook the boy's hand.

"Boy," he enthused. "That's quite a grip you've got there, Young Fella."

"That's what Mister Groome always says," answered the boy – in disgust.

"Fletcher Groome … an acquaintance of mine …. is 'too nice'," explained Janet with a smile.

Joan arose from the sofa and walked to where the trio stood.

Steve shook her hand – and decided to withhold any assessment of the strength of her handclasp..

"Enchanted," he said. "You're almost as pretty as your mother. And, really, I'm not being 'too nice'. I call 'em as I see 'em."

Joan – clad in an oversized shirt and tight-fitting, faded, jeans – bowed.

"I doubt that I'm really that pretty, but, thank you anyway," the young woman said at the height of her exaggerated curtsey.

"I swear, Joanie," observed Janet. "You're going to rip your jeans doing that."

"MUH-ther," responded Joan – in feigned exasperation.

She returned to her seat – in front of the television.

"What can I do for you, Mister Francis?" asked Janet.

"Well … if you wouldn't mind … I've got something that I'd like to talk to you about, Mrs. Bolton. Is there somewhere where we can … uh … could …uh … speak in private?"

"That serious?"

"Well, no. Not really serious. Nothing really earthshaking. But, if we could, maybe, duck into the dining room, I'd … "

Janet bent down and kissed Rickie once more – then, swatted him lightly on the bottom and said, "Scoot, Love".

As the boy seated himself on the floor – next to his sister's legs – Janet and Steve adjourned to the dining room. She offered to put on a pot of coffee, but he declined. They seated themselves at the huge table.

"Now, what is it, Mister Francis? Something to do with Jim? I thought that … well … that everything had been pretty well taken care of."

"Oh, it has," he replied with a sheepish grin. "Everything's in order … with regard to that. Uh … I'd be grateful if you'd call me Steve."

"Oh, I doubt if I could do that."

"Well, Mrs. Bolton, truth to tell, I'm not here in an official capacity."

"You … you're not? I … I don't understand."

"Again, I wish you'd call me Steve."

"I really don't know if that'd be proper," she answered, her voice dripping with wariness. "Now, what is it I can do for you?" She wished she'd phrased the question differently.

"Well, this is rather personal, I know. But … "

"Look, Mister Francis! I don't know what kind of … of … uh … signals I may have been sending to you, at the cleaners, but I assure you … "

Steve burst into laughter! Gales of raucous laughter! His crooked smile seemed to light up the whole room. He ran his right hand through the unruly shock of red hair – a goodly portion of which had curled down over his forehead. He was clad in a pair of khaki slacks and a matching shirt. His tanned arms seemed to bristle with muscular energy – as he succeeded in throwing his mop even further out of kilter. His laugh was infectious.

"It's nothing like that at all, Mrs. Bolton! Honest! What I'm trying to say … and doing it very badly … is that I have to admit that I've been quite upset with the fact that you have to work for that damnable cutthroat at the laundry. No one should have to work that hard! Not under those conditions. Especially not for the piddling little bit he pays! Not in this day and age! Not in some damn sweatshop like that!"

"Oh ... Mister Francis. Look, this is all very flattering. But, you see ... "

"Anyway," he interrupted, "my brother-in-law ... he has this management consulting firm. Over in one of those office buildings, over by Northland Shopping Center, y'know. It's right on Greenfield. Just off Eight Mile Road."

"Your ... your brother-in-law?"

"Yes. My sister's husband. He mentioned to me yesterday ... he said that ... well, he needs a receptionist. Says he can't find a halfway decent receptionist. Can't find one ... and keep her, anyway. It's a really busy switchboard. I guess the position is quite demanding. Plus, there's a steady stream of visitors ... in and out of the joint. The job would probably pay thirty-five- or forty-bucks-a-week more than what I'm guessing you're making over at Ol' Simon Legree's dandy little palace. And ... ta-DAH! It's five days a week. Not the six that you sweat ... ah, perspire ... out now."

"Why ... why, I don't know what to say. I mean, I'm sorry, if I thought ... "

Again, Steve's crooked smile.

"No problem, Mrs. Bolton," he responded. "I should've come to the point quicker. Much quicker. I'm the one who's sorry. Especially if I scared you. Really especially ... if I offended you."

"There are times," she sighed, "times when I really don't know if my head is screwed on properly ... or not. I'm ... well, I'm ... I'm flattered, Mister Francis."

"Steve? Please?" He clasped his hands in a praying position. "Please?"

She laughed. "Steve," she said softly.

"There, now. That wasn't so bad ... wasn't so painful ... now. Was it?" I was beginning to wonder if you might need a shot of Novocain or something ... just to get you to be able to pronounce my first name."

"No ... Steve. Perfectly painless. Please ... call me Janet."

"I thought you'd never ask."

"Steve, look. This is all very nice of you. And, believe me, I do appreciate your concern. I really do. But, I … well, I couldn't … I could never take a job like that."

"Oh yes you could!" The voice came from behind Janet! It was Joan! "Mister Francis," the young woman persisted, "we've been trying to get my mother out of that damned … "

"Joanie!"

"I'm sorry, Mom! But, that's what it is! Exactly what it is! It's a damned laundry! Working for a damned old reprobate! Who won't pay her any damn money."

Steve laughed. "Our little girl is growing up," he observed.

"Yeah," muttered Janet. Too fast … our little girl is growing up."

"Oh, Mother!" Joan sounded almost exactly like Barbara. "Mister Francis? My mother would be very good … very, very good … at that receptionist job. She just doesn't quite know it … yet."

"Nothing like the Bolton household," groused Janet. "All kinds of privacy."

"I think your daughter's right," said Steve. "You would be very good at it. Like she says … you're just not aware of it yet. Janet, listen. They take girls, fresh out of high school. Brand spanking new. Put 'em right on the reception desk. I'm not kidding."

"What's wrong with girls out of high school?" asked Joan – in mock anger.

"Oops!" responded Steve. "Nothing! Nothing that I've seen around here, anyway."

Turning his attention back to Janet, he advised, "Look … they train you. They're not going to throw you to the wolves. But … for heaven's sake, Janet … give yourself credit. You're a smart lady, and … I can tell … you've got a great telephone voice. You'll pick it up. They're certainly not going to turn you lose … not till you've mastered the thing."

"If I ever would master it. If I ever could master it."

"My God," he replied – louder than he'd intended. "I ought to put you across my knee! Of course you'll master it. Look! This guy needs a receptionist … like yesterday! Why don't you go over and see him? Monday morning? He could … "

"Oh … I couldn't do that! I'd have to give notice at the laundry … and that would take … "

"Give notice?" It was Joan again. "Give notice?" she repeated. "What has that old son of a … ?"

"Joan! That's enough! I will not have you using that kind of language!"

"Well," offered Steve, "the language may be a little ripe … but, Joanie's got a point. A more-than-valid point. She's got the right idea. Why should you give notice to that clown? Any notice at all? What's he ever done for you?"

"He gives me a paycheck."

"Yeah," snarled Steve. "Some damn paycheck."

"He hasn't given you zilch, Mom … and you know it," agreed Joan. "He hasn't done one thing … not one hairy thing … for you! Ever!"

"She's right," chimed in Steve. "Whatever piddling little stipend he may have given you … if you can even call it that … he's more than extracted! Extracted several times over! Many times over … in blood, sweat and tears!"

"Especially sweat," interjected Joan.

"You owe him?" mocked Steve. "You owe him? Hah! You owe him zilch! Zilch … as Joanie so graphically put it."

"It's not right," maintained Janet. "It's just not right. You always give notice."

"The only notice that old clod deserves," said Joan, with a sardonic laugh, "is a notice … in suppository form!"

"Joan! That's enough! Enough!"

"I hate to keep siding with your daughter," said Steve, with his patented smile, "but … "

"Oh, you don't hate it at all," observed Joan.

"Okay," he agreed, laughing heartily. "You win. I don't hate to keep agreeing with your daughter. Janet … you've got to listen to me! Listen to the both of us! Listen to someone! You've simply got to get out of there! Get out of that damned laundry!"

"Who writes your material?" asked Joan, with an overdone chuckle.

"You guys are ganging up on me," muttered a perplexed Janet.

"Seems like the only way to get through to you," answered Steve.

"Look. You owe this jerk nothing! Zero, do you owe him! Nada! Zilch! Now, really Janet. I want you to go over to Northland … on Monday morning … and talk to this guy. His name is Richard Brock. He's CEO of the company. I've already spoken to him about you. I can practically assure you that he'll hire you. Not only that … but, you can go right to work. Start right then! Monday morning! Be on the ol' payroll … right from the git-go! He needs the exact type person … the exact type that you are … Janet. As for this rubby-dub at the laundry? Tell him to go take a flying leap!"

"I … I don't know," mumbled Janet.

"Mom!" said an exasperated Joan. "Do you want me to get Barb and Patti involved? If you think that Mister Francis and I are ganging up on you … "

"Okay! All right! I surrender! You've got me outnumbered! Surrounded! And … and everything else!"

"Good," responded Steve. "That way … you won't be making a liar out of me."

"A liar? A liar out of you?" asked Janet. "What're you talking about?"

"A liar," he affirmed. "I sort of told him that you'd be there … at nine o'clock, Monday morning." He reached into his shirt pocket and retrieved a mint-green business card. "Here. Here's his card," he said, proffering it to Janet. "Rich is a pretty good egg. You'll like him."

"Well, I certainly never thought … " she began. "I mean, I never figured … I don't know how to thank you, Steve."

"I do," said Joan.

She walked from behind her mother's chair to where Steve was seated. Leaning down, she kissed him on the right cheek.

"Thank you, Mister Francis," she half-whispered. "Thank you so much. I can't thank you enough. And … if you think that I'm making a big deal out of it … it's a good thing that my sisters aren't here! We'd bury you in kisses!"

Steve, obviously, was deeply moved. "You're a beautiful woman, Joanie," he rasped. "A fine young woman. And that young fella in the other room … he's quite a guy too. I'm sure that you must all be a real source of strength to your mother.

A tear trickled down Janet's face. "You'll never know how much," she said. "You'll never know how much strength."

<<>>

The following day – Sunday – Barbara, Patti and Joan took over!

Barbara drove the two boys to the movie theaters, at one of the shopping malls. She gave them instructions – and sufficient money – to attend three different features, effectively removing them for the entire afternoon and evening.

Patti gave Janet a permanent wave – early in the morning. Then – ever the artistic one – she restyled her mother's hair, later in the afternoon.

Joan took care of the housework – and the laundry. (Sunday was always laundry day in the Bolton household – a "busman's holiday", if you will – on Janet's only day off.)

Once Barbara had dropped her little brothers at the movies, she made her way to one of the ladies' smart shops, in the mall – and, with the money that she and Patti had been able to scrape up, bought her mother a brand new dark-blue, shirt-waist, dress, with full skirt, white collar and a hint of white cuffs at the bottom of the short, puffed sleeves.

On her way home, Barbara snapped to the realization that Janet was without a pair of "really nice shoes" to go with her new dress. She made an abrupt U-turn – and sped to the pizzeria where she'd worked for the past 15 months. She succeeded in persuading the owner to give her an unheard of salary advance.

Then, she returned to the mall – and selected a pair of beautiful dark-blue leather pumps. She was delighted to find that she had enough money left – to buy a matching purse.

On her way back to the parking lot, Barbara – hurrying past an exclusive lingerie shop – stopped in her tracks. She was captivated by the sight of the beautiful, frilly, black bra – a marvel of engineering – on display in the store's window. She didn't have nearly enough to buy the sexy undergarment.

Aware of the fact that her mother hadn't bought new undies in ages, Barbara looked, longingly, at the bra. Janet, she knew, had worn the same "tired" brassiere for months – washing it out, each night, in the bathroom sink, and hanging it over the shower curtain rail. It had, of course, reached a point where – to put it charitably – it had seen better days. Numerous better days. Clenching her fists, Barbara marched out to the parking lot, retraced her route to the pizza restaurant and "conned" the owner into extending her a second advance! <u>Really</u> unheard of!

Back at the shopping center, she bought the lacy, "front loader" bra – and a pair of sheer, almost-transparent, black panties.

At 6:00PM, that night, the three daughters came to a horrible realization: Their mother was without a really decent pair of pantyhose!

By scrounging up every smattering of change they could find – and bringing into play eleven soft drink bottles to return for the deposit – the young women pooled their resources. Joan walked up to the corner convenience store – to remedy the situation.

"Gonna be a long, cold, week" observed Barbara, with a smile – while her mother was downstairs in the kitchen.

"I know," agreed Patti. "I've got a couple babysitting gigs lined up for Tuesday and Wednesday. And the Mullets … they usually go out on Friday. So, I'll be able to contribute … when I get my gold-digging little hands on some of that money."

"I … I just wish that I'd be able to contribute a little more," said Joan, sadly. "I wish that I could contribute … you know … to the thing with the dress and stuff."

"You do more than your share," replied Patti.

"That's right," agreed Barbara. "You get stuck with the boys all the time. Don't think we don't appreciate it."

"Appreciate what?" asked Janet – as she swept into the bedroom.

"Oh," responded Patti, "we were just talking about how Joanie never gripes about getting stuck with the boys. Gives Barb and me a lot of leeway."

"You guys amaze me," said Janet. "You work out everything … just everything … among yourselves."

She seated herself at her dressing table – and began to brush her hair.

"I'll … I'll never be able to thank you girls enough for today," she acknowledged. A tear trickled from each one of the much-more-alive blue/green eyes. "Not for only today," she continued, "but … well, you know what I mean. The perm, the hairdo, the manicure, the clothes. Oh, Barb! That's the most beautiful dress I've ever seen! Even when your fa … when Jim … was around, I never had such a beautiful dress! And the matching shoes and bag! You guys are spoiling me rotten!"

"You didn't mention the racy underthings," observed Patti.

Janet grinned. "They're positively scandalous," she conceded. "I may not be able to concentrate tomorrow. I'll be thinking all kinds of obscene thoughts … with all that sinful stuff next to me."

"Well," said Barbara, "that'd be a step in the right direction."

"Barb!" In spite of herself, Janet was taken aback. "What do you mean by that remark?"

"You know full well what I mean, Mother. It's time that you began to date. Like I said before. Like I said … many times … before."

"Right," agreed Patti. "And with someone other than Fletcher Groome."

"That's for sure," chimed in Joan.

The direction that the conversation was taking, was leaving Janet totally bemused.

"I … I thought you guys liked Fletcher," she managed to respond.

"Oh, he's all right," replied Patti.

"He's an old poop," declared Barbara. "Mother … listen, Mother. You need romance! Romance!! Not din-din at some fency-schmency restaurant. There's nothing wrong with dinner at a glamorous joint, of course. But, you need the whole package, Mother. Don't you think we see how misty you get at those schmaltzie old, lovey-dovey movies? The ones on TV? You need to meet … maybe even seduce … some handsome guy! One who'll send you flowers. One who'll write you poetry … even if it's bad poetry. Hold hands with you all the time. That sort of stuff. Pat you on the fanny … every now and then."

"Barbara!"

Janet set her hairbrush down upon the vanity. What her oldest daughter had said was – to her – shocking!

"What do you mean?" She barely recognized her own voice. "What do you mean, Barb? The thing about some guy patting me on the fanny's bad enough. But, I should seduce someone? Seduce some handsome guy. What do you mean by that?"

"Oh really, Mother. You know exactly what I mean."

"Yes," murmured Janet. "Yes. Yes, I do. That's what really frightens me. I do know exactly what you mean." She was totally nonplussed.

"Come on, Mother," pressed Barbara. "In so many ways, you're just like a little kid. A little girl. You're like *Rebecca of Sunnybrook Farm* or someone. And … in other ways … you're an old crone. We're not telling you to sleep around! God forbid! What we're saying is … or what I'm saying, anyway … is that it's about time that you devoted some attention to romance. You're certainly not going to hop into the sack with the first guy who comes along."

"Unless, maybe, it's that Detective Francis," added Patti, with a broad grin. "Joanie says he's quite a hunk."

"Big mouth," responded Joan.

Janet felt akin to one of those small steel balls in a pinball machine – one that's buffeted about the entire game surface. By her own daughters! The conversation had taken a turn in a direction with which she was terribly uncomfortable!

"I … I don't believe this," she muttered. "I don't believe I'm hearing this. I'm barely on a first-name basis with the man."

"Well," said Patti, "they say that a trip of a million miles … they say that it starts with the first step!"

THREE

Barbara, Patti and Joan had done their work well. Janet walked, tentatively, into the offices of **Brock & Associates** – at 8:55 AM the following morning – looking as beautiful as she'd ever appeared. More importantly, she felt more beautiful than she'd ever felt – in her entire life. She was positively radiant!

The interview with Richard Brock – a tall, slender, distinguished-looking, man in his late-forties, with medium-length, salt-and-pepper hair – went well. Brock's personal office was the approximate size of an airport. His desk could easily accommodate a rugby game. His three-piece, medium-grey, suit exuded well-tailored elegance. His booming voice was empty-barrel deep – and incredibly attention-getting. His presence seemed to fill every nook, cranny and desk drawer in the immense, mahogany-paneled, lavishly-furnished, office.

Steve Francis had obviously spoken with his brother-in-law – at length – about Janet. And about her situation. Her new employer alluded to her state – albeit almost in passing. A couple "throw away" lines. Steve's advocacy of the newest applicant had obviously swayed Brock. Swayed him significantly. Janet's beginning salary was more than generous. The stipend would be almost $50.00 more than her average weekly wage at the laundry! And for one day's less work! An entire weekend – off! Incredible!

There was, of course, the daunting task of actually learning the duties of receptionist. How to wrestle with the actual switchboard itself. At first sight, this modern wonder of seventies communication was terribly intimidating. Extraordinarily complex. The circuitry appeared to rival the instrument panel of a spacecraft.

Janet had managed to convey, she believed, an air of efficiency, during the interview. Once it came to put-up-or-shut-up time, though, she began to envision that her entire facade was fast evaporating! The image that she was striving so hard to deliver appeared to be going up in smoke!

The interview – and subsequent "Cooks Tour" through the massive suite of offices, conducted by Richard Brock, personally – took almost the entire morning. The company's headquarters encompassed every inch of the fifth floor of the modernistic15-story building.

At 11:45 AM, Janet found herself seated next to Peggy Sullivan – a young woman of 24, who'd hired in some 18 months before. She'd come aboard as a receptionist – but, was merely filling in on the board. She'd long-since been promoted. Had "graduated" to become a computer operator – some five months after going to work for **Brock**.

She'd lost none of her proficiency at the switchboard. Her ability to deal – in a pleasant and efficient manner – with the many visitors was also undiminished.

The entire situation seemed overwhelming to Janet!

"Oh, Peggy," she gushed. "I don't think that I'll ever be able to manage that thing! It's a monster! Dear Lord! It scares the dickens out of me."

"I'm sure it does," Peggy laughed. "It scared the dickens out of me too. Fact is … to be blunt … it scared the hell out of me. At first, anyway. But, you'll get the hang of it. No problem. You'll be all right. In a day or two … you'll be working the whole desk! Working it like a pro. You have an exceptionally nice telephone voice. Very sexy, don'tcha know. I wish that I could sound like that. Sound even half that sultry. Plus, you're a very beautiful woman. Mister Brock likes women with big breasts. The better to greet visitors. And that sexy voice is merely the maraschino cherry on top of the sundae."

"Sexy? My voice? Very sexy? Me? My voice? I think you may be listening to someone else. I never considered my voice … "

"It's very sexy. You could just about see Mister Brock's eyes light up … and say 'Tilt'! Just because of that voice of yours … and your body.

He'll deny it, of course, but he loves to have a busty woman ... with a really sexy voice ... as his receptionist. There are times when I think that it was probably my boobs that got me hired. Of course, I had to perform on this thing ... on this stupid switchboard ... to keep the job. The ol' boobies were a pretty good "in" for me, though."

"But ... but ... but, me?"

"Trust me, Janet. It's sexy ... your voice. And ... as chesty as you are ... you can't miss. Believe me."

"I ... well, if he thinks so ... I guess that's good. I do feel a little uncomfortable with it though. I hope he didn't hire me ... just because of my body. Or my voice. Dear Lord, Peggy! I'm so ... so ... well, I feel so overwhelmed. Especially overwhelmed, if Mister Brock is hiring me for ... well ... for all the wrong reasons. I just don't think I'll ever be anywhere near as good as you are ... when it comes to handling everything out here. When does your body ... or your voice ... stop canceling out ineptness out here?"

"Listen, Janet! You'll do fine. I can tell. You're not nearly as flaky as some of the girls we've had."

"Heavy turnover?"

Peggy nodded.

"That's putting it mildly," she advised. "You wouldn't believe some of those winners, we've had in here. I can't imagine where Mister Brock dug up some of those dingbats. Half of those ding-a-lings. Well, some of 'em, he hired strictly because they did have big boobs. I'm sure of it."

"Oh," groused Janet. "I can't tell you how excited that makes me. Big boobs."

"You'll do fine. I'm sure that he spotted a real potential in you. I think he's had his fill of full brassieres ... and empty heads. There are so darn many people out there ... people who just don't want to work ... these days. They like the paycheck. Love the paycheck. But, they have a hard time actually getting off their butts. Hard time doing whatever the work that's required ... to actually earn that paycheck."

"Well, of course, I'm willing to do the work. I just don't know if I'm ... if I'm qualified. All I've ever done is ... is to work in a stupid laundry."

"So I've heard."

"You ... you've heard? You've heard? From who? Whom?"

Peggy patted Janet on the knee. "We've got a topnotch grapevine in this here now establishment. The CIA should be that efficient. Half that efficient. Don't worry, Janet. You'll do fine. Like I said, I can tell. The switchboard ... it looks scary. Scary as hell. That's because there are so many lines ... so many extensions. But, see? You work 'em one at a time."

"You make it sound so easy."

"It is. It really is ... once you get your feet wet."

At that point, the switchboard seemed to light up like a night baseball game, at Tiger Stadium. The avalanche of calls effectively ended the conversation – and watching Peggy's hand glide, so effortlessly, over the keys served only to feed Janet's stark fear of total unworthiness.

Plus that, she had something else – a couple something else's – to worry about:

What had Steve said to Richard Brock? Further, what had Mr. Brock said to his employees? And which employees? Peggy had obviously gotten her "information" vis-à-vis Janet's previous job situation from someone. Her previous job situation – and how much else? And about what?

Did she get hired because of her potential efficiency in manning the switchboard? Or because of her bustline? Or her supposed sexy voice? Or was the whole thing a favor to Steve?

Would the company "carry" her – if she proved incapable of performing the duties of a receptionist? The receptionist was, of course, the company's first direct contact with the public. An overwhelming monster of a responsibility, as she was beginning to realize..

And Steve! He'd seemed so – so friendly. So in her corner. But, how much had he shared with his brother-in-law? Or with anyone else at her new place of employment? How much would've been speculation? How much would've been pure gossip? To say that all of this was a "bother" would be an understatement. Akin to stating that Marie Antoinette had died of a "sore throat".

How should she handle Steve's entire involvement in getting her on with this new firm? Getting her out of that damned laundry? She smiled inwardly. She'd come down on Joanie for using that same expression – vis-à-vis her former place of employment. A bit ironic, she thought. Shouldn't be that humorous.

The interior chuckle lasted a few seconds. There were, obviously, bigger things – much bigger things – about which to worry: Was Steve all he was cracked up to be? All he appeared to be? Why would a perfect stranger be so concerned about the well-being of another perfect stranger? It would be nice – it had been nice – to think that his motives had been nothing but of the most lofty pureness. But, who could tell? Who could really tell? On a more realistic – less idealistic – level, what could be in it for Steve?

<<>>

At 12:15 PM, Peggy left – to go to lunch. She was replaced by Gloria Tapp, a humorless woman of 38 – also from the computer room. Twenty pounds overweight, Gloria looked infinitely more than two years Janet's senior. Especially, decked out as she was in the ill-fitting, floral, pants suit – which emphasized the broadness of her derriere.

Gloria made it abundantly clear that she disliked her job as a computer operator – and especially abhorred the fact that she was required to cover the reception desk for even one hour, on any given day. The hour's stint with Gloria was excruciatingly long – and laborious – for Janet. The woman in the pants suit made absolutely no attempt to instruct her, to involve her in the operation – or to even speak to the newest employee.

Once Peggy had returned from lunch – and Gloria had made her way back to her bailiwick – an attractive brunette, of 34, emerged from the inner offices. Her expensive, well-tailored, business suit screamed "taste" and "class".

"Hi," she smiled at Janet. "My name is Terri Baun. Are you doing anything … anything outrageous … for lunch?"

"Uh … well, not really. I … uh … my name is Janet Bolton."

"Yes, I know." Terri's voice was low-pitched. Sultry. "I'm happy to meet you, Janet. I kind of run what we laughingly call the clerical staff around these parts. At least, that's what they lead me to believe."

"Oh. Oh yes. Mister Brock mentioned you. Quite frequently."

Terri smiled – and delivered a throaty laugh.

"I'll bet he did," she replied. "Look ... would you care to join me for lunch?"

Janet had all of seven cents in her purse. She would be unable to pick up her final check from the laundry, till Wednesday. She'd planned on simply sitting through her lunch hours on Monday and Tuesday – the better to absorb as much as possible about her new calling.

It didn't require much insight to note Janet's discomfort. Terri was able to see what the problem was. She'd been made aware of Janet's precarious financial situation. Peggy had been correct: The grapevine at **Brock & Associates** was state of the art.

"It's kind of a tradition around here," proclaimed Terri, with a broad, warm, smile, "that I take the new girl to lunch. My treat."

"That's ... that's awfully nice of you, Terri. But, really ... I don't think I ... "

"Sure you can. It won't be anything opulent. Believe me. Against my religious convictions. I'm a devout tightwad. But, I would thoroughly enjoy breaking a bit of bread with you. Feel adventuresome?"

<<>>

Terri had proved to be the perfect hostess. At lunch, she'd put Janet completely at her ease. She gave her newest hireling a whole host of thumbnail sketches. Rundowns of those with whom she would come in contact, on a regular basis. She impressed Janet as being positively brilliant. In a way, she seemed downright inspirational.

"After you get a buck or two ahead," she'd advised, once the waitress had set the second cups of coffee in front of the two women, "I'd think about maybe taking a course on computers at night. There are plenty of good schools around ... and it doesn't have to cost you an arm and a leg. It'd be a heavy-duty arrow in your quiver. You'd enhance your chances for promotion. Immensely. We're going to be converting the whole office ... over the next few months ... to an entirely new computer system. They keep using these frightening words like 'all-encompassing' ... and they're not lying. Very sophisticated. Very efficient. If you could become proficient in word processing or data processing ... or both ... I'd have to think that'd give you a leg up." Laughing, she held up her hand. "I know," she added. "That sounds obscene."

"It sounds more scary than obscene."

Terri took another sip of coffee. "I can tell more than a few things, Janet," she said. "I can tell that you've got all kinds of ambition. Not like a lot of the dippy ladies we've gotten to work here. Especially at that reception desk. I'm sure that … just like Peggy … I'm sure that you're not going to stay at that position all your life."

"I … I don't know, Terri. They may not want me at that receptionist position for very long. I don't really know if I'm going to be able to master it."

Terri delivered her patented throaty laugh. "You don't give yourself enough credit, Janet," she admonished. "Of course you'll master it. Of course you will. And faster than you imagine. A woman like yourself … with a little ambition and a little pizzazz … can move right up the corporate stepladder in this company. Make more money than you ever dreamed possible."

"I'm already making more money than I ever dreamed possible. Been making it for all of five or six hours now."

"It's only the beginning, folks! Only the beginning," responded Terri, in her best overdone carnival barker's voice. "Janet, you can do really well here. Really well. Now, don't think that you've got to run right out … go schlepping out … tonight, and enroll in some fangled computer course. Not just because I've suggested it. That's all it was. Just a suggestion."

Janet took a sip of her coffee – and was dismayed to find it lukewarm.

"No," she replied. "I think it's a good idea. I don't have any office skills."

Another of Terri's patented laughs. "You're probably much better," she declared, "much more proficient … than you think you are. After all, working for that tyrant at the laundry certainly didn't offer you much chance to hone your talents for anything! Except having to cope with that overheated, big, presser machine … or whatever it is. I can see you moving right up the mountain here."

Well, the meal had gone well till then. Terri, obviously, knew a great deal about her. About her past. How expansive – how frank – had Steve been, when speaking about Janet? And to whom? To how many people? Mr. Brock? Terri? The immediate world?

What could Steve really know about her? Nothing! That's what! That being the case, what could he say about her? That was troubling! And to whom – to what number of whoms – did he say it? That was even more troubling!

<<>>

The afternoon went quickly. Amazing! At the laundry – the "damned laundry" – every minute of every day had been sheer drudgery! At **Brock & Associates**, the hours had wound up simply flying by! Incredible!

Janet even felt as though she'd learned – had actually absorbed and retained – a modest amount of proficiency at the switchboard. At about 3:00 PM, Peggy had "thrown her in"! By quitting time – 5:00 PM – she had fielded almost 50 calls!

And not one disaster! Really amazing! Overwhelmingly incredible!

<<>>

At home, that evening, Janet was more ebullient than she'd been in years! Literally years! Although Barbara was not at home – a work night at the pizzeria – Patti and Joan had sat and, dutifully, listened to their mother ramble on, as Janet had related the most minute, most trivial, incidences of the day. And how efficiently she'd handled them.

It was obvious that Janet was thrilled with her new position. If any of the nagging doubts, as to Steve's role in her new situation persisted, they were not apparent to her daughters. The latter were positively thrilled at their mother's new-found enthusiasm. Even the two boys, as they'd buzzed into and out of the room, could sense something special.

It was a nice feeling.

<<>>

The future – despite Janet's new and wonderful work situation – would not be all peaches-and-cream. A number of adjustments would have to be made.

While it was true that she was making substantially more at **Brock & Associates**, it was also a fact that the money orders from Jim had ceased. Although the semi-monthly stipends from her late husband had been, by no means, the least bit generous, the money orders – combined with the pittance Janet had been paid at the "damned laundry" – had been enough to sustain the family. Barely enough. But, nonetheless, enough. Well, enough – when one considered that Barbara and Patti had provided a goodly amount of help. On numerous occasions.

Still, Janet's new and improved paycheck would not equal the combined income from Jim's money orders and Janet's wages at her previous place of employment.

Added to the immediate problem was the fact that, whereas Horace Truesdale had paid his "privileged" workers on a weekly basis, employees of **Brock & Associates** were paid twice monthly. Janet's first paycheck would not be cut – until she'd worked at her new job for two weeks and three days.

It was true that she had been due one more paycheck from the laundry. Barbara had picked it up two days after Janet had started her new employment situation. The amount of the check was infinitesimal. It was used, almost exclusively, to buy food – and hope that the family would be able to withstand the coming onslaught. The coming onslaught – known as starvation.

Barbara, of course, would be unable to help. A substantial amount of her earnings for almost ten days would be withheld. It had been advanced for Janet's new shoes, bag and racy undies.

A pitiful few dollars had been squirreled away – for Janet to use for gasoline. Fortunately, the old Maverick didn't require an inordinate amount of fuel. The crunch, of course, would have been lessened – had Janet been able to use a gasoline company credit card. She'd applied for six different cards – from six different companies – over the years. She'd been turned down by all six. At least there are some consistencies in life, she'd deduced each time the rejection notice had arrived – as expected. It was definitely belt-tightening time, in the Bolton household!

FOUR

Halfway through the second "hungry" week, Janet had consented to date Fletcher Groome – more to put an end to his persistent phone calls than anything else.

They rode, in Fletcher's sumptuous Jaguar, over The Ambassador Bridge, across the Detroit River, and into Windsor, Ontario – where he'd made reservations for dinner and the floor show, at the area's most posh nightclub.

Once inside the club, Janet was overridden with guilt. There she was – dining on sinfully opulent fare, while her children were "scoffling down fish heads and rice", as Patti had so teasingly put it.

Having had a chance to scan the menu, Janet decided to order the largest steak in the house. She'd have to gather up her courage, at the end of the meal – and ask for a doggie bag. She was planning on taking at least 80% of the steak home to the kids.

Fletcher and Janet dined, while the spectacular floorshow entertained. It was a wonderful revue. More lavish than any Janet had ever seen.

The highlight turned out to be a crooner – Eddie Montini – who had been Janet's girlhood idol. After some 27 years in the business, though, the singer now had to exert considerable effort to approach those high notes, that he'd hit so easily, in years past. In many cases, the efforts had resulted in near-misses.

Still, Janet was enthralled – just to be in the same place as the Eddie Montini! The room, itself, while by no means small, turned out to be rather intimate. When the singer asked for requests, Janet spoke up – in as loud a voice as she'd dared:

"Would you sing *As We Are Today?*"

The song – an obscure ballad from a long-forgotten movie, from the early-fifties, *The Daughter of Rosie O'Grady* – had been a moderate hit for the singer, when he'd recorded it in 1958. This revival of the tune – six or seven years after the movie had become a pleasant memory for Janet – had been marginally successful. But, by 1979, it had completely faded from memory. Just about everybody's memory. Except for that of the crooner. And of the woman who'd made the request.

"Wow!" he exclaimed, smiling broadly. "That goes way back."

Janet stifled the impulse to say, "And so do I".

It had been Janet's favorite song. She was fifteen, when the record had been released, in 1958. She'd had a massive crush on one of the football players at Cooley High School. Had worshipped him from afar. *As We Are Today* had been "their song".

The football player just hadn't been aware of that fact.

The orchestra, at the club in Windsor, was not at all familiar with the song. After humming a few bars to the pianist, the crooner made his way through the ballad – forgetting one line along the way. The fluff made Janet cringe!

The number had undeniably "struck a nerve" with the singer. He crooned the song with incredible feeling. With a measure of tenderness – which had been missing from his most recent, all-up-tempo, recordings. The audience clamored for him to sing it again. That, of course was most heartwarming. Twice he reprised the song – each time to thunderous applause.

From the very beginning, Janet's eyes had teared up!

"Why did you request that?" asked Fletcher – once the crooner had moved on to another, more swinging, melody.

Janet explained her schoolgirl crush. She was ready to dismiss the Q & A, when it occurred to her that Fletcher's straight-laced, almost carved-in-stone, face had taken on the strangest look – an expression she'd never seen before.

"Why do you ask, Fletcher? Does the song have some kind of special meaning for you? I've never seen that look on your face. Not like what you're looking at me … right now."

"No," he replied – almost too quickly. "It's nothing. Just … just curious is all."

Janet laughed. It was the first time all evening. Well, the first time she'd laughed at Fletcher.

"You know," she observed, "I'm probably the least perceptive person in the history of the world. Everybody tells me I'm too naïve. That … way too often … I take everything at face value. Never look behind anything. Never look beneath the surface. But, when I see a look … a look like the one you just had on your face, Fletcher … I can't just accept it as nothing. If you don't want to go into it … why, that's fine. I'd be the last one … the last one in the entire world … to pry into your private affairs. I've never pried. When I stop to think, though, I realize that I don't really know all that much about you, Fletcher Groome. But, please. Don't tell me that it's nothing."

Janet wondered why she was being so combative. And over something so trivial. Something so insignificant.

He laughed nervously.

"I … I don't know whoever told you that you're not perceptive, Janet," he said, at length. "As it happens, that was my wife's and my song. We'd had it played at our wedding, as a matter of fact. Back in the early-fifties. Nineteen-fifty-three to be exact."

Fletcher Groome had seldom mentioned his wife. Almost never.

He had assured Janet, when they'd begun dating – if you could call it that – that he'd been divorced. He'd made vague references from time to time, of having been married "a goodly number of years". Outside of that? Nothing.

Janet didn't know what to say. It was a surprise that a song as close to her, as was the ballad Eddie Montini had just sung, would've meant so much to Fletcher. Would've meant anything to him. The couple sat, in a stiff, stilted, silence – till the floorshow ended.

As part of his encore, the singer had, once again, sung *As We Are Today*. Two of the reed men and one of the trumpet players had remembered the tune sufficiently to join the pianist in accompaniment. While the song was being sung, for the last time, Janet riveted her gaze on Fletcher's face. Even in the subdued lighting, she could tell that he was experiencing a highly-emotional reaction. Of some sort. As the crooner walked past their table, the spotlight fell upon the couple –

and illuminated her date's face – serving to solidify, beyond a doubt, Janet's perception.

Once the vocalist had exited, the orchestra began playing soft, dreamy, dance music. Fletcher and Janet had finished their meal – doggie bag safely ensconced in the latter's purse – and were lingering over after-dinner cordial drinks. Although they'd partaken of only three rounds of cocktails, the alcohol seemed to be having an alien effect on Fletcher. At one point, they'd gotten up to dance and, while they managed to survive the number, Janet felt as though she'd just gone through The Battle of Anzio.

The Brandy Alexanders also seemed to loosen Fletcher's tongue. He began to tell Janet of his former wife: Fletcher and Clara Groome had been married seven years – when she'd left him – deserted him – for another man. The shock had crushed the man. Apparently! Obviously! There appeared that same indescribable expression again. That "look" – which, for some reason, had continued to make Janet terribly ill at ease.

It had been years after Clara had departed – he assured her – before he'd even dreamed of dating. By that time, he'd "let himself go". Had wound up almost 75 pounds overweight. He'd managed to lose about half the added suet – but, had never succeeded in getting back down to his "fighting weight".

He'd compensated for the lack of feminine companionship by acquiring ever-more-luxurious symbols of the opulent lifestyle. He'd also immersed himself into his business – to pay for them. He'd become one of the wealthiest men in Detroit.

"You know?" he'd asked, after the spastic dance had been survived. "You know what? You're actually only the second woman that I've ever dated … ever since Clara went and left me. Second woman. Just two of you. Can you believe that?"

Actually, Janet did find that difficult to believe. She was troubled, at that moment, with his entire demeanor. Much more concerned than she ever would've been, with his love life – or lack of same. He was beginning to speak too loudly. His voice was becoming terribly thick. The tone deteriorating into a high nasal pitch.

"Fletcher," responded Janet, her blue/green eyes taking on a hardness that few had ever seen. "Something tells me that you'd probably do well to ask the waitress for a cup of coffee. I think the drinks are starting to get to you a little."

"Okay, Doll. Anything you say. Waitress? Waitress!"

He'd called with too much force. People at neighboring tables were beginning to stare – and laugh. And he'd never called her "doll" before. Why was that so troubling?

"Please, Fletcher," whispered Janet. Her voice contained much more irritation than she'd intended. "Try and keep your voice a little lower."

He forced his brow to over-knit and – with an exaggerated gesture – raised his forefinger to his lips.

"Shhhhhhhhh!" he slobbered.

The waitress established a new Olympic record in placing before him an over-sized cup of strong, steaming, coffee. Fletcher thanked her – profusely. For the briefest of moments, Janet was certain that her date was going to pat the waitress on the derriere.

Shifting his attention to his partner once more, Fletcher rambled on:

"Yeah. Clara was a good ol' girl. She really was, Janet. She was, y'know."

"I'm sure she was." Janet was doing her best to rein in her exasperation. "I'm sure she was."

"No you're not. You ... you're just like ever'one else. You don't think I'm capable of gettin' a nice lady."

"Well, I'd like to think that I'm a nice lady."

He waved his hand. An expansive gesture.

"Oh, you are, Janet ... except I ain't 'got' you. Ain't never 'got' you. But, you sure as hell are. Hell of a nice lady. Only real nice one I ever had ... 'cept for Clara, of course. She took up with this kid. This damn kid! He worked for one of those door-to-door outfits. Sold coffee and tea and household stuff. Soap and wax and mops and stuff. He had nothing! Nothing! Not one damn thing! Not a goddam thing! Nothing!"

His voice was rising again – in both tone and volume. Janet managed to make him aware of his loudness once more. He resumed in a coarse, whispered, overdone, confidential, tone:

"This kid didn't have a pot or a window! Nothin'! I coulda bought and sold him … out of my petty cash drawer. Only thing I c'n figure is that he musta been … "

Fletcher looked to his left, then to his right. Both moves highly exaggerated.

"He musta," he continued, "that kid musta been good in the ol' sack, boy. He musta really been somethin' … in bed. His you-know-what musta been … "

Janet was becoming more and more uncomfortable. She did her best to change the subject. It didn't work. Fletcher – with great flourish – placed the back of his right hand close by the left side of his mouth. It was an overdone "just between us" gesture.

"Do you know what, Janet?"

"No, Fletcher," she responded wearily. "What?"

"I never … " An exaggerated shake of his head. Then, he continued. "I never been to bed, y'know … not with no one. No one but Clara. Never! No sir! Uh-uh!"

She patted his hand – despite the fact that such a statement would be difficult to believe. Even for someone as supposedly naïve as Janet.

"I'm proud of you, Fletcher," she said, feeling uncomfortable in her insincerity. "Maybe we'd better go."

"Ahhhh," he brushed off the suggestion. "Hell. The night's still in rompers. Don't be an ol' party-pooper, Janet. Don't be a damn party-pooper."

"It's almost midnight. I have to go to work tomorrow … and it's an awful long way to get home."

Once more, an overdone wave of his hand.

"Say no more, my sweet," he intoned. "If you wanna go home, then … dammit … it's home we'll go."

He withdrew his wallet, fished a sheaf of bills from it – and plopped the pile of currency down on the table. Then, he arose.

Janet was appalled at the more-than-generous tip! She was convinced that their waitress had more than earned it. Still, it was difficult for her to gloss over that amount of currency. To pay no attention to the monumental total of money, that laid there. To Fletcher, it was a mere throw-away stipend. Nothing important. Not to him.

It would've fed Janet's entire family for the better part of a week.

Fletcher was more unsteady than Janet had anticipated. She

managed to assist him to his car. It was a struggle. She found herself wishing that he'd dropped another 25 or 30 pounds.

She decided that she was going to drive. She helped him – over his many, varied, dramatic, and obscene, protests – into the passenger's seat and closed the door. Then, she got in behind the wheel. Reluctantly, he produced the keys – and handed them to her. Then, he settled back into the soft Corinthian leather upholstery.

<u>Maybe he'll fall asleep.</u> <u>I should be so lucky.</u>

Fletcher, of course, remained wide-awake. The nearer they got to the Detroit-Windsor Tunnel, the more talkative he became. As Janet wheeled off Oulette Street – heading toward the tunnel – he continued to babble on.

"You know what, Janet-Doll?"

"No, Fletcher-Doll. What?"

"That's the reason I never insisted on it with you."

"On what with me? What're you talking about?"

"On you goin' to bed with me," he answered with a mock-sinister stage leer. "Tha's what I'm talkin' about. I musta been no damn good in bed. Otherwise, ol' Clara ... she never woulda left me. Not for that piddlin' little S.O.B. So, I says to myself, I says, 'Fletch, you ain't worth a damn ... in the ol' sack-a-roo'. Tha's why I never tried it. Never tried to seduce you."

"Oh, I don't know about that," she replied in an amused tone. "I'm sure that the thought's occurred to you ... from time to time."

"Yeah," he agreed – with an insipid smile. "Yeah. But, I wa'ant doin' any of <u>this</u> kind of stuff, y'know!"

He put his left hand on her right breast! She picked it off her bosom – and slammed it down into his lap! Once they reached the middle of the long, narrow, tunnel, he put his hand on top of her right thigh – and tried to press his fingers down between her legs! Janet was wearing her beautiful new blue dress – with a silken half-slip underneath. As she reached to lift his hand a second time, he pulled her skirt upward!

"Lessee," he slobbered, "less jus' see what you got on underneath there!"

The traffic lanes in the Detroit-Windsor Tunnel are extremely narrow – built as the facility was to accommodate Model-A Fords. Janet was doing her best to concentrate on keeping the Jaguar in its own lane. Fighting to keep the car on its side of the two-lane tube. She made three futile swipes – in an attempt to pull his hand away! She kept missing! He'd move his arm slightly – just enough to evade her thrusts!. As narrow as the tunnel was, she couldn't divert her attention from her task of steering the car. Not for more than a second or two at a time. Fed up, she eventually uncorked a more outraged attempt to pry the hand loose from her leg! And practically collided with an oncoming car!

By then, Fletcher had her dress and half-slip rucked up to the tops of her shapely legs! His hand found the inside of her soft, milky, thighs once more! He slid it up over Janet's pantyhose – to the area where her legs come together!

Janet screeched the Jaguar to an abrupt halt! Another almost-disastrous move!

The luxurious car stopped on a dime! However the driver in the seven-year-old Mercury Marquis – immediately behind them – had been completely surprised by Janet's "panic stop"! The man managed to halt the huge sedan – a fraction-of-an-inch from the rear bumper of Fletcher's car! Fortunately, there had been no car close behind the Mercury!

Janet jammed the gear selector into "Park"! Grabbing her date's hand, she threw it, once more, into his lap! Then, she brought about her left hand – in a fierce roundhouse arc! It was a vicious slap! The blow connected – full-on – with Fletcher's nose and mouth! The clap filled the car! It also brought the man out of his drunken stupor!

He attempted to speak. However, while his mouth moved, nothing came out!

Still seething, Janet pulled the shift back into "Drive" – sending the Jaguar roaring toward the U.S. side of the tunnel once more!

To add to her discomfort, Janet was without the toll fee, once she'd surfaced in Detroit. She sat – steaming – for what seemed an eternity!

Fletcher – apparently drunk no longer, but terribly disoriented – fished for his wallet. Then, fumbling through the currency compartment, he finally withdrew a $5.00 bill. The woman in the booth glared at them! The already-rattled driver of the Mercury beeped his horn – incessantly!

By the time Janet had the Jaguar headed out Grand River Avenue, Fletcher appeared to have gotten hold of himself.

"I'm … I'm sorry, Janet," he rasped. "I'm truly sorry. I didn't mean to dive into the cocktail glass back there. I honestly didn't. I don't know what happened … what came over me. I guess hearing that damn song again … hearing that song … I guess that didn't help. I'm so sorry, Janet. I am. Believe me, I wouldn't … "

"It's all right, Fletcher," she replied, with a heavy sigh. "No harm done. I guess that there's no harm done, anyway."

Then, stretching her arms outward – locking them, rigidly, as she pressed against the top of the steering wheel – she sighed once again. Heavily. Gradually, though, her mood was softening, ever so slightly.

"Are you all right," she asked. "Are you okay, Fletcher? For a minute there, I was afraid I might've broken your nose!"

"Well, I'd have deserved it. No … my nose is fine. A little sore, though. You've got quite a left hook, there, Lady."

"Ladies shouldn't need left hooks."

"You're right. They shouldn't. Only when they're on a date … with the south end of a horse headed north."

Janet laughed at the analogy – in spite of herself.

"You … you just surprised me, is all," she said.

"Yeah, well … I surprised myself. Janet, you know that I don't … that I've never … that I haven't ever acted that way. Never before."

"I know, Fletcher." Her frame of mind, by then, had softened – considerably. "I apologize … if I made a heavy-duty federal case out of it."

"Well, you had every right to. I'm sorry, Janet. Truly sorry."

"It's all right. It's oh-KAY, Fletcher. No problem."

"Will you … will you see me again."

"I don't know, Fletcher." Another industrial-strength sigh. "I don't really know. I suppose so. I guess, maybe, I will."

"I wouldn't blame you if you didn't. I wanted tonight to be so … so … so special, Janet. I really did. And then … to just go and screw it up like I did, I just … "

"It's all RIGHT, Fletcher. No problem."

"You see, Janet," he persisted, "I wanted everything to go so well! So damn well! I was … well I was … I was going to ask you to … to marry me. And, damn! I guess that … when they started to do that song … I guess it just … it just … well, somehow I guess I let the whole entire evening go straight to hell! Sent the whole thing … right into the old dumper!"

"Marry you? You were going to ask me to … to <u>marry</u> you?"

She dropped her foot off the gas pedal – a reflex action.

"Yes," he answered, his voice assuming its normal firm tone. "Yes, marry me. Oh, Janet! I need you! I really do! Need you badly! And … listen Janet … you need <u>me</u>! Whether or not you know it, you do need me! Maybe not as bad as I need you, but you do need me! You do! Dammit … if you'll be honest with yourself … you'll have to admit that you do need me! I know that things are … well, they're in such a mess for you now, but … "

"Oh, they're not in such a complete mess, Fletcher."

"Oh no? Listen. Listen, Janet. Listen to me. You've got seven pounds of meat in that damn doggie bag. I knew … knew damn well … when you ordered it … I knew that you'd never be able to eat it all. Not in a million years. Took me awhile to figure it out. Figure it out … that you were going to bring it home to your kids. I'm not too bright, sometimes. Oh, Janet! Why do you want to keep fighting? It's a losing battle. Don't you see? You told me before … told me about your husband sending you money from time to time. Obviously, that's stopped. Janet? Can't you see? It's a … well, it's a losing battle for you."

She negotiated the left-oblique turn from Grand River onto Seven Mile Road.

"It's not a losing battle," she replied, firmly. "Really. I'm doing quite well at **Brocks**. For the first time … practically in my whole life … I feel good about what I'm doing. I feel … for the first time in my life … I feel like I'm competent. That stupid switchboard … it just about caused me to lose my appetite, when I first saw it. But, everybody told me that I could master it. Well, I did! I've mastered it! In just two days! Two days, Fletcher! Can you imagine how that makes me feel? What a rush that gives me? I feel good about that, Fletcher. Damn good!"

"I'm sure it does, Janet. But, can't you see that … ?"

"I'm even looking to take a course or two at night. Learn about computers. It took a heap of convincing by a couple of women at the office ... Terri and Peggy ... but, I'm really convinced that that's where my future lies. Big things ... computers. Terri says it's our future."

"Yes. And where are you going to get the money for those computer courses? They don't give 'em away, you know. Be honest now, Janet. Are you making as much as you were? When you had the money from ... from what's-his-name, from Jim ... coming in? You may be making more than you were at that bastardly laundry. But, are you taking home as much money as what you were totaling a month-and-a-half ago? Two months ago? Even though your wage is substantially more than old 'Scrooge' was paying you, that's really not saying a hell of a lot. How're you ever going to make it? Listen to me, Janet ... "

"No! No ... you listen to me, Fletcher! I can make it! I can bloody-well make it! I realize that it's ... that it'll be ... close. But, let me tell you. For the first time in my life, I've got a good ... a really good ... feeling about myself. I'm someone, Fletcher! A real, living, breathing someone!"

"Of course you're someone. Of course you are. You've always been someone. To me ... and to your kids."

"Yes. But, now I'm someone ... to me! To myself! As selfish as that probably sounds, it's important! Important as hell! I never really realized exactly how important! But, it's fair-thee-well vital! Critical!"

She snapped off a left turn at her street.

"Janet," he persisted. "Marry me! Listen, Janet! I can give you everything! Every damn thing! Anything that you'd ever need ... anything that you'd ever want ... you can have! I can give it to you! I would give it to you! I will give it to you! Look! Ask yourself this: Ask yourself if it's being fair to your kids! Is it fair to ask them to continue? To continue with the struggle? Listen, I could buy Barbara a car! New car! Buick Regal or something. Maybe a Camaro. Patti too ... in a year or two. Whenever she's old enough. Janet ... listen to me! Please! Listen to me. They wouldn't ... your kids wouldn't ... they wouldn't have to worry about scrounging nickels and dimes at some damn pizza restaurant. Or babysitting. I understand that the jerk at the pizzeria ... that he's always got his hands all over the help! All over the help! All the help! All the time!"

Fletcher's offer had touched Janet – deeply! From a pure-logic point of view!

It was true, of course. All of it. He was right. Things had been terribly difficult for the children – most especially for the girls. Even if she didn't love him, marriage to Fletcher Groome would make a certain amount of sense. Perhaps an overwhelming amount of sense. She was certain that many women would jump at the proposition. Jump at the proposal. Why had she used that word – "proposition"?

Wouldn't it be nice – for Barbara to live a normal life? To have a nice car! Have some really nice clothes! Patti too! And Joan! And her sons! Well, the boys really hadn't been called upon to fight any of those battles yet. Not yet! She could save them all that. It was within her power to alleviate a whole lot of problems for her children! "In one swelled foop", as Patti was prone to say.

The potential Utopia evaporated – "in one swelled foop" – as Fletcher's remark about Barbara's boss hit home! Although everyone was aware of the fact that the man was a womanizer, she'd never heard her daughter complain about him. Well, not in that area, anyway. She was certain that Barbara would've "squared him away" – right from the beginning. Still, it was a worry.

"Fletcher," she heard herself say, "there's not really any way that you ... or anyone else ... can protect us from the real world. In the real world, guys are always trying to put their hands on girls. All over girls' bodies. We know that's true. Just look at what happened in the tunnel. The money, the new car, the nice clothes, the so-called normal life ... they all sound great. But, the fact is ... the fact is, Fletcher ... the fact is that ... that I don't love you! I'm sorry, Fletcher! I'm sorry ... but, I just don't love you. I don't know that I could ... that I could ever ... love you."

"I've ... I've never required that, Janet. I've never required that you love me."

"I know. I know that. But, Fletcher, it ... it just wouldn't be right. It'd be totally dishonest."

"Dishonest? Not to me. I know that you don't love me. I'm aware of that ... going in. I can accept that. I do accept that."

"Yes. But, I can't accept it. Fletcher, what you tried to do to me, tonight ... in the tunnel ... "

"I told you, Janet. I'm sorry about that. I'm just as sorry as I can be. I wish it'd never happened. You know that I don't normally do things like that."

"It's … it's not only where you had your hands. I just can't let anyone touch me … touch me there, or practically anywhere else … if I don't love them." She sighed once again – even more deeply. Tears welled up in her eyes. "I'd … I'd be prostituting myself," she rasped. "Prostituting myself. Whoring myself."

"Janet … for heaven's sake! You're looking at it all wrong!"

A tear trickled down her cheek – as she thought back to her daughters' remarks about seducing a man.

"No I'm not," she said, steadfastly. "I'm not looking at it all wrong. I know that this sounds cruel, Fletcher. And I don't mean it to. But … don't you see? I couldn't face the prospect of your hands on me! Your hands all over me! Especially … well … especially if we didn't have any clothes on! I … I couldn't face the … couldn't face the prospect of … of going to bed with you."

He was stunned!

Janet forced herself to continue. Once she'd brought up the subject of having sex with him, it would be folly to simply leave the entire proposition (that word again) hanging. Her eyes had dried.

"On the surface, Fletcher, it sounds like the answer to my every prayer. A dream come true. But, don't you see? That's all it is. Just a dream. The reality is that I'd feel like … dammit, I'd feel like a … like a … like a whore! I know that my kids would be shocked … if they thought I was prostituting myself."

"You … you're not prostituting yourself, Janet. Nothing even close!"

She realized – with a start – that she was about to pass her house! Slamming on the brakes, she immediately looked into the rear-view mirror. Looking for a '72 Mercury? Happily, there was no one behind them. Warily – and wearily – she swung the Jaguar into her driveway. It had been an exceptionally exhausting night. She was totally drained. More so, in a way, than on those many (thankfully, long gone) days, when she'd drag herself out of the laundry – the "damned laundry" – at the end of a long, never-ending, sweaty shift!

She patted Fletcher on the knee – as she unbuckled her seatbelt. She opened the door and crawled out.

Then, she turned and said to him, "I appreciate the offer, Fletcher. I do. I really do. No one has offered to marry me in years. Decades. Not since Jim proposed. I'm flattered. I truly am. Extremely flattered. But, you see? I don't love you."

He got out – and met her, in the illumination of the left headlight.

"It's not important." His voice was a hoarse whisper. "It doesn't matter … not to me … whether you love me or not, Janet. I love you! Probably enough for the both of us! But, consider this: You've got to think of your children's well-being. That's something that you can't turn your back on. Do you want them to go on like this? Go on living … if that's what you can call it … living the way they've been living?"

"Somehow," she snapped, "I'm not ashamed of the way my children have been living."

"That's not what I meant … and you know it."

"Yes." She sighed once more. Her entire body seemed to deflate. "I know it, Fletcher. But, it never occurred to me before … to wonder what the kids would be like, if Jim had never deserted me. Deserted us. Listen to me Fletcher. If they hadn't had to … how did you put it? … scrounge for nickels and dimes, they couldn't possibly be any better kids than they are now. It'd be impossible. No, Fletcher. If I loved you … that'd be one thing. But, I don't. I like you. You're a nice man. And I have a good deal of … of … of affection for you. But, no matter which way you slice it, it's not love. I flat don't love you. Not in a let's-get-married sense, anyway."

"Janet, listen. I've … "

She pressed three fingers over his lips!

"It may very well be totally selfish on my part," she said. "But, I'll take my kids … just the way they are now. Maybe you're right. Logically, I guess, you may be right. Maybe it's unfair to deny them the benefits of new cars and nice clothes … and not having to scratch for every single, lousy, stinking, damn, nickel! Not to have to make every damn nickel stretch … to the breaking point. To where they're choking the poor buffalo. If that makes me selfish … then, so be it. I never pretended to be perfect, anyway. On the contrary … "

He started to say something. Again, she shushed him with her fingers to his lips.

"Logically," she resumed, "it would work. I'd be the first to admit that it just reeks of logic. But, Fletcher, if I've learned one thing in my young life, I've learned that love … true love … is anything but logical. If it was, I'd have accepted your offer … in a New York minute. I don't know that I've ever been in love. Five kids notwithstanding. I just don't think that I've ever experienced it. Not true love. I just don't think I've ever had that happen to me. Not even close."

"Well," he replied, "I'll have to do something about that."

He pecked her, lightly, on the cheek and said goodnight.

As he backed the Jaguar out of the driveway, Janet had the strangest feeling! She'd never heard him use that tone of voice before. It sent a chill, tingling up and down her spine! Why should that be?

She shuddered! It was involuntary – but, it definitely was a shudder! Strange! Almost eerie!

<<>>

An hour later, Janet lay awake in her bed. Her attempts to placate her churning mind amounted to a never-ending series of failures!

<u>How do you shut this thing off?</u>

Had she been correct, in what she'd told Fletcher Groome? Had she, indeed, never been in love before? She fluffed the pillow – then, rolled over. Finding a comfortable position seemed out of the question. The runaway movie projector – which had taken over her mind, and was showing no mercy – seemed unable to stop grinding out a plethora of disjointed images.

Maybe – just maybe – she actually had been in love. Maybe she'd experienced it dozens of times. Maybe she actually <u>did</u> love Fletcher – and didn't know that either.

And why did the smiling face of Steve Francis keep popping up? Inserting itself? And at the damndest times? Why was there no rhyme or reason to his "guest appearances"? He just "was there"! And then he wasn't! No pattern. No nothing.

She tried to concentrate on love – and whether there was the faintest chance that she might've experienced it. In whatever degree. For how ever long. She supposed that she must have loved Jim. After all, she did marry him. On the other hand, what did that prove? She could marry Fletcher too.

Of course, she'd never cringed at the thought of Jim's hands on her body. Well, obviously, she was a different woman back then. A young woman. A girl, really. Fresh out of high school. What could she have known at that age?

Through the years, she'd come to believe that she'd married Jim for security. More for her peace of mind than anything else. Jim would be, for her, a shelter from any possible storms.

Yeah! Right!

Well, he should've been a shelter. He was positively brilliant – especially with figures. There had, at the time, seemed to be a peace of mind that came with such a marriage. With being wed – "till death do you part" – to a stalwart accountant.

Yeah! Right!

Well, if I'm so hell-bent on security, it's there for me now. With Fletcher. Mine for the asking. No – mine for the taking!

Barbara and Patti – and, to an extent, Joan – had urged her to seek out and find romance! Be swept off her feet! Even to seduce someone!

She shuddered! The image of Detective Francis pole-vaulted back into the center of the whirlpool, which was passing for her mind! She shuddered again!

Dear Lord! That's all I'd need! Some tawdry affair ... with someone I don't even know!

Why should his form keep popping up? Well, Joan did suggest that he was a "hunk". That he might be a likely target for a good seduction? Again, she shuddered!

Dear Lord!

She rolled over onto her tummy. But, the whirlpool of images just wouldn't stop!

God knows, she certainly didn't want to seduce Fletcher Groome! The very thought of being in bed with him gave her goose bumps! And sent a massive shudder – yet another one – coursing through her body! Hoo! That one was almost a convulsion!

Why should that be?

Oh, here we go again!

Fletcher was an attractive enough man, she supposed. In his own way. Could her revulsion toward intimacy with him be a result of the fact that sex had never been particularly satisfying to her? Five kids notwithstanding?

She had known only one man. Jim. They'd both been virgins when they'd married. She was certain of that. Actually, Jim had never seemed to show much interest in that area of their marriage. Again – five kids notwithstanding.

When everything was stripped away, their sex life – what sex life had existed – had proved to be deadly dull.

She flipped onto her right side.

She wondered if Jim had found another woman – had taken a lover – in Fort Worth. He'd evidently never married. Would he have found a woman – and slept with her? Would that woman have excited him? More than Janet ever had?

Probably! Couldn't hardly help it!

Onto her back once more.

Janet was trying, desperately, to jump off that track. Why should she, all of a sudden, be caught up in wondering about her late husband's love life? Seven years after he'd deserted her? Why should the thought of Jim being in bed with another woman bother her – after all these years?

Well, she didn't think that it was really bothering her.

Then what the hell are you doing thinking about it?

Back onto her right side.

She didn't really desire anyone! Amazing! Was that normal? Was she normal? She'd never really desired Jim. Not if she was to be totally honest with herself. Certainly not in the manner that all the confession magazines, the movies – and even some of the television dramas, these days – had always depicted desire.

Maybe I'm a eunuch! Oh, dear Lord!

Maybe – as some had suggested – sex was nothing more than a weapon. Simply a basis for exerting leverage! Would she use it that way if she married Fletcher?

No! Certainly not! Of course not!

And yet –

She rolled over onto her left side. The illuminated dial of the old clock/radio reminded her of the lateness of the hour. She simply must get to sleep! Otherwise, she'd be in no condition to go to work in the morning. She was really going to have to put all this stupid sex nonsense behind her! Put it right out of her mind! There was no sense trying to stare down the stupid clock.

She rolled onto her back once more. That was better. Well, she hoped it was better. She tried to snuggle down into the mattress.

Stupid sex nonsense? There had to be more to it than that.

<u>Yuk</u>! <u>Here we go again</u>!

Drowsiness, thankfully, was beginning to sweep her up. Engulf her in its merciful arms. There simply had to be more to it – more to life – than that! Than just sex! She drifted into a troubled sleep – trying to convince herself of that fact.

FIVE

The big day had come at last! Payday! A kinder, gentler, paycheck! A whole lot kinder! Hopefully, the first of many at **Brock & Associates**! At 3:30 PM, all the anguishing, endless, guessing games came to a screeching halt. All the stomach-churning concern about the size of the check dissipated! That amount – that torment-producing figure – was shown in a little white space, on the right side of the light-green check. The light-green check – with the dark-green squiggly lines printed across the entire front side. That beautiful, gorgeous, piece of green paper. The number of dollars listed brought a warm glow to the heart of the very grateful – very relieved – recipient.

Visions of loading up the old grocery cart, at the supermarket, danced in Janet's head! As she knew – as everyone in the family knew – the Bolton budget would remain terribly strained, without Jim's money orders. Still, to behold a check in that amount – and to know, in her heart of hearts, that she'd earned every glorious penny of it – filled Janet with a sense of pride! A satisfaction – financially, anyway – that she'd never known before. Five o'clock couldn't come too soon!

At quitting time, Janet was one of the first employees out the door – the total opposite of her normal posture. Terri Baun and Peggy Sullivan stood together in the far corner of the reception area – and smiled at one another, at their newest employee's hasty departure.

As Janet wheeled her Maverick out into the westbound traffic onto Eight Mile Road, she was grinning from ear to ear. She'd spent the final hour-and-a-half at the switchboard, practically biting holes in her lips – and the insides of her cheeks – in a concerted, monumental, effort to stifle the constant, industrial-strength, grin.

Safely away from the office – weaving in and out of the congested traffic pattern – she allowed herself the luxury of a raucous, exaggerated, stage-cackle. The outburst sounded almost as though it had come from none other than *Snidely Whiplash* – which brought on gale upon gale upon gale of boisterous, genuine, laughter!

At the supermarket, the euphoria she'd experienced at the office, and even in the car, paled – something she'd have thought impossible – as Janet watched the woman behind the window of the courtesy booth count out the amount of her wondrous check, in crisp tens and twenties. It was probably her imagination playing a trick on her, but the lady in the booth seemed to look at Janet in a new light – as she'd shoved the currency through the slot under the glass in the window. A more respectful light. Much more respectful.

During her tour through the store, Janet fought a thousand battles. The temptation to simply go ahead and fill her cart with steaks, filet mignons, roasts, lobster, etc. etc. etc. was overwhelming. Well, almost overwhelming. It was a tough fight, but Janet's more practical side prevailed. It was a tough fight though.

By the time she'd piled the six bags of groceries into the back seat of the Maverick, some of the glow had vanished. When the young man at the checkout counter – who'd been completely unimpressed – had mashed the "Total" key on the cash register, Janet had been afraid that her entire life was passing before her eyes. She'd blinked! Then, swallowed hard! It took a Herculean effort – but, she'd managed to peel off "a couple of yards" of cash and hand it to the stoic young man! Well, at least three-quarters of her glorious paycheck was still intact!

Coaxing the engine back to life, she pulled out, once more, into the flow of traffic on Eight Mile Road – and began humming to herself. Then, she began singing. The song was *As We Are Today*.

"Hmmmm," she muttered to herself. "Gonna have to get the radio in this jalopy fixed one of these days."

<<>>

As Janet approached the light at Beech-Daly Road, it flashed yellow – then, quickly turned red. She slowed the Maverick – taking great care not to spill her backseat booty from the supermarket. She was totally unprepared for the molar-rattling jolt! The car behind her – had slammed into the Maverick!

Great! Dammit! Just what I needed! A damn accident! Obviously, things have been going too well for me! Running too smoothly!

She sighed – and unbuckled her seat belt.

The cars on her left were still stopped for the light – but, there seemed to be enough room to walk back and assess the damage. She opened the door and got out!

The huge, burly, man – whose tank of a 10-year-old Chrysler New Yorker had rammed her – had already emerged from his car, and was looking over the results of the collision!

Janet joined him! She was almost afraid to look. Once she did, she wished that she had not! The compact Maverick had sustained a good deal of damage: Bumper, splash pan, both tail lights, trunk panel and trunk lid! All goners! The battleship that was the Chrysler was not damaged! Not in the slightest!

Janet glared at the unkempt giant of a man! Before she could say anything, he spoke:

"I'm awfully sorry, Ma'am. I don't know how it was … that I didn't stop in time. I musta been not payin' enough attention. Not thinkin' about what I was doin'."

"Just … just look at my car! Look at it! Just look at it!" She was on the verge of tears! Her glorious feast day was turning to ashes! With a rush! "Just look at it!" She couldn't stop uttering that same sentence. "Look at it! Do you realize what you've done? This is my only means of transportation! Now look at it! Just … just look at it!"

"I know, Ma'am. I know … and I'm sorry. Real sorry. I really am. Now, don't you worry none. I got insurance. Good insurance. I'll have your car fixed right up! Lickety split! I'm guessin' that the insurance company … that they'll give you a rental car, while yours is laid up. That's what they alweeze do. Ever since I been with 'em."

Janet glared at him – her blue/green eyes blazing. Could this – this person – could he possibly have insurance? On that old aircraft carrier of a car? On that deadly hunk of iron? And, even if he was covered, would the policy be elaborate enough to actually provide rent-a-car coverage? It didn't look to be really encouraging.

"I know what you must be thinkin', Ma'am," he said. "And you're right. You're right as can be. I don't have collision coverage on this ol' heap. Car ain't worth it. But, I really do have all the other stuff … the liability and the property damage and the rent-a-car stuff and all that. Honest! Tell ya what! These here people … they're all tryin' to get 'round us. Why'n't you just go ahead an' pull into that next side street, up there? And then, we'll just go ahead and exchange information. I'll write down who you should get in touch with … at my insurance company. Okay? I ain't gonna run off on ya, now. I'll be right behind you. I'll even put on my four-way flashers … so's you can tell it's me in your rear view mirror. How's that sound?"

Janet sighed. Then, she gave him a resigned nod. What was coming over her? The man seemed sincere enough. Was she undergoing some kind of change? Some sort of metamorphosis? Was she converting from an admitted *Pollyanna*? To a cynic? To a skeptic? To a curmudgeon? She'd thought that only a man could be considered a bona fide curmudgeon. She'd certainly not accepted, at face value, the things Fletcher had told her a few nights before. Especially how chaste he'd been through all the years. The man in the Chrysler was now also filling her with doubt. Was she becoming what she'd always dreaded becoming? A full-fledged cynic?

Once back in her Maverick, Janet proceeded past Beech-Daly, eased the car up to the next side street. Then, she pulled around the corner. Sure enough, the huge car – flashers blazing, as promised – was following. Janet coasted to a stop – about 100 feet from Eight Mile Road. The Chrysler pulled up behind.

Darkness was falling very quickly – as Janet emerged from her car. There were no streetlights in the area. Another spooky ingredient!

She wondered if there'd be ample light – to even see to exchange information. Probably, they'd have to use the headlights of the Chrysler. Might as well get on with it.

She was almost all the way to the driver's door of the tank – when the behemoth got out! He was wielding a knife! Before Janet could react, the hulk grabbed her!

In a purely reflex action, she managed to turn away from him! However, he caught her – in the middle of the turn – and, while he clamped his arm, ruthlessly, across her breasts, he held the immense knife at her throat!

<u>Dear Lord!</u> <u>What now?</u>

"Now you listen to me, Little Lady," he hissed. His breath was as foul as everything else about him. "We gonna go back to your car an' get your purse! Then, we gonna get in my car! An' we gonna go somewheres! An' we gonna have us some fun! You hear me? Gonna have us some fun! Some real fun! You got that?"

"Y ... yes."

"Good! Now, just kinda slow-like, we gonna walk up to your car!"

Janet was trembling from head to toe! Her body shivering violently! She was certain that she'd have been unable to stand – had the gorilla not had her firmly in his grasp!

At that moment, a man's voice filled the semi-darkness:

"All right, Sucker! Freeze!"

The would-be kidnapper threw Janet to the pavement – and began running! He barreled between the cars and up over the curb! He ran awfully fast, for an anthropoid of his dimensions!

As the fleeing man reached the edge of a field – some 60 feet away – the familiar form of Detective Steve Francis rushed to her side!

"Are you all right?" he shouted.

She nodded – shakily!

Steve set out after the man with the knife!

"Stop!" he shrieked. "Police!"

Paying no heed, the thug ran further into the field – overrun with hip-deep weeds!

A shot rang out!

In the gathering dusk, Janet was unable to see either man! She had no way of knowing what was happening! No way of determining the result of the gunshot!

She'd pulled herself to her feet – and was crouching behind the wounded Maverick! She couldn't imagine what those ghastly – those ghostly – sounds were! Couldn't fathom from where they might be coming! Then, it occurred to her: They were the rasping sounds of her labored inhaling and exhaling!

Her eyes straining, she could barely make out the silhouettes of two shadowy figures – as they were emerging from the field! Who had gotten the best of whom in their life-and-death confrontation? What if the robber – or rapist or whatever – had subdued Steve?

<u>Dear Lord</u>! <u>Please</u>! <u>Please don't let anything happen to him</u>!

The figures approached Janet's car!

To her immense relief, the would-be attacker was being prodded from behind – by Steve's service revolver! The giant's wrists were tightly secured in a gleaming-silver pair of handcuffs!

"Thank God!" Janet heard herself saying. "Thank God!"

"You sure you're all right, Janet?" was Steve's greeting.

She nodded – tentatively.

"Yeah. Yes. I'm fine … now. Well, almost fine. How can I ever thank you?"

"No thank you necessary. Look, is your car drivable? I guess it must be. You got it this far. I can't see … can't hear, can't smell … anything leaking. You didn't hear anything did you? Like, maybe, a tire rubbing? Something grinding? Any other kind of really funky sound?"

"No. No … I don't think so. I think it might be all right. It … it just looks like it's … ! Oh, damn! I don't even want to think about it."

"You can stop shivering now," he allowed – flashing that patented smile.

She'd thought that she <u>had</u> stopped!

Steve marched the immense bozo back to where his State Police cruiser was idling. Janet couldn't tell exactly what he was doing. The captive seemed passive enough – but, one never knew.

How close had she come? And to <u>what</u>? Specifically – to <u>what</u>?

She was still shaking – badly – once the pair approached again.

"Listen," said Steve. "I just radioed for backup! Local cops! Ought to be here in a second! In a couple of minutes. They can take this yahoo in. Then, why don't I follow you out to your house? That way, I can be sure that you'll make it. Can't have all those groceries spoil now, can we?"

As Janet opened her mouth, to ask how he knew about her groceries, two patrol cruisers – red-and-blue lights flashing – careened onto the street! Each cruiser roared to where the trio stood – then, slammed on their brakes! Guns drawn, two Southfield Township officers burst out of each squad car!

Once Steve had shown them his credentials – and explained what had happened – the wanna-be assailant was stuffed into one of the patrol cars. Then, the two cruisers roared off into the night.

Janet climbed into the Maverick. She was managing to stop her head-to-toe shivering. For the most part, at least. Even so, it was a monumental chore – to simply place her still-shaking hands on the steering wheel.

It was at that moment that it occurred to her – as she'd turned the ignition key – that Steve's presence might have been more than a fortunate coincidence. It had certainly taken long enough for that possibility to sink in. She climbed back out – and called to her benefactor, as he was about to enter his vehicle. She ran toward him.

"What were ... what are ... what're you doing here, Steve?" she panted, as she approached the detective. Her voice was a strange combination of breathlessness, huskiness – and a pronounced emotional drain.

"Saving you, Me Fair Damsel," he replied, with that unique smile of his.

"No. I mean, how did you happen to be <u>here</u>? Now? At this time? At the exact moment when I needed you? Needed help, anyway. A lot of help. How did that ... how could that ... happen?"

"Well, you know, sometimes I try and keep an eye on you ... a little bitty."

"Keep an eye on me?" Her voice took on a combat-ready sharpness – a frigid dimension which scared her. "What do you mean ... keep an eye on me? Steve? Are you ... are you ... would you be <u>spying</u> on me? Because, if you are ... "

"Spying?" His voice betrayed outrage! A whole lot of outrage! "Spying? Of course not!"

"Well, it certainly <u>seems</u> like you are!"

"Listen, Janet. My job takes up probably eleven or twelve hours a day. On some days ... sixteen or seventeen. I really don't have all that much time to spy on <u>anyone</u>! Unless we suspect that they're, maybe, engaged in some kind of criminal activity. And we do that on company time."

"Well, you seemed to have taken this opportunity to spy on me."

"I was <u>not</u> spying. Just checking. There <u>are</u> times, y'know, when things aren't quite so wild and crazy … and we've got a little more time to ourselves. I usually try and look in on you during those times. Doesn't happen all that often, but … "

"Oh?" she responded coldly. "And just how often are 'those times'?"

"Oh, maybe once or twice a week, I'd guess. Sometimes nowhere near that often. Sometimes it could be two or three times in a given day. Just all depends. I did contrive to be here tonight, though, truth to tell. I'm not saying that I know you like a book or something … although the idea has some appeal … but, I've … "

"What are you talking about?"

"Well … for openers … I know you well enough to know that you'd be on Cloud Nine today. Payday! I figured that you'd probably cash your check at the drive-in window … at the bank across from the office. That would've been bad enough. But, the grocery store was worse!"

"Grocery store was worse? What do you mean … the grocery store was worse?"

"Well, I knew that you'd be walking three feet off the ground … with your new-found wealth. If you happened to flash a roll of bills, it's … well, there are guys out there that look for that! That watch for such things. That's the way they make their living! They do exactly what this S.O.B. just did! What he just did to you! They look for a lady … preferably one they outweigh by eighty or maybe a hundred pounds. If they can find one who's good-looking, why that's a helluva bonus, for such a schmuck. Most important, it's got to be a woman … one that's got a great big wad of green stuff. And, listen. They're damn good. They come up and smack you with their battlewagon of a car … just like this clown just did … and, while you're rattled, they get the upper hand! Take advantage of you. Rob you! Maybe even … God forbid … rape you!"

Janet began to shiver once more!

"Dear Lord!," she exclaimed. "He did say … he said … well, he told me that we were going to go somewhere. Go somewhere … and have some fun! I think that's what he said! I'm pretty sure he said that! Dear Lord!"

Steve reached over and took her right hand. Then, he pressed it tightly – in both of his! Something inside of Janet moved! What she felt – the emotion she experienced, for just the most fleeting of seconds – was something she'd never known before!

"Look," he said, pressing her hand even more tightly in his. "It didn't happen! Did <u>not</u> happen! Okay? It flat-out did not <u>happen</u>! Did not happen!"

She nodded absently.

"Were ... were you there?" She didn't recognize her own voice. "Were you there ... all the time? The full time?"

"Yeah. Pretty much. Didn't you see that animal? Didn't you see him follow you out of the parking lot at *The Food Fest*? He saw <u>you</u>! Pegged you ... when you cashed your check! He just went on out to his nuclear bomb of a car ... and he waited for you!"

"I had no idea! Dear Lord! He was following me? All the way from the store?"

"Yup. He was good. Damn good. Took me a few minutes before I was sure that he was up to ... up to what I thought he was up to. He followed you ... all the way. Had a chance to pull around you! Twice, he had an opportunity to catch up and pass you. He had better opportunities than I did! Once I was able to get close enough ... it was too late! I can't tell you how many cusswords I spouted! I knew that there was no way he was going to do anything on Eight Mile. Once I saw that the two of you were going to pull off onto this street, though, I knew he was about to make his move! So, I turned off my lights ... and coasted onto the street. Stopped here ... a few yards back. He pulled that knife on you ... at just about the time I got out of the car."

She felt her legs turn rubbery once again. She didn't collapse – or even semi-collapse! But she found herself more or less draped up against his body.

"Good Lord, Janet," he muttered, half caressing her – and half holding her up. "If I'd been too late ... well ... I don't know what I'd have done!"

"Just the same," she muttered, as she'd regained her footing, and pulled away from him – more briskly than she'd intended – "it's very disconcerting. Awfully damn disconcerting ... to think that you're being spied on. That you're living in some kind of stupid fish bowl. It's creepy. Did you follow me ... three or four nights ago? I went on a date that night ... with Fletcher Groome. Over to Windsor."

"No! Certainly not! Of course not! I would never do a thing like that! I ... I was going to say that it's no concern of mine ... who you go out with. But, that ... really and truly ... wouldn't be quite accurate. Not accurate at all." He reached for her hand again. She deftly dodged the move "I really haven't spied on you, Janet," he said. "I really haven't. Tonight? Tonight, it just seemed to be a good time to look in on you, is all."

"Well," the shaken woman observed, with a massive sigh, "I guess we'd better get this show on the road. Is there somewhere ... someplace I have to go? To press charges and all that?"

"Not right at this moment. I think we've got this S.O.B. pretty well dead to rights, and ... "

"Speaking of dead! Dear Lord! I heard a ... look, Steve ... I heard a shot! Did you shoot him?"

"Naw. Warning shot! Let him know that I bloody-well meant business. The second shot would've been a bit more business-like! But, I just fired the one shot into the air. It fell to earth. I know not where."

Janet laughed – in spite of herself.

"Like Joanie always says, 'Who writes your material?'."

"She's a fine girl ... Joanie. You're very lucky, Janet. Especially lucky. I envy you."

Something in what he'd said moved her. Touched her deeply. Another feeling she couldn't explain. How could he – how could <u>anyone</u> – envy her?

"Look, I'm going to have to make a report" he advised her. "But, listen, once that little duty is taken care of, if you'd happen to have a spare cup of coffee lying around your house ... not doing anything constructive ... why, maybe you'd invite a ne'er-do-well police officer over. To see that it doesn't go to waste, don't you see."

"You talk in riddles sometimes, Steven Francis. Just so I know what's going on ... which would be a real upset ... are you inviting yourself over to my house? For a cup of coffee?"

"Yeah. But, I thought that 'mooch' sounded so ... so crass."

Once more, she laughed.

"Yes," she replied. "We must remain refined. Mustn't we?"

"Well, maybe not at all costs. But, if you're game, I'll creep in, scoffle down some coffee ... and creep out."

Janet could only wonder what he may have meant – by his "maybe not at all costs" comment.

And she wondered why she was so disappointed in his not following her to her house, as he'd first suggested. Ah well. He probably had gotten caught up in the heat of the moment. It was understandable that he'd be required to make reports. Still ...

<<>>

Once she'd arrived home, Janet seemed the epitome of the calm self-assured woman. She enlisted Joan to help her carry in the groceries.

"Good God, Mom! What happened to the car?"

"Little accident, Honey. I'll tell you about it, when we get inside."

"Little? Looks like a pretty big one to me. Are you all right?"

"Of course. Of course I'm all right. Why shouldn't I be all right?"

"Okay, Mom. I was just askin'. I'm sorry, if I ... "

"No, Baby. I'm the one who's sorry. I didn't mean to bite your head off. Actually, it was pretty ... as you kids say ... pretty hairy. I'm telling myself ... over and over again ... that I'm all right! That I'm okay! That I'm fine! I just got a little carried away with my hokey little self-deception deal!"

They lugged the groceries up into the kitchen, and set the six bags down on the battle-scarred, badly-chipped, porcelain table next to the refrigerator.

Janet turned to Joan. Taking the 14-year-old into her arms, she kissed her daughter above her left ear.

"I'm so sorry, Baby," she rasped. "I really didn't mean to snap at you. It's just ... it's just ... just ... "

She began to weep, silently.

Joan held her mother tightly – patting the older woman on the shoulder.

"Take it easy, Mom. Everything's all right. Just ... just take it easy. It's okay. Everything's okay."

At that point, Robbie walked in from the dining room. He had never seen his mother cry before. Well, a tear here and there – but, nothing even close to what he was witnessing at that moment! He ran to Janet and Joan!

"Mom! What's wrong?" he shouted – wrapping his little arms around the buttocks of both women.

Joan answered for the distraught Janet:

"Nothin', Kid," she assured. "It's just girl stuff. I'll fill you in on it later."

The youngster stepped back and asked, "Are you guys sure there's nothin' wrong?"

"Yeah, Kid," sniffed his mother. "Us guys are sure. Why don't you go back and watch your tee vee?"

"Nah. There's nothing really good on. Are you sure that someone didn't beat you up, or sumpthing? 'Cause ... if anyone beat you up ... I'd ... "

Janet pulled away from Joan – and picked Robbie up. It was more of a struggle than she'd anticipated. The boy was only nine – but, he was growing. Growing so quickly. Growing so tall.

"My man of the house," she said – her manner brightening noticeably. "I just pity anyone who'd do anything to me ... whenever you're around, Boy."

He kissed her on each moist cheek.

"I'd stomp 'em," he assured. "I'd stomp 'em good!"

"I'm sure you would."

She put him back down, and tapped him lightly on the bottom.

"My goodness," wheezed Janet. "You're getting to be such a big boy. A big guy. Such a young man."

"Well," he said – as he headed back to the living room, "you just tell me ... if anyone tries to beat you up. I'll get 'im!"

"My hero," said Janet, smiling broadly. "You'll always be my hero."

She put on a pot of coffee, while Joan busied herself putting away the groceries.

"Boy," observed the younger woman. ""I don't remember us ever having this much stuff in the fridge or the pantry. Man, we'll be able to eat on this stuff ... forever!"

"Wrong, Grocery Breath," replied Janet, laughing. "We're going to have to be extremely careful. Hopefully, though, we won't have to scratch and claw ... like these last two weeks. I don't ever want to do that again. That's why I ... how do you guys say? I let it hang out a little ... at the market tonight. Before the car got bunged up."

"Are ... are we going to be able to get it fixed?"

Janet dropped into the chair by the table – the very picture of exhaustion.

"Yeah," she answered after a long, long pause. "Somehow ... one way or another ... we'll get it fixed. I don't know exactly how we're going to do it ... but we damn well will. We'll manage. Somehow ... someway ... we'll manage. It'll get repaired."

"I know we will, Mom. Look ... why don't we call Uncle Scott?"

Scott Carmichael was not really the children's uncle. He'd been a close friend for years – as had his wife, Wanda. Scott was Janet's insurance agent.

"Good idea," sighed Janet. "It's too late tonight. I'll give him a call ... first thing in the morning. In the meantime, why don't I whomp us up some supper ... now that we've got a few vittles in the house? No more 'fish heads and rice'! At least, hopefully, no more 'fish heads and rice'. Where's Rickie?"

"Upstairs. In his room. He's mad at me."

"What inhuman torture have you subjected your poor little brother to now?"

"Nothing. Just a toothpick or two under the fingernails. Jeez! You'd think I was hurting him or something."

"Seriously, Joanie. What's up?"

"Oh ... he and Robbie were having a squabble over who was going to watch what on television. So, I changed the channel to something neither one of 'em wanted to look at. Rickie threw a tantrum. So, I spanked him ... and sent him to his room. He swears he's never going to speak to me again."

Janet laughed.

"Did you ask him to put it in writing?" she asked.

"Yeah. But, it went over his head."

<<>>

As she went about cooking dinner – and as soon as Patti had gotten home – Janet called Patti and Joan into the kitchen. Barbara was still at the pizza restaurant. After closing the door from the dining room, Janet – as calmly as she was able – told her shocked daughters of her frightening encounter with the would-be robber/rapist earlier in the evening.

Joan seemed to be handling the narrative better than Patti. The latter's eyes seemed to glass-over, as Janet continued to relate the harrowing encounter. As the narrative depicted more and more horror, Patti seemed to be becoming more and more withdrawn!

"It's just a good thing that Steve was around," Joan kept remarking. "Just a really good thing. I'm glad he was there! Glad he was following you!"

She seemed not to have been the least bit upset by the fact that the police officer had been "looking in on" Janet. In fact, three or four times – during the relating of the horrible experience – she'd related her unbridled pleasure, at the prospect, to her mother.

"You're the luckiest lady in the world, Mom," she kept repeating. "The very luckiest lady."

Patti seemed not to have formed an opinion. Not insofar as Steve's apparent attention to her mother was concerned. She sat, stoically, silently, at the old porcelain kitchen table – and simply stared off into space.

Janet was becoming more and more certain that she'd been ill-advised to tell her daughters. At least until after dinner. It was so important to her that the kids should enjoy the upcoming meal.

That'd sure be different! Real different!

SIX

Ninety minutes later, the Bolton family was finishing dinner. The bill of fare had provided a rare treat: Pork chops. Outside of the Fletcher Groome-generated steak – in the doggie bag – it had been meager pickings till then. Both Robbie and Rickie snarfed down three pork chops each. The girls were every bit as eager to wrap themselves around the long-awaited tidings. Janet was glad that she'd bought what she'd estimated would be two or three meals worth of the cuts. Gladder still that, at the last minute, she'd had foresight enough to have prepared each one of them. The ravenous repast, however, created some doubt that the newly-bought foodstuffs would last till the next paycheck. The old saw about, "At the end of the money, there's always some month left."

Janet sat – almost transfixed. She watched her children – all of them absolutely thrilled – as they devoured the pork chops, mashed potatoes, peas, salad and an entire box of chocolate-covered doughnuts. The latter, of course, had been a bit of a luxury. Well, the whole entire meal had been a bit of a luxury. Maybe more than a bit. A warm glow of satisfaction engulfed Janet, as the kids – happily, including her two daughters – continued to dig in.

Had it not been for liberal amounts of *Hamburger Helper* – and the pizzas that Barbara had brought home most nights – Janet had no idea how they would've made it through the previous couple of weeks.

Barbara had explained that the pizzas were "left over" – and Janet had bought it. Well, she'd accepted her daughter's explanation – for the first week. After eight or nine days had passed, it finally occurred to her that never before had there been that many "leftovers". The young woman had never brought home that many pizzas. Not that often. Not in an entire month! Finally, the younger woman had broken down and confessed that she'd managed to make a few more pizzas than she knew the restaurant would sell. The owner – marginally aware of the Boltons' plight – had given the pies to Barbara! A nice gesture. A very charitable one. On the other hand, every one of the Boltons was certain that he/she would never be able to look another pizza in the eye.

Janet's thoughts turned to the owner of the pizza joint. Fletcher had told her that the man had a reputation for putting his hands all over the help! All the time! Did that, she wondered, include Barbara? Was her daughter having to put up with a whole host of indignities at the hands – literally – of this owner? Was Barbara being forced to continually withstand certainly-unwanted sexual advances? Just because she believed that she could not afford to give up her job there? An affirmative answer to that question would, of course, be devastating!

Janet made her way out into the kitchen – to refill her coffee cup. The deep, brooding, highly-troubling, ponderings followed her:

Was she being a good mother? Was she properly fulfilling her maternal duties? Was her dire financial situation causing her oldest daughter to have to contend with outrageous "attention" in the workplace? She wound up splashing as much coffee outside her cup as inside!

Her head ached! Her mind was an out of control whirling-dervish! If she were to marry Fletcher – or, possibly, simply sleep with him – she could completely extricate her family. Rescue each one of her kids, from a seeming hell! Tempting? She didn't know if considering "hooking up" with Fletcher constituted an actual temptation! But, it was certainly something to think about! In addition, there would be more than only that one stupid, antiquated, black-and-white television in the house. Robbie and Rickie wouldn't have to squabble over which program they'd view.

Not only would Barbara not have to put up with the guy at the pizza parlor – especially if the creep was using the Braille System – Fletcher had offered to buy the young woman a car. A brand new one.

A Buick Regal, she remembered him specifying. Was it a Regal? Or was it a Camaro?

Barb isn't the only one around here who could use a new car!

Her mind was swept back to the accident! Her harrowing escape from that – that subhuman! There was no doubt in her mind that he was going to rape her. Rob her and rape her! Then? After that? Who knows? Her body was caught up in a brand new series of "Shivering Willies"!

Wresting her mind away from the evening's horrible experience, she forced her thoughts back to the multitude of immediate possibilities. Mostly, the inevitable advantages which would accrue to her family – were she to wed (or go to bed, on a regular basis, with) Fletcher Groome: For one thing, she wouldn't have to work. Even if she would decline to marry him, she still probably wouldn't have to work – if she "played her cards right". Which, of course, translated out to "merely" sleeping with him.

Merely?

Again, she was overcome with a mind-boggling series of shudders! What kind of thoughts were those that she was entertaining? She'd never – ever – allowed herself to even think along any of those lines before! Not in her entire lifetime! Let alone to seriously consider them! Why now?

Well, for one thing, there were four kids in the other room – wolfing down the only decent meal they'd had in God-knows-how-long!

Further, there had been that narrow escape – just hours before! A woman can't even cash her stupid check at the stupid supermarket – without getting robbed or raped! Or – dear Lord – killed!

There was her poor, badly-wounded, Maverick, out in the driveway! How would she ever replace it? How could she ever replace it? How will she ever get it fixed? Even if Scott Carmichael advises her that the insurance will pay for the damage – far from a foregone conclusion – she'll be without a car, while the Maverick is being fixed. A rental car would probably be out of the question.

Her eyes began to tear up, once again! Thoughts of Barbara – having to fend off advances at the pizzeria – took over the movie screen of her mind!

The hell with it! I ought to just go ahead and marry Fletcher …

and have done with it! Quit putting Barb ... and everyone else ... through all this hell!

Still, she was horribly repulsed at the thought of being in bed with Fletcher!

Dear Lord! His hands! His hands ... all over me!

"Oooohhhh!" Another massive shivering spell!

"Mom! What's wrong?" It was Patti. She'd just entered the kitchen.

"Nothing," Janet answered – far too quickly! "Nothing at all! Just ... just got a chill up my back, is all. Someone must've walked over my grave."

"Mother! Don't say things like that. Don't even talk like that."

The remark had obviously upset the young woman. She almost never called Janet "Mother". Barbara always did. But, the others always called her "Mom".

"I'm ... I'm sorry, Sweetheart. I didn't mean to ... "

She was interrupted by the doorbell.

She'd all but forgotten that Steve Francis had indicated that he was going to drop in. It was a bit of a shock – that she'd relegated the man who'd, quite probably, saved her life to an emotional back burner.

She guessed that the detective was probably – as Joan had described him – a "hunk". She had – she was forced to admit – experienced a new and wonderful sensation or two, just standing there, talking with him. Especially when he took her hand in his.

The bell rang once again!

"I think that may be your buddy, Steve," she said to Joan – as she hurried through the dining room, toward the front door.

By the time Janet had let the detective in, Joan and Rickie were standing close behind her. Apparently, Steve had made quite an impression on both of them. He mussed Rickie's hair – as Janet led their visitor into the dining room.

"I don't think you've met my Number-Two Daughter, Patti. Patti? This is Steve Francis."

The young woman got to her feet – and allowed the officer to take her hand.

"Mister Francis," she bubbled. Only the second show of emotion that the girl had exhibited – since Janet had told her of the attack. "I've heard so much about you," she said to their visitor.

"Oh? And from whom would that be?"

"Joanie. She said you were a hunk."

"Patti!" seethed Joan. "Shut up!"

"Well, you did," answered Patti with a laugh. "And you're right. He is. A real-life hunk."

Janet hurriedly injected, "And this is the other love of my life … the man of the house, Robbie."

"Hi there, Robbie!"

Steve was careful not to compliment the boy on his grip, as they shook hands. He didn't want to wind up in the same category as Fletcher Groome.

"Sit down, Mister Francis," invited Joan. "I'm glad to see you again."

"I can tell," he replied, smiling brightly. "I'm glad to see you again too."

"What about me?" asked Rickie.

"Oh! And especially you, Champ." He winked at Joan. "And it's nice to meet you too, Patti. You too, Robbie. I hope that I'll be able to meet Barb soon."

"Oh," informed Joan, "she's working. Won't be home till a little past midnight. You're certainly welcome to stay … until she gets here."

"That's a little past my bedtime." Steve answered, obviously pleased.

"Do sit down, Steve," invited Janet. "I'm sorry that I don't have any pork chops or potatoes left to offer you. In fact, I don't have much of anything from dinner to offer you. Not even a chocolate doughnut. If you have time, though, I can put on some … "

He put up a hand.

"No," he responded. "No, please. I had an awfully late lunch today … and I'm still stock full."

Patti jammed the last of her doughnut into her mouth – and gulped down the bottom third of her cup of tea.

"Why don't Joanie and I clear away the table?" she asked – far too loudly. Looking at Robbie and Rickie, she continued, "You two hard guys, I want you to go on in and watch tee vee."

"We wanna stay here and talk to Mister Francis," replied Rickie.

Patti put her hands on her hips and replied, "Well, I don't <u>want</u> you to stay here and talk to Mister Francis. I want you to go in the other room … and watch tee vee. Mister Francis and Mom have lots of things to … to talk over and discuss."

Steve – who'd been seated only a matter of minutes – rose, and looked at each of the Bolton children and said, "I'd really appreciate it if you'd all call me Steve. Mister Francis is my father. Well, was my father. Really … Steve is fine."

"I don't know," interjected Janet. "I've always tried to teach them to treat their elders with respect. God knows, there's precious little of that around today."

"Elders?" That craggy smile again. "You make me sound eighty-seven years, and four-months, old. I agree that, in most cases, an … uh … elder should be called mister or missus or miss or whatever. But, there are other ways of showing respect. Besides, this is a special thing. At least, I hope it is. Isn't it, gang?"

Robbie and Rickie shouted – in unison, "Yeah!"

Joan smiled warmly at their guest and said, enthusiastically, "Yes. Yes, it is."

Patti merely smiled – and nodded.

"Then, it's settled," proclaimed Steve. "Steverino it is."

"Well, I don't know about 'Steverino'," conceded Janet. "But, Steve, I guess, does sound like a winner."

"I'm glad that's settled," said Steve.

"Now, listen up guys," pressed Janet, "I think that Patti had a really shining idea". Looking at her two sons, she prodded, "Why don't you two men go in and turn on the tee vee … and let your sisters see if they can restore some order out of the chaos out here?"

Once the boys were ensconced in the living room – and the girls, having cleared the table, had repaired to the kitchen – Janet poured a cup of coffee for Steve and herself. Then, she rejoined her guest at the dining room table. Patti had, diplomatically, closed the door between the two rooms.

"I'm sorry," began Janet, "if I sounded ungrateful back there … out there … this evening. I honestly am. It was just a little unsettling … to think that I was having all of my movements chronicled. Let's face it

… there are things that each of us human types don't particularly want publicized. Stuff we'd rather keep to ourselves."

"It was a natural reaction," he replied. "No apology needed. I probably could've been a little more suave about it. It's a fine line, y'know. How do I tell some person … especially in a situation like that one … that I care enough about her to try and keep a bit of an eye on her? And yet, not cross over the line … and tell her that I've been following her around? Snooping around? Invading her privacy?"

"You … are you saying that you care for me? You are saying that you … you actually care for me?"

"Yes. I believe that's what I said. It pretty well sums up how I feel. What I feel. Of course I care for you. Of course I do! I think I have … from the time I first met you, at Uriah Heap's handy-dandy little sweat shop. Don't ask me why."

"Oh, please let me ask you why," she pressed, with an impish smile – squiggling her nose slightly. "Being serious for a minute, I wouldn't want anyone caring about me … simply because they might … that they might be feeling sorry for me."

"Feel sorry for you?"

Janet wished that he hadn't spoken so loudly. She was positive that Joan and Patti would have had their ears plastered flush against the kitchen door.

"Feel sorry for you?" he repeated. "How can I feel sorry for you? How could anyone feel sorry for you? You've got the five nicest kids I've ever seen. You're one of the luckiest women in the whole furschlugginer world!"

"You've only met four of 'em. Only four of my kids."

"Don't get technical. Listen, I don't have to be a rocket scientist to see what a great relationship you have with them. I could see it in the way that Joanie and Rickie interacted with you that Saturday … back when I came here to tell you about the position at **Brock's**."

"Aren't you going to ask me how I'm doing over there? Or is that another thing … something else … that you already know? Because you've been … uh … looking in on me."

"No. I don't have to … quote-unquote … look in on you for that. I know that you're doing well. Mainly, because I knew … from the moment I met you … that you packed the gear to do a helluva job.

Secondly, if you were not doing well, you wouldn't still be there. My brother-in-law is a great guy. Salt of the earth ... and all that. But, he will not tolerate inefficiency. If you weren't doing the job, you'd have been out on your bottom. Your very beautiful bottom ... if you'll allow an unsolicited testimony to be entered into the record. No. No, whatever else ol' Richard is ... whatever he may do ... he sure as the dickens doesn't run a charity hospital over there. You pull your weight ... or he'll find someone who will."

"Well, that's nice to know."

"What's nice to know? You've got a beautiful bottom? Hell, anyone could've told you that."

She laughed – obviously uncomfortable with the remarks about her derriere. Especially since she could picture her daughters – stifling a whole series of giggles – on the other side of the kitchen door.

"You're obviously Irish," she observed. "Are you sure, Steven Francis, that you're not carrying the Blarney Stone around with you? In your pocket, somewhere?"

"Ah, me Darlin'! It wouldn't be blarney I'd be handin' ya, now!"

She gave him an overdone wince.

"That's the worst Irish dialect I've ever heard," she responded. " Maybe you're really Italian or something. Swedish, maybe?"

"Well," he responded, "getting back to what we were talking about ... "

"My bottom?" Janet had just shocked herself with the question.

"Well, that too," answered Steve – not missing a beat. "But, one of the reasons Richard has such a turnover, at that receptionist's desk, is that it's a damn demanding position. It's the first contact that a prospective client has with the firm. And it's so critical that the receptionist knows what the hell she's doing."

"Well, it's nice to know that <u>someone</u> thinks I know what the hell I'm doing."

"Ol' Rich has had a few good ones. That Peggy, now. She was a real gem. But, the good ones have always moved up the old corporate stepladder. People keep telling Rich that he should just be happy to get someone who can do a passable job ... just a passable job ... on the desk out there. But, he doesn't want to know from passable. He wants efficiency. And, with you, he's damn sure got it. Otherwise, I'm sure you'd … "

"Be out on my bottom?" Again, she shocked herself. "I know. You told me."

His craggy face took on a seriousness she'd never seen before. His square jaw seemed to set itself – almost like a stone sculpture.

"Are you doing all right now?" His voice had taken on a surprising huskiness.

"Right now? Right at this moment?"

"Yeah. You seem pretty well settled down … after your little adventure this evening."

"Yes," she answered – with a monumental sigh. "I don't really think that the impact hit me … really hit me … until we sat down to dinner. Dear Lord! When I think of what that gorilla was going to do … going to do to … do to me!"

"Well, I realize that it's easier said than done … but, you're going to have to try and put it behind you. Put it right out of your mind. That's going to be very difficult … especially when you'll have to file a complaint against the S.O.B. Probably tomorrow or the next day. I'll take you over to the station, in Southfield … if you want. I'm sure I can kind of help you walk through the thing. Know a few shortcuts, I do."

"Yes. Yes, thank you. Yes, that'd be nice. You're a … a really nice man."

"Not really. Just concerned about you. That's all."

"It's funny. All these years, I haven't really been all that concerned about myself. I always figured that things would just … well, they'd always just work themselves out."

"Haven't they?" He'd seemed nonplussed by her statement.

"Well, yes. Yes, they have. But, dear Lord, I look back now … at some of the things I thought and did … and I almost have a kitten. How could I have been so naïve? So unquestioning?"

"And now? You're losing your naïveté? You're starting to question things?"

She nodded.

"I guess I am," she answered. "I was sitting here … watching the kids digging into the first halfway decent meal they've had in … in what seems like … seems like decades. You talk about buzz-saws. Here were four kids … just shoveling it in! Scoffling it down! Just as fast as they could! Even Patti. She's sixteen … and so mature, you know. So ladylike. So sophisticated. And yet, there she was … setting intramural records, for packing away vittles. Just like Robbie and Rickie. Well, so was Joanie. And I'm thinking to myself, 'Why am I subjecting them … to all this?'"

"Oh, c'mon. I don't think you're subjecting them to anything that's so all-fired terrible."

"That's just it! Yes I am! I've always allowed myself to think that I wasn't! But, yes I am! Apparently, Barb's boss at the pizza joint has a reputation for patting all the girls on the fanny. If not worse! And here's my oldest daughter … working for him! Patti's gone … virtually every night … babysitting every kid in the neighborhood! Joanie is practically raising my sons! My sons … who haven't had a father for as long as they can remember! And here I am! Starting to doubt everything I've ever believed in. I used to accept things. Accept just about everything … at face value."

"I don't think you're starting to get all that cynical, Janet. I hope not, anyway. I'd rather take everyone's word … and get my butt kicked every now and then … than to be so damn skeptical that I don't believe anything. So damn cynical … that I'd have to look behind everything I hear. Even everything I see. To me, <u>that's</u> demented."

"Well, I … I guess I've never looked at it quite that way. But, I still think that I'm too naïve for my own good."

"That's one of your charms, Janet. Please … don't lose it. You have such a … well, such a … such a refreshing manner about you. Such a … I don't know … it's almost like a Christmas morning look, that you get sometimes. And I see that … and I say to myself, 'Myself,' I say, 'there ain't enough of that commodity in this old world we live in'. Ever the philosopher, ol' Steve-o. Ol' Steverino."

She took a long drag at her coffee cup. She'd never had a man – or anyone else – tell her that she'd projected a "Christmas morning look". Never before. Of course, she'd never had a man – or anyone else – tell her that she'd had a good-looking bottom before either. God knows, Jim had never said anything that had even come close. In either area.

"Steve," she said, at length, "it's funny you should say that my …

my manner ... that it's refreshing. I've been fighting a lot of battles lately. It's not that I think ... or that I feel like ... like I've had a long row to hoe. That my situation was that overwhelming."

"Ah, but you have, Janet. It has been a long row to hoe. A lesser woman ... a lesser person ... would've found it damned overwhelming. You haven't. And ... because of that ... you've done well. Extremely well."

"Maybe. Sometimes ... most times ... I find myself doubting that. I doubt that I'm doing well at all. I don't know. Maybe I'm getting old, or something, but ... "

"How old are you? All of thirty-two? Thirty-three?"

"Try thirty-six ... and that's something you don't ever dare to ask a woman. Any woman."

"Well, you certainly don't look it. Actually, you don't even look thirty-two or thirty-three. I just figured that ... with your having children as old as Barb and Patti ... I figured you had to be in your early-thirties. At the very least."

"That's nice of you," she said, with a half-smile. "Maybe I'm finally out of my adolescence. About damn time. But, lately, I've been tempted ... tempted to just chuck everything ... and just go ahead and marry Fletcher Groome."

The "look" crossed Steve's face! For only the briefest of seconds! If Janet hadn't been looking directly at him – her gaze affixed on his craggy countenance – she'd have missed it. Would never have seen the expression. No, not an expression. Actually, it <u>was</u> a "look"! A strange – well – "look"! Probably couldn't be called anything else..

If she hadn't known better, Janet reasoned, she'd have sworn that the "look" was almost one of – of horror. Stark <u>horror</u>! Could that be?

"Well ... uh," stumbled Steve, "I've never met the man. Don't even know what the man looks like. But ... well ... I think I remember the last time I was here that the little one ... Rickie ... thought he was ... how did he say? ... too nice."

"Yeah. It's not only Rickie. They all think that he's too nice."

"Do you love him?"

Instantly, she was engulfed in a top-to-toe shudder.

"Love him?" she managed to say, hoarsely. "Love him? Of course not."

"You say 'Of course not' … as though loving him would be the most illogical thing in the world. Yet, you're obviously thinking seriously in terms of marrying him. I'm … I'm sorry … but, really, I don't understand."

"You wouldn't." She wished her voice hadn't contained such a large amount of impatience. Her answer had made her guest – literally – wince.

"I suppose you're right," he replied – doing his best to rally.

"My problem is that … that I understand it all too well. As I said before, Steve, you're a nice man. Too nice to know what's percolating in my evil, twisted, demented, little mind. What I'm thinking of doing is, of course, the next thing to … to prostituting myself. Maybe not even the next thing. It's probably even more reprehensible. At least a whore makes no pretense. She is what she is. No illusions about what she's doing. At least with a prostitute, everything is all out in the open. But, me? In order to take the onus off my kids … and, let's face it, off myself … here I am, seriously considering the sanctified state of Holy Matrimony! Besmirching a sacrament … with someone I doubt I could ever love. There are times when … when his touch … when it makes my skin crawl"

"Then I don't see how you could possibly consider … "

"Don't you see? If I married him, the kids wouldn't have to celebrate an ordinary … a stupid, damn, run of the mill … meal! Celebrate it like it was some kind of a damn banquet or something. My oldest daughter wouldn't have to worry about getting her fanny patted … or something even worse … every time she walked past her boss. My kids wouldn't have to fight over one stinking, lousy, stupid, damn, black-and-white, television set. And none of this would … " Janet couldn't hold back the tears! "Oh, God!" she wailed. "Dear Lord! Sometimes I don't even know what I'm thinking!"

Steve reached across the table, and grabbed her hands up – encasing them in his own! It was at the same moment that Patti and Joan burst through the door from the kitchen!

"Mom!" cried Patti. "What's … what's wrong? Are you all right?" Janet nodded.

"Yes," she sniffed. "Yes. Fine. I … I just got carried away. Would one of you ladies bring me a *Kleenex* or a paper towel or something? Before I destroy my make-up completely? Or maybe flood the joint out?"

"I didn't do nuthin'," their visitor proclaimed to the girls – holding both arms out in an overdone shrug. He'd had to remove both of Janet's hands to produce the gesture. "Honest."

"We know," smiled Joan. "We know. You wouldn't do anything to hurt her."

The manner in which her daughter had said, "You wouldn't do anything to hurt her" caused Janet to break down once more! Patti hurried to get some tissues – while Joan, standing behind her mother's chair, wrapped her arms around the neck of the distraught woman.

"Mom," she soothed, "we don't want to see you hurt. When you're hurt … we're hurt. Even the boys … little blankety-blanks that they can be, sometimes … they also hurt."

Janet placed her right hand over her daughter's right hand.

"You're sweet," she sniffed, again. "You're … all of you … you're great. I don't deserve you."

She began to weep once again, as Patti rushed back into the room!

"Here," she exclaimed. "Here's fourteen pounds of *Kleenex*. Now you can cry till your heart's content."

Patti's expression had presented an uncontrollable paradox for Janet – who began to laugh and cry, at the same time. Patti knelt next to her mother. Put her head in Janet's lap.

"You'll have to excuse Mom," she said to Steve. "She's had a pretty hard day. An extremely hard day. I think that, maybe, a lot of things may have … may have come to a head tonight."

"I know," Steve answered, nodding slowly. His voice was scarcely beyond a whisper. "I know. You're a very perceptive young woman. I wish I could have your insight. I wish there was something I could do … some button I could push … to help."

"You've helped a lot now," replied Patti. "Thank God you did what you did tonight … or Lord only knows what would've happened."

Joan left Janet's chair – to stand behind Steve's. She put her arms around his neck. Then, she leaned down – and kissed his right cheek.

"Yes," she agreed. "Patti's right. If you hadn't come along, things would've been ... well, they would've been ... they'd have been God-awful horrible! I can hardly stand to even think about it! Thank you, Steve. Thank you again. And again and again."

She kissed his other cheek.

"Aw gorsh, Ma'am," sputtered the flustered visitor. "Yer flat embarrassin' me."

"She's right," added Patti. "Sometimes we don't count our blessings enough around here. To think of what could've happened ... what would've happened ... to her, if you hadn't been there ... I ... we ... well, we just thank God that you were there."

At that point, both boys walked in from the living room.

"What's the matter, Mom?" asked Rickie. "Is something wrong?"

Robbie looked at his mother. Then, at his two sisters. Janet was crying. Joan and Patti both had tears running down their cheeks. "C'mon, you guys," he insisted. "What's wrong?"

"Nothing," sniffed Janet. "Nothing at all. We're fine. We're all fine."

Robbie shifted his gaze to Steve. His eyes narrowed – a stare well beyond his years.

"What's goin' on, Mister Francis?"

"It's Steve. Remember? Nothing, Old Buddy. Nothing's going on. Honest. You know how girls are. They get together ... and they all start bawling, y'know. I'm surprised they haven't thrown me out."

"Yes," interjected Janet. "On his bottom!"

Then, she started to laugh. Uncontrollable gales of laughter! Robbie looked at his mother, then at Steve. The latter simply shrugged. Shaking his head, the boy retreated to the living room – followed by his brother.

It took fully two minutes – but, Janet managed to regain her composure.

Joan returned to the kitchen. Patti also headed there. But, before leaving the room, she turned to Steve.

"Thank you," she said to him. "Thank you for being here. For being there ... and for being here."

Alone once more, Janet and Steve merely sat at the table – studying one another. It was a situation unlike any that Janet had ever experienced.

Clumsy? Yes, certainly clumsy. Clumsy – yet comfortable. Strangely comfortable.

Steve took her hands in his once more and asked, "Should I leave?"

Janet shook her head.

"No. Please don't. I'm so sorry to have gone off the deep end, like I did. Last thing you need … is for someone like me to come apart at the seams. I apologize."

"Don't! Please … don't apologize! Don't ever apologize! Not for that!"

Steve's eyes began to water. He let go of her hands. Janet left them in the center of the table.

"I don't know," he rasped. "Can't remember, when I've ever been more … more moved. Moved … by anything! Not in my entire life!"

A tear trickled out of his left eye – and down his cheek. He did nothing to wipe it away.

My God! He's crying! This big brave policeman … who probably saved my life! And he's crying! He's actually crying!

"Have … have I done something wrong?" she asked.

"Wrong? Of course not. On the contrary. You got a little upset … and started to cry. Four kids came barreling in! Four kids to comfort you! Four kids who'd positively do anything … anything in their power … to make you not cry!" Another tear. "Like I said, I've never been more moved in my life," he rasped. "Never. Do you realize that millions of people … millions of 'em … go through their entire lives? And they don't know what that feels like. They'll never know the feeling that someone actually cares … cares that deeply … for them. And you can multiply yours by four. By five, y'know. I'm sure that Barbara would've been in the middle of the whole thing … if she'd been home. Can you realize how totally empty some people's lives are? How much they'd give to have one person … just one, man or woman, boy or girl … who'd show that they care?"

His tears – while by no means a flood – seemed to be coming with greater frequency. Janet – despite being deeply touched by what Steve had just said – seemed to be rebounding. Regaining control.

"Do … do you have any children, Steve? You know something?

This it totally amazing! You know practically everything there is to know about me. About me and my family. And I know practically nothing about you. Your name and occupation ... and that's about it."

"No," he answered. "I don't have any kids. Not anymore. I had a daughter once. But, I don't have her anymore."

He was fighting a losing battle – a futile attempt to stem the tide of tears.

"I ... I don't know what to say," responded Janet, in a voice barely above a whisper. "I didn't mean to ... to, you know ... to pry. I certainly didn't mean to ... to open ... uh ... to open any old ... any old wounds."

"Of course you didn't. I'm two years older than you, Janet. There are times when I feel like I'm twenty years older than you. Right now ... the way I'm acting ... you probably feel like you're twenty years older than me. On merit."

"No," answered Janet – making a heroic attempt to affect a casual tone. "Not at the moment, anyway. I'm ... I'm sorry, if I said something I shouldn't have."

"You didn't," he answered, letting go a gargantuan sigh. "You didn't. My daughter was eleven-years-old ... when she died. I surprise myself. I actually said 'died'. I usually say ... even to myself ... that she 'went away'. It was eight years ago. We were living in a little apartment ... in Farmington. My wife, my little Sharon and me. We had a situation where we were working with three different police departments. A horrible spate of late-night armed robberies. They had me staking out these different convenience stores, you see. And so, I was in the back room of this *Twenty-three Skidoo* store ... over on Nine Mile Road. Right near Middlebelt. When I got home ... back to my apartment ... about eight-thirty in the morning ... I found the whole damn complex, in a smoldering ruins!"

"Burned down? The complex had been burned down?"

He nodded slowly – as he plucked one of Janet's tissues. He blew his nose. A loud honk. The noise seemed to help him turn a corner. Slightly, anyway.

"Some idiot ... some horse's ass ... in the next apartment," he expanded. "Some clod! Smoking in bed! The whole damn building went up! Like some kind of damn tinder box! Wind blew the embers ... blew 'em onto the other buildings! But, those people ... those that weren't in my building ... they had enough warning! They all managed to get out! Thank God! Betty ... my wife ... and my little Sharon! They ... they had no such warning." Tears resumed cascading down his face. "They ... Betty and Sharon ... they didn't make it." It hadn't been that much of a corner.

"They ... they didn't? Oh, Steve! I'm so sorry! So ... so ... "

"No," he sniffed. "No, they didn't." Then, his voice took on a rock-like quality – which, Janet assumed, was the product of years of dealing with such an overwhelming loss. Such a mind-boggling tragedy. "They died," he continued. "So did the guy with the damn cigarette." He reached for another tissue. "So," he rasped, "did four other people."

It was Janet's turn to take his hand.

"I'm so sorry, Steve. So sorry. I think I remember that fire. It was all over the news on tee vee. What a tragedy. What a terrible, terrible, terrible tragedy! I'm ... really ... I'm so sorry. So terribly sorry."

"I guess that's why ... when I see kids relating really well to their parents ... I guess that's why it sort of sets something off inside me. In my line of work, you see so much crap! So much out and out crap! You see kids ... kids killing their parents! You see parents abusing, raping, sodomizing, their kids! Killing their kids, for God's sakes! Some of the most God-awful atrocities!" A chill roared up his back – bringing on an all-consuming shudder! Once again, he blew his nose. "Awful, awful atrocities," he went on. "And that's just the really outlandish stuff. It's <u>supposed</u> to upset you. Upset anyone! How could it not?"

"And does it?"

"Of course! Of course it does. You see parents having to come down and bail out their kids ... after the kid has gone ahead and done something completely rotten! Something terrible! Something atrocious! And hell, most of the time, the kid could care less ... doesn't give one tinker's damn what their parents might be going through. Could care less. It's really upsetting! Sometimes, it's the parents who're the bastards. And <u>that's</u> even worse! Neglect their kids! Harm their kids! Starve their kids! Hell, even rape their kids!" It was his turn to sigh – heavily. "It's a damn cumulative effect."

"Yes. Yes, I guess I've never thought much about it ... but, yes. I can certainly see where it would be terribly depressing. To have to deal with this stuff ... day in and day out. Day after day."

"It is. Believe me. And ... as a state cop ... I don't get involved in that many of those situations. Not on a percentage basis. The local cops ... they catch it all! But, I see enough. Too damn much. So much ... that I get sick to my stomach! Physically sick to my stomach! And I'm supposed to be a wondrous detached ... a dispassionate ... officer of the law."

"I really don't see how you ... or anyone else ... could be dispassionate about those things. Any of those things. How could you be dispassionate about those things?"

"Well," he answered, "it's kind of hokey ... but, I've appropriated one of Satchel Paige's life-long sayings. Only thing that gets me through. Well, one of the things that helps me deal with all the ... all the ... all the crap. All the out and out crap ... that comes my way. Comes any cop's way."

"Satchel Paige? Who was Satchel Paige? I don't think I've ever ... "

He was a man ... a guy, who labored away in the old Negro Leagues. Before Jackie Robinson broke the color line, in Major League Ball. With the old Brooklyn Dodgers ... back in nineteen-forty-seven. Satchel was an old man ... some say in his fifties ... when he was finally signed on by the Cleveland Indians. That was in forty-eight, I believe. He was a special guy. Helluva special guy."

"In what way? Other than, you know, he was in his fifties ... and was still playing ball?"

"My dad used to go down to Tiger Stadium, y'know. Briggs Stadium, as it was known in those days. He said he got to see Satchel Paige pitch a couple or three times. They'd had him ... the Indians did ... had him as a relief pitcher. The bullpens ... both of 'em ... were in deep centerfield at that time. Deepest part of the ballpark."

"I ... I don't understand. Don't see what this old pitcher has to do with ... with how you handle all this ... all this crap, as you so delicately describe it."

"Well, whenever ol' Satch would come in from the Indians' pen ... way in deep center ... it always seemed like it took him an hour-and-a-half to get to the pitcher's mound. Of course, he'd always said that all he had to do to warm up … was to shake hands with the catcher. He was a really funny man. Great human being. And, when people would ask him why it was that he always moved so slowly, he'd always say … I'm paraphrasing now, but he'd say … 'I always take it slow. And I never look back. You should never look back. No one should ever look back. Might be something gaining on you.' So, I simply try to never look back."

"Does it work?"

"It <u>seems</u> to. Most of the time, anyway."

"That's … that's amazing. Who'd have thought that … ?"

Y' know, Janet? You just might try and adopt that … ah … that philosophy for yourself. Listen, you've had so much to go on in your life. You've had so much … well, so much crap … to deal with. And you've handled it beautifully. I'm not trying to borax you. You <u>have</u> handled it beautifully. And you'll <u>continue</u> to handle it beautifully. I'm positive of that. But, I believe that you should … also … never look back. Can't tell if something actually <u>is</u> gaining on you. You don't need something <u>else</u> to worry about. Concentrate on what's ahead of you. There's enough stuff in the present to keep you busy … and off the streets. And if you don't look over your shoulder … if you can just pull that mindset off … I have no doubt that you'll do fine. Continue to do fine. Listen, Lady. You have nothing else to feel … nothing else but pride, and a sense of accomplishment … for all the things you've jacked with. All the things you've had to contend with. And … all the things that you've flat-out accomplished. Let me tell you … <u>that's</u> a helluva lot. If you continue on … keep right on … the way you've always kept on, you'll do all right. <u>Better</u> than all right. Plus, there might not be <u>anything</u> … not a damn thing … gaining on you, y'know. Not one damn thing."

Gently, he removed his hand from hers – and arose.

"I've got to be leaving." Janet began to speak, but he raised a palm – cutting her off. "We have to see one another, Janet. We simply have to. I don't think I could hack walking out your front door … and feeling as though I was walking out of your life."

She looked up – into his deep, rich, blue eyes. Why had she not noticed the vibrant colors before?

"Yes," she answered, softly, as she got up from her chair. "Yes. We do."

Steve pulled her gently around the corner of the table – and into his arms. He held her tightly. Her arms wound around his neck. His arms wrapped around her waist.

He didn't bring his lips down hard – certainly not hard – upon hers. For fully 30 seconds, their lips barely seemed to touch. Janet was not absolutely certain that their lips <u>were</u> touching. They may have been inches apart! But, she could still feel the electricity crackling – as though between two electrodes! How could that be? Did that lightning – or whatever it was – make actual touching unnecessary? Superfluous?

Her train of thought evaporated – as his kiss became more and more fervent. As he pressed his eager mouth against her lips with much more urgency! The electrodes were becoming terribly overworked! Were they on the verge of burning out? Maybe even exploding?

She felt herself melt against him! Her kiss answered his! She stiffened, momentarily, as she felt his tongue pry open her lips – and flick into and out of her mouth! No one had ever done that before! The very thought of a "French kiss" had always appalled her! Yet, she found herself responding to something deep within herself! Some sort of awakening! Some sort of incredible awakening! An arousal! Yes, it was an out and out arousal! One with which she was far from sure that she could cope!

She made an attempt to pull away! She was frightened! Frightened by what was happening to her! Frightened by what Steve was doing! Frightened by the way she was reacting! The manner in which she was responding to his tenderness! His tenderness – and his passion! Should she be answering either emotion this way? <u>Any</u> emotion this way? Strange, wonderful, overwhelming forces were charging through her body! Galloping through her entire being! She needed, she knew, to break the embrace! To end it – immediately!

As he held her even more tightly, she could feel his urgency! With his body so solidly pressed against her – pressed taut against her – there was no mistaking his need!

She knew – in her less frenzied moments – that, at this point, she should really put on the brakes! That this was out and out madness!

Why was she losing control? Why had she lost control? While what was happening to Janet may have been the oldest story in the world – the raw emotion was all so new to her! So amazingly, incredibly, new!

Finally, she broke away!

"Uh ... Janet ... I think I should ... uh, maybe ... I guess I'd better go."

"Yes." Her voice was a hoarse whisper. Much huskier than she'd ever heard herself. "Yes," she repeated. "Maybe you ... maybe you'd better."

They stood there! The pair of them! Transfixed! Not moving! Neither one of them. Just looking into one another's eyes! For two or three minutes! An eternity! Was it possible for eyes to – to kiss?

He took her hands into his once more. Finally, he spoke:

"Janet," he rasped. "Janet, you are the most beautiful woman I've ever met. So beautiful! So beautiful ... inside and out! If you could only <u>imagine</u> how beautiful you are! I've never been so captivated by anyone! Ever! Not in my entire life! I really don't know how to ... how to ... to behave around you. There are times when I haven't been able to think of anyone else. Of anything else. I'd see something ... and immediately wish that you were there to share it with me. Stupid things. This morning ... out on Orchard Lake Road ... there was this rusty old Thunderbird. Eight, nine, ten years old. And it'd run off the road. Sitting there at the damndest angle. Straddling a ditch. Don't know how it could ... possibly ... have gotten there. And I found myself wishing you could be there with me. Be right beside me ... looking at that stupid car, at that stupid angle, hanging across that stupid ditch."

Janet seemed to be regaining her composure.

"You're so romantic," she replied, with a semi-laugh.

"It's true. I don't know why, but ... ever since I met you ... you've just simply dazzled me with your footwork. From that first day ... when Busch Claiborne and I went to see you at that slave-labor laundry ... I haven't been able to get you out of my mind. What's left of it. Claiborne even mentioned it ... on the way out to the airport. And this was a couple days later. I guess I must be awfully ... awfully transparent."

"I don't know about that. Everyone says that I'm supposed to be the transparent one. And ... and, whether I am or not ... I certainly couldn't see through you. I really couldn't. Still can't."

She ran the backs of the fingers on her right hand lightly over his left ear – and down his left cheek.

"Steve! I'm frightened!"

"Frightened? Yeah. I'd be too ... after going through what you did, over there on Eight Mile Road. I know that I'd certainly be all kinds of ... "

"No! Not about that! Well, I am! I was! Still am! But, that's not what I'm talking about. It's just ... listen ... when you kissed me, just then, I ... I felt something! A lot of somethings! Things I've never felt before! And here I am ... a grown woman! Supposed to be, anyway! A woman who's been married! Thirty-six years old ... with five kids! And ... and here I am, Steve. Here I am ... carrying on like some little snot-nosed teenager or something. It scares me! Steve ... it scares the hell out of me."

"I'll let you in on a little secret. It scares hell out of me too. I'm thirty-eight ... and I'm feeling stuff I've never felt before, either. Just like you are. Well, I can only assume that it's just like you're feeling, anyway."

"Steve? Is it right? Should we ... ? I mean ... what are we to do?"

He laughed. It was forced – but, it was a laugh.

"A cold shower would probably be a logical priority. Look! Why don't we make a date? Have a date? For, like, Friday. Day after tomorrow. *The Starlight Theater Group* is putting on a remake of *Kiss Me Kate*. Live production. Out at that little theater in Farmington Hills. How 'bout I get us a couple of tickets to that? And then, maybe we can stop at some restaurant ... and open a keg of gas ... afterward."

"I've never been to an actual live stage production. *Kiss Me Kate*. That's a musical, isn't it?"

"Oh sure. Cole Porter. *So In Love, Always True To You In My Fashion, Why Can't You Behave, Wunderbar*. All kinds of great music. I'm sure you'll enjoy it."

"I'm sure I will. I'm ... I'll be looking forward to it."

Steve released her hands – and started for the living room.

As he did, Janet half-shouted – in the direction of the kitchen –

"Steve's getting ready to leave, gang. If you want to say goodnight to him ... "

Both Patti and Joan burst out of the kitchen – before Janet had finished. Each young woman approached the detective – and kissed him on the cheek.

The four walked into the living room.

Both Robbie and Rickie were asleep on the floor – in front of the antiquated black-and-white television. The TV picture was flip-flopping. The sound – never a bargain under the best of conditions – was too garbled to understand. Joan shut the set off.

"Shhhh," cautioned Steve. "Don't wake 'em up."

"It'd take the roof falling in to wake 'em up," replied Patti, with a laugh. "You could dribble a basketball on their chest. Nothing! They'd never know."

"How about if I carry 'em up to bed?" suggested Steve.

"Tell you what," offered Janet. "Why don't you carry Robbie? He's the heaviest. See how nefarious I am? Patti can take Rickie."

"Thanks a batch," responded Patti – in mock sternness. "That's really nefarious."

"No," the guest said. "I'll just go ahead and carry 'em up. You'll have to show me where to stash 'em, though."

Steve lifted Robbie into his arms – and followed the girls upstairs. Once they'd gotten above the landing, Janet gathered up her other son – and joined the rest, on the second floor.

Since Patti and Joan decided to remain upstairs, Janet and Steve made their way back down to the living room – then, headed for the front door.

"What time is it?" asked Janet, as they stepped down into the vestibule.

He looked at his watch.

"My God! Almost eleven-thirty! I'd have guessed nine o'clock or something. It's ... it's been quite a night."

"Yes," she responded, with a smile and a nod. "Quite a night."

Once again, he took her in his arms – and kissed her. A warm kiss. A tender kiss. A kiss, however, totally lacking the frenzy of the initial encounter in the dining room.

The crackling urgency seemed to be lacking, during this "encore".

That made Janet feel a bit more comfortable. Maybe the furious, passionate, need would not have been present, in the dining room either – had they broken their embrace sooner. Much sooner.

Paying heed to that lesson, she disentangled herself from him. It certainly wouldn't take much, she feared, to push her over the precipice!

"Uh … Steve. I think we'd better say goodnight. I really and truly appreciate your coming over. And I can never … never ever … repay you, for what you did for me on the way home. I always felt that I could imagine what it'd be like … being in that position, I mean. But, I was wrong. Way wrong. A person can't possibly know what it's like! Not until it happens to you! Until you experience it for yourself! Dear Lord!"

"Yeah. I hear that all the time. <u>All</u> the time. Too damn often."

"I shudder at the thought … the thought … of what that creep could've done to me! What he would've done to me! Dear Lord! I can't … I can't thank you enough!"

"Janet? You know … you do know, don't you … that I care. That I care deeply for you. You do know that … don't you?"

She nodded. Her eyes stared down at the front of her shoes.

"Yes," she answered, softly. "Yes, I do. I do know that. And it's … it's a little scary."

"Don't let it be. It's natural for boys and girls to care about one another. Your kisses … well, they tell me that you care about me, too. More than just a little bit."

"Yes." Her voice was back to being exceptionally husky again. "Yes … and that's what makes the whole thing even more scary."

"Don't worry. It'll work out. We'll make it work out. You'll see."

Once more, he kissed her – without taking her into his arms. A soft, tender, loving, kiss – full on her lips!

Then, he was gone! It was as though part of Janet had gone with him!

<<>>

As had happened on the night that she'd gone to Canada with Fletcher Groome, Janet found herself experiencing great difficulty in dropping off to sleep. Without a doubt, there were even more unanswered questions – boodles more unanswered questions – after her encounter with Steve. Abundantly more uncertainty – than the prospect of having to deal with Fletcher could ever pose. She supposed that this was a blessing.

After her return from Windsor, she'd merely tossed and turned – from one uncomfortable position to another. Her adventure with Steve, though, was causing her to out and out thrash about. It was a wonder that the bed was able to contain her!

<u>Dammit! Why do I have to be so damned naïve? Any eight-year-old kid probably knows all the answers. Not me, though! Here I lay! Like some kind of a stupid little schoolgirl! And nothing! I don't know a damn thing</u>!

The questions were so basic! Why should the answers be so complicated? Why should Steve's touch send chills up and down her spine? Send them rattling up and down her whole, complete, entire, body? Why should she yearn for his embrace! Lust for it?

She shuddered when the word "lust" popped into her consciousness. But, try as she might, she was unable to pop it out!

<u>Think of something else, Janet! You've got to think of something else</u>!

Yeah! Right!

Why should the thought of Fletcher's embrace make her skin crawl? Fletcher was a nice enough man. A little selfish, possibly. A little overbearing, maybe. He made no bones about the fact that he would love to take her to his bed. On the other hand, outside of the episode in the tunnel, he'd never really pressed the issue. When she'd thought about it – really considered it – Fletcher had offered to provide for her. To provide for her and her children. No strings attached! No strings? Well, she would have to marry him! Or "shack up" with him! That would seem to present a string! A very substantial string!

On the other hand, he had offered to put her through business school. No strings there! He'd not made the offer contingent upon her marrying him – or even sleeping with him. Still, the implication had never been all that far from the surface!

Steve, on the other hand, had never really offered anything.

<u>What do you call his saving your life, Idiot? That's not chopped liver, y'know</u>!

Well, yes. He did save her from that horrible man! But, wasn't that his job? He was, after all, a police officer.

Yeah. But, nothing in his job description says that he has to follow you about. It's not his job to protect you twenty-four hours a day seven days a week.

Twenty-four hours! Seven days! The room was filled with her sigh – as the significance of twenty-four hours hit her! Someone once said – who was it? – that it's impossible to analyze true love. Was what she was feeling for Steve – that frightening, overwhelming, longing – was that true love? Could that be true love? Another monumental sigh!

How the hell should I know?

SEVEN

The next day, at Brock & Associates, the story of Janet's harrowing escape from the mugger/rapist made her the uncontested star of the office. She'd related the terrifying adventure to Peggy Sullivan, first thing upon arriving. It didn't take the newest employee long to have come up with all kinds of second thoughts. It would, of course, have been exceptionally difficult to keep such a hair-raising confrontation to one's self.

Janet's major oversight: She had grossly underestimated the significance that virtually every one of the women at the office would place upon Steve's presence, in the "caper". One by one, each of the ladies – and, ultimately, some of the men – stopped by the reception desk to quiz Janet about the frightening incident. Even surly Gloria Tapp engaged her in a lengthy conversation. Virtually unheard of.

As Gloria was about to return to her own office, she raised one eyebrow – and, in an over-syrupy voice, allowed, "Steve Francis. That's Rich Brock's brother-in-law, isn't it?" Only Gloria could make such a statement sound obscene.

Shortly after ten o'clock, Steve called.

"Do you have a minute?" he asked. "A minute ... to where you can talk?"

"Yes. You managed to catch me in a lull. May have to cut you off, in mid-sentence, but ... "

"I wouldn't touch that line with a ten-foot pole," he replied, with a sinister laugh. "Or with an eleven-foot Swede."

"Oh, poo! Did you call to talk to me? Or to harass me?"

"Oh, good! I have a choice?"

"You're in a rare mood this morning, Detective Francis."

"Probably because I had a rare evening last night, Ms Bolton."

"So did I," she answered, her voice taking on a much more serious tone.

"Which part? The part with me? Or the one with the bad guy?"

"Both parts. I hope, though, that the portion I spent with the bad guy ... portions like that ... will be extremely rare. Them, I can do without."

He laughed once more.

"Good save," he conceded. "Actually, he's the reason I'm calling."

"He ... he is? Why?"

"Well, the boys over at the police station, in Southfield, would like for you to come by. Today, if possible. Fill out a few forms, although ... I have to say ... your form is already pretty well filled out."

"I thought you were just paying attention to my bottom."

"Not really. It just happened to be the portion of your anatomy that was under discussion last night. However, we can certainly ... "

"What about the bad guy?" she interrupted, laughing. "He's the reason you called. Remember?"

"Oh. Oh, yeah. How quickly we forget. Anyway, the coppers would like you to come down to headquarters, in Southfield, and ... uh ... complete some paperwork. How 'bout that?"

"Good save! Does it have to be today?"

"Well, they'd like for it to be. See ... they checked this playful little rascal out. The sweet little dickens. And it seems as if the boy has a record as long as your arm. Referencing yet still another portion of your anatomy. For one thing, he's wanted ... in Arkansas ... for murder. Two of 'em, actually."

"For ... for murder? For two murders?"

"Yeah. Pretty frightening. He apparently did the same number on some lady down there ... in a town called Arkadelphia. And then, another in Benton. They have suspicions that he was behind a couple other ladies dying, in Little Rock. And one in Hot Springs. But, they don't have enough evidence ... not yet, anyway ... to be able to ... "

"Dear Lord! And this was the man who ... ?"

"Yeah. Plus he's got twelve or fifteen arrests in some of the other southern states! For such things as armed robbery, assault, carjacking, and a breaking-and-entering charge or two. Oh, he's a real sweetie."

"Oh! Oh, Steve! Dear Lord! Steve ... to think that he almost ... "

"Yeah. But, he <u>didn't</u>! You have to keep remembering that. Keep it foremost in your mind. He didn't! Did <u>not</u>! The thing, y'know, about not looking back. But, it is important that you go to the police station and fill these things out. As far as we know, they don't have anything on him in Michigan ... but, you know how the legal system works. They're still checking, of course. Would hate to have his lawyers ... assuming he's got some, or gets some ... spring him on some formality, or technicality. We think that the district attorney's office is simply going to let Arkansas extradite him ... murder being a much more serious situation and all that. The Southfield guys would like to get all the papers cleared away today, though. Get all their ducks in a row. In case some quirk comes up in the extradition thing, and ... "

"Where did you ever get that expression?"

The question seemed to surprise him. Perplex him.

"Which expression?" he asked. "'Ducks in a row'?"

"Yes. It's one that my husband always used. Not the best of connotations."

"I could cut out my tongue." He was trying to lighten the mood – but, cringed at the image he'd just depicted. "I'll never use it again," he added – hastily. "Strike the ducks. But, to get back to the subject at hand, you're going to have to fill out those papers sometime. Have to go over there sometime. Oh, I guess they could come see you. But, that's never the best of situations. It'd just be easier if you went there. They've got all kinds of stenographers, over there ... and all that sort of good stuff. If you'd like, I can pick you up ... and run you out there."

"That's ... that's nice of you."

"What time's lunch?"

"One o'clock."

"Wanna do it then?"

"Will we be late coming back?"

"Maybe a little bitty. Can you fix it? Square it with the powers that be?"

"Yes. I think so. I'm sure I can. Terri's pretty understanding."

Once the connection had been broken, Janet fielded a number of calls – then, asked Peggy to cover the board, while she spoke with Terri.

After Terri had advised Janet that she was free to take how-ever-long the police report would require – and then take her full lunch period – she said, "Janet, there are a couple things I'd like to speak to you about." She indicated one of two leather chairs, across from her tidy, well-organized, desk. "Why don't you have a seat? Much more comfy."

Oh Lord! Dear Lord! What've I done now?

"Don't panic," advised Terri, with a warm laugh. "There's nothing wrong. Go ahead. Sit-see."

Janet seated herself. Try as she might to say something – anything – she was at a complete loss for words.

"On the contrary," continued Terri. "We've very pleased with your performance. You're doing fine … doing a fine job … Janet. Mister Brock, myself … and everybody else … we're all pleased with the way you've been handling the reception desk and the board. In fact, that's what I'd like to speak to you about. Remember that first day? At lunch? I suggested that you might want to take a course or two … in computers? Do the night school thing? Remember that?"

"Yes. But, as yet I really haven't been able to … "

"I know," replied Terri, with a reassuring smile. "What I wanted to tell you was that Mister Brock … he's agreed with my suggestion. My suggestion that you take a course over at *Wolverine Business Academy*. The good news is … the company'll pay for it."

"They … they will?"

Terri nodded. "Yes, they will," she said. "I'm sure that I'm not laying a bulletin on you, when I tell you that it's not an offer we make to everybody … although a few of our people have taken advantage of the opportunity. I think it's about an eleven-hundred dollar course, nowadays. It'll be hard work, Janet. You shouldn't think it won't be hard work. Damn hard. If I remember correctly, it's something like an every Tuesday, Wednesday and Thursday night situation. From something like seven-thirty to ten o'clock. And there's a lot … a hell of a lot … of homework. T'ain't easy. Some of it you can do up here …

when the board goes quiet. I think that board gets really quiet, about … oh, about … about every other year. Without fail."

"I … gee, Terri. I can't thank you enough. I really can't."

"It'll be well worth your while … if you can hang with it, Janet. They teach the same programs we have here … plus the ones that we'll be using on our glorious new system. And, probably, a few we've never even thought of. Or heard of."

"Terri, I … I really don't know what to say. I mean … "

"Again, let me warn you: It's a tough go. A real fanny-dragger. The next session starts next Tuesday … and runs for something like six weeks. Do you think you're up to it? Up for it? This soon, after … ?"

"Yes. Yes, of course. At long last … I'll have some kind of <u>skill</u>! A real <u>skill</u>! An actual <u>skill</u>! It's really bothered me, over the years, that I've had absolutely zero … as far as office skills go. Or any other skills, I imagine. I could operate that lousy steam presser, over at the lousy laundry. But, that was about it."

"You're way too hard on yourself, Janet. You've done a heck of a lot in your life … and I'm not merely talking about your job here. Raising those kids … raising 'em, under the circumstances you found yourself in. Well, I'd have to say that I admire you … admire the bejeebers out of you."

"The kids practically raised themselves, you know. I can't tell you how … "

"I'm sure it wasn't anywhere near that cut-and-dried. I'd hate to have had to cope with your situation." Terri's smile was reassuring. "Look," she continued, "if the computer thing is what you want to do, we'll cut a check for the school this afternoon. Get you enrolled. And, once again, don't worry about getting right back today … after your little tour of duty at police headquarters. God! I can't believe what happened to you … well, almost happened to you … last night. You're lucky … lucky as you can be … that you were able to walk away from it. Walk away from it … unscathed. With me, only my laundry-man would know. I think I'd have been in bed for a week. Maybe even wound up at the funny farm. Lucky that Steve happened along."

There was an unspoken something in the inflection Terri had given to the word "happened". It made Janet the slightest bit uncomfortable.

<u>Probably my overripe imagination working overtime.</u>

<<>>

The encounter at the Southfield Township Police Headquarters went well. Far better than Janet had expected. Steve, of course, had been a big help – "walking her through" the various reports.

They'd stopped at a kosher delicatessen for lunch – on their way back to **Brock & Associates**. Over corned beef-on-rye sandwiches and coffee, they made small talk. For one thing, Steve informed her that he'd reserved tickets for *The Starlight Theater's* live performance of *Kiss Me Kate* the following evening. Janet – while certainly not having forgotten about the date – had relegated it to "the back burner". She didn't know why.

Well, maybe she did. What would happen – once they got home? Would Steve kiss her again? Probably. She hoped so, anyway. The kiss wasn't the problem. How would she react to it? And what might the kiss <u>lead</u> to? <u>That</u> was the problem!

<<>>

The following evening, Steve presented himself at Janet's door – corsage in hand – promptly at 6:30 PM.

The Starlight Theater, in suburban Farmington Hills, was an amateur group – one which produced four shows each summer and fall. Traditionally, one of the four had to be a musical. It was always more lavish than the others. Always their final production. This year it would be Cole Porter's delightful *Kiss Me Kate*.

Since the previous night – another adventure in trying to get to sleep -- Janet had begun to look forward to the upcoming date. Of course, Friday afternoon had ground on and on. And on and on and on.

Dress for the theater was casual. Janet chose her favorite ensemble – before Barbara's celebrated Sunday shopping spree: A pale-green, silken, blouse – worn with her dark-green skirt. The skirt was slightly out of style. Well, she opined, so was the blouse. So, for that matter, was everything else. Both items would be considered by many to be far too heavy for late August. Janet's wardrobe, of course, had been severely limited over the years. The green combination had been her best "Sunday Go To Meetin'" togs – for as long back as she could remember. She'd originally intended to wear her "new blue dress". But, she'd worn it virtually every other day at work. Besides, she'd worn it to Windsor – with Fletcher. She most certainly didn't want to "jinx" this date! Not when she would be with Steve! The latter was decked out in a pair of tan, light-knit, slacks and matching cotton shirt.

The performance was a delight! Janet, who had never before seen any sort of live production, was thrilled! It didn't hurt that Steve had taken her hand in his – even before the curtain had gone up.

When the soprano and the baritone had dueted on the very beautiful *So In Love*, Steve had switched her hand from his right hand to his left – and wrapped his right arm around her shoulders. The arm had remained there till the final curtain. Janet found herself wondering if it might have fallen asleep. Apparently not! When a particularly romantic interlude would occur in the play, his arm would tighten around her – and she'd "snuggle in" toward him. When the spanking scene had played out – "Fred Graham" had put "Lilli Vanessi" across his knee, on stage, while they'd been performing Shakespeare's *Taming Of The Shrew*" – Janet had felt ill at ease for some strange reason. However, Steve's "grip" seemed to not change. Was that normal? Or was she being abnormal?

As the soprano reprised *So In Love*, he kissed her hair – close above her left ear!

<<>>

After the theater, they ate and drank Irish Coffee (laced, abundantly, with what is known as an "adult beverage"), at a charming little out-of-the-way restaurant – a converted and refurbished old farm house – in nearby Novi. Steve had always called the town "November First" – which, somehow, Janet found exceptionally funny.

They held hands – constantly – across the heavily-lacquered knotty-pine table. The jukebox contained three old time favorites: *The Twelfth Of Never,* Cole Porter's immortal *Easy To Love* – and *So In Love*, also by Porter. The latter, of course, had been the love song from the production they'd just attended. Steve dropped in coins for each of the numbers! Numerous times! Each time *So In Love* would pour forth, the couple would spend the entire three minutes – simply gazing into one another's eyes, and shamelessly holding hands..

As they drove back down Grand River, toward Janet's home, the latter decided that she had, indeed, borrowed trouble. She should never have worried about her date with Steve. Of course, three Irish Coffees and a schmaltzy, wonderfully-romantic, ballad from a simply-phenomenal show may have helped her relaxed mode along. That and all that beautiful music from the jukebox. Plus, an abundant amount of hand-holding.

Even before they'd gotten to the restaurant, there had been yet another pleasant surprise. As soon as they'd left the theater – had just gotten into Steve's car – he had, with great flourish, pushed a cassette into the player in the dash: The Original Cast recording of *Kiss Me Kate*! He'd thought of everything!

Upon leaving the eatery, of course, the tape had continued. She snuggled close to him, as he drove – her left hand resting on his right thigh! He'd placed his right arm across her lap – wrapping his hand around her right thigh! Every time *So In Love* would fill the car, each would tighten his/her hold!

It was almost one o'clock, when he pulled his huge Ford LTD into the driveway – behind her poor, still-battered, Maverick – and killed the lights. There was the faintest glow emanating from the kitchen window. The hood over the stove contained a 40-watt bulb – which was literally never turned off, despite the family's struggle to pay the electric bill every month.

"My eternal flame", Janet had called it. It had been lit – from the day that Jim had left! Through the years – and a copious number of light bulbs – it had illuminated the kitchen and parts of the dining room, and landing, with a warm, peace-producing, glow. Even more warm and peace-producing – once Patti had bought, and installed, a soft-pink bulb. Janet loved the effect – and had kept the pink hue "in the act".

Janet was to discover – as she sat with Steve – that, as an important bonus, the pink light provided a soft, romantic glimmer, for a couple of "crazy kids", parked in an LTD, in the driveway.

Steve did not kill the motor – and, by so doing, didn't stop the music. He turned to her – and tilted her chin upward, with his left hand.

"Hello there, Pretty Lady," he rasped. "Whatcha doin' out here ... all alone at this time of night?"

"Waitin' for a streetcar," she responded, smiling warmly.

"Mind if I join you?"

"I'm not coming apart."

He laughed. The laugh was deeper than any other she'd known from him. She was glad. It had become more and more important, as the evening had progressed, that he enjoy himself. That he have a good time. That he be pleased. She didn't want the date to be all about her.

"Now," he responded, "who's in a rare mood? Besides, how do you know that you're not coming apart? You shot a pretty good stick, back there ... with that Irish Coffee ... y'know."

"Are you suggesting, Sir, that I'm a little tipsy?"

"I should be so lucky. Do you know ... My Little Fathead ... that you're about the most beautiful woman I've ever seen?"

"No. But, hum a few bars ... and we'll fake it."

"Hmmmmm. Maybe you inhaled a little too much of that wretched brew back there." He kissed her lightly on her forehead. "Either that," he went on, "or your mother was frightened by an old Henny Youngmann record."

"Are there any <u>new</u> Henny Youngmann records?"

"How come?" was his response.

"How come what?" she asked.

"How come ... all of a sudden ... how come a nice, romantic, evening is turning into something out of *Abbott and Costello*? Or *The Marx Brothers*?"

"Why, I don't know what you're talking about. After all, aren't you the one who called me a fathead?"

"Yes you do ... and yes I did. In that order. Janet? Janet, you've been nuzzling next to me all night."

"You noticed?"

"Yes. I'm not made of wood, y'know. From the neck up ... yes. But listen. Listen to me. All evening you're real affectionate. Now when we get home, it's ... all of a sudden ... the comic hour. *Showtime!*

How come? And ... as for the second part ... I don't know why I called you My Little Fathead. I really don't. Just kind of came out."

"Your little fathead. I think I like that. I guess I must <u>really</u> be tipsy."

"You may have a little bit of a glow-on ... but, you're not tipsy. Tell me true, My Little Fathead, what are you afraid of? This?"

He swung around toward her – as much as the steering wheel would permit – and took her in his arms. His lips pressed against hers! Immediately, his tongue sought out the hidden treasures of her warm, willing, mouth! Janet responded in kind – not stopping to consider her reaction! Flicking her tongue, gently, against his, she opened and closed her mouth. Gently. Tenderly.

His left hand found the curve of her right breast! She began to moan, slightly – as he lovingly caressed the lush, full, mound! Her right hand began to softly massage the hair behind his left ear!

He broke the kiss! Both were breathing deeply! Janet's inhaling and exhaling was substantially more labored than that of her date. He ran his lips over her closed eyelids – planting light kiss after light kiss upon them! He kissed the tip of her nose! Then, her cheekbones! After numerous busses, he returned to her yearning mouth once more!

His hands had decided to be stubbornly uncooperative – as he sought to unbutton her blouse!

Janet surprised herself – by being amused at his klutziness! She surprised herself even more – by acknowledging her awareness of his difficulty! Being aware of it – and not doing a thing to halt his fumbling progress! Or maybe she was even helping him – encouraging him – considering all the wondrous things his lips and tongue were doing to her!

Finally, he managed to open "the key to *The Magic Kingdom*"! She was unsure whether he'd intended to pull the blouse completely out of her skirt! But, that was what he'd accomplished! She tensed – as his hand began fondling her breast, over her bra!

It occurred to her that she was wearing the flimsy, transparent, black, number that Barbara had picked out for her – on the magical day, when she'd gotten her "new blue dress".

It was rather silly, she thought, to pick that exact, precise, strategic, moment to wonder why she'd chosen to wear that particular brassiere

– rather than her trusty, much-more Spartan, white-cotton, creation. The answer was obvious, of course. But, until that moment, Janet hadn't wanted to acknowledge it. Hadn't wanted to deal with it!

Her head was beginning to swim slightly. Was it the Irish Coffee? Or was it the fact that Steve had – at that moment – slipped his hand beneath that esoteric creation?

His right hand had been, more or less, locked – along with her left hand – between their bodies. She felt him push her slightly away from him – toward the far side of the front seat. His lips were still locked upon hers – the kiss becoming more and more breathlessly fevered by the second.

He withdrew his hand from her breast – and wrapped both hands behind her, beneath her blouse! A futile attempt to unhook her bra. She broke the kiss – and laughed lightly.

"It unhooks in the front, Silly," she whispered.

Then, she really surprised herself – shocked herself, actually – by unfastening the garment! Her round, firm, pink-nippled, breasts burst loose from their confinement.

He leaned back – holding her at arm's length – and drank in the wonder of the soft, white, coral-tipped, beautifully-sculptured, mounds.

"My God, Janet! You ... you're just so beautiful! So very, very, very beautiful!"

Then, his lips were upon her breasts! His tongue flicked lightly – then, pressed firmly against – first one of the hardened nipples, and then the other!

Her derriere had remained, for the most part, on Steve's half of the front seat. However, the top part of her body had been pushed back toward the passenger's door.

Janet found herself "balanced" – positioned, very precariously. Ultimately, she lost that precious equilibrium! She wound up twisted onto her right side. Steve landed – rather gracelessly – on top of her left hip! At that same precise instant, they both began to laugh! Wave upon wave upon wave of uproarious laughter! The so-called hilarity filled the car! They sat straight up.

Janet made no attempt to cover her nakedness.

"We must be a sight," observed Steve. The genuineness of his laugh had given way to a nervous twitter. "Like two crazy school kids," he said. "Making out in a car."

She seemed less affected.

"Pretty suave and subtle, we were, hah?" she responded.

"Janet? You know and I know that we can't continue like this. Not here. Not now. Not like this." Despite that declaration, he began caressing her breasts, once more! "I ... I never could've imagined breasts like that," he rasped. "Never in a million years. Never in my wildest dreams. Janet, Janet, Janet! You're incredibly beautiful!"

"Aren't they too big?"

"Too big? Lord, no! They ... they're perfect! Letter perfect! Janet, they're ... they're just ... just so ... so beautiful."

"Sometimes," she said, matter of factly, "I think I might be better off ... with a little less there. I keep worrying about them sagging. Fortunately, they haven't ... yet."

He smiled. "I noticed," he allowed. "I sure as hell noticed."

"Barb is always telling me that she wishes she was as ... how did she put it? She says she wishes she was as chesty as I am. One of the few things I've got to be proud of, I guess." She came up with as evil a smile as she was capable. "Well, two things, actually."

"That's not true ... and you know it! Now I remember why I called you a fathead."

"Oh, yes? And why would that be?"

"Because, dammit, you're always putting yourself down. Obviously, your breasts are something you can be proud of. Damn proud of. If it was up to me, I'd probably have them bronzed! But, Janet, you've got so many other things. So many other things going for you."

"Bronzed? Yeah. I can see it now! My boobs hanging from the chandelier, in the living room."

"You see? You really <u>are</u> a fathead."

"Steve?" Her voice betrayed a storm of questioning, frightening, emotion, which had just swept over her. "Steve, what're we going to do?"

"About what?"

"Now it's <u>my</u> turn to say you know about what! You know damn <u>well</u> about what! About us! That's about what! Part of me wants you to take me somewhere! Make mad, passionate, love to me ... as they say! And part of me is scared as hell! Another part of me is so damn confused! Steve ... I don't know what I want!"

"I know," he muttered. "I know. I'm in the same fix. I would love to take you somewhere ... and make mad, passionate, love to you, and ... "

"<u>Now</u>, who's writing your material?"

"Yeah. We're a million laughs. It's funny ... and it's not! I love you Janet! I really do! I'd vowed that I wasn't going to tell that to you ... say that to you ... in a heated-up situation like this one. I wouldn't want you to think I was just simply angling to get you into the sack. I was sorely tempted to whisper it ... whisper it into your ear ... at the show tonight. When they were singing *So In Love*."

"So, why didn't you?"

"I'm damned if I know. I certainly should've. I guess you don't have a copyright on being a fathead. There are two of 'em in this car, on this night."

"Well, I'm glad to hear that," she said, in mock-seriousness.

"Look, Janet. If we were to wind up in bed, this very night ... we <u>wont</u>, but if we <u>did</u> ... I wouldn't be rationalizing when I say that it would be right! It <u>would</u> be right! In my heart, I know that it would be <u>right</u>! I <u>know</u> it!"

"Steve, look! I ... "

"No! Let me finish. You and I both know that we can't make love out here! We can't make love in a stupid car. Like a couple frenetic school kids! We both know that it has to be something special! Something extra-special! Especially, the first time!"

"I ... yes. I agree. It should be special. Especially the first time ... whatever the implications of what I'm saying might be shouting out."

"I ... I don't know if you'll believe this or not. I would hope that you would. But, I've only had one woman in my life. My wife! When she was taken from me, I felt as though I could never love anyone else. Would never love anyone else. Not like I loved my wife."

"Steve, don't ... "

He pressed on, undaunted: "Now, I find that I love you. Janet, you have to believe that I'm not trying to lure you to bed. I out and out <u>love</u> you! In a way I've never loved before! I don't know what <u>you</u> might make of it ... but, as for me, <u>I'm</u> amazed!"

It was at that point that he seemed to discover where his hand had been! An even more stark discovery – something he'd been totally unaware of: Her hand was atop his!

He pulled back – an effort to remove his hand! But, she held it – pressed tightly to her bosom!

"Steve, you're not alone. I've, also, only been intimate with one person in my whole entire life! Just like you. Same as you. And Jim and I didn't have that much going for us ... ah ... in that area. Despite the fact that we had five kids. There's no need for me to go into detail, but we just ... we just didn't have that much going for us. I'm convinced now ... right at this moment ... that it was because we really didn't love one another. I'm sure we did ... at least we thought we did ... when we got married. And probably for a few years afterward."

"Janet, there's no need to ... "

A humorless smile crossed her lips

"I've looked back many times," she pressed on, "since Jim left. And it's long since occurred to me that I really didn't love him. Never really loved him. I don't think he loved me either. In fact, I'm sure of it. I'm not even convinced that we liked one another ... which is even worse." She sighed deeply – and exerted even more pressure on his hand! "We were both awfully young," she continued. "Awfully damn young. We thought we were in love. I'm sure of that. And it must've seemed like a good idea at the time. Our getting married, I mean."

She removed her hand from his – and found herself surprised at the decrease in pressure upon her breast! As he began to speak, she put her fingers up to his lips.

"I'm ... I'm surprised that I'm telling you all this," she admitted. "I think I'm in love with you too. There are times, though, since we kissed the other night, when I'm afraid that maybe ... well, it might be that you just went and unleashed a whole torrent of pent-up emotion! Some caged-up sexual feeling! Deep inside me! Sexual desire! That you might have awakened something in me. Like you, there are things that I've never felt before! And I can't help but wonder if it's not just purely sexual! Purely ... completely ... physical! I don't really think it is. Obviously, I don't. But, Steve ... it's a whole new ballgame to me. I'm in uncharted territory ... as they say. And, like I told you before, it scares the hell out of me. I'm ... I just ... just don't know how to react."

His laugh was brittle. "I guess," he replied, "that we've both got a lot of things to think about. A lot of stuff to rummage through ... don't we?"

She removed his hand from her bosom – and kissed each knuckle as well as the area just above. Then, she pulled it up to her cheek – and held it there.

"Yes," she responded. "Yes, we do. Like you, I want it to be ... to be perfect." She lowered her eyes, kissed his hand again – then, squeezed it hard. "I want it to be perfect," she repeated, "the first time. All this grappling ... and fumbling around ... out here in the stupid driveway is a far cry from being jolly well perfect. I do want to see you again, Steve. Like every day. Did I just <u>say</u> that?"

"I would hope so. Would <u>hope</u> you'd want to see me. Every day sounds <u>fine</u> with me! I definitely want to see you ... also like every day."

"But, Steve, listen. I worry that ... if we see too much of each other ... I worry that ... well, I worry about what may happen. We could very well have wound up ... as you so discreetly put it ... in the sack tonight. And I can't say that I'd have been sorry. At least, not tonight I wouldn't. In the morning? Hah! That might be a whole different thing." She smiled – and leaned over, kissing him on the nose. "I'm glad," she went on, "that we didn't make love tonight. Klutzing around out here in the car is one thing. We took it just about as far as we could, though. If we'd have wound up in the back seat, well, we might have taken the ... well, the luster ... off a very beautiful night. We'd better quit, I'm thinking. Quit while we're ahead. I do worry though. Maybe the next time, we won't quit. Maybe we won't quit ... while we're ahead."

"Or that we might not be ahead at all? Might not be ahead in the first place?"

She smiled – warmly. "Yes," she answered. "I guess I didn't look at it that way ... but, yeah, I guess I am worried about that."

He took each cup of her brassiere in his hands – and gently covered her with the soft, silken fabric.

"You'd better buckle up for safety," he suggested.

He watched her – intently – as she hooked the cups together. Once she'd buttoned her blouse – and made a valiant effort to tuck it back into her skirt – he continued:

"I really don't know what to say, Janet. I love you. I'm certain that you love me. By rights, we should be shooting off firecrackers! Waking the town and telling the people … like the song says! All the really neat stuff that lovers are supposed to be doing! Handstands! But, I'm afraid that we both feel like we've got a tiger by the tail! If our love's as strong as I think it is … as strong as I believe it is … it'll be around for awhile, y'know. For a good long time. We certainly don't have to consummate it tonight. But, I'm just as scared as you are … of tomorrow. We'll just have to … to play it by ear, I guess. I really think that we've done pretty well … so far."

"We're doing pretty well … because there's no bed handy."

He shook his head – in emphatic disagreement. "No," he said, firmly. "That's not true. Look … we're not all that far from our friendly, neighborhood motel."

"A roll in the hay … at the 'Whoopie Motel' … wouldn't be right. And you know it, Steve. You know that."

"Of course it wouldn't be right. So, here we sit … with no bed handy."

"Okay," she sighed. "You've convinced me. Now what do we do? What do we do about the future? We've got the whole weekend ahead of us … although there won't be anything left of it, if we don't say goodnight, and get the hell out of the car."

He laughed. He seemed much more relaxed. "There are worse places to spend the weekend, Fathead," he observed.

"Want me to unhook my bra again?"

"No!" he half-shrieked, and half-laughed. "I may be made of stern stuff … but, not <u>that</u> stern."

"How about … what about … tomorrow?" Her voice was terribly shaky.

"How about we take the kids to the movies," he suggested. "We can find some flick, I'm sure. One that's not rated Zilch! Something, I'm sure that'll interest the sophisticated tastes of all you girls … and even fit the Bugs Bunny needs of us boys."

"Us boys? Bugs Bunny?"

"Certainly. Of course. I'm a Bugs Bunny junkie. Also a Daffy Duck junkie. Also a Porky Pig junkie. Also ... "

"All right," she answered, laughing. "All right. I get the picture. Sounds good. Why don't you look in the paper and see what's playing? I don't know who ... outside of Robbie and Rickie ... will be available.

He kissed her once more – then, got out of the car and made his way around to let her out.

As they walked to the side door of the house, he patted her lightly on the bottom.

"Don't tell me you're one of those awful fanny-patters," she said, with an overdone stage-sigh.

"Okay. I won't. I'll <u>never</u> tell you that. Wild horses couldn't drag it out of me," he answered – patting her once more.

Seconds after she'd inserted her key into the lock, he took her, once again, into his arms. This time, the kiss was long, languid – and incredibly tender. He ran his hands up and down her body! Three or four times! Then, he caressed her derriere – through her skirt! With both hands!

They said goodnight.

Janet stepped inside and walked up into the kitchen, past her "eternal flame", Then she made her way into the dining room. She watched – as the LTD backed out of the driveway. Her eyes stayed affixed to the glow of the large tail lights – till the car disappeared, down the darkened street.

Once more, a gargantuan sigh. She'd thought that she'd had a multitude of toxic questions, after her date with Fletcher Groome. She'd thought she was in the middle of a muddle then. It was to laugh! The things she'd grappled with on that night – which now seemed, suddenly, to be so long ago – were nothing! Nothing compared to the emotions that her first date with Steve had engendered! Fortunately, she believed that – when it came to Steve – she just might be able to come up with a few answers.

She certainly hoped so!

EIGHT

Saturday evening: **Janet, Steve, Robbie** and Rickie were the only movie-goers.

Barbara had been scheduled for a shift at the pizzeria. She'd left before Steve had arrived. Patti had lined up a babysitting job – and was walking out the door, as Steve had pulled into the driveway. She'd stopped – and run to his car. As soon as he'd gotten out, she'd hurried over to kiss him, on the cheek. Then, smiling broadly, she'd made her way up the block. Joan had nowhere to go. She'd preferred, however, to remain at home.

"I think Joanie just wanted the night off," explained Janet – as she'd herded Robbie and Rickie into the back seat of the LTD. "Truth to tell, she winds up sitting on the men, here, most of the time. Tonight'll give her a chance to kind of let her hair hang down. Kick back, y'know. Just do whatever it is she wants to do. She'll have the whole house to herself."

A theater in Dearborn was rerunning two *Walt Disney* features – *Pete's Dragon* and *The Absent-Minded Professor*. Steve had assured Janet that the double-feature would be a nice outing for "us boys". He was right. Steve laughed as loudly – and as often – as anyone in the audience. Probably more so. In both cases. Janet found herself wondering what he'd have been like, had they actually attended the threatened Bugs Bunny festival.

It was almost eleven-thirty, when the second picture finished. Robbie and Rickie had both fallen asleep, on the way home. While the boys slept in the back seat, Steve and Janet held hands in front. They'd "shamelessly held hands" – as Steve had described it, on numerous occasions – for the entire time they'd been seated in the theater.

The boys seemed to pay no heed. Janet shuddered, slightly, as she recalled more than one incident when Robbie, especially, had been troubled while she'd held hands ("shamelessly" or otherwise) with Fletcher Groome. The display of affection between Steve and their mother had been considered, apparently, to be quite "natural". Certainly, it had not rated even a trace of disapproval from either one. Janet found herself wondering if one of their sisters might have "coached" the boys as to what to expect. And how to react – or not react – to it.

Why do I see Barb smirking at me … in my mind's eye?

Janet suddenly snapped from her reverie. Steve was speaking. For how long, she didn't know. " … got a VCR at home … and I'm kind of a movie buff. Some of 'em were made before I was even born."

"Oh? A VCR? That's pretty heady stuff, I'd say. Especially opulent … to someone, like me. Someone who owns merely a ratty old black-and-white set. I guess you can play whatever movie you want, hah? Whenever you want. Pretty snooty, I'll tell the world."

"Yeah … but, I will remember you little people, Dahling. Listen, I've even got a couple old *Andy Hardy* movies … ones that Mickey Rooney made in the thirties and forties. God! He was just a kid! And now? To see him in *Pete's Dragon* … to see him as an old man … really makes you stop and think! Ain't none of us gittin' any younger. Shore ain't none of us gittin' younger."

His voice seemed to betray a more-than-slightly troubled dimension. A surprise.

<<>>

When they'd finally reached Janet's house, it was after midnight. Joan was already asleep. Once they'd carried Robbie and Rickie upstairs, Janet seemed exhilarated. Steve, in contrast, appeared a little fatigued. Had it anything to do with his remark about getting old?

As they walked back downstairs, into the dim, semi-lit, living room – shamelessly hand-in-hand (again) – Janet asked, "Can I sell you a cup of coffee."

"It's awfully late, Fathead. I should really get on out of here. Let you get some shut-eye."

"I'm really not tired. I'd be glad to put on a pot."

"Yeah. If we brew a pot … and then sit around and drink it … we're probably looking at two o'clock. Maybe three o'clock. That's just too damn late. I'm not in as good a shape as I usta was. Not in as good a shape as you are, Fathead."

They stood there, in the almost-eerie glow of the small lamp atop the television. He held her at arm's length. Then, gently, tenderly, he placed his hands on her breasts!

Since they'd dressed casually for the evening, Janet had worn a pale blue sweater and a pair of jeans. The sweater had seen better days. Although it was, thankfully, "still in one piece", the color had faded through the years. Underneath, she'd worn one of her few remaining Spartan, white cotton, bras. Even through the two layers of material, his hands felt so warm! So comfortable?

"Yes," acknowledged Steve. "I can see … and feel … that you're in much better shape than I am."

She laughed – and, immediately, wondered if she should have.

"Oh, I don't know," she replied – after fighting a thousand battles, "I could go feeling around on you … and, I'm sure, I could come up with some things that're in pretty good shape too."

The minute she'd said it, Janet wished that she'd had it back! Steve seemed completely flustered by the remark – and didn't reply.

"I'm … I'm sorry," she hastened to say. "I didn't mean that. Not the way it sounded. I was just … was just trying to be flip, I guess. I should know better. I apologize. I'm not that kind of girl, y'know … and what I said was inexcusable."

"No apology necessary. It just … well, it just … it came out of left field, is all."

"You really have some kind of effect on me, Mister Francis. I guess you hit the nail on the head last night … and tonight. I am a fathead. A true fathead."

He wrapped his arms around her.

"You're _my_ fathead, Fathead. My special fathead. And there's no need to apologize. Women have just as much right to make suggestive remarks as men. And let's face it. What I said was pretty racy."

"I guess I must still be the product of my upbringing. From the time I was a little girl, it was acceptable for a man to say things like that. But, not for a woman. And it spills over into other things. Lots of other things, you know."

"Other things? Like what?"

"Well, I know that I shouldn't admit it ... but, I love the feel of your hands! The feel of your hands ... on me." She pulled his hands tighter to her bosom! "There," she rasped. "I like the feel of your hands ... right there. But, you see, I haven't reached the point ... not yet anyway ... where I'd feel comfortable with my hands on ... on ... on you."

His laugh was without mirth.

"I guess," he allowed, "that we've had the ol' double standard for so long ... that we've all adapted to it. Don't even give it a thought. I never thought much about my having my hands on you ... and the lack of you having yours on me. Well, that's not true. It's just ... hell. You know what I mean. I always figured that everything would just simply work out. Would just come naturally. I'm not really that analytical. Look, Janet. For heaven's sakes, say what you want to say. Do what you want to do. I would hope that you'd feel comfortable ... as you say ... no matter what you'd ever do with me. Just be your wonderful self. Don't worry about saying. Don't worry about doing. Don't worry about not doing. Just go on being my wonderful Janet. My sweet fathead."

"Are you ... are you doing anything tomorrow?" she asked.

"No. Not really. Why do you want to know? ... asked the boy wonder, hopefully."

"Well, for one thing, you've never even met Barb. Almost the only time we can all really get together ... as a family anymore ... is for breakfast, on Sunday mornings. It's usually about noon ... once we get back from church. But, if you're interested, I'd love to have you come by for breakfast. I can't promise it'll make you forget *The International House of Pancakes*, but ... we do pretty well. Am ... am I being too forward? Too pushy? "

"Push all you want, Lady. Push all you damn please. Of course I'd love to come. Wild horses couldn't keep me away. Uh ... you don't happen to have any wild horses lurking around here, do ya?"

"No. But, I could lay in a few, if you'd like."

"Lay in a few? Hadda go and talk dirty, didn't you?"

"Oh poo! Listen, if you want to come, you're more than welcome tomorrow morning."

"I'll be here with bells on. I'll look a little ridiculous … but, dammit, I'll be here with bells on."

She smiled broadly. "You <u>will</u> look a little funny. I wonder," she mused, "what Barb's first impression will be."

"She'll love 'em. She'll go ape over the bells. The chicks love the bells. She'll probably tell me to keep them in the act."

"Oh, you," she laughed, as she tapped him lightly on his left shoulder.

The little tap seemed to drive home to both, the fact that they'd just conducted an entire conversation – in an embrace.

Suddenly, his lips were, once again, seeking hers! The kiss became an almost-desperate coupling! His tongue was into and out of her mouth – an insatiable hunger! She pressed ever closer to him! Gently removing his hands from her breasts, he ran them up and down her body! They came to rest on her behind! As he gently massaged her bottom, she began to undulate – melding her body even more tightly to his!

Finally, the kiss was broken! Neither of them could be sure which one of them had actually disengaged the locked lips!

He tugged at her sweater – negotiating it out of the waistband of her jeans! He pulled the top up beneath her chin – exposing Janet's bra-clad breasts! Their lips melded, once more – as he caressed her bosom, again. This kiss was lest frantic. Less urgent.

Reaching behind her – underneath her sweater – he managed to unhook her bra. Sliding the undergarment up above her firm, sculptured, breasts, his hands began to caress, to fondle, to press, to knead. At no time did their lips part.

The couple stood in the middle of the living room – clamped tightly in each other's arms. The embrace lasted three, four – maybe five – minutes. An eternity. All the while, she had pressed her lower abdomen tight against him! His need was, of course, spectacularly apparent!

His hands – beneath her sweater and brassiere – continued to manipulate her breasts. The nipples, as expected, had long hardened under his soft, gentle, caring, touch.

It was at that moment that Barbara let herself in the front door! The young woman was unaware of the couple's presence – until she'd stepped up from the vestibule, and into the living room. Neither Steve nor Janet heard her – until she'd practically run into them, in the subdued lighting.

"OH!" gasped Barbara. "I'm sorry, Mother! I ... didn't see you ... see you there."

"Uh ... well ... uh ... that's all right. We didn't mean to startle you. Uh ... Barb, I'd like you to meet Steve. Steve Francis."

The detective had done his best to slither his hands down – and out from under Janet's sweater and brassiere. It was spectacularly obvious that he'd felt extremely awkward shaking Barbara's hand – considering where his own fevered palm had just been. Janet did her best to appear unaffected. Not an easy task, when straightening one's sweater – especially without re-hooking one's bra.

Barbara made a mighty effort to put her mother – and her newest acquaintance – at their ease:

"I'm ... I'm glad I finally got to meet you, Steve," she'd managed to blurt. "After all I've heard about you. I'm so grateful for the other night. That you came along when you did. Otherwise, I shudder to think of what could've happened."

"I ... uh ... invited Steve to breakfast tomorrow," Janet advised her daughter. "You don't mind, do you?"

"Mind? Of course not, Mother. I've wanted to meet him ... to actually meet Steve ... for a long time. I think it'd be great ... having him over for breck-breck. Did you two have a good time at the movies tonight?"

"Yes," answered Janet. "We took the boys to see the *Disney* thing. Double feature." She was rallying – quickly regaining her composure. She was doing better than Steve, in that area. "The boys seemed to enjoy it," she said.

"How about Joanie," asked Barbara.

"She didn't go," replied her mother. "I think she was just as pleased to escape your darling little brothers for a night."

Barbara laughed. "I can understand that," she said. Looking up at

Steve, she explained, once again, "Joanie's the one who usually pulls the duty ... where Robbie and Rickie are concerned."

"I know," said Steve, in a half-whisper. "Well, I've really got to leave."

Barbara extended her hand, once more.

"It was certainly nice to meet you, Steve," she said brightly. "I'm looking forward to breakfast tomorrow. Good night now. Good night, Mother."

As the young woman started up the stairs, Janet and Steve made their way to the front door – an obviously highly-discomfiting moment for the both of them – Steve more so than Janet. Much more so.

"I'm ... I'm sorry, Steve. I should've realized that Barb'd be getting home about now. I completely lost track of the time. Lost track of everything. I truly am a fathead."

"No. I'm the one who's sorry. If there's a fathead present, it's moi. I shouldn't have embarrassed you like I did. Should've kept my hands to myself. There's a time and a place for the things we were doing. Standing in the middle of the living room is not one of them. I'm the one who's the fathead."

Janet sighed – heavily. "There are times," she rasped, "when I'm convinced that our roles are reversed ... Barb's and mine. Sometimes, I'm convinced that ... well, half the time, anyway ... I'm convinced that I'm the daughter. That she's the mother."

"You may not be all that far off. She sure handled the situation a hell of a lot better than you and I did. Well, better than I did, anyway. She's quite a young lady, y'know. Quite a young lady."

Janet opened the door, as he leaned down – and kissed her, lightly.

"Till tomorrow, My Love," she whispered.

"Till tomorrow, Fathead," he replied.

Her head-to-toe laugh was therapeutic. It seemed to dissipate the overwhelming tension.

"Just what I need," she allowed. "An incurable romantic."

<<>>

Sunday breakfast went well. Steve had shown up at twelve-fifteen. The meal was without any manner of disaster. There'd been no apparent discomfort on the part of Steve or Barbara – much to Janet's relief. Well, she thought, there <u>seemed</u> to be no unease. Still, she couldn't help but feel a tinge of apprehension or anxiety – she didn't know which – as the seven of them attacked a plethora of fried eggs, an immense stack of toast and enough bacon to have fed a regiment.

Immediately after breakfast, Janet's apprehension accelerated – slightly. As Patti and Joan began to clear the table, Janet's gaze narrowed in on Barbara. She wondered if her daughter's conduct ought to dictate the events of the next few hours. Barbara, though, was her normal, loveable, self. She gave no indication of anything out of the ordinary.

Whatever tension that may have existed was broken by Rickie. He asked Steve if he'd like to play catch. The detective – noticeably off the hook – invited Robbie to join them. The three "boys" headed out the side door.

Janet watched through the dining room window – as the trio headed for Steve's car. Amazing! He'd had a baseball glove, two bats and a number of balls – in various stages of repair – in his trunk.

<u>He is</u>! <u>He's a kid</u>! <u>A great big kid</u>!

She was startled, somewhat, to see Rickie running toward the house. Janet hurried into the kitchen – as the boy burst through the side door. He breathlessly informed his mother and two sisters that, "Steve is gonna take Robbie and me to the mall! Get us a couple of gloves! He didn't know that we didn't have none."

"Didn't have any," corrected Patti.

"Have any," repeated the youngster. "Okay, Mom?"

"Yes, Honey," laughed Janet. "Of course."

The boy started back outdoors! Then, he stopped – and stuck his head back inside.

"He's neat, Mom!" proclaimed the youngster.

"Yes, Honey," agreed his mother. "He's neat."

Janet poured herself another cup of coffee – and snagged a fresh cupful for Barbara, who'd remained seated at the table in the dining room. Setting both cups on the table, Janet closed the door to the kitchen – and seated herself.

"Barb," she began. "About last night ... "

"Oh, Mother, for heaven's sake. Don't give it another thought. I certainly haven't. I'd probably be worried if … well, if … if nature wasn't beginning to take its course."

"That's another thing that bothers me, Barb. You worry so much. You worry so damn much … about me. You worry about your sisters and brothers. About … things."

Barbara's smile was as warm and as infectious as Janet's. "You've got me as a blue-haired, bingo-playing, little old lady in sneakers, Mother. I'm not quite there yet."

"Well, I still may be closer to the truth than you know. I might not be that far off. You're matured … far beyond your years, Baby. Far beyond them. Like I told Steve, last night, there are times when I don't know whether I'm the mother or the daughter. You … you've taken over so many things, Barb. Lifted so many things … so many burdens … from me. From my back. Barb … Barb, I'm so sorry."

Tears glistened in the older woman's eyes.

"Sorry? Sorry about what, Mother?"

"Sorry that you've had to become a woman. Had to become a woman … before you were ever really a girl. Before you were even a kid, for heaven's sake."

Barbara laughed – and patted her mother's hand. "I'm fine, Mother. I really am," she assured. "Our situation for the past few years … ever since your husband left … has probably had more positives than negatives. Not only for me … but, for Patti and Joanie too. I look around at school … and all I see is how immature some of the students are. How most of the students are." She laughed – heartily. "Not only the students," she continued. "Some of the faculty too. Probably most of the faculty … when you stop and think about it."

"Barb? Barb … this is so hard for me to ask. We've never really had much chance to talk any … uh … any girl talk. Things have been so hectic, sometimes."

"Things have been so hellish sometimes," emphasized the young woman.

"Yes," nodded Janet. "Yes, they have. They've been nothing else … if not hellish. Barb, you seem to … well, you seem to go to school, go to work, work around here, and … "

"So?"

"So … do you have any boyfriends? I know that must be the most stupid question in the history of the world ... to ask a seventeen-year-old girl. A seventeen-year-old woman. A <u>beautiful</u> seventeen-year-old woman. But, that's just it. I don't know what a seventeen-year-old even does, these days. Or who she does it with. I feel quite ... quite inadequate, actually. Almost left out ... when it comes to being a mother. In some areas, anyway. Just so damn ... so damn ... well, so damn <u>inadequate</u>."

"Oh, Mother. What do you mean by inadequate?"

"Well, when I was seventeen, I don't think I'd ever had a date. Not an actual date. Couple girlfriends and I, we'd go to the dances on Friday nights ... over at Saint Cecilia's parish hall, which is where we all lived, when I was growing up. And, I suppose, I must've kissed a couple guys. I remember that, one time, a boy put his hand ... well, he put his hand here." She indicated her right breast. "And I was ready to out and out scream! I almost slapped him silly! Did, actually, land one pretty good one." She allowed herself a rather satisfied smile. "I probably would've slapped him silly ... if a couple of the other girls hadn't stopped me. But, what I'm saying is that I'd never had a real, true, one-on-one relationship when I was your age. I really don't know what's normal ... or what's abnormal ... these days."

"Oh, I guess most girls, nowadays, they probably date ... when they're fifteen or sixteen. Not usually anything terribly heavy."

"Well, it just seems like you read and hear of more fourteen- and fifteen-year-old girls getting pregnant these days. Twelve- and thirteen-year-old girls, even. Television is so much more ... well, so much more ... explicit these days. Much more so than when I was growing up. We still had *Howdy Doody* and *The Mickey Mouse Club* and *Kukla, Fran and Ollie*, in those days. Right now, I'm so damn mixed up. I never really thought about these things. Well, not as much as I probably should have. Not until last night."

"I think you're probably putting too much importance on last night, Mother."

"I don't think so. After all these years, I've been going around ... just all wrapped up ... wrapped up, in my own little world. I think that, in some areas ... in a lot of areas ... I've been completely oblivious of what may be going on in your lives. Yours and your sisters. Maybe something inside me is afraid to think about such things. To even wonder about such things. Maybe I've never wanted to face up to things."

"Face up to things?"

"Yes. The three of you ... you're young women now. Not little girls, anymore. I guess I just never thought about the different things ... the different situations ... that you have to cope with. Cope with as young women. But, see? When you walked in on Steve and me, last night ... "

"Mother! Don't <u>worry</u> about last night. You're building last night ... building it into something ... something that's <u>way</u> all out of proportion."

"Maybe ... in a way. You're probably right. You usually are. But, still, it made me stop and think. Barb ... this sounds dumb ... but, do you date?"

Barbara started to laugh – then, thought better of it.

"No, Mother. I don't really date. A couple times Jimmy Roundtree and I've stopped for coffee on the way home from the pizzeria. But, that's been about it."

"Jimmy Roundtree?"

"Yeah. You've never met him. The few times you've come to the pizzeria, he's not been there. He works many more hours than I do. Many more hours. He brings me home, from time to time. Most of the time, of course, Marcia brings me home. Her, you've met. She's been there ... for years. Sometimes, Guido does."

"Guido? Isn't he the owner?"

"Yes."

"Barb ... there are, you know, rumors. Rumors that he can't keep his hands off the help. Is that true?"

"Well, yes. He's a fanny-patter." She smiled. "From the word 'go'."

Janet winced slightly. She'd used the same term Friday night – when Steve had patted her own bottom.

"Does he," she asked, "does he ever ... uh ... ?"

"Pat me on the fanny? Oh, he has. A couple or three times. When I first started there, he did. But, since then, we reached a sort of ... well, kind of ... an understanding."

"An understanding?"

"Right. I didn't make a big fuss or anything. I just flat out told him that I didn't appreciate it. I told him that my fanny was my own personal property. Maybe it was the way I said it ... or the way I looked at him or whatever. I'm not really sure. All I know is that he stopped. It was no big deal. I work there ... and he doesn't pat me on the fanny. I've never really worried about riding home with him. He's a pretty good guy. Every time some rube, at the restaurant, makes some stupid, silly move on me ... which the idiot usually thinks is suave and sexy ... Guido'll jump all over him. I think I'm probably the only girl over there, that he looks out for. The rest? Why, I guess ... I guess he just pats 'em on the fanny."

"This Jimmy what's-his-name?"

"Roundtree? He's a nice enough kid. Kid! He's actually not a kid. He's twenty-three or twenty-four. Got a couple of kids of his own. Both babies. Two- and three-years-old, I guess."

"Have you ever ... ?"

"Dated? Dated Jimmy? No. Never. We've never dated. Or anything else! He's got too many hang-ups."

"Hang-ups?"

"Yeah. For one thing, he's not into any long-term relationships."

"That's bad?"

"No. Not at all. Not in his case. If I were him, I wouldn't want a long-termer either. But, he's so afraid that he's going to fall for someone ... that he's as stiff as he can be, with a woman. With any woman. Kind of creepy sometimes. Can't see his kids! Doesn't even know where they are! That'd kill me! I guess his wife must be a real bitch ... although he never talks about her. Well, hardly ever. But ... poor guy ... he's going through all kinds of changes ... over the fact that he doesn't know where his kids are. Or how they are. Sometimes, all he needs is a sounding board. So, from time to time, we'll stop at *Denny's* for coffee ... and I go ahead and let him bounce his frustrations and anxieties off me. He shouldn't think that every woman in the world is a ... is a bitch."

"It figures," said Janet, with a soft smile.

"It figures? What figures, Mother?"

"Even when it comes to boy-girl stuff, you wind up playing the

Good Samaritan. Playing the mother figure. That'd probably be more accurate. The mother figure."

"Oh, it's no big deal."

"That's just it. Yes it is, Barb. You've probably been some kind of lifesaver for him. And for God-knows-how-many others."

"Oh, Mother. Sometimes you get so overdramatic."

"Barb? Have you … do you … ever get involved in a … well, a situation … one like Steve and I were in last night? I'm sure you're aware of what was going on."

"Or what was coming off," responded Barbra, with an obscene laugh. "Or almost coming off, anyway. I don't think I've ever seen a bra as rumpled as yours was Mother."

Janet began to blush. Barbara patted her on the hand, once more.

"I … I wasn't sure you'd noticed," muttered Janet.

"How could I miss it? As big as you are there? It almost looked like you had three boobs." Barbara began to laugh once more – but, brought herself up short, as her mother's blush deepened. "Mother," the younger woman admonished. "Don't be so up-tight! Loosen up some! As it happens, no! No, I've never found myself in that position. That's not to say that I couldn't have. Or never will. I'm not really such a pillar of morals, y'know. Not as pure as the driven snow."

"This is becoming … well … it's becoming a real education. For me, anyway. What do you mean by that? By 'pillar of morals'? By 'not as pure as the driven snow'?"

"Not to worry, Mother. I'm still intact. Still a virgin … if that's what you're referring to. I've never been in that situation … mainly, because I've never met anyone that I've ever <u>wanted</u> to get into that situation with. The boys at school are all such drips. When they grow up … <u>if</u> they ever grow up … I suppose they'll be all right. I'm not especially looking for anyone. I've read that … when you go looking for it … it never comes. Sooner or later, I believe, someone'll come along … someone I care really deeply for … and then, I suppose, I'll be available. Then? Who knows? So, if it happens that I do meet Mister Right, and you walk in on the two of us … and find us in the same situation that you and Steve were in last night … I'd expect you to understand."

"Well, I probably wouldn't," replied her mother, glumly. "Wouldn't have. Not before last night, anyway. I guess that I would … possibly would … now. I guess you have to have been there. At the risk of telling tales out of school, I'd never really ever gotten there with your … uh … with Jim."

"Why doesn't that come as a big shock to me?"

"Barb, we're going to have to talk more in the future. I'm just as sorry as I can be that it took me so long to … "

Once more the younger woman patted the hand of her mother.

"There's nothing to apologize for, Mother. Absolutely nothing. Look, we haven't been able to talk … mainly, because things have been so damn hectic."

"I think I like your word 'hellish' better. But, I do have to apologize. I really feel as though I've been neglecting my duties. Neglecting an important part of your … your … your … "

"My sex education?"

"Well … yes."

"Don't give it another thought. I don't know of many girls … ones that can talk this frankly with their mother. I supposed the same thing would hold true for boys … talking with their fathers. I hope you'll put your mind at ease. I'm still as virginal as can be … and I can safely say the same thing for Patti and Joanie."

"Joanie? Dear Lord! Joanie's only a baby!"

Barbara laughed.

"There's a line," she informed her mother, "in *Fiddler On The Roof* … where 'Yenta, the Matchmaker' talks about such things to 'Tevye's' wife. She says, 'From such babies … come other babies'."

Her daughter's remark – obviously intended to place their discussion in a lighter dimension – sent a chill down Janet's spine.

"Whooooo!" she exclaimed. "We're going to … for sure … have to talk more. Maybe I can pick up a few more gems of wisdom from my blue-haired, bingo-playing daughter. My blue-haired, bingo-playing daughter … in sneakers."

<<>>

Once they'd finished their coffee, Janet and Barbara busied themselves cleaning upstairs – while Patti handled the housekeeping chores on the first floor and Joan did the laundry.

Much to Janet's surprise, it would be almost five hours before Steve and the boys would return. She had begun to worry. It was practically five-thirty in the evening. How long could it have taken to buy a couple baseball gloves? On the other hand, she was certain that – had they gotten into an accident – she'd have heard by that late hour.

At 5:45 PM, the "boys" drove up. All three of them.

"Sorry we were so long," apologized Steve. "There really isn't all that much room to bat a ball around here. We'd have taken out a window or two, for sure. Maybe a windshield or two. So, we stopped at the playground. Those guys are getting pretty good. Some athletes you got there, Fathead."

"Don't call my mother a fathead," bristled Rickie.

"It's okay, Honey," assured his mother. "He says it in love. Steve doesn't mean that I'm really a fathead. At least I hope not. It's just a … a kind of a nickname."

The boy seemed somewhat placated.

Robbie seemed to understand a little better. Besides, he was bubbling over with enthusiasm.

"Mom!" he shouted. "Guess what! Steve bought us the neatest gloves! And two bats! And three baseballs! Brand new! All this stuff is brand new!"

"Well," explained Steve, "one of the baseballs isn't so new. Not anymore. And I guess you could say that neither are those guys' gloves. Man! They were hawking balls all over the yard, over there."

"What did you go and do that for?" asked Janet. "Buy them all this stuff?"

He shrugged his broad shoulders. "Wasn't all that big a deal. My bats were too big … too heavy … even for hard guys like them. So, I figured that we needed some lumber. Bats that they could swing. And, who knows? We could've lost a ball or two at the playground. Always best to be prepared, don'tcha know."

She kissed him.

"Thank you," she rasped. "Thank you so much."

"We thanked him too," advised Rickie.

"We sure did," agreed Robbie. "The stuff cost him seventy-dollars. A little more than seventy-dollars."

"Seventy dollars?" gasped Janet. "Oh, Steve! That's too much! I can't let you do that! It's too much! Far too much!"

"Nah! Future major leaguers like them … they need proper equipment. Right, men?"

Both boys nodded, enthusiastically.

Janet's demeanor softened. She reached up and kissed Steve once again.

"I … I really don't know how … how to … to thank you," she said.

"Oh, we'll think of something," he whispered in her ear.

<<>>

Dinner time was fast flying by – so Steve went out and got a red-and-white "barrel" of fried chicken – along with a cauldron of mashed potatoes-and-gravy, plus a vat of coleslaw, a dozen ears of freshly-cooked corn-on-the-cob and too many biscuits to number.

Barbara was not scheduled to work that night. Patti had no babysitting obligations. The seven of them sat in the living room – munching chicken and "fixin's" and watched the venerable Judy Garland movie, *Meet Me In St. Louis*, on the family's equally-venerable black-and-white television. Once the picture had finished, both Robbie and Rickie had lain asleep on the living room floor. Steve insisted upon carrying them up to their bedroom. The three girls retired to their room.

Barbara, Patti and Joan shared the master bedroom. The boys were ensconced in the second-largest room. Janet had taken the remaining one – which was very small. It seemed the only logical disposition of valuable sleeping space.

Steve and Janet, remained on the couch, once the children had dispersed, and watched another schmaltzy old musical – *Three Little Words* with Fred Astaire, Red Skelton and Vera-Ellen – while they "shamelessly" held hands..

It was 11:20 PM, when Janet walked Steve to the front door.

"Thank you, My Love," she said. "Thank you so much for today."

"Aw shucks, Ma'am. T'weren't nuthin'."

"Yep it t'were. I don't think I've enjoyed a Sunday so much. In my whole <u>life</u>, I don't think I've enjoyed a Sunday so much. The kids …

oh, Steve. They love you so! Robbie and Rickie had the times of their lives. What with you playing ball with 'em and all. You shouldn't have bought out the entire sporting goods department at '*Monkey Wards*', though."

"Yes I should have. I most certainly should have. They're fine boys, Janet. But, they do need to have a man's influence in their lives ... to a point, anyway. You might want to remember that ... as time-and-a-half goes on."

"I know," she sighed. "It's just that ... "

"Look," he expanded. "My parents divorced ... when I was eleven or twelve. All I had ... all there was around the house ... were my mother and my four sisters. Two of 'em are older than I am. The other two ... one's just a year younger nor me, and the other's not quite three years my junior. I love 'em all. Love 'em dearly. But, there were just too damn many women around there. They all treated me like I was seven-years-old, or something. Even my kid sisters. Both of 'em. I joined the Navy ... when I was a couple days past my seventeenth birthday ... just to get the hell away from all the feminine influence. It sounds like a knock against 'em ... but, it's not. How could they know? How could they ever know what I wanted? What I needed? They couldn't. The first thing ... and I'll remember this till my dying day ... the first thing that happened, when I got to Boot Camp, up at Great Lakes, was this chief petty officer. We were all standing there like a bunch of idiots ... not knowing one of our vital body openings from an excavation in the earth. And this CPO, he asks the white-hat guy who was trying to line us up ... he asks, 'Are these men ready yet? To go for their physical exams?' Hey! He'd called me a <u>man</u>! <u>Me</u>! A <u>man</u>! I ate that stuff up!"

"I ... I guess I've never really looked at things that way."

"How could you? You've never been a little boy ... unless there's something very significant you've never told me. Hell, I'm not altogether certain what they ... what your boys ... what they may be thinking, at that age. And I was a little boy ... rest assured ... at one time. But, I had a father ... at least till he and my mother split the sheets. He didn't come around much, after that."

"I'm sorry, Steve. I had no idea that ... "

"It wasn't anything to get worked up over. We never got along all that great, anyway. But, he did play ball with me ... every now and then. Took me to a Tigers or Lions or Red Wings game ... every once a quarter. Rob and Rick ... they need that. I think that most kids ... most boys ... their age, have a ball glove. And, probably, a bat or two. And, certainly, a couple of baseballs. When I was a kid, eventually we'd have knocked the cover off the ball ... so, we'd bind it up with that black electrical tape. Every time the tape split, we'd just add another layer on top of it. Some of those balls, I remember, they must've weighed eleven pounds. Next time you're at *Walgreen's* or *K-Mart*, pick up a roll of black tape for your budding pros. Oh! And just so you'll know ... I'll probably lay a football on 'em ... and maybe even a couple hockey sticks and a puck or two. You don't actually knock the cover off a hockey puck."

"That's ... that's too much, Steve. Way too much. You shouldn't do all that."

"Oh, c'mon. It's not 'all that'. They're boys, Janet! Listen, Fathead. There are certain things that are important to boys. If not now ... then, in the future."

She sighed – and brushed back a tear. One from each eye.

"Like everything else," she lamented, "I've never thought much about it. Much about <u>anything</u>, I guess. Steve, I can't tell you: These past few days have ... well, they've been a real education. One hell of an education. I guess what you say makes sense ... about having too many women around. But, I'd like to think that, eventually, I'd have gotten Robbie and Rickie gloves and bats and balls and hockey pucks ... all those things."

"Of <u>course</u> you would've. I know you would've. I'm sure you would've. But, you know something? I thoroughly enjoyed myself with 'em today. Probably won't be able to move tomorrow ... but I had a helluva time with them today. I honestly did." His eyes began to well up. "In a way," he continued, his voice taking on a hoarse-whisper quality, "it kind of almost reminded me of my daughter. Not really the same, y'know. There's something about daddies and daughters." A tear trickled down his cheek. "That's why," he expanded, "well, it's why I can't ... not for the life of me ... I just simply can't imagine your husband just simply splitting! Just up and leaving! Leaving his daughters! His little girls, for God's sakes! Three precious little girls. I guess they <u>were</u> little then. And, to go ahead and leave your <u>daughters</u> … I just can't fathom that!"

She reached up – and brushed away his tear. Then, the one that overflowed his other eye.

"I guess," he said, trying to halt the flood of emotion, "I guess that part of me has always longed to have a son or two. Kids I could actually play ball with. Look, I really had a ball with Rob and Rick today. I really did. And … let me assure you … I wasn't indulging 'em. I really wasn't. I was … truth be known … indulging my-own-self."

She kissed him once more.

"You are sweet. So sweet."

"Nah. A little selfish, maybe."

"No," she insisted. He couldn't remember her voice ever having taking on that degree of certainty – of authority. "Not selfish! Sweet! Sweet," she repeated, emphatically. "When are you going to think of some way that little ol' me can repay you? Hee hee!"

"Well, we can't effect a payment plan here! We got into enough trouble last night. Did Barb have anything to say … about our little departure from decorum?"

"Oh, we talked about it a little. She completely understood. Said that, if I walked in on her, in the same … how did you say it? … found her in the same little departure from decorum, she hoped that I would understand. I told her that I probably would." She shrugged. It was a gesture of pure helplessness. "But, you know what?" she asked. "If push actually came to shove, I … well, I … I don't know. I just don't know if I could be quite that understanding."

"I don't think you give yourself enough credit. I'm sure you'd … "

"I guess it's the old do-as-I-say-not-as-I-do double standard thing." I don't know, Steve. I wish I did. I wish I knew about a lot of things. I'm finally realizing how stupid … how dumb … I am."

"Not dumb, Fathead. Not stupid. Nothing close. There you go again … being too damn harsh on yourself. I'm sure that you'd be more capable of dealing with it … or anything else … than you realize. More adept than you think."

"Maybe. Maybe not. All I know is that … when she told me that she was still a virgin … I can't tell you how relieved I was. How relieved I still am."

"As well you should've been. As well you should be. Don't worry about it. You'll do fine. Whether it's Barb or Patti or Joanie ... or the men. You'll do fine."

"Patti? Joan? God, Steve! Don't even say that! Don't even think it."

"They're young ladies, Fathead. And the boys aren't that far behind."

"I' know," she groaned. "Barb drove that fact home ... painfully home ... this afternoon." She heaved a massive sigh. "Painfully home," she repeated.

"Our little girls are growing up," observed Steve. It was not an original thought.

"Don't I know it. Don't I ever know it." She kissed him again – tenderly. Sympathetically. "Look, Steve," she rasped, "I'm sorry ... I'm truly sorry ... about your little girl. Your daughter. Your little Sharon. Dear Lord, I spend so much time worrying about myself ... and about my kids ... that I wind up not being aware of my blessings. Not being aware of how thankful I should be, for those blessings."

He pulled her close to him and kissed her on her lips. Then, he released her – before the kiss had a chance to "build". She wound her arms around his neck. However, he disengaged himself from her embrace – and patted her, once more, on the bottom.

"Well," he said, "I see by the ol' clock on the floor that it's time fer me tuh hitch up muh wagon and head fer the ol' door, thar. I had a wonderful day, my dear little fathead. A wonderful day. You're one hell of a woman. And you've got one hell of a fam-blee. I'll give you a growl ... at the office tomorrow."

He kissed her once more. And patted her once more. Then, he turned and left.

Janet would have, she knew, many additional complexities to ponder – while lying in her bed, alone, that night.

NINE

The next morning, Steve phoned shortly after nine-thirty. The call was brief – by necessity. He advised Janet that his unit of The Michigan State Police was to be involved in a special investigation.

"I can't really say too much about it ... not at the moment, anyway," he advised. "It's a biggie, though! A real biggie! Stake-outs! Following people! Skulking around. All that kind of good stuff."

"Steve? Steve, be ... be careful. Please. For God's sakes! Please be careful."

"You can depend on it. Gotta go now. I'll call you from time to time ... during the week. But, I can't really tell you when. Not right now. Don't really know."

"Well ... starting tomorrow ... I'm going to be pretty busy my-own-self."

"Oh? How so?"

"How quickly we forget. Don't you remember? I start school tomorrow night. Gonna learn how to grapple with ye olde computer. I hope they'll be able to cram some real smarts into my punkin haid."

"Oh. Oh yeah. I guess I got all caught up in this thing ... plus there were a few distractions over the weekend ... and the whole thing slipped my alleged mind. I'm proud-a ya, Kid! You'll dazzle 'em with your footwork."

"Yeah," she answered, with a soft laugh. "Or baffle 'em with something else."

"Nah. You'll do fine. There's lotsa smarts in your punkin

haid, already. Look, Fathead. I really gotta go. Break a leg ... or whateverinhell they say in classroom biz."

<<>>

The night course was a good deal more than Janet had bargained for. However, she seemed to be adjusting reasonably well.

The Wolverine Business Academy had been founded in the mid-thirties – and had only recently moved to newer, more modern, quarters in Garden City. Originally, the school had specialized in bookkeeping, accounting, shorthand, and other secretarial skills.

In 1974, they'd branched into the "new fangled" computer field. By 1979, computer sciences had become the virtual main thrust of the school's curriculum. *Wolverine's* computer training classes had come to be recognized as among the finest in the Detroit metropolitan area. Indeed, in the entire state of Michigan.

At the outset of her school adventure, the workload had seemed overwhelming to Janet. Fortunately, the student-to-instructor ratio was only about 10-to-1. Terri had advised the newest student that she expected that the ratio would eventually be reduced – probably to 8-to-1 – or possibly 7-to-1. A couple or three students could be expected to drop out – before the six weeks would elapse. Possibly even more – than the standard two or three.

"I've known of situations where it's been five or six cop out," she'd told Janet.

The course was of a "hands on" nature. Fortunately for her there wasn't as much pure "book-learnin'" as Janet had feared. Still, by the end of the first three-hour class, she'd wound up totally exhausted.

At home, she'd found that it had taken till almost midnight – after her first class – to complete her homework. The exercise had been comprised, for the most part, of simply memorizing the myriad of terms she would need – beginning Wednesday night.

She virtually fell into bed – and dropped, immediately, into a deep, troubled, sleep, in which a disjointed, frenzied, bedlam of terms, commands, keyboards, screens, and floppy discs seemed to take turns "making a violent, strafing, run" at her.

The following night, the course seemed to go much easier. By the time the class was dismissed, Janet's confidence had increased! Tenfold!

And there'd already been one dropout. Her instructor, Ron Warren, told her – as she was leaving the classroom – how pleased he was with her progress. Why would he have picked <u>her</u> – out of the entire body of students?

"You're probably at the head of the class," he'd advised her, "insofar as command of terms are concerned. And, more importantly, I think you have a bit of a leg up on the others ... when it comes to relating them to the functions they perform on the old computer."

She'd tried to brush it off, but Janet felt distinctly ill at ease – due to the manner in which he'd said "leg". Just something about – she didn't know – the tilt of his head, or his limped-lidded gaze. Something! No – obviously, she was reading too much into something that shouldn't make her even pause.

Terri had used the same term, on that first day. Yes – but, <u>she</u> was a woman. <u>That</u> would tend to make a difference. No – it all had to be in her head. The instructor was, after all, being very complimentary toward her.

"You're head and shoulders ahead of everyone else," he'd continued. She thought that this, maybe, was a bit much. Far too complimentary. "You must really have done your homework," he'd rambled on. "You'll find that not too many of your illustrious fellow students do. Many of them will not crack a book ... once they get away from my evil clutches. They're only fooling themselves ... only hurting themselves."

While he was speaking, he'd put his hand on her arm – just below her shoulder. Janet found the touch to be exceptionally disconcerting. As before, she didn't know exactly why. Or how she should react to it. Wasn't that being a bit forward? Well, probably not, she wound up thinking.

<u>I'm acting like a teenager. Like some kind of a high school girl.</u>

Ron was fortyish, tall, blond – and had worn the same rumpled suit on both nights. His vivid, penetrating, deep-blue eyes seemed to compliment his crooked, boyish, smile. His gaze was penetrating, though. Disturbingly so!

"You're a joy to work with," he'd assured her – as he'd, thankfully, removed his hand.

Flustered, Janet blurted a "Thank you" – then, hurried from the building.

Tooling along, in her beat-up Maverick, on the way home, she found herself wishing, once again, that she would have been better versed in boy/girl relationships. Wished that – for all her life – she'd been more astutely advised about such things. Was Ron "coming on" to her? That <u>was</u> the term she'd heard Barb or Patti use. Wasn't it?

There were six other women in the class – all significantly younger than Janet. Was the fact that Ron was closer to her age – the only one in the room who was in that bracket – would that have been the reason that he'd seemed to devote more attention to her? Platonic attention? Or something else? The situation had all kinds of potential to become terribly troublesome.

<u>But, not if you don't let it, my girl</u>.

<<>>

On Thursday, Janet felt adventuresome enough, at the office, to attempt to "call up" a few of her newly-learned techniques. Apply them to the company's complicated computer system. These attempted workings would entail programs that she was not certain existed. Or – even if they did exist, in the **Brock** system – she was unsure whether she'd be allowed access to them. On the other hand, with her vast font of experience in the field – six whole entire hours – she felt certain that the programs had to "be in there somewhere". Most seemed to be! How about <u>that</u>?

After each successful entry, Janet became slightly more courageous. Three different times, she was instructed – on screen – that she would need a password to progress further into the program. Those results, of course, failed to bother her. She was out and out <u>thrilled</u> – that she'd managed to have gotten that deeply, into the far reaches of her employer's system. Maybe she <u>wasn't</u> such a "fathead" after all!

Whenever time permitted, she studied her textbook at the receptionist's desk. She even blundered across two different tutorials – in one of the bottom drawers of her receptionist desk – which pertained to the **Brock & Associates** system. She wasn't able to get very far with them, however. <u>Very</u> complicated material. Stuff on which she'd had yet to touch, in class. She'd, most certainly, have her work cut out for her.

<<>>

After class, on Thursday night, Janet had a very definite spring in her step. She'd swept out of the room – while Ron had been occupied. He'd been speaking with another student. One much younger than she. That was fine.

One week down! Five more to go! Wolverine Academy ... I'll lick you yet!

As she climbed into her car, Janet heard her name! It was a shout from way across the parking lot! It was Ron! He was bearing down upon the crippled Maverick – running full tilt!

"Hi," he panted. "You got away from me, there. Look ... " he continued to puff. "Listen. I just wanted to tell you that it's such a pleasure to work with you. To work with someone so obviously devoted. Half of these other ya-hoos don't really give a damn. Taking the course ... just so they'll have one more arrow in their quiver ... resume-wise. You, though ... you seem to throw yourself right into the thing. You really do."

He was still having a problem catching his breath.

"Look, Miss Bolton ... Janet," he went on. "Would you think it forward of me to invite you for a cup of coffee? I'd really like to, well, get to know you, a little bit better. I'd really like to make you my own little project. Would like to find out where you're going. What the course means to you ...from a professional standpoint, of course."

Janet smiled, self-consciously. "Uh ... that's very nice of you, Mister Warren. But, it's ... it's really awfully late. And I really have to ... "

"Ron. Please call me Ron."

"I ... I don't know if I could do that. In any case, it is awfully late ... and, really, I'm very tired. Morning comes so soon. I appreciate the offer, but I'm going to have to ... have to decline. With thanks."

The instructor appeared crushed! Janet was in a quandary. How to say something nice? How to buck up the man? He was obviously hurt. How do you cheer him up? Without encouraging him to pursue an amorous route? This whole discomfiting scenario, playing out as it was, was far from being her strong suit, she knew.

She bade him an awkward goodnight. Ron's "night-night" was equally as clumsy.

As she drove away, it occurred to Janet – hit her suddenly, with the impact of a sledgehammer – that she now had something new to worry about: Would her rebuff affect her scholastic relationship with Ron? Would it affect her final grade in the course? Or any other grades? Bring down her GPA? She didn't even know if such a course would project a Grade Point Average.

Damn! <u>Why can't a person just go to school? Take a stupid course?</u> <u>Get an honest grade? Without having to get involved with the stupid</u> <u>teacher?</u>

<<>>

Once Janet arrived at home, she found a new crisis waiting! As she pulled into the driveway, she saw the light snap on in the dining room. Then – within seconds – the kitchen lit up! Patti was waiting for her at the side door. The young woman was obviously rattled!

"Patti! What is it? What's the matter?"

"You'd better call Aunt Anne right away! I think something's happened to Uncle Roger!"

"Uncle Roger? What?"

"You'd better call her, Mom! She said she'd be waiting for your call … not to worry about the time. They're an hour behind us in Chicago, anyway."

Janet swept up the steps – and hurried into the kitchen. She opened her "junk drawer", next to the one in which she kept the silverware – and began to rifle for her sister's phone number.

"Dammit! I can never find my stupid address book … when I need it. Trying to remember Anne's number is a lost cause … as often as I ever call her. As often as we ever talk to one another."

"That's all right," comforted Patti. "I wrote it down. It's on the tablet … by the phone."

Janet kissed her daughter on the forehead.

"I should've known you'd be so efficient," she said. "I should've known."

She rushed into the living room, snatched up the phone and dialed her sister's number. The call was answered before the first ring had been completed.

"Hello?" The voice on the other end had obviously been crying.

"Anne! What's wrong?"

"Oh! Oh, Janet! Listen! It's … it's Roger! He's dead! He's been killed!"

"Killed? Roger? How? What happened?"

"Long story! It'll be splattered all over the papers here tomorrow! He was …was … was murdered!"

"Murdered? Dear Lord! Anne! Just like … just like Jim! Do they know who?"

Anne's sigh practically filled the receiver! "Yes," she replied at length. "They know who did it."

"Dear Lord! Dear Lord, Anne! Who … who was it? Where'd it happen?"

Anne's response was barely audible: "His mistress. At her apartment."

"His <u>mistress</u>? Roger has … had … a mistress? Oh, Anne! What happened?"

The newly-minted widow began to cry. It was apparent that the breakdown was not the first – nor would it probably be the last. Once she regained some portion of her composure, she began to speak once more:

"I'm sorry, Jan. I can't help it. Can't … I'm having trouble coping. I really am. What happened was that he was trying to break up with her. Oh, he wasn't coming back to me. Not back to my bed, anyway. God forbid he'd ever come back to my bed. That'd never happen." She broke down once more! "I … I've been aware," she resumed, "that he's had one mistress or another for … I don't know … maybe five or six years. Maybe longer. Probably longer. Who knows? Who the hell <u>knows</u>?"

"Anne! I never knew!"

"Well," sniffed her sister, "it's really not something you go shouting from the highest steeple. I really didn't care. I knew it was all over with us … years ago. Almost before it was even started … now that I look back on it. But, I figured that … as long as he'd continue to support me … what the hell? I'd had it pretty good. I had this nice house, all these years. And, you know, a reasonable amount of money."

"Yes. But, there's more to a relationship … a marriage … than money."

"Well, every three or four years, he'd buy me a new BMW or

something. The house was … like I said … really nice. Still is … though it's under foreclosure. I'd always had a few bucks to spend. So, if he was out sleeping around … if he was out there screwing around with this one or with that one … well, it didn't really bother me. Not that much, anyway."

"You never cease to amaze me, Anne."

"Nothing amazing about it. About me. About anything else, Jan."

Her voice was, all of a sudden, remarkably devoid of emotion. Janet was shocked at the sea-change in her manner. And how quickly it had occurred. Janet had been truthful: Her sister – truly – had never ceased to amaze her.

"I knew," said Anne, matter-of-factly, "which side of the bread the butter was on. Always knew that. Knew it for years. Hell, I had a good thing going. I've never pretended to be anything but mercenary. I got pretty much what I was after. Didn't have to do a damn thing. Sat around on my butt all day. Didn't have to put up with him … with him wanting to make whoopie at night. He was a real dud in bed, anyway. Well, maybe that's not true. Maybe he wasn't such a dud. He certainly seemed to be doing all right … hopping into and out of other ladies' beds."

"Anne! I can't believe this is my own flesh-and-blood sister talking!"

Anne's voice took on an ice-cold, extremely hardened, quality – a dimension Janet had never heard before. Would the surprises never end? "You and I know, Jan," she said, "that we've been different. Totally different. From the time we were little kids, for God's sakes. Different as night and day. I moved heaven and hell to try and get you to apply for welfare … when Jim split! I'd have applied for welfare, AFDC, food stamps, mortgage subsidy … and everything else I could've gotten my grubby little hands on! In a New York minute! You can either be idealistic … my idealistic sister. Or you can be pragmatic … and add in, maybe, a little deviousness. Guess which one of those ol' Anne is?"

"I … why I never … I never thought of myself as being particularly idealistic."

The conversation had reached a point where there was not a trace of sorrow – or any other emotion – in Anne's reply: "You are, Jan. Idealistic as hell. I don't know if my pragmatism has gotten me any farther than you, though. Maybe not even as far. Hell, probably not even as far." Anne's voice had switched once again – to a flat, totally-drained, monotone. "Who knows?" she added. "Who the hell knows? Anyway, I guess dear Roger tried to drop this broad. Had cancelled all of her credit cards. He was in the process ... as I understand it ... of cleaning out his stuff! She pulled a gun!"

"A gun? She had a gun? She pulled a ... a gun?"

"Yep. Big one, too! Can you believe it? She pulled a damn gun! Pulled this really powerful gun! And then, she shot him! Three or four or five times! Right in the face! Oh, Jan! Jan ... it was ... it was terrible. God-horrible!"

Anne was beginning to cry once more. Janet hadn't the foggiest idea what her sister was experiencing. Not after her shocking description of her marriage – or non-marriage. Certainly not after having run the gamut of emotions – in a matter of minutes. In a matter of seconds, in a couple instances.

The funeral was to take place the following Monday – four days hence. Would Janet be able to attend? Given her sister's lack of love toward her brother-in-law, it would seem like a hollow gesture. Janet herself had never experienced any real feelings toward Roger. But, then she hardly knew him. Anne obviously had known him! Known him well!

Whatever, under the best of circumstances, the situation still had to be terribly traumatic for her sister. And if Anne had any friends in "The Windy City", Janet had never heard of them. Her sister had never spoken of any acquaintances out there. None! Ever! Janet knew that Anne needed her. Despite whatever relationship the poor woman might've had with Roger, her sibling was, at that juncture, in a horrible emotional state.

"I'll ... I'll get there someway or another," Janet assured. "Right now, I'm kind of financially embarrassed ... but, I'll think of something."

"Well, I'd send you some money. But, I've got about sixteen bucks in the house. Apparently, they're in the process of tying up our checking account. I was gonna say 'our savings account too' ... but, I find there isn't one. I guess this latest floozie was quite an expense for poor, dear,

Roger. I really don't know what the hell's goin' on here, Jan. I honestly don't. I don't know one damn thing. Look, if I'm able to lay my hands on some extra money, I'll … I'll wire it to you."

"No. No, you've more than got your hands full. Look, I'm not thrilled with the prospect of trying to nurse my poor, decrepit, old Maverick out there. I haven't told you what happened. Had a bit of an accident. That's not all! Not by a long shot! I'll tell you about it, when I get out there. Only problem is … the rear end of my car has been drastically redesigned … and I can't seem to find out if my insurance company's going to do anything for me. I can't get anything out of my agent. And I've known him forever. The car gets me to and from work all right. But, a three-hundred mile trip … one way … that may be … " Her voice trailed off. "Don't worry," she assured. "Don't worry. I'll … I'll think of something. Maybe I can get an advance or something. Rent a car. It'll work out. I'll probably leave after work tomorrow."

"Look, if you're going to drive, don't you dare leave until Saturday morning! At the very earliest! If you fly, you can wait till Sunday. Let me know … if I need to pick you up at the airport. Otherwise, just come when you can. You've got the whole damn weekend. I've got the whole damn weekend. We all have got the whole damn weekend. Funeral's at nine-thirty, Monday morning."

After hanging up, Janet started upstairs. Halfway up the staircase, she stopped and returned to the lone phone, in the living room. She dialed Steve's residence. <u>His</u> number she could remember – though she'd only had occasion to dial it once before. No answer.

<u>Damn! Must really be some kind of a super-duper thing he's involved with!</u>

She realized that she was no longer tired. She decided to brew a cup of tea. Asking Patti to put on the kettle, she began to remove her blouse – on her way up to her bedroom. Six or seven minutes later – after she'd removed her clothing and makeup, then donned her robe – Janet swept into the dining room. Patti had placed a cup of boiling hot water on the table – and had set a tea bag in the saucer. She kissed her mother goodnight, as Janet seated herself.

The latter was to languish there – for almost an-hour-and-a-half. She was locked in a Herculean effort to sort things out. Never an easy situation. Not even under the best of circumstances. And Roger's death, of course, had hardly contributed anything positive. Obviously, Anne would have her work cut out for her, over the next weeks and months. Janet pondered the intrigue – and how it all could've taken place, while she had been completely in the dark. She thought back to the only time that Anne had visited Detroit in the past 10 or 12 years.

Dear Lord! Could it have been that long? Probably not!

Anne had actually visited – a day or two after Jim had left. Since Janet had never been to Chicago, that had been the last time she'd seen her sister. Was Roger sleeping around then? Anne had given no indication that she'd been aware of such tomfoolery.

Tomfoolery. Do people still say tomfoolery?

Would Janet be able to get an advance? Time off? She'd only been employed at **Brock & Associates** for a heartbeat. What about her computer course? Would she have to miss too many classes to successfully complete the study? Would Ron Warren interpret her absence as an outrageous overreaction to his offer to go to coffee with him?

How would she even get to Chicago? Fly? Finances just about made such a proposition out of the question. Drive? Her poor Maverick, she felt certain, would rebel at being asked to perform that far above and beyond the call of duty.

If only she could talk to Steve!

She got up and made her way into the living room. Dialing Steve's number, once more, she waited nervously – as the phone rang and rang and rang and rang! After three more attempts – over the next hour – Janet finally gave up and went upstairs! To toss about – fitfully – in her bed!

<<>>

At nine-thirty the following morning, Janet fidgeted at her desk – doing her best to summon the courage to ask Terri for Monday and Tuesday off. In addition, she would have to ask for an advance. How big an advance? Enough for her to fly? Driving seemed out of the question.

No sense asking for the time off … if you can't get there.

Her troubled plotting was interrupted by the phone. First call she'd had to field in almost fifteen minutes. It was Steve!

"How's my fathead this morning?" he asked, brightly.

"Quite upset."

"Upset? Janet, what's wrong?"

"Death in the family. My brother-in-law. In Chicago. Messy. Awfully messy. Apparently his mistress shot him. Shot him up pretty good. More to it than that, so I understand. It was, I think, lack of affection and lack of money. Money mostly. I guess Anne has her money ... what there is of it ... pretty well tied up. Probate ... or maybe the authorities are just simply sitting on it. I don't know."

"Anne?"

"Yeah. She's my sister."

"That's a shocker. I didn't even know you had one. I'd have thought that ... " his voice trailed off.

"You'd have thought what?" Janet was in no mood to verbally thrust and parry.

"Nothing. I'm sorry. Is there anything I can do?"

"No. I don't know. I've got ... I've just got to see if I can get there. For the funeral. They're burying him on Monday. Getting ready to ask Terri for a couple days off ... and, dammit, an advance."

"Are you going to fly?"

"I ... maybe. I think so. I'm not sure. I don't really know. Depends on ... "

"Look, Janet. If you need some money, I'd ... "

"No! Absolutely not! You've done so much for me now. Probably too much. It was so ... so nice of you to have done all the things you've done already. The theater, the movies ... all that stuff you bought the boys. I won't hear of it. If I can't get Terri to advance me a few bucks, I'll ... I'll ... I'll ... think of something."

"Hoooo! Slow down, Gal! In the first place, what little bit I did, I did for purely selfish reasons. Wasn't all that much anyway. Listen, you wouldn't be thinking about ... thinking seriously, anyway ... of driving out there, would you? Not in your poor old bedpan of a car."

"Well, I ... "

"I'll be damned! Yes you are! I can smell the wood burning from here."

"Well, it would ... y'know ... be a heck of a lot cheaper than flying. Plus, Anne'd have to pick me up at the airport ... and she lives a pretty good way from O'Hare. Something like twenty miles, I think. Maybe twenty-five."

"Look, Janet. Why don't you do this?"

"No! Absolutely not!"

"You haven't even heard what I've got to say."

"It's going to wind up with you giving me some money ... or something."

"See that? You're wrong. Not that at all."

"Oh? Then, what is it?"

"I don't know if I'm gonna tell ya now." He was trying to be funny. It plainly did not work.

"Fine," she said curtly. "That's fine."

"Aw c'mon, Janet. I was just trying to be a damn comedian. Seven-trillion comedians out of work ... and here I am. Being funny. What I was going to say ... what I was going to ask ... is why don't you take my car?"

"Your car? Take your car?"

"Yeah. My car. It's a nice big, fat, four-door LTD. Plus, it's not all that outrageous ... when it comes to slurping up gas. And it rides awfully nice. Like a rocking chair. Radio works. Tape player does too. Look ... I'll even leave the *Kiss Me Kate* tape in the player. You said you loved that music. And this is the original cast."

"Oh, Steve! I couldn't do that. I mean ... "

"You most certainly could."

"That's ... why, that's ridiculous. What would you use?"

"I'll swap you ... for the weekend. Or for next week, or whatever. How-ever-long you need the Ford."

"No. Really, Steve. I couldn't do that. I wouldn't have you running around in that atrocious-looking dumpster of mine."

Steve laughed. Janet hadn't abandoned levity altogether.

"Well," he replied, "truth to tell, I won't really be needing your ... how do you say? ... your dumpster anyway. I'd have it there, if I needed it. But, this surveillance thing is apparently going to keep us all hopping. Well into next week, I'm sure. Bigger ... much bigger ... than any of us had ever thought. So, I'll be using police vehicles most of the time anyway."

"Oh, Steve. Really. I couldn't."

"Of course you could. Look, Fathead. It'll be absolutely no imposition. None whatever. Zero imposition. The LTD's just sittin' there ... doin' nuttin'. Rusting away. Gathering barnacles. Tell you what. I can bring it by your office ... probably sometime around noon. Wait for me ... before you go to lunch. I won't be able to take you to lunch. I'm on a hell of a tight schedule ... but, I can drop off my car and pick up the ol' Maverick. Why don't you ... as soon as you possibly can ... why don't you go down and put the keys in the Maverick? Put 'em in the ashtray! Leave the doors unlocked. I'll just switch cars ... on the fly. When you see my car out in the lot, you'll know that I made the ol' switcheroo. I'll do the same. Leave my keys in the ashtray. How's that sound?"

"Oh, Steve. I wish you wouldn't."

"Well, I wish I would. C'mon now, Fathead. Ain't no big deal. You'll be doing me a favor, actually. Driving it. Keeping the ol' battery charged, and all that."

"Yeah," she responded glumly. "Just like I've been doing you a favor these past few days ... by lightening your bank account. Your banker shouldn't get a hernia."

Once more he laughed. More heartily this time.

"Like Joanie says," he responded, "who writes your material? Then, it's settled. I'll pull the ol' switcheroo caper. You'll wrestle the LTD to 'Chi' ... as me an' Big Looie alweeze calls it. Do me another favor, though, will ya?"

"I don't know if you can afford for me to keep doing you favors."

"Yeah I can. Yeah you should. Do me a favor. Look, I have trouble sleeping nights ... most of these nights ... and ... "

"_That_ kind of favor?"

"No, Fathead! Not _that_ kind of favor. You're going to be in Chicago. Remember? And I'm going to be out catching bad guys. Hopefully, anyway. I was building to something ... but, I think I've forgotten what it was. Besides, I think I like your idea better."

"You were saying something about not being able to sleep," she offered, stiffly. "Not being able to sleep nights. That was ... well ... you ... you kinda scared me."

He laughed once more. "The way _you_ interpreted it, I think I scared myself. Naw, I was saying that I have trouble sleeping nights

... and you being out on the turnpike, well, it ain't gonna help. Don't need the extra worry. So, what say I leave you a couple credit cards, in the ... ?"

"No! Steve! I absolutely draw the line there. It's ... "

"You don't have to use 'em, y'know. In fact, I hope that you don't have to. Against my religion ... me being a devout cheapskate and all."

"That'll be the day."

"Look. You'll just have 'em for backup. Okay? It can get kind of scary ... out in the middle of nowhere ... if you break down. And I'd never forgive myself ... if you had a bad problem. A really hairy problem ... because of my car."

She sighed heavily. "You're too much," she rasped.

"Well, that's substantially better than you telling me that I'm not enough. Look. Here's the move, 'Muggsy'. I'll put my *Mobil* card ... and, I guess, probably my *Citgo* card ... in an envelope. I'll just stick 'em up over the visor on the driver's side. Okay? For an emergency. Of course, if you happen to run short of cash ... why, hell, that's an emergency. Isn't it? I'd have to think it is."

"Thank you," she said softly. "Thank you, Officer Francis. I ... I don't know what I'd do ... do without you."

"I fervently hope that you're not going to want to find out. Okay, Fathead. Gots to run. I'll swing by ... with my glorious LTD ... as soon as I possibly can. Should be before one o'clock. If it's a little after that ... well, you'll know that I got detained, a little bitty. I'll try and call you tonight. You're not going to leave till the morning, are you? It'd take you all night, and ... "

"No. I've already caught hell from my sister ... for even thinking of such a thing."

"I think I like her."

"You like everyone. You must really like me ... the way you're doing all these wonderful things for me. Steve, really. I'm ... I'm most grateful. Truly grateful."

"Aaaaah. I'm the one who's grateful, Janet. I can't tell you what you mean to me."

"Oh, you do fine. With tender, loving, little endearments ... like 'Fathead'."

"That's me. An incurable romantic. Gots to run. I'll try and call you tonight. If I can. If I get hung up on this thing … and can't get away … let me wish you a bon voyage now. And tell you how much I'll miss you. I really will, Janet. You don't know how much."

"I can guess," she responded, softly. "Thanks again. I love you."

"What? What'd you say?"

"I … I said that I love you."

"You totally snuck up on me there, Gal. I wondered if I'd ever hear you say that. I don't know if I could ever hear you say that too much. Say it too often. Gotta run. I love you too! I … oh, God! I wish I didn't have to scoot. But, really … I gotta. Bye! Bye, now … and good luck. You're truly a valiant lady."

Once the connection was broken, Janet immediately rose and – after asking Peggy to cover the board – she made her way to Terri's office. It was obvious to the latter that her employee was troubled. She invited Janet to be seated.

"Now," Terri soothed. "Suppose you tell me what's on your mind."

Janet explained the circumstances of Roger's death, and asked for Monday off – as well as part of Tuesday.

"Part of Tuesday?" asked Terri, cocking an eyebrow.

"Well, yes. I figure I can be back by late Tuesday morning … or, maybe, early in the afternoon. I've got to be back for my class, at *Wolverine*, on Tuesday night. Tuesday evening."

"Well, Janet, I'd appreciate it if you could make it back for class on Tuesday … but, go ahead and take off all day Tuesday, from here. Not a problem. I won't look for you till Wednesday morning. It'd be far too hectic for you to try and get back here … if the funeral's going to be Monday. You'd have to get up in the middle of the night. I'm afraid you'd wink off in class. I know that I certainly would. I almost did … a couple times. And I wasn't blowing in from Chicago, either."

At that moment, Gloria Tapp sauntered in – and placed two long, green-bar, computer printouts on Terri's desk.

"Go ahead," continued Terri. "Take the two days off. Leave early today … if need be. I'm assuming that you'll be needing an advance."

Gloria stood there – looming over Janet, as she responded, "Well, yes. If I could. It would certainly come in handy."

"No problem. Will a hundred dollars be enough?"

Janet nodded – enthusiastically.

"Oh, yes," she gushed. "Yes, certainly! More than enough! I'm sorry, Terri. Sorry to have to come in and ask for these things ... when I'm still a rookie."

"Hey! Is it your fault that your brother-in-law met with such a ... such a demise? Don't give it another thought." Then, Terri looked up at Gloria. "You're doing well here, Janet," she continued. "When an employee gives more than is asked for ... above and beyond the call, don'tcha know ... well, we try and give a little more too."

"I ... you know ... I can't get over it," replied Janet. "Everyone here is so nice to me ... so kind to me. Let me tell you: Steve's going to let me take his car. He insisted on it. Mine would probably make it, but ... "

"That was nice of him."

"It sure is. He's going to drop off his car in the parking lot. Around noon, I guess. In fact, I've got to go down and put the keys to my Maverick in the ashtray ... so that he can just switch cars and leave. He's on a big, fat, old assignment ... and isn't quite sure when he can get here to make the switch. Might be later in the afternoon. So, I'll be here all day anyway. I've been threatened ... under pain of hairbrush ... not to attempt to leave before tomorrow morning. Neither Steve nor my sister'll hear of it."

"Well, just so that you know you're entitled to leave early." Terri glared at Gloria. "Is there anything you need, Gloria?" she asked, testily.

"Uh ... no. Here's yesterday's figures. Is there something wrong? With Janet, I mean."

Janet briefed Gloria on her situation – as the two walked out together. Before exiting, Janet turned to Terri, once again, and thanked her – profusely. Back at her workstation, she got the key ring out of her purse – and pried her ignition and trunk keys off.

<u>Don't know what good the trunk key's going to do. Can't even get the damn thing open.</u>

She hurried down to the parking lot, and dropped the two keys in the ashtray.

<u>Well, he'll be grateful that I don't smoke. At least the ashtray'll be</u> <u>clean.</u>

Then, she rushed back up to the office. As Janet approached the switchboard, Peggy rose – and offered her condolences.

"Thank you, Peggy. I guess Terri must've told you."

"No, actually it was Gloria."

"Gloria? Really? I think I must've misjudged her. She never seemed as though she was ever all that interested in anyone … other than … " Her voice trailed off.

"Other than herself?" asked Peggy, with a warm smile. "If you've misjudged her, then, so has everyone else in this here now establishment. Maybe she's mellowing, in her old age. On the other hand, maybe she was just unloading a juicy hunk of gossip."

<<>>

The rest of the day passed slowly. Unable to view the parking lot from her perch at the reception desk, Janet would periodically stride to the windows across the waiting room – to see if Steve had switched cars. He had not – and the afternoon was beginning to turn into evening. That was a worry! Could something be wrong? Could something have happened to him? He hadn't said so – not in so many words – but, his new assignment seemed fraught with danger!

She was forced to put her anxiety on a back burner, shortly before two o'clock. The switchboard lit up – one final flurry, before the weekend. At three-thirty, Janet rushed over to the window – just as Peggy was entering the reception area.

"There yet?" asked the latter.

"I don't see it. But … my Maverick's gone! Wait! Oh! Yes, there it is. There it is. Way over there … over there in the far corner."

"The Maverick?"

"No. Steve's Ford. It's way over on the far end of the lot. He probably couldn't find a closer spot. That was nice of him."

Janet felt much better – much more secure – as she returned to her switchboard.

It was at that point that she realized she'd not eaten lunch. She was famished! With less than an hour-and-a-half before quitting time, it would behoove her, she felt, to "tough it out" – and not take lunch. She was, after all, getting Monday and Tuesday off.

TEN

The sun was just beginning to rise, as Janet passed the city of Monroe – some 30 miles south of Detroit. She was proud of herself – for having gotten up at four-thirty that Saturday morning. She was on the road – just a few minutes before five o'clock.

She'd even had the foresight to have done her packing on Friday night – an important ingredient in her resolution to "hit the road … early". By her calculation, if she could maintain a speed of 55-miles-per-hour – and allowed herself a total of one hour for refreshments and "pit stops" – she should be in Chicago by 3:30 PM or 4:00 PM.

She was, she knew, flying in the face of her personal history – being as fastidious as she'd become over the past 12-or-so hours. Maybe more of Jim had rubbed off on her than she'd thought. Naw! That was ridiculous! She'd not seen her late husband in years. The sudden voyage into the wild and wonderful world of the practical had seemed to have occurred concomitant with her employment at **Brock & Associates**.

Or maybe it happened with her having become acquainted with Steve Francis?

She changed the station on the radio. It was so nice to have an FM set to listen to. Aw well, she reflected. She should be grateful, she knew, that her Maverick was still function able – more or less. The radio had been out for almost a year.

She was a little disappointed, though, that Steve had not left the original cast recording of *Kiss Me Kate* in the tape player – as he'd promised to do. Probably an oversight. We <u>was</u> a busy man. Maybe it was just as well. Listening to that wondrous music – especially *So In Love* – by herself, might not be the best of all worlds. There would, of course, be one important element missing: One Detective Steve Francis.

She punched another button on the radio, and picked up another station. One with a bit stronger signal. It was a "Beautiful Music" station. She was pleased, six or eight minutes later, to hear them playing a medley from *Kiss Me Kate*. It was, of course, not that unusual. The local stations – especially this one – usually played music from a particular musical, if a production of that show was in town. Could that be a harbinger? Of something nice? An omen of positive happenings?

Given the purpose of her trip, that didn't seem likely.

As the LTD made its way into Ohio, Interstate 75 narrowed – only to widen back up. Then, it narrowed again – to allow for exit and entry lanes on the northern edge of Metropolitan Toledo.

Janet strained to read the various traffic signs – as they confronted her with a cacophony of black-and-yellow, muddled, warnings and instructions. Some of them had silhouettes. Some featured "stick people" illustrations. She had no idea as to what some of the new-fangled pictures/symbols meant.

She seemed to be doing pretty well – until an old Volkswagen van decided to make a panic exit from the Interstate! The raggedy-looking old bus-type vehicle was speeding – at no less than 85 miles-per-hour! He was hurriedly overtaking the LTD – which bothered Janet not at all. That was when the driver decided to sweep across – hurtling from left to right – smack-dab in front of Steve's Ford.

Janet managed to tromp down on the brake pedal – in time to avoid a nasty – probably <u>fatal</u> – collision! To just barely keep from colliding with the recklessly-driven vehicle! Fortunately, at that hour of the morning, there had been no cars behind her – or, she was certain, she'd have gotten "creamed"! Shades of the adventure with Fletcher Groome – in the Detroit/Windsor Tunnel. Thankfully, <u>not</u> shades of that subhuman – in the huge Chrysler!

She was terribly shaken, of course. She did her best to compose herself. She allowed the car to coast ahead. The rusted-out old van had sped almost halfway up the exit ramp. It would serve no purpose – to shout the oath, which was bursting to be let loose!

Son-of-a-pup! He was probably on something!

Doing her best to take mental inventory, Janet stared first at her shaking, white-knuckled, hands – clutching the wheel, in a death grip! Making a concentrated effort, she managed to reduce the trembling – somewhat!

It was at that point that she noticed the door to the glove box. It had snapped open – when she'd practically stood the Ford on its nose! She glanced, hurriedly, into the rear compartment. Her overnight bag had toppled from the seat to the floor. So had her little toiletry case – which had been sitting next to the suitcase.

No damage done! At least she was in one piece! She'd not have to explain to Steve, what had happened to his nifty car! She could always reposition the two items in the back, when she stopped. All in all, she was, she felt, lucky to be alive!

By the time she was driving through downtown Toledo, she began to feel better.

Hope the rest of the trip isn't this eventful! I don't need this much adventure!

The sun had risen to the extent that brilliant beams were pouring through the window in the driver's door. She swept the sun visor around – blotting out some of the glare. The warmth – from beneath the visor – served to have a comforting effect.

Once the highway began to curve in a southwesterly direction, the sun reflected off of something – something very shiny – half-hanging from the glove compartment. What could that be? Looked like something white. No, on a second and third hurried glance, it seemed to have some sort of coloring.

She'd stop south of Toledo – maybe once she'd entered the Ohio Turnpike – and grab a cup of coffee. She sure could use a jolt of caffeine. Maybe a tad of ham and eggs. Sounded good. Plus a "pit stop" would be called for. Once she'd pull off, she'd be able to straighten out the glove box – and stash her luggage, once more, on the back seat.

Twenty minutes later, she guided the LTD into a *Waffle House* parking lot, coasted into a vacant parking spot – and killed the engine.

Sitting with her hands still extended – tightly clutching the top of the wheel – she began a series of deep, deep, breaths.

<u>Dear Lord</u>! <u>I'm lucky to be here</u>! <u>Maybe lucky to be alive</u>! <u>Damfool idiot</u>! <u>He could've killed me</u>!

She unbuckled her seat belt – and leaned across to restore some semblance of order to the glove compartment. She picked up the mysterious item – the one which had been reflecting the early-morning sunlight. It was a glossy *Polaroid* snapshot. There were several others in the glove box. Only that one had dangled out.

Janet picked up the snap – to replace it. Out of reflex, she glanced at it! It was <u>pornographic</u>! In spades! The self-developed picture depicted a naked man and woman – sharing sexual intercourse! Janet closed her eyes! She shook her head slightly – then, looked again! The same XXX-rated photograph stared back at her! She shuddered – violently!

It was impossible to identify the man. The shot was taken from the lower part of the bed! Evidently with a self-timer! The upper part of the man's torso was outside the photograph – from his left ribcage to his right shoulder! His back, buttocks and thighs were clearly – vividly, explicitly – depicted! The woman was a different story: While her face – more or less from the chin up – was not shown, her left breast was graphically pictured! Both people were completely naked! There could be no doubt as to what they were engaged in!

Janet felt the relentless clutches of pure, outright, nausea begin to swirl inside her stomach! The color had drained from her face! Her hands were shaking badly – once more! To think! To think that Steve – her brand spanking new "white knight" – would take pictures such as those! That he'd keep pictures like that! It was a mind-boggler!

Even learning of Jim's death had not sent anything remotely resembling the overwhelming waves of dizziness, queasiness – and out and out disgust – which were cascading through her entire being, on that early Saturday morning!

She couldn't remember ever having experienced anything close to the tidal wave of pure nausea – brought on by the discovery of the God-awful photograph she was holding, in her trembling hands! And there were more of those horrible pictures!

<u>Dear Lord</u>! <u>What's happening</u>? <u>What's happening to me</u>?

Drawn by some power – an overwhelming force – one with which she couldn't cope, Janet reached into the glove compartment! She withdrew the other snapshots! There were four additional photos – each, presumably, depicting the same couple in the same act! In none of them, was the face of the man shown. In only one of the pictures was more than a small portion of the woman's face depicted. Janet was certain she'd never seen the woman before.

The last photo came within a whisker of sending her full-fledged nausea boiling over! It seemed to have been taken from a point further removed from the bed. It showed the man lying on his side – facing the woman. His back was to the camera. The vision of the back of his head, though, was absolutely damning! The man's hair was, unmistakably, the same color as that of her policeman "benefactor"! The hairstyle – the back of it, anyway – was the squared-off-at-the-collar-line type. the same style, as sported by Detective Stephen Francis! To add to Janet's stomach-twisting, overwhelming revulsion, the figure in the picture appeared to be about Steve's height and weight! Who else could it be? Janet hadn't realized that she'd begun to weep! Not until one of her teardrops fell upon the fifth – the most damnable – of the disgusting snapshots!

She jammed the pictures back into the opening in the dash – and slammed the door to the compartment! It popped back open! She whipped it closed – with even more velocity! It bounced open, once again – equally as violently! Janet took a deep breath – and gently closed the door. It was no use. It would not stay closed. The clasp at the top had come loose. Apparently, one of the screws had dropped out.

Probably when I jammed on the brakes back there! Dear Lord! Maybe I'm the one who knocked the lock loose … when I slammed it so damn hard!

She yanked the keys from the ignition, then, pulled herself out of the car – and onto her woefully wobbly legs! She opened the back door, fastidiously placed her luggage back up on the seat – then, slammed the door! The almost-deafening sound from the shaken woman's all-her-might act resounded throughout the parking lot – causing three or four people to stop and stare at her.

Too damn bad!

She made her rubber-kneed way across the lot and into the eatery. Entering the *Waffle House*, Janet perched on a stool – at the far end of the counter – and ordered a breakfast that she was not sure she'd be able to consume. Once the waitress had set her coffee in front of her, she made her way to the restroom – to "repair the damage"!

Inside the ladies' room, she headed straight for the mirror on the opposite wall. The Janet who looked back at her – while certainly not the most ravishing countenance she'd ever laid eyes on – appeared to be in far better shape than anticipated. She looked none the worse for the wear. A real surprise!

Five minutes later, Janet returned to her all-too-quickly-cooling coffee. Part of her was famished! And, while she'd been visualizing a steaming plate of bacon and eggs and toast – ever since she'd crossed over the Michigan/Ohio state line – she was less than certain that her churning stomach would accommodate even a bleak, unbuttered, slice of toast! Let alone the bacon and eggs that the waitress had just placed in front of her.

Toying with her toast, Janet was becoming more and more distraught. Mostly, because she realized that she was unsure as to what she should do. Those photographs sure changed things! Probably she should simply turn around – and head back to Detroit. She was far from positive that she'd be able to make it all the way to Chicago and back – knowing that those despicable photographs were merely a few feet away! Without a door, even, to close them off! She <u>should</u> destroy them! That'd take care of <u>that</u>!

On the more practical side, she realized that she really <u>must</u> go on! When all was said and done, she knew that she actually <u>had</u> to get to "The Windy City"! Returning home would add at least four hours to her trip. And, she'd have to explain to her daughters the reasoning behind her abrupt return. And, she'd undoubtedly have a problem running down Steve – to exchange cars once again.

<u>Hmmmm</u>! <u>Running down Steve</u>! <u>An interesting prospect</u>! He was supposed to be involved in some super-secret investigation! <u>Yeah</u>! <u>Right</u>! <u>Super-secret</u>! <u>It ain't all been police work</u>, <u>Stevie</u>, <u>has it</u>?

Even if she could locate the detective, how could she be sure that the Maverick would survive the trip? Clearly, from a practical standpoint, the only logical answer would be to press on to Chicago – the filthy pictures in the glove box notwithstanding.

She'd deal with her "White Knight" later! When she returned!

That settled, she managed to stuff down the cold, blah, toast – along with two more cups of coffee, necessitating a second trip to the ladies' room. She never touched the bacon and/or eggs.

<<>>

Once she'd negotiated the cursed LTD onto The Ohio Turnpike, Janet settled in – as much as possible – for the long drive. The turnpike ended where The Indiana East-West Toll Road began. An unending stretch of super highway – all the way to Chicago.

The miles of flat, boringly familiar, terrain were far from the ideal situation – when it came to keeping Janet's mind from wandering back to the vile *Polaroids* in the glove box. How <u>could</u> he? How could he have <u>done</u> such a thing? Where did that leave her? What kind of a relationship could one ever expect? Look forward to, with a – a pervert?

<u>Dammit!</u> <u>Damn it all!</u> <u>Things were just going too well!</u> <u>Too damn well!</u> <u>The job!</u> <u>The way the kids took to him!</u> <u>The way he took to them!</u> <u>The fun we all had</u> … <u>all last weekend!</u> <u>The things I feel for him!</u> She shuddered! <u>Felt for him!</u>

That's what you get, she supposed. That's what you get – for letting yourself be so vulnerable. So damn vulnerable.

She had, she knew, no legal – no moral – right to be so upset with Steve. He was certainly free to do exactly as he wanted. When he wanted. He'd made absolutely no commitment to her. Well, not in so many words, anyway. Actions, though! They were another story. And truthfulness! He had told her that he'd never had another woman – had never been intimate with another woman – since his wife had so tragically died. That was how many years ago? Eight? She thought he'd said eight. That's a long time.

<u>How can I believe him?</u> <u>That he lost his wife?</u> <u>Dear Lord, and his daughter!</u> <u>Lost them</u> … <u>that way?</u> <u>That horrible way?</u> <u>If he'd lie about not being with a woman</u> … <u>what would stop him from lying about losing his wife and child?</u> <u>Even in such a God-awful way?</u>

Eight years! Well, she'd not been intimate with a man for probably that long. Maybe even longer. She couldn't remember the last time she and Jim had made love. Their sex life had been mediocre – at best. Five children notwithstanding. Toward the end, what people coyly referred to as a "love life" had simply dried up. Just dried up – despite the fact that they'd continued to share the same bed. No one had circled a date on the calendar – and proclaimed, "This is it! From now on … no more sex!" He had simply stopped coming to her – and, of course, she'd stopped going to him!

But, with Steve! With Steve, it had seemed so – so different! Or, at least, she thought so. She'd never felt those things before. Any of them! Never before had she ever experienced the overwhelming emotions! Never like the ones that Steve had brought raging forth – from the very depths of her mind! Her psyche! Her body! Her loins! He had so excited her, from an intellectual point of view! From a companionship point of view! And – seemingly most especially – from a sexual point of view! Sexual? She shuddered, once again! Even more violently!

Dear Lord! We could've just as easily wound up in bed! Three or four times we could've wound up … as he'd said … in the sack!

Her knuckles were snow white! She had to force herself to relax the traditional-by-now death grip on the poor, innocent, steering wheel!

She'd been foolish! So damnably foolish – and naïve – to believe that Steve (or any other man) could (or would) remain chaste over eight years! Fletcher Groome had made that same claim! He'd, supposedly, not been to bed with a woman in … was it decades? Although Janet had, herself, been chaste for a period of years, men were far different! They were! Were they not? Obviously, Steve was! Steve is! Steve has been!

Well, she'd simply have to "grin and … " No! She wouldn't say it!

Ahead was another of the "pit stop" areas. Janet glanced down at the fuel gauge – for the first time during the entire trip. She still had a quarter-tank. The LTD obviously had a much larger tank than her poor old Maverick. She pulled in and filled up.

It occurred to her that she'd also not seen the credit cards Steve had told her he would leave for her. She'd pulled down the visor on the driver's side – early that morning. The cards had not been there. Most assuredly, they'd have poured down all over her lap or onto the floor

– or somewhere. They'd, obviously, not been there. And they were <u>certainly</u> not in the glove box!

<u>Dear Lord!</u> <u>The glove box!</u>

She flipped the passenger's visor. Nothing! He'd either forgotten to put them in – or this was simply another one of his strange exercises. It was, probably, just as well. The last thing, in the world that she would want to do would be to use one of his stupid damn credit cards. She'd have problem enough reimbursing him for all the baseball equipment that he'd bought the boys.

She tooled the car over to the adjoining restaurant, cut the engine, unbuckled her seat belt, pulled the keys from the ignition, got out of the car, slammed the door – and locked it! She resisted the overwhelming urge to <u>kick</u> it!

Janet had to wait fifteen minutes for someone to take her order. Twenty minutes after that, she'd had to advise the gum-chewing, blank-stare, waitress of what she wanted. At long last, the woman bounced a plate – containing a lukewarm hamburger in front of her. Half of her tepid coffee was sloshing around in the saucer, when it finally arrived. A fitting meal for her trip thus far. She forced the burger down – but, insisted on a fresh cup of coffee.

Once she'd finished her "meal", she trudged into the ladies' room. The image looking back at her, this time, appeared very weary. Extremely haggard. The opposite of the surprisingly semi-vivacious Janet, of *Waffle House* fame – just outside Toledo.

Her makeup bag was in the car. She'd wedged it into the obscene, not-a-moment's-peace, glove box opening! Anything to close off that yawning cavern of pornography! Any port in a storm! She rifled through her purse for a lipstick. Finally locating it, she applied a coat to her surprisingly-parched lips.

Then, she made a few passes at her hair, with the tiny brush she'd always carried. Having completed the semi-repairs, she hurried back out into the parking lot.

Minutes later, she swung the LTD back out onto the Toll Road. The last leg of her trip. Thank God!

<<>>

It was almost five o'clock, when Janet guided the Ford into the driveway at Anne's house, in Chicago. It had taken almost an hour-and-a-half – and three hurried, harried, (pre-cell phone) pay station calls – to finally locate the long, narrow, two-story residence on "The Windy City's" north side.

The reunited sisters sat up till almost four o'clock in the morning. (Almost five o'clock – according to Janet's eastern-time zone body chemistry.) Despite the latter's state of almost-total exhaustion, they talked. On and on and on and on. There simply never seemed to have been a lull in the conversation.

Anne's situation was fraught with mind-boggling complications: Apparently, Roger's adventure with his mistress had proved to be an exceptionally expensive undertaking. As the affair had gone on, he'd sold virtually everything which had any significant cash value!

The problems didn't end there: He'd borrowed heavily! He'd refinanced his car! And Anne's! He'd even renegotiated the mortgage on their home – sacrificing a remarkably-beneficial interest rate! To add to the mix, he'd defaulted on the new note – and the home was now under foreclosure! Both car notes were <u>way</u> in default! Anne had found the notices in her husband's personal papers, in his study, after his death.

"There's nothing!" she wailed. "Absolutely nothing! Not one damn thing! I don't have a pot … to put flowers in! I'm broke, Jan! Flat-out broke! Ka-POOT! As in I don't have a damn penny to my name! I don't know, Jan! I don't know what the hell I'm going to do!"

Janet spent most of the night – until she was simply unable to keep her eyes open – doing her best to convince her sister that she should move back to Detroit. The widow, after all, had absolutely no relatives in Chicago. She'd married Roger when both had lived in "The Motor City". Seven months after the wedding, Roger had been transferred to his company's national headquarters, in "The Windy City".

At the time of his demise, he was Executive Vice President of Sales Strategies. His annual salary was $212,000 – a considerable stipend in this day and age, but quite monumental in the seventies.

As Anne had discovered, he'd left nothing. He'd cashed in his insurance policies. His company policy had remained in good standing. But, the money would barely cover funeral and cremation expenses.

<<>>

Monday evening, after the funeral – attended by Anne, Janet and four other barely-known people – the widow agreed that her best move would be to simply "walk away" from her situation in Chicago. She would join her sister in Detroit.

The entire plan almost went up in smoke, when the sisters – both, by then, totally exhausted – engaged in a full-blown, top-of-the-lungs (on Anne's part) argument: Anne was bent upon taking her car to Detroit – despite the fact that it was about to be repossessed.

"Screw 'em," she'd snarled. "Let 'em come looking for the damn thing!"

"You can't do it that way, Anne. For one thing, it's not honest. It's simply not the responsible ... the honorable ... thing to do. For another, I'm just simply not up to facing a situation ... where the finance company comes knocking at my door, somewhere down the road. My kids <u>certainly</u> don't need ... don't need the hassle. And, quite frankly, neither do I. Plus that I'm not ... physically or emotionally ... I'm not up to playing tag with two cars, out on the turnpike. Or anywhere else."

"Oh, it wouldn't be that difficult."

"Yes it would. Maybe you don't remember my telling you this ... but, I'm under a bit of a deadline. I've got to get back home, tomorrow. Get back in time to go to my computer class, tomorrow night. It would be one hell of a lot easier ... given the shape we're both in ... if we just simply went in one car. We could take turns driving. Anne, I'm just too fried ... too badly whipped ... to try and do it any other way. Call the finance company's eight-hundred number You can call 'em ... when we get to Detroit. Tell 'em where the stupid car is ... like right here ... and that you've left the keys in the tailpipe or the ashtray or something."

<<>>

At 4:00 AM, on Tuesday morning, the two haggard women crammed "everything that wasn't nailed down" into the LTD. Anne's clothing took up most of the room. The rest of the space – precious little, as things developed – was devoted to favorite knick-knacks and a few appliances, such as her new microwave, blender, table-model stereo, clock/radio and a rather elaborate popcorn maker. In addition, they'd managed to squeeze in a copious number of Anne's favorite LP albums. The Maverick would never have come close to handling such a load. Especially with no trunk available.

<<>>

They arrived in Detroit – in time for Janet to take a quick shower, change clothes and run off to class.

Only Joan and the two boys had been at home, when they'd arrived. Janet was dismayed at her daughter's seeming lack of enthusiasm – when Anne walked into the Bolton home. Of course, the young woman scarcely knew her aunt.

<<>>

Back at *Wolverine Business Academy*, Janet struggled to keep her eyes open. She literally forced her fingers to obey the fuzzy commands from her semi-numbed brain. It was a gargantuan battle – to simply maintain a reasonable level of concentration.

Ron Warren seemed not to act any differently. Well, it gave Janet a start – when he called her back, as she was about to leave the room, once class was dismissed. She felt her temper begin to flare.

Fine! Great! Just what I need! I don't have my hands full enough!

"Janet," Ron began. "Is there anything wrong?"

"Wrong? No. Nothing I can't handle. I just had a little trip over the weekend. Well, not really little. Had to go to Chicago. It absolutely drained me. Death in the family."

"Trip? Where? Chicago? What happened?"

She sighed. As much from impatience – and maybe frustration – as from exhaustion.

"Chicago," she answered wearily. "My brother-in-law … my sister's husband. He … passed away."

"Strange. Your daughter didn't say anything about your being out of town."

"My daughter? What do you mean, my daughter? When did you see my daughter?"

"Not see. Didn't see her. Talked with her on the phone. Barbara."

"When did ... when did you call? <u>Why</u> did you call?"

"Saturday. No big deal. Just wanted to talk to you. I didn't think you'd mind. Your daughter said that you were out. Didn't say anything about Chicago. Not one thing about Chicago."

Janet bristled.

"What are you saying? Are you telling me that you don't trust me? That I'm lying to you? Lying ... about going to Chicago? You must think you're some special kind of ..."

"No! <u>No!</u> No ... heavens no. You're making a big thing out of nothing. I was just a little ... a little surprised. That's all. Surprised that Barbara wouldn't mention that you were out of town."

"Well, for openers, Barb doesn't know you from Adam. I'm sure that she wasn't anxious for just anyone ... someone who she'd never heard of ... to know that only my children were at home. I didn't tell her to do that ... but, I think it was a rather clever move on her part. Damn smart."

"Oh ... oh, sure. Of course it was. You're right, of course. She doesn't know me from Adam. I don't know what I was thinking about, when I ... "

Janet wondered if she looked as dragged out – as she felt.

"Look," she interrupted. "I'm terribly tired. I really need to get home. I haven't even unloaded the stupid car yet."

"Certainly. Of course. I didn't mean to hold you up. I was just ... sort of ... well, a little bit curious. You just didn't seem your lovable self tonight ... and I just wondered if I'd done something, or said anything, that ... " He let his voice trail off.

She managed a faint – highly fatigued – smile.

"No," she assured. "Nothing. I'm just very tired. Very tired. I really have to be going."

As she turned to make her way to Steve's car, she had to acknowledge that she was puzzled by Ron's expression. She had never, she believed, seen such a look. It was pure confusion. At least, that was her mind-weary interpretation. She would have to straighten things out, with him, later.

<u>On the other hand, why should I bother? Why should I be concerned by what he thinks? He's my instructor. Period! Just my instructor ... and nothing more! Isn't he?</u>

<<>>

Once home, Janet was not really surprised to find that Anne had gone to bed. Barbara had "suggested" that she take Rickie's bed. The latter could bunk in with Robbie.

Patti and Joan were sitting in the living room, watching television, as their mother entered. Joan explained the sleeping arrangements – and advised who had devised them. Barbara would not be home from the pizzeria for another hour or two.

"I really don't think Barb is all that fond of Aunt Anne," observed Joan.

"Yeah," joined Patti. "And she's not the only one."

Janet was taken somewhat aback.

"Why?" she asked. "Why would you or Barb be at … be at loggerheads with your aunt?"

"Oh, we're not at loggerheads," answered Patti. "It's just that she never … well, she never seemed to care about anyone. Except herself, of course."

"Patti!" responded Janet. "That's not true! Simply not true!"

"Yes it is, Mom," maintained Patti. "With the God-awful situation that you've had to hack … since Dad left … has she ever sent you one dollar? One lousy, stinkin' dollar?"

"Well, no. But, that's not … "

"Mom," persisted Patti. "Listen. Aunt Anne and Uncle Roger had all kinds of dough. You've always taught us that there's nothing closer than brothers and sisters. Or sisters and sisters."

"Or brothers and brothers," added Joan.

"Right," resumed Patti. "And here you are. Your own sister … and she couldn't care less. Never gave a damn."

"Oh, Patti." Janet's exhaustion was fast becoming a totally-debilitating force. She really didn't need this discussion, she felt. "Anne's always just been kind of … kind of wrapped up. All in her own little world, you know."

"Well," replied Patti, "as Barb pointed out, when she needed you, you were there. There for her. It took some doing … a good bit of doing. But, when you needed her … "

"Oh, Patti. I've never needed her. Not really."

The two daughters looked at one another. Joan shrugged. Patti just smiled.

"Why don't you go take a shower, Mom?" asked Joan. "Go take a shower … and get ready for bed? Patti and I'll unload the car. Aunt Anne was kinda upset … that all her stuff was in Steve's car. The only thing she had here was that small suitcase that she'd brought in."

"Yeah," agreed Patti. "You look like something the cat dragged in, Mom. You must be absolutely unconscious. That thing dragging behind you … is your fanny."

"Yeah," giggled Joan. "I saw the two ruts in the mud, outside."

"For the time being," advised Patti, "we'll put Aunt Anne's stuff in the cellar."

Janet wished that her eyes wouldn't become so moist, in such situations.

"I'm the luckiest mother in the history of the world," she rasped, a tear coursing down her cheek. "The luckiest mother on the entire planet."

Patti leaned over and kissed her mother.

"We're all lucky," she observed.

<<>>

The next morning, at work, Janet found a note on her desk. Steve had called just ten minutes before she'd arrived. She scrunched the paper into a ball – and peppered it into the wastebasket! With such force – that the missile bounced back out. Sighing deeply, she retrieved the message – and dropped it, softly, into the wire-mesh receptacle.

She was going to have to confront him – eventually!

Throughout the course of the morning, though, she was thankful to be able to immerse herself in the numerous projects which had accumulated over the two days she'd missed. Still, every time the phone rang, the prospect of hearing Steve's voice on the other end of the line kept her in a constant stage of "rattlement". At 11:10 AM, he called again.

"Hey!" he bellowed. "World traveler! How the hell are ya?"

His voice was so filled with enthusiasm! Further, it contained more than a hint of his having missed her.

"I'm … uh … I'm fine. How are you?" Her voice was curt. Her words clipped.

"I'm great! I'd … hey, wait a minute! Janet? Is something wrong?"

It would be impossible to overestimate the way his voice had suddenly deflated.

"Wrong?" she responded, her voice faltering. "No. Of course not. Why should something be wrong?"

"Well, you just … uh … you just don't sound like you."

"I'm very much myself. Who else would I be?"

"If you say so." He was trying to brighten up. "Hey, Fathead? How about lunch? Our big old caper has kind of hit a lull … I guess you could say. We got a couple of the bad guys. Few more of 'em still out there, I guess. But, we <u>did</u> nail a few."

"I'm sure you did. I'm sure you nailed more than a few. I'm so happy for you."

"Janet? Janet … look! Janet … what's wrong?"

"There's nothing wrong Steve," she said, stiffly. "Nothing. Nothing in the world. Everything is … is fine. Just fine."

There was a lull. Steve was obviously trying to cope with the unexpected, almost-hostile, tone emanating from Janet. With the disturbing tenor – coming from her side of the plainly-discomfiting exchange.

"I dunno," he finally replied. "I was never all that perceptive, y'know. But, something tells me that you're doing what old Willie Shakespeare used to talk about. Methinks that thou doth protesteth … too damn much."

"Steve, I guess I might as well tell you. I'm no good at playing games … at beating around the bush. I was never any good at that sort of thing."

"Hey! Great! Wonderful! I'm all for that! Why do I have the feeling that I'm lost in some kind of fog or something?"

Janet let go a massive sigh! She seemed to be spending half her life, of late – just sighing.

"I found them, Steve." Her voice was much weaker than she'd wanted. "I came across the pictures. I … I didn't mean to. I really didn't. But, the glove box snapped open … when I had to slam on the brakes! So … really … I wasn't snooping. It's just that the … "

"Pictures? What are you talking about? What pictures?"

"Oh Steve," she said, her voice steeped in disappointment. "Come off it. You know damn well what I'm talking about. What pictures. Those pictures you'd left in the stupid glove compartment. The pictures of you and the naked lady."

The … the naked <u>lady</u>? What, on earth, are you <u>talking</u> about?"

"Oh, please! Please, Steve, don't make things worse." A tear trickled down both cheeks. "Why don't you," she rasped, "just come and get your car? The keys are in the ashtray … and the pictures are in the glove box. The damn thing won't … it won't close." The tears were coming with a rush. She knew that she was on the precipice – once-removed from breaking down altogether! "Just leave my car," she managed to say. "Just leave the Maverick …and we'll be done with it. Done with <u>everything</u>!"

"I don't … Janet, listen to me … I really don't know what the hell you're talking about! I honestly <u>don't</u>! Haven't the foggiest … ! Listen, I didn't have … I don't have … any damn pictures! Not with naked ladies in them! By all I hold holy, that's the honest-to-God truth! I swear! On my mother's eyes! I really … really and truly … don't know what you're talking about! I don't! I swear it! What … what naked lady? Who's the naked lady? I totally don't understand! Don't have the faintest idea what you're … "

"Please, Steve! Don't screw things up! Not any more than they are already. It's bad enough that they were there. Look, you're … you're a big boy now. You don't have to account to anyone. Least of all me. You're certainly free to frolic and cavort with girls … ones who don't have any clothes on. But, spare me all the <u>crap</u>! Spare me the <u>crap</u> … the out and out <u>crap</u> … that you don't know what the hell I'm talking about."

"That's just it, Janet! I <u>don't</u> know what you're talking about! I don't! I haven't the foggiest idea! Zero clue! Whether you choose to believe it or not, I don't … I do not … frolic and cavort with girls who don't have any clothes on! I never have! Ever! Now I'm the one who's beginning to get a little steamed! Janet? Janet … this whole thing is a bad rap! A bum rap! A phony rap … for me! <u>On</u> me! <u>To</u> me!

Whatever! I swear that … swear this … to you! I swear it! Swear on my precious daughter's memory! I'll tell you this, though! I'll tell you this! I'll damn well get to the bottom of it."

The word "bottom" struck a nerve with Janet! It had been almost a buzz word, when they'd first gotten together.

"I'm sure you will," she replied curtly. "Right to the bottom! You're a whiz … when it comes to getting to bottoms!"

His protest had dried up her tears – somewhat! The denial– obviously a hollow refutation – had served to rile her! His demeanor had her even more upset. Rather than having further saddened her.

"In the meantime," she continued, "I've got two days work to try and make up. I'm grateful for the use of the car. I really am. My sister came back with me." Her tone was softening – in spite of herself. "We never would've made it," she added, "without a car of that size. But, I really don't have any more time to talk. Whenever you get the chance, I would appreciate it if you'd exchange cars again."

"Look, Janet! Listen …. I don't … "

She cut him off! "I'll look for my keys in the ashtray," she said, stiffly. "Please don't … I'd appreciate it if … just don't, Steve. Don't … please … come up to the office. I … I just have too much … too much to catch up on. Because, you know, of the two days I've had off."

She was back to fighting off the sobs – welling, once again, in her concrete-coated throat!

"What … what about tonight?" His voice was a husky whisper.

It was almost impossible for her to answer! But, she did:

"I … I have school," she rasped. "Steve, I really have to go now. Goodbye! And thank you for the use of your car. For everything you've ever done for me. Ever."

She broke the connection!

Ringing Peggy's desk, she managed to blurt, "Peggy? Can you cover for me? I have to go to the john!"

She ripped the set from her head! Her hair looked as though it had been styled with a *Mix Master*, as she bolted toward the ladies' room! Not a moment too soon! As quickly as she'd closed herself into one of the stalls, the wracking sobs began! The dam had broken! The convulsive spasms overcame her! Reduced her to a quivering mass of broken-hearted humanity! It would be fifteen minutes – before the icy grip of heartbreak would even begin to loosen!

Twenty minutes later – her makeup and hair passably repaired – she made her way back to the reception desk. Peggy's expression was one of pure horror – when she saw Janet's face! The latter would simply have to cope with the embarrassment of the redness – and puffiness – of her eyes! But, for how long? Who knew? Who the hell knew?

<<>>

That night, after school – as Janet pulled her tired Maverick into the driveway – she was dismayed to find Steve's car, parked in front of her house. It was almost eleven o'clock – and there he <u>was</u>! In his stupid LTD.

<u>Wonderful! Dammit! Just what I need!</u>

She'd rallied, somewhat, during the afternoon. To her surprise, she'd salvaged what had begun as a lost day – with a monumentally productive class at *Wolverine Business Academy.*

The evening had been made even more productive – by the mere fact that Ron Warren had not gone out of his way to speak to her. That had been a plus. She didn't want to deal with the reason – the reason that not having to cope with her instructor had so pleased her. She was, as usual, terribly confused – especially whenever it came to "boy/girl stuff"! So, it was great – that she'd not had to try and grapple with the added complication of Ron attempting to relate to her. At least, it was a blessing, at that point.

Now this! She was going to have to grapple with Steve – obviously.

Before she could pull her suddenly-tired-once-more body out of her car, Steve was standing at what was left of the back bumper.

"Janet! Janet! I've simply got to talk to you, Janet!"

"There's nothing to talk about, Steve. Oh, Lord! That sounds like something out of some stale ... some stupid ... soap opera."

"Well, this whole damn thing is something out of some stupid soap opera! Janet, look! You've got to believe me! You've simply got to! Those pictures! They weren't <u>mine</u>! Weren't <u>me</u>! <u>Aren't</u> mine! That's <u>not</u> me! I <u>swear</u> to you! I've never seen them before! Have no idea who those dipsticks are! No idea who's even <u>in</u> the damn pictures! They're just not my pictures! I swear that to you!"

"Oh? And whose might they be?"

"I ... damn ... I don't know! Look, I just told you that I haven't the foggiest idea who they belonged to. Plus that, I don't have the foggiest ... don't have the foggiest idea ... how they could've gotten themselves into my glove compartment! Janet! You've <u>got</u> to believe me! You've simply <u>got</u> to! Janet, they were <u>planted</u>! Put there by someone! As God is my judge, Janet, they were planted!"

"Steve, please. You're just making a bad situation worse. No one would ... as you say it ... plant something like that. That's a piece of your cops'n robbers world."

"But, they <u>did</u>! Someone <u>did</u>! Janet, I swear it! They did! Look! If you want to come and look at it ... well, you probably couldn't see it too well at night ... but someone pried the top catch loose. You can see where a screwdriver ... or maybe a chisel or something ... where some instrument was used! They <u>wanted</u> the thing to fly open! <u>Someone</u> wanted it to fly open! They wanted you to see those damn pictures! They must've figured that, on a trip that long, the thing'd eventually give way. And, when it did, you'd ..."

"That's patently ridiculous, Steve! And you bloody well know it! It's totally absurd!"

"Janet! Janet ... it's <u>not</u>!"

"There's no one ... no one that I know of, anyway ... who'd want to pull an off-the-wall stunt like that! Not one single person! Why would anyone <u>do</u> that? What would they hope ... hope to accomplish?"

"Well, to come ... maybe to come between us."

She sighed – again. Her legs seemed made of soggy, wilted pasta. She had no idea how long they'd continue to support her body! She leaned back against the car!

Her head was beginning to pound!

"Steve," she began. Speaking was becoming a real labor. "Steve ... it's stupid for you to give me all this lip service. All this hooey. I'd probably have been more receptive to you ... to your saying ... 'Hey, I don't know what came over me, but I got carried away, with this broad, and yah-yah-yah. But, it was a long time ago ... and I don't do those things now.' That, I could maybe understand. But, for you to try and hit me with some kind of a totally cockamamie story! Some fairytale about someone sabotaging your stupid glove box, well it's … it's damn … it's damn ludicrous! I don't know if I'm more upset at the stupid pictures … or about the fact that you obviously think that I must be a total airhead. That I really <u>am</u> such a fathead. That I'd go ahead and actually <u>believe</u> such an idiotic story."

"Look, Janet! I love you!"

"Yeah." Her voice had come back sufficiently – to where it simply dripped cynicism. "So you've said."

"I mean it, dammit! Janet, I love you! There must be someone who's trying to make time with you! Someone … some guy … who'd like to make me look bad! Make me look like some kind of jerk!"

"Oh? And who would that be? Fletcher Groome? He's the only other man I've dated. He may be a bit of an ass … but, he'd certainly never resort to anything as underhanded as that. As nefarious as this. He's always wanted me to be nothing but happy. Always seemed to have my best interests at heart. You heard what Rickie said about him … about him being too nice. I don't know if he's too nice. I don't know that anybody can really be too nice, but … "

She pulled herself away from the car – starting for the house. Halfway to the side door, she turned toward him – and lashed out: "It just won't wash, Steve. It won't wash! I'd appreciate your not insulting my intelligence … insulting me … with that stupid 'plant' scheme. I've got to get in the house. I'm tired. I'm fair-thee-well exhausted. I've had a tough day. A tough three or four days. Five maybe. I don't know, anymore. I don't know anything! Not a damn thing!"

"Don't say that Janet. You're <u>always</u> putting yourself down."

"Come <u>off</u> it, Steve. I'm not up for another lecture. Another sermon … about how I don't realize how wonderful I am. Right now, there's only one thing I know. One thing I'm sure of. I only know that I'm so tired! So damn tired! So exhausted! So beat! And I'm so damn bloody disappointed! I'm upset! I was doing all right … till just a few minutes ago! School turned out to be good therapy for me tonight. Even the pain-in-the-fanny instructor left me alone. I managed to get my mind … what I laughingly refer to as my mind … off all the other stuff! Of all the other <u>crap</u>! I was almost even happy! Till I got home … and found you waiting for me."

"Am I that much of a ... that much of a ... of a turn-off for you?"

She sighed, once again – even more deeply. "It's not a question of turn-on or turn-off, Steve. I ... I guess that was my problem. My problem was ... was that you were a complete and utter turn-on for me. Complete and utter turn-on ... dammit! I was so happy ... "

"We can still be happy, Janet! We can!"

"No." Her response was barely audible. "No, we can't. It's my own damn fault. I led with my chin! Not too brilliant! And I got knocked on my fanny! No one to blame but myself." She seemed to draw herself up – almost to his size. She glared at him – her fiery eyes locking onto his: "But you can be sure," she seethed, "that my guard will never ... never, ever ... be let down again! Never! Never, never, never! Never! Ever!"

"Just because of some stupid damn pictures?"

"Yes! No! I don't know! It's everything in the whole wide world! Every damn thing in the whole damn world! My sister ... she's a wreck! Because her husband turned out to be a total S.O.B.! He cheated on her! He hocked everything he could lay his grubby, cheating, little hands on! So he could keep on laying his mistress! His mistress! The one who took him for everything he had! And when there was nothing left to take from him, she ... she killed him! <u>Shot</u> him! She was a bitch! And <u>he</u> was a son of a bitch!"

She couldn't believe her choice of words. Those were two expressions she'd never used. Well, practically never used. In addition, her voice was rising – in both volume and tone!

"And here I am," she half-shouted. "Here I <u>was</u>! Dancing down some stupid primrose path! Then, I see those stupid damn pictures! And here you are! Here you stand! Trying to borax me into believing some stupid story about some stupid plot! I've had it, dammit! I've jolly-well had it! Had it ... big time! Had it with <u>you</u>! Now, get out of my way! Get out of my driveway! Get out of my life!"

At that point, an upstairs window opened! A youthful head protruded!

"Mom? Is that you?"

"Yes, Patti. It's me."

"Is ... is everything all right?"

"Yes, Honey! Everything is fine! Everything is just ducky! I'll be right up, Baby."

Turning to Steve, she hissed, "Now, will you get your lying, cheating, no-good, butt the hell out of here? Get out ... and leave me alone?" She was shocked at the gravel in her voice.

It was obvious that Steve had been terribly hurt by her outburst! Hurt visably! Hurt deeply! He gave her a curt semi-bow – from the waist! Then, he turned on his heel – and headed for his car!

A pale, drawn, drained, shaking, Janet turned her key in the side door – as the LTD roared off into the night!

ELEVEN

The following morning – practically before Janet had gotten a chance to sit down at the reception desk – Steve called, once again.

"Janet." His voice was filled with pleading. It succeeded in striking a chord with the woman, whether she'd wanted it to or not. "About last night, Janet. Listen. I apologize ... apologize all over the place ... for upsetting you. I'm so sorry. So very sorry. You're the one thing ... the one thing in my whole life ... that I want. The one person who I was terrified of upsetting! And it kills me that I've upset you."

She sighed – heavily. What else? "Steve ... look. You're just making it worse. Making things worse. Infinitely worse. Please stop making things so difficult. Please. I've hardly slept. It took me practically all night to get to sleep ... despite being as exhausted as I was. And when I did manage to drop off, it wasn't any bargain. Now, I've got a mountain of work, here. A mountain of work. I really can't afford to get all upset ... and bent out of shape ... again. I really can't. It won't work, Steve. It's not going to work. It can't."

"The only reason it won't work, then ... is because you don't want it to work."

"Yes. Fine. Yes. That's true. It's all on me. Now, please! Please let me go. Let me get to work ... before I get myself so upset. Like I was last night. And like yesterday ... when I had to make a mad dash for the john! The john, for God's sakes! Just because I can't control myself! Couldn't control myself! Please, Steve! Please don't call me anymore! And please ... dear Lord, please ... please don't tell me any more of your lies."

"All right," he replied – his voice overflowing with dejection. "No sense beating a dead horse."

"Oh. Thanks a <u>lot</u>!"

"You know what I meant. I really can't <u>say</u> anything to you, can I? Can't say one single word! Not one damn ... not one single ... word to you. Not without you totally misinterpreting it ... and then, jumping down my throat. Isn't that right, Janet?"

"You catch on quick."

"Okay. Just one question."

"Oh, please. Spare me."

"Did you see my credit cards?"

"Credit cards? No. No, as a matter of fact. No, I didn't. I just figured that that whole charade was just another one of your little ... little escapades. And neither was the cassette. *Kiss Me Kate*. That wasn't in there either. What else is new?"

"Stop and <u>think</u>, Janet! Why would I tell you that? Tell you <u>any</u> of those things? Why would I tell you that I was going to stash my credit cards in the car? Leave the *Kiss Me Kate* tape in the car? Why would I tell you those things? And then not do it? Why? Why would I do that, Janet? Those were the simplest things in the world to do. Why wouldn't I <u>do</u> them? I practically had to break your arm to get you to agree to be in the same car ... as the damn plastic. Why, in heaven's name, wouldn't I leave 'em? Leave 'em ... and the cassette? I'm not totally stupid, y'know. It just <u>seems</u> that way."

"Dammit, Steve! Here we go again! How should I know? How could I <u>possibly</u> know that? I <u>don't</u> know! I don't know beans! I don't know anything. I've never known anything. Not one damn thing! Can you understand that? I don't know why the stupid credit cards weren't there! I don't know why the stupid cassette wasn't there! I don't know why the stupid sun comes up in the stupid east. Or that it <u>does</u> come up in the east. I don't know <u>anything</u>! I only know that the stupid pictures <u>were</u> there! And I don't know anything else! Don't know zilch about anything else! About this ... or about anything else!" She burst into tears again – in spite of herself! "I don't know why you even took the damn pictures! I don't know anything! Not one damn thing! Nothing! Get it? This is old, stupid, ignorant-as-hell, Janet that you're talking to!"

She broke the connection!

Then, as had happened the previous day, she broke for the ladies' room!

<<>>

That evening, Janet swept out of *Wolverine Business Academy*, in a rush. Another of her patented escapes. Calculated to discourage Ron Warren from pursuing her down the hallway. Or even out into the parking lot. It was unfair, she knew, to judge Ron by other men. By any other men. He <u>had</u>, in fact, been awfully nice to her. He'd always seemed genuinely interested in her progress. But, of course, he was probably interested in other things. What else? Well, what was wrong with that? Men and women were <u>supposed</u> to be interested in "other things". They were <u>supposed</u> to be attracted to one another. If things were, maybe, a little different, well, it wouldn't be totally outrageous for her to consider cultivating a relationship with someone such as Ron.

<u>Only</u> just <u>not now</u>. <u>Not tonight, anyway</u>.

Hurrying to her car, she jumped in, slammed the door, cranked the engine to life, jammed the gear selector into "Reverse" – and squealed out of her parking spot! Then, in true pedal-to-the-metal fashion, she left a copious amount of rubber on the blacktop – as she roared out of the lot! She sped all the way home – something she never did!

Twenty minutes after barreling into the driveway – and standing the poor Maverick on its nose, as she'd come to a screeching halt – she sat placidly at the dining room table, with a freshly-brewed cup of tea in front her. She was making a Herculean attempt to read the paper. It wasn't working.

Joan and Patti were in the living room – perched in front of the venerable old television set. Barbara was still at the pizzeria. Anne was out. She'd lost no time in dating the owner of a nearby convenience store.

"Mom?" Patti was calling from the living room. "Why don't you come on in and watch this movie with us? It's pretty good."

"Appreciate the invite, Baby. But, I'm trying to catch up with what's going on in the outside world. Haven't read *The Free Press* in a week, now. Thanks anyway."

She halfway expected one – or maybe both – of her daughters to join her at the table, but they'd remained in the other room. It was probably just as well. She didn't really feel up to explaining her situation to them. They were aware, obviously, that something had gone terribly awry in her relationship with Steve. Best not to delve into it. Not for awhile, anyway.

Back to the newspaper. She wound up reading the same headline four times. She'd gotten halfway through the first paragraph of the article – and still had not the faintest idea what it had said. She sipped her tea – then, leaned back in her chair. Her thumb and forefinger found their way up to her heavy-lidded eyes.

<u>Tired</u>! <u>So damn tired</u>! <u>Eyes sore</u>. <u>Gonna have to see about maybe getting some glasses</u>. <u>Yeah</u>. <u>Sure</u>. <u>And where would I get the money?</u> <u>Oh, hell</u>! <u>Why does everything have to be so screwed up?</u>

She jumped a foot, when the phone rang – despite the fact that the instrument was in the living room!

Joan answered on the third ring. Janet could hear the rasp of her daughter's voice – but, was unable to determine what the young woman was saying. And to whom.

Joan appeared in the archway between the two rooms.

"It's Steve," she announced in a voice as soothing as she could manage. "He wants to talk to you. Should I give him the bum's rush?"

"No, Honey," Janet answered with another stock-in-trade sigh. "I'll take it."

Pulling herself up from her chair, she made her way into the other room. She was certain that each muscle, fiber and membrane in her body was raw. Or sore. Or completely fatigued. Every step seemed more a labor than the last one. But, not as difficult as the next one would be. She picked up the phone.

"Hello?" Resignation oozed from her voice, when she spoke the greeting.

"Janet!"

"What?"

"Please, Janet."

"Please what?"

"You know damn well what! Please ... let me see you."

"Oh? And just how much of me did you have in mind? How much of me were you wanting to see?"

"Stop! Stop it, Janet. Please stop it."

"Come on, Steve." Fire was creeping back into her voice. "I've asked you ... pleaded with you, tried to explain to you ... everything I can think of. And still you keep on calling."

"Yeah. I keep hoping against hope... that you'll consent to see me. Janet, you love me. I know you do. I know it. I know it in my heart. Know that you love me."

"Uh huh. Tell me more."

"You ... don't want to hear it."

"That's the first intelligent thing you've said. When did you figure that out?"

"All right." All the fight seemed to have seeped out of his voice. "All right, you win. I won't ... won't call anymore."

"Will you put that in writing?"

"Please, Janet! This is damn well killing me!" She managed to stifle another flippant retort. "Janet," he pleaded, "all I'm going to say ... all I'm going to tell you at this point ... is that you're mistaken."

"Of course I am. Like I said this morning, it's all on me."

"Please, Janet! Please! You're greatly mistaken. Horribly mistaken. Horribly ... for me. I never saw those pictures! Ever! In my entire life! I haven't the foggiest idea as to what's happening ... but, that's not me in those damn pictures! I'm going to ... rest assured, I'm going to ... going to get to the bottom of this thing."

"I know. You said that before. We've discussed bottoms ... a number of times."

"Good night, Janet. I have only one thing to say to you: I love you."

"Good night, Steve."

<<>>

Janet stood – not unlike a statue – with the receiver in her right hand. She was covering the mouthpiece with her left – in a futile attempt to stem the tide which was building! To hold back the tears! Joan arose from the sofa – and took the phone from her mother. Replacing the receiver in its cradle, she put her arms around the distraught woman.

"I'm sorry, Mom," she soothed. "I don't know what's happened … but, I'm sorry."

Patti arose and flicked off the television. Then, she joined her mother and sister – as they headed toward the dining room.

Janet seated herself once again and rasped, "I'm the one who's sorry, girls. I'm just so sorry. So damn sorry. Always so damn sorry … to be getting you all involved in … involved in … "

She began to weep, once more. Patti seated herself beside Janet – while Joan headed for the kitchen to fire up the teakettle once again. Seeing that her mother had nothing in which to blow her nose, Patti reached back behind her – to the ponderous buffet. She removed a box of heavy paper napkins – and handed one to Janet.

Once the three women were seated – a fresh cup of tea in front of Janet and a mug of cocoa for each of the young women – Janet told her two daughters of the discovery of the offensive photographs. She was much more explicit – in her vivid descriptions of the pictures – than she could ever have imagined. And even more surprised at the ensuing developments. She was completely unprepared for either of her daughters' reaction. Neither Patti nor Joan seemed to indicate that the matter was an especially big deal.

Dear Lord! There must be more of a generation gap, here, than I'd thought!

Both girls, of course, sided with their mother, in the dispute. But, each expressed the wish that Janet and Steve would – eventually – "get back together".

"You were never happier, Mom" observed Patti. "Never happier than when Steve was around."

"That's true," agreed her sister. "He really made a heck of a difference around here. He really did."

"Well," sniffed Janet. "I don't mean to be a drag on you guys."

"Oh, Mother! You're not." Patti seldom called Janet "Mother".

"I really think," soothed Joan, "that it'd be the best thing in the world for you to go on up to bed, Mom. You're pooped. Pooped as can be. I'm sure that Aunt Anne won't mind your not waiting up for her."

"Besides," added Patti – with a liberal amount of cynicism, "who knows when <u>she'll</u> be in? If I were you, Mom, I'd grab as many Z's as I could. Joanie's right. You look terribly, terribly pooped."

"Yeah, well. That I am. You're right … both of you. As usual. I think I will drag my fanny upstairs … and hit the sack. Although … with the way things are going … the sack'll probably hit back!"

Once she was in bed, the fatigue which had overwhelmed Janet was still not enough to overcome the swirling, churning, avalanche of thoughts, images, questions – and just about everything else in her life! None of which she wanted to deal with.

What to do? Should she accept Steve's assurance that – somehow – someone actually <u>had</u> planted those horrible, those God-awful, photographs? Should she simply accept his word? On blind faith?

Everyone – well, almost everyone – had told her that she was incredibly naïve. She'd been told that – ever since she was a young woman. Even when she was in high school – if her memory served her. Maybe even grade school. Hell, maybe in the womb.

<u>Yeah</u>. <u>Well</u>, <u>I'm not that naïve!</u>

The entire scenario defied all logic. Steve had seemed so genuine. He'd assured her that he'd never had another woman. Not since his wife had died. That had been eight years. Obviously, he'd not told her the truth. And when you'd add in what he'd told her about his daughter. About how horribly his daughter had died. The whole situation was a disaster! An absolute disaster! Maybe it was a blessing – finding the photos.

<u>Those snapshots!</u> <u>Those damn *Polaroids*!</u>

She shuddered as picture after picture after picture assaulted her consciousness once again! Obviously, he'd <u>not</u> been truthful! Obviously! Maybe he was a compulsive liar. He hadn't seemed to be one of those. But, then, those are the hardest people ever to detect. To ever catch in a lie. They're bona fide professionals. They're letter-perfect at what they do. Have perfected lying, to a science. Still, who knew? Who really knew?

On the other hand, he'd have to stay pretty "straight", she imagined, to maintain his position with the Michigan State Police. Possibly. But, how anxious would the State Police be – to pry into a man's private sex life?

As long as he wasn't causing 'em any trouble?

Still, there were the thoughts – and words – of her daughters. Two of them anyway. Probably all three of them. If Patti and Joan felt that she should resume her relationship with Steve, then it was probably a solid-gold bet that Barbara would feel the same way. The boys too. They'd completely flipped over Steve. The entire time that they'd been exposed to him.

Dear Lord! Exposed? Why did I have to go and think of that word?

<<>>

Finally, mercifully, Janet fell off, into a deep – highly troubled – sleep. Punctuated by the towering presence of Steve! He'd invaded each and every one of her disjointed dreams! In every nook and cranny of those disjointed dreams!

She awoke at 4:45 AM and took four aspirin tablets. She'd never done that before. Then, she crawled back into the bed. Sleep, though, was proving terribly illusive! Again! Yet! Still! She tossed for an hour – then, gave it up as a bad job.

She wound up back downstairs, in the dining room – with a freshly-brewed cup of tea. And the ever-present copy of the *Detroit Free Press*. As had happened the night before, she would read four and five paragraphs – and absorb absolutely nothing.

"Mother? Are you all right?"

Barbara stood in the archway, clad in her slightly-tattered chenille robe and her nightie. Janet closed her eyes – and nodded. The young woman seated herself, across from her mother.

"Steve?" she asked.

Janet nodded. "What else?" she answered.

"Patti told me. I'm sorry, Mother. I truly am."

"I know. We're all sorry. Fat lot of good that does."

"Mother, this whole thing … it just doesn't sound at all like Steve. I'd have bet the rent money that he'd never do a thing like that."

"So would I, Barb." She sighed – heavily. "So would I. Just goes to show you. You think you know someone … even after just a short

- 184 -

time. But, do you? Do you really? How can you know someone ... in so short a period of time? How can you?"

Barbara shook her head – in obvious puzzlement.

"I don't know, Mother. Even if Steve was goofy enough to get into a situation like that ... taking all those stupid pictures and everything ... I just can't see him being so idiotic as to just leave the darn things lying around. I mean, he had to know that they were there ... in the glove compartment. Those aren't something you can just forget where they are. I just can't see him leaving them there. He is a policeman, after all. And I'd have to believe that his job consists of paying attention to details ... no matter how minute. Paying rapt attention to details. Zillions of details. The smallest ... most insignificant ... details. I mean, he deals with that stuff ... with out and out minutia ... every day. I'd have to imagine that he does, anyway."

A tear trickled down Janet's cheek. She sighed – again. Heavily – again.

"I ... I guess I never really thought that much about it," she admitted. "Not in the light of his job anyway. I don't know. Maybe, it's the old saw about the guy who shines shoes for a living. His own shoes ... they always look terrible. The mechanic's car ... it always needs a tune-up or something. Maybe the same thing applies to police officers. I ... I just ... I just don't know. I wish I did. I sure wish that that I did."

"What're you going to do?"

"What can I do?"

"Well, I guess you're going to have to decide if it's really that serious. If the thing is so terribly serious ... that you want to blow a whole, entire, relationship. You were happy with him, you know, Mother. Very happy."

"Yeah. I know. So I've been told."

"I'm ... I'm really not trying to lecture, Mother. I'm not. I'm sure that Patti and Joanie must've told you just how ... how different you were. How very happy you were. How out and out thrilled you were. Once you and Steve began to hit it off."

"Yes. Yes, I think even Robby and Rickie probably have had something to say about it. Something to say along those lines."

"Well, to me, the real question would be ... whether it's worth blowing such a relationship. Over some stupid pictures. Stupid pictures … that are probably part of his past. Probably part of his <u>way</u> past. Stupid pictures that … I'd have to bet … were taken a really long time ago. Before he ever knew you."

Barbara arose and strode over to her mother. She leaned down and kissed Janet, on the cheek.

"I really can't say what I'd do, if I were you," the young woman continued. "It's something that you're going to have to weigh for yourself. Something you're going to have to decide for yourself. I really don't envy you."

Janet raised her tea cup – a toast to her daughter.

"I can't get over your … your maturity, Barb," she said. "Not really maturity. I guess the word I'm looking for is … is … is wisdom. Barb, Honey? You're wise … the mind boggles at just how wise. Wise … well beyond your years. <u>Well</u> beyond your years." She laughed, softly – and reflected even further: "You're really wise … beyond <u>my</u> years. Everyone tells me that we have the mother-daughter thing completely backward. Even your Aunt Anne. She's … "

"I don't know that I'd put too much stock in anything Aunt Anne has to say," replied the young woman, seating herself again.

"No, Barb. She's right. It probably stems from the way I grew up. Compared to the way you've had to grow up. The way <u>all</u> you kids have had to grow up. I was so … so sheltered. So damn sheltered. And you … you've had to fight for every damn, lousy, stinking, stupid, rotten, thing you've ever gotten." The tears began in earnest. "I'm sorry, Barb," she sniffed. "You've never had anything close to … anything even remotely resembling … a normal childhood."

Barbara moved back to her mother's chair. She rubbed Janet's shoulders – then, leaned down and kissed her, once more.

"I don't think there's any such thing as a normal childhood, Mother. I really believe that I'm better off … for having grown up the way I have. I'm sure it's put me in much better position to face that big, fat, mean, old world out there. I think the whole thing … the thing with your husband splitting, the way he did … I believe it has helped me to realize what's important. What's important … and what isn't."

"You mean … like pictures?"

Barbara nodded. Her quick response was not unexpected.

"If they're that upsetting ... that troubling ... to you, then you have no choice but to not see Steve anymore. Not see him again. Like I said, I don't really know what I'd do. It's just simply something that you're going to have to decide, Mother. Something you're going to have to work out for yourself. Either way, I'm behind you. We all are."

Janet sighed. "I guess," she groused, "I've already decided. I ... I just can't go back to him, Barb. I just can't. Not after all the things he'd told me. And then to ... "

She was fighting a losing battle! There was no stemming the tide! A sob caught in her throat!

Barbara kissed the top of her mother's head

"Okay," she said – exuding a bogus cheeriness. "You've made your decision. If he's out ... then, he's out! Now, you've just got to do your best to forget him. To get him out of your mind."

"Out of my mind," Janet reflected. "That's probably a very accurate statement."

TWELVE

Over the following month, Janet managed to more or less avoid Steve. She dodged his calls, as best she could – and was painfully curt with him, whenever he was able to "catch" her.

After nearly four weeks, the calls finally stopped! Finally! Mission fulfilled!

She did her best to convince herself that Steve's absence had left absolutely no void in her life. None whatever. She had her kids, after all. No one could be more blest than Janet Bolton – with her five wonderful children. Every night – without fail – she thanked God for them.

Who needed a man in her life? Certainly not this self-same, totally independent, Janet Bolton! Otherwise, she most assuredly could've/ would've gone out with Ron Warren, her instructor at the computer gig. Heaven knew, he'd asked her often enough.

Or even Fletcher Groome. He'd begun calling her – virtually every day. Literally every day. Ever since she and Steve had parted ways. Janet had reached a point where she'd almost dreaded coming home from the *Wolverine Business Academy* – and being forced to field Fletcher's "sure as hell" calls. On more than a few occasions, Joan had (gladly) fibbed – telling him that her mother was not at home.

Even Ron was becoming a pain. He was always – always and ever – after her! It practically took a crowbar to pry herself away from him after class. Although he'd never made a veiled threat – had, apparently, never come close – Janet wondered if her constant rebuffs would affect her final grade.

Why does everything have to be so damn complicated?

Anne had moved out – less than two weeks after she'd arrived, in Detroit. She'd taken a really beautiful apartment in opulent Bloomfield Hills – despite the fact that she'd had no job. Nor much prospect of going to work – anytime soon. The place was exquisitely furnished. She'd advised Janet that a "gentleman friend" was "helping her out". She'd never identified her benefactor(s). It/they could've been, theorized Janet, any one of the (at least) three or four men that Anne would have dated, since moving from Chicago. And those were only the ones of which Janet was aware. Guys that the woman was obviously "cultivating" – while still operating out of the Bolton household. All were (also obviously) exceptionally well off. Wealth had always been one of her sister's etched-in-stone, no-exceptions, requirements.

Janet actually had no time to be concerned with her sister's living arrangements, her employment status – or her sex life. Since moving out, Anne had called one time – to advise of her new phone number and make a correction in the address she'd given them.

Janet had poured herself into her job at **Brock & Associates**. Her expertise – with the basic program on the computer at the reception desk – was beginning to become more and more evident. She began asking Terri Baun to assign her to some of the less-complicated computer projects. When the latter provided them, Janet had successfully integrated them in with her other duties.

On Monday nights – when she was not attending school – she'd always stayed late, at the office, volunteering for still more projects. Her devotion to duty paid off! She was awarded a $200.00-per-month pay raise! An amount of staggering impact! The increase had been totally unexpected. She'd doubted that many of the senior employees had ever received a more lucrative increase in wages.

She'd paused, from time to time, to wonder whether it was her expertise – or her family situation – that had been responsible for her newly-expanded paycheck. The specter of Steve always seemed to be looming, in the background. (In the shadows? In the high grass?) She did, after all, work for his brother-in-law.

Her proficiency with the computer – along with the "obscene" increase in wages – <u>did</u> serve to boost her self-confidence! Buoyed it, immensely! For the first time in her life, she decided that she was "good at something"!

<<>>

At long last, her final week at *Wolverine Business Academy* arrived!

<u>Three more days</u>! <u>I can't believe it</u>!

Those last three classes would be devoted to what Ron Warren called a "survey test". The examination consisted of a project of staggering proportions: Each segment of the curriculum was represented – and was the focus of a mind-boggling series of theoretic "problems". An unsatisfactory performance, or less than the most thorough knowledge – in any phase of the "survey" – would be sufficient to cause a failure grade, at that juncture! Such a "falling short" would not allow the student to complete the mind-warpingly complicated exercise! By that time, four of her fellow students had already dropped out. Another point of extreme satisfaction: Janet had "hung in there" for the entire course. No mediocre accomplishment.

On Tuesday night, Janet managed to fight her way through the first third of the "survey". She'd done passably well, she believed. But, it had been a monumental struggle! The exercise had left her with a splitting headache!

As she'd handed her papers to Ron Warren, he smiled broadly, and asked, "Janet, can you spare a couple or three minutes? There's something that I'd like to discuss with you."

Her forehead crinkled – and her eyes scrunched shut.

"Not tonight, Ron. I'm pooped! Really waxed! Tonight's been a tough haul ... a really tough haul ... for me."

He nodded, sympathetically.

"I know," he answered. "I could tell. That's what I wanted to talk to you about. Please, Janet. Please. Just have a seat. Won't you ... <u>please</u>? I just have to take in the rest of these things. It's ... well, it's important. Really important."

She sighed deeply – and plopped down into the student's desk-type seat, in front of Ron's desk. Within four or five minutes, the classroom had emptied. The instructor arose – and placed one thigh over the front corner of his desk. Then, he gazed down at the haggard woman.

"You've been keeping quite a schedule, you know," he began.

Groping to retain a smattering of patience, Janet closed her eyes – softly – and nodded.

"It's not really necessary, y'know," he soothed. "Not necessary at all."

She kept her eyes closed. Scrunched them even more tightly – if that was possible. It was a Herculean struggle – to merely talk. Let alone having to get involved with – or, maybe, even match wits with – her instructor. It was almost painful – to simply form words and to move her lips. Each word seemed to drain just a little more from her. She began the necessary reply:

"It may not be necessary," she half-whispered. "It may not be necessary ... for someone as bright as yourself, Ron. Someone who knows what he's doing. But ... for a poor civilian like me ... it's necessary. Believe me ... it's necessary."

"I didn't mean that," he said with a soft laugh. "I didn't mean anything like that. Nothing having to do with your being a 'poor civilian'."

"Ron, look. I don't know what it is you're talking about. Haven't the faintest idea. I'm so tired. And I have a God-awful headache. A headache ... like I don't ever remember having a headache. As much as I'd like to sit here and talk to you, I simply have to go. Simply have to leave. I've got to get home. Really."

"Look, Janet. Listen to what I'm saying. If you were to consent ... consent to go out with me ... it wouldn't be ... well ... it wouldn't be necessary for you to slave over this stupid 'survey'."

She snapped bolt upright!

"What're you talking about?" Her voice had suddenly returned. Full-volume! "What the hell are you talking about? Are you saying that ... if I'll date you ... are you saying you'll give me a passing grade? No pain, no strain?"

"Uh ... well, no. Actually, I wouldn't put it that way, Janet. But, hell. Listen. I know your circumstances. You're trying to work all day, go to school here at night, be mother and father ... and everything else ... to your children. You have a ... well ... such a large family. And I just thought that ... "

"You just thought that I'd prostitute myself! Is that it?"

"No! No! Certainly not! Not that at all! Nothing like that! No one's said anything about your going to bed with me. About your … ah … sleeping with me."

"Ron," she seethed, "if I had the strength, I'd get up from here … and I'd slap you silly! There's more than one way to prostitute yourself."

"Janet … I just meant … "

"You only meant to take advantage of what you perceived to be a situation … one where I'm vulnerable! Vulnerable as hell! No thank you, Mister Warren! I'll take my chances on doing … and passing … that damn test or 'survey' or whatever you choose to call it, in your warped little mind. I can't tell you … can't tell you … can't tell you how despicable I think you are! How very … "

"C'mon, Janet! You're making a big thing out of nothing!"

"Maybe it's nothing to you! That's an even <u>bigger</u> insult! Maybe you've been able to trifle with other students in my position … in other classes … but, I'll be <u>damned</u> if I'm going to let you hold my mark, in this class, over my head! I'll be <u>damned</u> if I will!"

She arose – with new-found stamina – and bolted from the room! As she raced across the parking lot, she was virtually blinded by the tears!

<u>What's the use? What in heaven's name is the use? Knock yourself out! And for what? To become a damn whore? A damn whore … or maybe a plaything for someone like Fletcher Groome?</u>

She'd not realized it – but, she was standing next to her Maverick. Leaning against it, actually. After a few seconds, she snapped to the fact that Ron was barreling across the lot – in her direction! Fumbling, frantically, in her purse, she filched out the ignition key and pulled open the unlocked door! Then, she threw herself inside! Jamming the key into the ignition switch, she turned it – with a vengeance! The engine roared to life!

<u>Good old Maverick! At least, I can depend on you!</u>

She jammed the gear selector down into "Drive"! Everyone in the neighborhood heard her squeal out of the black-topped lot!

<<>>

It took more than a little resolve for Janet to return to *Wolverine Business*

Academy for the Wednesday night and Thursday night segments of the "survey"! Both evenings, Ron made untold attempts to speak to her. She'd ignored every one of them!

Finally, it was over! Her grade – along with her certificate of completion – would be sent to her employer the following week. She handed her final assignment to Ron – and hurried from the room! Hesitating, as she reached the door to the parking lot, she was surprised to find herself actually considering returning to the classroom. Actually speaking to Ron. The obvious hurt in his eyes – as she'd handed her papers to him – had rather haunted her. Maybe it should not! Maybe she'd misjudged him! But, maybe she had <u>not</u>!

<u>No! I'll be damned first! There was nothing subtle about his offer! His offer? Hah! Call it what it damn well was, Janet! It was a damn proposition!</u>

She would be done with *Wolverine Business Academy*! It was <u>over</u>! She'd completed the stupid course! She'd fought the good fight – exhausting as it had been! And she'd <u>won</u>! She'd jolly-well won! She was certain – more certain than ever, since completing Ron Warren's stupid, hokey, "survey" – that she'd passed! Passed with an above-average grade point! With an excellent grade point!

Ron most certainly would <u>never</u> let their episode of Tuesday night – or her refusal to speak to him tonight – influence his grading her test! He wouldn't even consider lowering her mark for the entire course – because she'd rejected him! Would he?

<<>>

The following Tuesday morning, Terri called Janet into her office. It was ten-fifteen. And it was good news! Janet was to be <u>promoted</u>! The promotion would bring another "obscene" pay raise! She would be earning almost half-again her starting salary! "Bales" more than her combined wage from the laundry – coupled with Jim's semi-monthly checks! Until that moment, such a stipend had been totally unthinkable!

Once she will have trained a new receptionist – Richard Brock was interviewing candidates, even as they spoke – Janet would be assigned to a desk in the "computer bay"! She would report directly to Peggy

Sullivan! (Another bit of good news. She and Peggy had become quite close, over the months.)

The first potential replacement proved totally inept. The second woman – who would require a good deal of patience, but seemed passably capable – didn't show up for work on Thursday morning. Finally, by the following Monday, a new receptionist had been trained, and was – seemingly – permanently in place.

That afternoon, Janet was shown to her new desk – next to that of Gloria Tapp. (A bit of alarm, there.) There was something terribly disconcerting about Gloria. About her entire personality. Her close proximity was <u>not</u> helping. Why should there be such a feeling of unease? Janet didn't know. But, plainly, it was there. Maybe the unmistakable foreboding was simply a misconception. Hopefully, that was the case. It probably didn't help that Peggy had warned Janet that Gloria was a world-class back-biter – as well as the least-productive of the six women who toiled in the "computer bay".

"Anyone who even looks like they might want to get ahead, Gloria'll tell you that she's brown-nosing," Peggy had cautioned. "She can be a real pain-in-the-butt. But, she does do her work. Whatever we assign her, she does. No more and no less. Does it efficiently … and in a reasonable amount of time. So, we all put up with her. She knows that she's not going to advance any further. Knows that it would not be a good business decision, on our part. Not without a monster change in attitude … and I don't see that happening. So, when she perceives someone as a rising star, she does her best to shoot that person down. I don't know if it's some kind of psychological need … or if she's just simply a pain-in-the-butt. She never lets me forget how much more … ah … mature she is, than me. I just nod and say, 'Yes, Gloria' … and let it go at that."

Fifteen minutes before it was time to go home – to leave for the day – Terri marched into the "computer bay"! She made a major production of presenting Janet with her certificate of completion, from *Wolverine Business Academy*!

Janet had passed with the highest honors! The document was emblazoned with enough oak-leaf clusters and gold seals – to make it resemble a presidential citation. Terri had taken the liberty of having the certificate lavishly framed. By Tuesday, it would be hung on the wall – close by Janet's desk. (Close by Gloria's desk as well.)

Ron had proven to be an honorable man after all!

<<>>

On the way home, Janet's head was still swimming. A few months before, she could never have dreamed that her situation would have changed. Could have changed. Could have changed so drastically!

Part of her "success story" was due, of course, to Steve. She had to acknowledge his role in her new-found opulence. Well, for her, it was opulence. And though the admission was rather grudging, she had to allow for the fact that – without Steve's never-ending encouragement (and his "aid" in securing her the position at **Brock's**) – she'd undoubtedly still be pressing that horrible steam machine at that God-awful laundry for the sainted Mr. Truesdale. And continuing to produce untold buckets of perspiration – six days a week!

However, once situated at her new employer, she <u>had</u> progressed on her own. Steve may have gotten her the job – but he most certainly couldn't have kept it for her. To be honest, he'd told her as much, when he'd first posited the change in employment. And he had been absolutely correct. Nor could he ever have gotten her that glorious promotion. Or all that wonderful money! No! <u>That</u>, she'd done on her own. Sweating out those endless "fanny-dragging" nights at the computer class had proved so worthwhile.

In her new position – once she got a paycheck or two under her belt – she could even consider buying herself a much newer car. It seemed as though her insurance company was going to be of no help in getting her trusted friend – the Maverick – fixed. Her agent – supposedly an "uncle" to her children – had continually ducked her calls. For lo, those many months. Eventually, she'd just given up – despite Barbara's consistent pushes for her to continue following up the campaign. She'd simply continued to send her premium check off every month. As always. Good old dependable Janet Bolton. But, maybe now would be a good time to think of a newer – much newer – car! And – most definitely – a new insurance agent.

Mr. Oglesby, up the street, always traded in his car every year. This year's Buick for next year's Buick. Janet didn't know quite what model it was – but, it was beautiful. And not a really big beast. And it <u>was</u> a Buick! She'd always wanted to – someday – own a Buick. Would Mr. Oglesby consider selling the car to her? Could she ever get a loan to pay for it? She shook her head – a futile attempt to make the image of her, ensconced in that gorgeous Buick, leave! But, her warm smile confirmed to her that it was great fun – for a change – to even seriously imagine such a scenario!

The fact that it was becoming slightly annoying to have to drive the banged-up Maverick – wonderful as it had always been to/for her – was not a product of her imagination. She loved the Maverick – poor thing. But, she'd come to hate to have to drive her dear old friend – in that condition.

Well, she supposed, she could afford to have her old friend fixed. Repaired. Made to look as good as new. But, that brought other problems. It would take a goodly amount of time to fix the sainted car. A goodly amount of time. What would she use for transportation – while it was in "sickbay"? Even her most lavish imaginings wouldn't allow for the rental of a car. Not for any extended period of time. It was a pickle. Not a really rotten pickle. On the contrary. Still, it was a pickle all the same.

Another unwanted image penetrated her reverie! Just when she was wafting along in peaceful contentment. Chewing on the cud of her successes! Then, why did the thought of her asking Steve if he could help her out – transportation-wise – have to intrude? That would be a non-starter! She'd jolly well <u>die</u> first!

<u>Steve</u>! <u>Sure</u> … <u>he could've been a help</u>. <u>So could Fletcher</u>. <u>For that matter, so could Ron</u>. <u>Probably</u>. <u>But, dammit, everyone has his price</u>! <u>And I'll be damned if I'm going to pay it</u>!

She'd probably be better off just buying a newer car – Mr. Oglesby's Buick or something else. Just buy a car outright. They'd never give her anything for her poor dilapidated, faithful, Maverick. Just keep the beast of burden and maybe have it fixed – eventually. Then, she could give the trusted friend to Barbara. She wouldn't have to worry about her daughter riding home every night – with her bottom-patting boss.

Maybe she could get Anne to help her. Her sister seemed to know a lot about cars. Just a couple of weeks ago, she'd gotten herself a two-year-old Pontiac Grand Prix. Janet was mystified as to how Anne could've come up with such a fine car – merely a week after having taken a commission-only sales position. Anne had, she'd said, "put to sleep" some guy who'd owned a used car lot over on Livernois.

Janet whipped the tired old Maverick onto her street.

Ask Anne? It is to laugh. When do I ever see her?

Well, apparently, she was going to see her that night. Anne's Grand Prix was parked in front of the Bolton house.

What can she want? She never comes to see us!

Janet was upset with herself – for thinking ill of her sister.

Been listening too much to Barb.

Joan had prepared dinner – and began to serve the meal, as soon as she saw her mother pull into the driveway. Seated at the dining room table were Anne and Patti. Barbara had left for the pizzeria. Patti would soon have to depart – for a babysitting "gig". Robbie and Rickie ran to greet Janet – as she walked up the stairs into the kitchen.

"Anne," greeted Janet, as she entered the dining room – wearing her two sons. "What brings you to this neck of the woods? I thought that you worked evenings."

"She came ... because Barb told her of your promotion, Mom," volunteered Joan. "Said she wanted to be part of the celebration. Even brought three huge ... I mean humongeous ... sirloin steaks with her."

Once again, a slight pang of guilt engulfed Janet. Why was she so quick to judge her sister's motives? She did notice that Patti was not as enraptured with her aunt's presence. Not as thrilled at Joan, certainly.

"Gee," exclaimed Janet. "Unaccustomed as I am to sirloin steaks ... of all things ... I want to thank you, Anne. Thank you so much. I more than appreciate the thought. But ... can you really afford them? Afford sirloin steaks? I mean, didn't you only just start work? Just start your job?"

"Been a little over three weeks now," answered her sister. "I've done good. Now that I've got a car, I can get to more places. Get there faster. Don't have to depend on someone else for a lift here ... and a ride there. Picked up a few coins over the past couple weeks. It's a great plan, Jan. You should try it. You can make a lot more money

... a hell of a lot more money ... than you are now. Even with your new-found wealth."

"Not all that much wealth, I'm afraid. But, I have to say that I too have done good. If you'd told me, just a three or four months ago ... if anyone had told me back then ... that I'd be a fency-schmency computer person, I'd have told them to sober up."

They dug in. Janet was mildly surprised to see her children devour the expensive cuts with such verve. As soon as she would be able to get a few paychecks under her belt, she'd most certainly have to start springing for some steaks – and maybe even a roast or two.

"I don't know how you do it, Jan," expounded Anne – around a mouthful of mashed potatoes. "I could never do what you do. Especially dragging my butt off to school every night and ... "

"Oh, it wasn't every night. Only three nights a week. And it's finished now. All behind me ... speaking of butts. But, you're right. My fanny <u>was</u> dragging at the end."

"Not only at the end," corrected Patti. "You were dragging pretty good ... from the time you ever got back from Chicago."

Janet was gratified that Anne seemed not to notice the obvious barb.

After dinner, Joan and Patti began to clear the table. Once the dishes were soaking, Patti left for her babysitting job. Joan closed the door between the kitchen and dining room, and began washing the wonderfully-streaked-from-all-that-steak dishes, pans and utensils. Robbie and Rickie stood by her side – dishtowels at the ready.

"I still don't see how you do it," Anne said, once she and her sister were alone. "Gawd! A nine-to-five job? I couldn't do that. Was never cut out for nine-to-five. My compliments, Jan."

"Shucks, Ma'am. T'weren't nothin'. Listen, Anne. I was <u>glad</u> to have the job. To <u>get</u> the job! <u>Thrilled</u> to get the job. <u>Any</u> job. But, <u>this</u> one ... well, it's proved to be a real <u>blessing</u> for me."

"I still think, though, that you should look into the plan I'm involved in. I could show it to you. But, it'd be better if Mike ... he's my boss ... if he could show it to you. Jan, believe me! You could make loads and loads of money! A <u>ton</u> of money! Really!"

Janet smiled. "Anne," she said, "I don't even know what it is that you do. You sell stuff. That I know. But, I don't think I've ever heard you ever talk about your product or service ... or whatever it is."

"Products," answered her sister. "Plural. We sell lots of things. Everything from laundry detergent to ironing boards to jewelry to fine china. But, listen. The real money is in recruiting new members. New employees. See, I'd get a percentage ... of whatever you'd sell. And you'd get a percentage of the sales ... of any people that you'd get to join. Of course, I would too. And, likewise, you'd get a piece of whatever action would be generated by the people that your people recruit. See? It's an endless thing. And as it goes on ... "

"Anne! That's a <u>pyramid</u> thing! A ... a <u>pyramid</u> scheme!"

"No it's not, Jan. Really. It's not. I'll have to get Mike to really explain it to you. Show you what the difference is. He does it so much better than I do. He's been in the business ... eons longer than I have. But, it's really <u>not</u> a pyramid scheme. Believe me. There's a difference. Hell of a difference."

"Not from what you're telling me."

"Well ... trust me ... there is. Mike could put your fears ... all your doubts ... to rest. But, all that's beside the point, Jan. There's a lot of money to be made! Just a hell of a lot of money! Scads of money! What difference does it really make? As long as you're not out knocking over gas stations or robbing banks, what difference does it make ... where it might be coming from?"

"Well, I just don't think it'd be my bag, Anne. I think I'm probably going to be taking another course. Accounting. In January. Over at *Wolverine* ... the place where I took the computer thing. I think that's probably more my speed."

"Well, it doesn't have to be, Jan. It doesn't have to be your speed. That's what I'm trying to tell you. You've worked so hard. So damn hard. All these years, you've worked your tail off. And, when I think of that S.O.B. at that laundry, I could just ... "

"It's in the past, Anne. Listen, I'm not a glutton for punishment. I'm really thrilled that I've come this far ... this fast. I can't tell you what it's done for my self esteem. I guess that ... before getting on at **Brock's** ... I guess I didn't have much."

"Well, you didn't have much of anything. That's why I've always been so concerned about you."

The remark rang hollow. Before her husband's demise, Janet had seldom heard from (or of) her sister.

"Well, like I said, that's all in the past. This position ... well, it's given me a whole <u>lot</u> of self esteem, y'know. And the fact that the company's going to spring for another course ... why, it's great! Hopefully, I'll be able to get even further ahead. Progress even <u>further</u>. This upcoming course ... it runs a little longer. But, hopefully, by next May or June, I'll really be ... "

Anne smiled. She seemed caught up in her sister's enthusiasm. Entertained by it, anyway. "Well," she observed, "I guess that's where you and I are different. We're sisters ... but, we sure are different. In so many ways. I'm not willing to go through all the ... to put in all the time and the tons of agony that it takes to get anywhere near the top. The top in your world."

"C'mon, Anne. It hasn't been agony. Not even close. In fact, it's been one of the most satisfying periods in my entire life. You can't believe the satisfaction that comes with ... "

"Nope. Can't see it, Jan. I suppose it has a lot to do with my experience with Roger ... the bastard." Her laugh was bittersweet. "I have to admit, though," she began again, "that I probably never was overwhelmed by the Judeo-Christian work ethic. I pretty well sat around on my behind ... when Roger was doing so well, financially. Just let the filthy old money come a-rollin' in. I knew of his hokey little peccadilloes. I'd have to have been a total idiot not to. I didn't admit it, back then ... even to myself. Not for the longest time. But, deep down, I knew. I damn well knew. I'd always figured ... what the hell. Keep a smile on your face ... and your big mouth shut. And I did. I was fat, dumb and happy. Didn't know nuthin'. Then, when all this crap came down ... with Roger's death, you know ... it all exploded in my face. I made up my mind that I was going to do whatever it takes ... whatever is called for ... to get ahead. Whatever is required. Just like Scarlett O'Hara. I wasn't <u>ever</u> gonna be hungry again! Not ever! Was gonna do whatever it takes." Her eyes narrowed – and her lips became a thin, taut, line. "Whatever it takes," she reiterated. "And, damn it all, that's what I've done. That's exactly what I've done. I've out and out become Scarlett O'Hara."

Janet was becoming terribly ill-at-ease – and couldn't understand why. "Oh," she replied, as lightly as possible, "I really think you're being too hard on yourself, Anne. How long has Roger been ... been dead? Just a short time. In terms of history, it's just the blink of an eye. And look how well you've done. You've got a nice car. Much nicer than mine. Of course, that wouldn't take much." Why did she have the feeling she'd just blasphemed? "You've got that wonderful car," she tried to rally. "That awfully nice car ... and, of course, a really neat apartment. You're doing well enough that ... "

"Oh sure! In fact, I do better each week. I'm getting, I guess, two or three people recruited. Three, actually. I've talked 'em into selling our stuff. Got these three people ... all of whom are moving a lot of pots and pans. A hell of a lot of pots and pans. And, see? Every time they unload a bunch of pots and pans, I make a percentage of that. And they're also bringing in people. Well, this one couple, anyway. And I'm getting an override on that too. On them too. That's the way you really make money, Jan. A hell of a lot of money. If you can get to where you've got maybe twenty ... or, hell, even thirty ... people under you, you can make a fortune. Just off what they're doing. Don't even have to bother getting off your butt. Let them do all the work. Let them work for you. Jan, look. I'm a hustler ... let's face it. I guess I've always been s hustler. I've never really faced up to it before. Didn't want to admit it ... even to myself. But, that's what I am. I'm a damn hustler."

"Oh, Anne."

"It's true, Jan." She lowered her voice to almost a whisper. "Look, Jan," she asked, "how do you think I got that Grand Prix, outside?"

"Why, you told me. You said you'd put some owner of some car lot ... put him to sleep."

"Yeah. Well, that's not quite accurate. The key word there, Jan, is 'sleep'! I slept with him. Slept with him ... more than a few times."

"You _what?_"

"Shhhhh! It's not necessary to wake the town and tell the people."

"I'm ... I'm sorry, Anne. You ... you just surprised me. No. Shocked me ... is what you did."

"I know I did. But, think Jan! Think about it! Do you really believe that I've got enough BS ... that I can just talk some jerk who I'd never met before ... con him into giving me a really nice car? With no money down? No, Sister dear. That just doesn't happen. Not in the real world. I don't sleep with him anymore, of course. I finally got him paid off. Thank God. He's really a creep! Yuck! A real sleaze-bag. I paid the damn car off ... last week! In bed! Now I'm rid of him. But, I'll tell you something else: I made the same offer ... to five or six car lot owners ... before this clown took me up on it. At first, this bozo wanted to give me a twelve- or fifteen-year-old Pinto, or something. For one roll in the hay. Car looked like it would never make it off the lot. I had to go to bed with him once or twice a week ... but, I massaged the Grand Prix out of him. Idiot."

"Anne! I can't believe this! I can't believe what I'm hearing!"

"Believe it, Jan. Believe it. I don't sleep with ... well ... I don't sleep with just <u>anyone</u>. I'm not about to hop into bed with any Tom, Dick or Harry. I only sleep with those that I have to."

"Those you ... you have to?"

Janet could feel the color begin to drain from her face.

"Don't fall off your chair, Jan. There haven't been all that many. The owner of the apartment complex that I'm in. Plus that, he ... "

"Him too?"

Anne nodded emphatically.

"Of course! By the time I got to him, though, I'd raised my sights considerably. I began looking up companies ... firms that own a lot of complexes around town. This guy is president of **Prescott-Kramer Incorporated**. He's loaded! Has a huge house ... a mansion, I guess you could say ... out in Grosse Pointe. He's probably got a whole platoon of sweet young things at his beck and call. But, he sure wasn't above a romp in the old hay with dear old Annie! He gave me a check ... for the amount of deposit on my apartment. Called the property manager out there. Told him to make damn sure that I got the nicest apartment available ... and that it'd better be damn clean!"

"I ... I can't believe I'm hearing this. And ... dear Lord ... from my own sister."

"Don't go into cardiac arrest, Jan. I always figured you'd have to be dragged ... kicking and screaming ... into the twentieth century. But, I also believed that ... by now ... you'd have gotten educated enough to know how the world spins, these days. Don't get upset. Since I got rid of that creep from the car lot, I don't sleep with anyone now. Except, of course, for Mike. Him, I sleep with."

"Mike?" Janet's voice was barely audible.

"My boss. I went to bed with him ... not so much to get the job. Hell, they'll take you ... if the body's warm. Why wouldn't they? I mean ... what the hell ... it's strictly a commission-only deal. If you sell something ... and recruit a few people ... they make a buck or two. If not? They're not really out anything. They cover their butts ... by getting a two-hundred dollar deposit on the kit."

"The ... kit?"

"Yeah. The kit. Samples of most of the stuff we hawk. Plus brochures and pamphlets ... and all their motivational BS. Well, I didn't have the money for the kit. So, Mike and I wound up in the feathers."

"<u>Anne</u>! This is ... "

"Despite what you may think, I didn't prostitute myself, Jan. Well, I guess maybe I did ... a little bit, anyway ... going in. But, there's something there, Jan. Something there ... between Mike and me now. These days, it's a whole different relationship. I don't really <u>have</u> to sleep with him now. I'm making a few bucks, these days ... so I don't really need to sleep with him. But, I do. I guess that makes it different."

"Oh, Anne." Janet was the picture of total dejection. "Anne, how could you?"

"Janet ... c'mon. Don't be so damn overdramatic. Look, after my life with Roger, I just made up my mind that I'm used to the finest ... and that I deserve the finest. And whatever it takes to get the finest ... well, that's what I'm going to do. Scarlett-Baby ... that's me! And that's exactly what I've done. Precisely what I've done."

"That isn't how you've done ... done so well ... in your sales and your recruiting ... is it? I mean you don't ... you don't ... uh ... "

"I don't wind up in the feathers with my customers? Is that what you're asking? No. Not anymore, anyway."

"Not ... not anymore?"

"Well, I've only done what I felt like I had to do ... to get started, don't you see. In other words, I laid that car lot guy often enough ... that I don't have to be bothered with him anymore. And, once I started making a buck or two ... and once I got my apartment, the deposit and all ... I've been able to pay my rent. On time, even. I haven't seen the prez ... the owner of the complex. Not since he got me into my apartment. I haven't needed to. Once I got myself established ... really established ... with the company, I didn't even need to sleep with Mike anymore. I do, though. Because I want to. Not because I have to. To get my brand new career launched, though, I <u>did</u> seduce ... quite literally ... the owner of one of those physical fitness studios! After a couple rolls in the hay, I got him to lay in the whole line of our herbs. Gave him the whole schpiel ... about how they'll help his customers lose weight. And they will. They do! I wasn't lying, Jan! They will! They have! It's really good stuff. I believe in it. This guy ... he makes a few bucks off the concession. But, the <u>people</u>! The people ... <u>love</u> him! Just from the results of our herbs! I didn't tell him any lies. The line has gone over really well. In fact, he's given me three or four other leads! Other managers ... or, hell, maybe even the owners ... of a whole lot of other studios. And he gave me those leads ... no strings attached. There hasn't been any more hoonkle-doonkle between us."

"How about the other studios? Are you ... Oh hell, Anne. This is none of my business. In <u>spades</u>, it's none of my business. There's no need for me to be giving you the third degree. It's just not any of my business. You're a big girl now."

Anne smiled – and stared at her sister's bosom. "Yeah," she agreed. "And in the same places that you're a big girl."

Janet blushed. "You know what I meant," she groused.

"To answer your question, Jan, those other guys, they're starting to take the stuff ... the herbs ... in too. A couple of 'em ... are stocking the whole product line. Without benefit of any ... ah ... side advantages. Now that I've gotten to where I'm pretty well established, I don't have to do anything ... not one damn thing ... that isn't on the up-and-up. It's gotten to where it's all strictly business. Nothing going on ... nothing on the side ... so to speak."

"Yes. But, getting there ... "

"Was half the fun," supplied Anne – with the most obscene leer Janet had ever seen.

"You ... you haven't ... you haven't told the kids ... my kids ... have you? I mean, they don't know anything. Do they?"

"No. I don't think so. <u>I've</u> certainly never said anything to them.

I think, though, that Barb ... and maybe Patti too ... they might have an inkling, about what's going on. What <u>went</u> on. Past tense. Maybe even Joanie does too. Possibly more than just an inkling. I have the feeling that Barb never did buy the old song-and-dance that I gave you ... when I got the Grand Prix."

"She never said anything to me. None of them have," replied Janet, still shaken.

"They wouldn't. Neither Barb nor Patti. Or Joanie, for that matter. Face it, Jan ... those girls of yours ... they're much more worldly than you are. Hell, maybe the boys are too ... even as young as they are. Ya never know."

Janet closed her eyes – and let go with a mammoth sigh. "I guess you're probably right," she acknowledged, at length. "I guess you must be right."

"Damn straight I'm right. Jan, look. I admire the way you've pulled yourself up by the ol' bootstraps. Admire the hell out of it. But, I'm just not built that way. Maybe it'll all come back to haunt me someday. Especially when everything (she placed her hands under her own breasts) <u>collapses</u>. Look ... I'm sure that you've got to be much more satisfied with your accomplishments ... than I am with mine."

"There haven't been all that many accomplishments."

"Are you kidding? Yes there have. You've done so well, Jan. And you've done it ... in the good way! Done it ... by playing by the rules. The hard way. No immoral, obscene, or fattening shortcuts, for you."

"Anne, I really don't want to talk about it anymore. Your accomplishments ... or mine. Just don't want to get into ..."

"Okay, Jan. I shouldn't have brought it up, in the first place. I'm not sure what you must think of me."

"You're my sister ... and I love you. It's none of my business ... <u>spectacularly</u> none of my business ... what you do. Or how you do it. I'm happy that you decided to have dinner with us tonight. And I'm grateful that you went out and bought all those steaks. That was nice of you. We don't get steak around here very often, y'know. Like practically never."

"Oh, it was my pleasure. There is one other thing, though, Jan. One other reason that I invited myself over tonight."

For some unexplained reason, Janet shuddered. "One ... other reason?"

"Yes. What're you doing Saturday night?"

"Well, I don't know. That's a long way away. I mean ... I probably ... well, I think I'll probably have ... "

"You've not gotten back with Steve, have you?"

"No," answered Janet – probably too quickly. "No. Of course not."

"Well, then why don't you go out with us?"

"With us?"

"Yes. Mike's boss ... Jeremy Bloodworth ... is in town. And he's gotten four tickets ... at the *Fisher Theater* ... for Saturday night."

"Oh, Anne. I don't know. I really don't feel like ... "

"Big ... really lavish ... production of *Carousel*, Jan. Remarkable show. Of all the shows that Richard Rodgers ever wrote ... he always said that he liked *Carousel* the best. Seats are scarce as hen's teeth. And expensive as hell. I guess Jeremy paid something like three-hundred-and-fifty bucks ... for the four of 'em. That's almost ninety bucks apiece. Forty-five dollars a <u>cheek</u>. I told Mike that I'd get you to go with us."

"Really, Anne. I don't ... "

"Come on, Jan. It'll do you a world of good! And it'll get me off one hell of a humongous hook. Look. If you don't go ... then, I don't know who I can get. I don't know that many people in town. Women people, anyway. I'd really appreciate it, Jan. I really would."

"I ... I really don't know, Anne. I've just ... "

"It'll do you good, Jan. It really will. Just so much good. You know, I'm really worried about you, Jan. I really am. So are your kids. They <u>really</u> are. They, maybe, don't say anything much to you ... but they're really upset. At least the girls are. Ever since you and Steve broke up ... they say that you've never been the same. You need to get out, Jan! Get your butt out of the ol' house! Live a little! Have a little fun! Unbutton a little! You've got no one to answer to. No reason that you should feel guilty. Why <u>shouldn't</u> you get out? Have a little fun? What's wrong with that? Tell me one thing that's wrong with that! Where's it written that you've got to go around wearing sackcloth and ashes? You're not in a convent, y'know. Why shouldn't you be able to let it hang out a little? Why shouldn't you be able to ... ?"

"All right! All right, Anne. I'll go."

Her sister fairly beamed.

It didn't occur to Janet – not till fifteen or twenty minutes later – that, having accomplished her mission, Anne had simply gotten up. Immediately! And had left!

THIRTEEN

Saturday evening. Janet and Anne double-dated with Mike Dumbrowski – Anne's boss – and Jeremy Bloodworth, executive vice president of the company which employed the pair.

Jeremy was a lean, dynamic, man of 45 – dressed in the trendiest of suits. He had a voice like an empty barrel – and was, by far, the most suave person Janet had ever met. Suave? Slick, maybe, would be more accurate.

The quartet partook of dinner at a sumptuous club – to which Mike had long belonged. Janet was not a total stranger to expensive, opulent, restaurants. Fletcher, after all, had taken her to a number of them, over the past couple of years. However, she'd never seen a menu which listed no prices. This was the epitome of "If you have to ask … you can't afford it".

During the meal, the men dominated the conversation. Never was Janet's opinion solicited. The few times that Anne was permitted to contribute smacked of both men merely patronizing her.

By the time that the waiter finally presented the check, Janet was certain that she had absolutely nothing in common – with either Jeremy or Mike. After her recent discussion with Anne, there seemed to be not much common ground there either. Mike signed the tab – and added a $50.00 tip. The total was almost $375 – causing Janet to gulp, as she was finishing her after-dinner Brandy Alexander.

The four of them arrived at the *Fisher Theater* – in the picturesque "Golden Domed" Fisher Building, on West Grand Boulevard and

Second Avenue – about ten minutes before curtain time. The seats Jeremy had secured were top-notch – located in the middle of the center section, downstairs, four rows from the orchestra pit. The production was Rodgers & Hammerstein's immortal *Carousel.* It was an industrial-strength lavish show. The costumes, the scenery – and the remarkable talent – were far beyond anything Janet could've imagined. There was absolutely no comparison between the dazzling production she was attending – and the hard-working, dedicated, amateur troupe which had staged *Kiss Me Kate*, in Farmington Hills.

Janet thought back to the intimate little theater – and to the special bond which seemed to have formed between herself and Steve, when the "Fred Graham" and the "Lilli Vanessi" characters had sung Cole Porter's brilliant *So In Love.*

Attending that production with Steve had been so different – so sort-of-intimate – as opposed to being seated next to the impeccably-dressed, groomed-to-the-n'th-degree, Jeremy Bloodworth, in the huge, ornate, lavish *Fisher Theater.*

As the show progressed, the "Billy Bigelow" and the "Julie Jordan" characters combined to sing the beautiful *If I Loved You.* As the superb rendition – the exquisite harmony of the two marvelous voices – wafted throughout the auditorium, Janet experienced a terribly hollow feeling! A haunting void – unlike anything she'd ever known. How could one feel so – so alone? In the midst of such a throng of humanity?

The ballad was one of the most beautiful songs on which R&H had ever collaborated. Troublingly, there was something about the manner of the male lead – an elusive ingredient – which reminded her of Steve. She was unable to determine why. The role of "Billy" was as male chauvinist as any man could be. He had a surly demeanor. None of that was remotely similar to what she'd known of Steve Francis. Maybe it was some inflection in the star's voice. Or even his body language. Possibly some subtle nuance. Janet found herself feeling even more alone.

At the intermission, the four stood in the lobby – sipping expensive wine and discussing the performance. Jeremy had allowed that he'd thought *If I Loved You* was "a bit of a drag". He'd been unimpressed by <u>any</u> of the music – except for the light-hearted *You're A Queer One, Julie Jordan.* The novelty song had been sung by "Carrie Pipperidge"

– a flighty, sexy, blonde of potentially-easy virtue. Hers was the most juicy role in the show. Until the intermission, anyway.

Janet tried her best to shut Jeremy's comments out. She could picture – much as she didn't want to – Steve having sat next to her. Holding her hand. Letting the romantic duet sweep them up on the wings of the gorgeous ballad.

As the curtain rose again, "Billy" sang the famous *Soliloquy*. His character has just learned that "Julie" – to whom he was married – was pregnant. The entire number consisted of "Billy's" ruminating as to what his son – or, maybe, his daughter – would be like. The final portion of the song had "Billy" singing about "My little girl … pink and white as peaches and cream is she."

It reminded Janet of something Steve had once said: "There's something special between daddies and daughters." He'd lost his own "little girl", so tragically. If, of course, he was to be believed. He'd been unable to fathom why Jim would've deserted <u>his</u> little girls! Again, if the detective was to be believed.

Janet – enraptured by the soliloquy – had thought of her own sons and daughters. Tears began to course down her cheeks. As she reached into her purse, for a tissue, she was aware of the fact that Jeremy was looking askance at her. Out of the corner of his eye. Disapprovingly, she thought.

Throughout the rest of the performance, she was terribly uncomfortable – and she imagined that it showed. In the play, "Billy" has been killed! When "Julie" comes upon her husband's body, her aunt begins to sing the very beautiful and inspirational *You'll Never Walk Alone*.

It was too much! The tears began to cascade down Janet's face! She was out-and-out crying! The weeping did not abate – as "Julie" was swept into the arms of her "aunt". On the contrary. Jeremy huffed his obvious displeasure! She was certain that Steve would most certainly have been moved by the poignant scene. Maybe even to tears. To complicate matters further, Janet was, once again, overcome with almost uncontrollable emotion – when, at the finale, the cast reprised *You'll Never Walk Alone*.

After the performance, the sisters repaired to the ladies' room. Janet was horrified at the destruction her makeup had suffered. She endeavored to do her best to salvage what she could. Anne smiled at her sister's attempt to restore order out of chaos.

"Kind of gets you ... right here ... huh?" she asked, pointing at her left breast.

Janet – presuming Anne was referring to her heart – sniffed and nodded. "Yeah," she replied. "You know me. Cry at telephone poles and parking meters. I don't think Jeremy's amused."

Anne patted her sister on the shoulder. "Oh, him," she responded. "Listen, he just runs around in a different world than we do. With Jeremy, everything is pressure-pressure! Money-money! To him, simply everything has a dollar sign on it. Never stops to smell the roses or the coffee ... or whatever the hell it is that you're supposed to stop and smell. Don't worry about it. Mike says he's sure that Jeremy thinks you're a very beautiful woman."

"Well, that's nice of him, but ... "

"But, what?"

"Oh ... nothing."

"Nothing my rear end! You're missing Steve! Aren't you? Well? Aren't you?"

"Yes." Janet's gaze seemed to be centered on her sister's shoes. But, Anne could tell, she was far removed from the ladies' room. "Yes, I am. Dammit, Anne! What's the matter with me?"

"Nothing. Absolutely nothing. Look though, Jan. You can be miserable tomorrow. But, tonight, I want you to do your best to have a good time. A damn good time. There's nothing you can do about your situation with Steve ... not tonight, anyway. Not one damn thing. So ... don't be a drag to Jeremy. Okay?"

Janet took a final swipe at her mascara and forced a smile – more a smile of resignation than agreement.

Mike drove them out to Anne's apartment – despite Janet's protests that it was too late. The clock was edging in on midnight. It was 12:30 AM, when they arrived. Anne fixed four highballs. Janet refused hers – and walked out into the kitchen to put on a pot of coffee.

The foursome seated themselves in the living room, for almost a half-hour. Janet had no idea as to where the small talk was leading. She couldn't understand most of it. At least the conversation to which she'd been paying even scant attention.

Then, Mike suggested that it seemed a little warm in the apartment. Janet couldn't fathom what he was talking about. The temperature was comfortable enough. However, Mike insisted that everything would be wonderful – if he simply opened a window in Anne's bedroom! He extended a pointed invitation to Anne – to join him in that little endeavor.

The two of them departed for the bedroom – leaving Jeremy and Janet alone, in the living room. Janet made a monumental effort to engage him in more small talk – despite her awareness that they'd had absolutely nothing in common. In addition, her continuing embarrassment was growing. Especially so – as it became more and more obvious what was going on in the bedroom.

Eventually, Jeremy decided to deliver himself of a spirited lecture – extolling the wonders of the company for which he worked. Janet could be doing oh-so-much better. Wouldn't have to work that "stupid nine-to-five crap". Income potential was limitless! Especially for someone as "good looking" as she was! She could set her own schedule. Wouldn't have to get up early – "unless you damn well want to". She'd have much more time to spend with her kids. Wouldn't have to burn the midnight oil – taking "silly-assed" business courses. Janet sat – coffee cup and saucer in her lap – and, patiently, listened to him drone on. On and on and on and on and on!

<u>When is this damnable night going to end?</u>

Finally – after about 20 minutes – Anne and Mike reappeared! Anne was still working on the side zipper of her dress. Mike – looking exceptionally flushed – was without his necktie and suit coat.

Just as Janet was about to insist on being taken home, Mike blurted, "Well, opening that window sure made a hell of a difference." He swatted Anne on the bottom. "Didn't it, Baby?" he pressed. "<u>Hell</u> of a difference!"

"Sure did," she panted. "Sure as hell did."

"Now," continued Mike – locking his eyes onto Janet's, "it's probably a little too <u>cool</u> in here. Why don't you and Jeremy go on back there ... and close the damn thing?"

"Go back there and do <u>what</u>?" Janet half-shouted her response. "You're out of your damn mind! I'm not going back there! With Jeremy ... or anyone else! It's after one o'clock! If no one's going to drive me home, I'm going to call a cab! I've about had all the enjoyment I can handle … for one night."

"Aw now, Janet," soothed Mike. "C'mon! It'll do you good! You're so damn up-tight!"

Janet – her blue/green eyes ablaze – focused them on her sister.

"Oh … Mike didn't mean anything," was Anne's muttered response. "Relax, Jan. We'll take you home … get you home … shortly." She exhaled! The sound almost filled the room! "In the meantime," she continued, "don't be an old stick-in-the-mud. Remember what I said … what I told you … in the ladies' john! Unlax! Relax, Jan! Relax … and have some fun! Have yourself a hell of a good time tonight. Tomorrow's another day. But, tonight … tonight … you should let it all hang out! Live a little!"

"Live a little? Live a little? You mean I should live a little … by going back there, and … and … and … "

"Janet," cooed Anne. "Jan, please. No one wants to upset you."

"Upset me? Upset me? Well, I fair-thee-well <u>am</u> upset! I want to go home! Now! Do <u>any</u> of you understand that? How <u>complicated</u> is it? I want to go <u>home</u>! I do <u>not</u> want to stay here? I <u>especially</u> do not want to go back to the bedroom! Especially with a total <u>creep</u> … like Jeremy! I do not want this night to go on any <u>further</u>. Read my <u>lips</u>! I want to go <u>home</u>! H-O-M-E! Right <u>now</u>! It's like they say: 'What part of no … do you not <u>understand</u>?'!"

When it became obvious that none of the three was going to make a gesture – give any sign which would indicate they were prepared to take her home – Janet stormed across the room and snatched up the phone! Dialing *Directory Assistance*, she secured the number of a cab company. Then, she phoned and ordered a taxi. Anne was almost loath to provide her sister with the exact street address.

When, Janet finally managed to extract that information from her sister, she barked into the phone, "Tell the driver that I'll wait for him downstairs. Out in front of the building."

Slamming down the receiver, she bolted from the apartment – and scurried down to the front of the building to await her cab.

<u>I hope that, at least, the driver won't be some kind of sex maniac! Maybe there's one person I come in contact with tonight that won't turn out to be a positive schmuck!</u>

<<>>

A half-hour later, Janet slammed the rear door of the taxi – and swept up the driveway to her home. Never had it looked so good. So welcome. So furious was she – with the events of the evening and night, that the fact that virtually every room on the ground floor was illuminated did not register. The minute she let herself in the side door, however, she knew that something was very definitely amiss! Barbara – clad in her light-blue waitress uniform – met her at the top of the steps, in the kitchen.

"Mother! Thank God you're here!"

"What … what's wrong?"

"It's … it's Patti!"

"Patti? Where? What? Is she hurt? Where is she?"

"I … we … we don't know!" It was Joan who'd responded – as she'd hurried from the dining room, her pale-green terrycloth bathrobe flailing in every direction!

"What do you mean you don't know?"

"Patti … she was babysitting up the block … at the Monteith's," began Joan. "And … and then, I got this … I got this call!"

She rushed into her mother's arms!

"What kind of call, Baby?" soothed Janet. "When?"

"Just about fifteen or twenty minutes ago," filled in Barbara.

"Who was it? What did he … what did they want? What did they say?"

Joan began to cry. "It was a man," she wailed. "He said that they had Patti!"

"There, Joanie," comforted Janet. "Easy, Darling. Do we know who 'they' are?"

She looked at Barbara for the answer.

"No, Mother," replied the eldest daughter. "But, they sure act like we sure enough <u>ought</u> to know who 'they' are."

"What do you mean?"

"Well, they told Joanie that 'they' had Patti, and … and if … if we ever want to see Patti again … if we want Patti back … then, we'd better damn well give them the money. Or turn the money over to them … or something like that. Words to that effect."

"Money? What money?"

"We don't know," sobbed Joan.

"Have you phoned the police?"

Barbara nodded – emphatically! "The Livonia Police," she said. "I'd thought they'd be here by now. I didn't know who else to call. I guess the local police ... they always get the FBI involved, anyway. Always get the FBI in on all the kidnapping cases. I ... I really wasn't sure if ... if I should've called Steve or not!"

"It would've been fine," said Janet, rather surprising herself. "It would've been ... been all right ... for you to call him. I can't imagine what ... what ... why ... anyone would want to kidnap Patti."

"They sounded like they knew what they were doing, Mother," said Barbara.

"But, why would they take Patti?" asked Joan. "I mean ... everybody who knows us ... everyone knows ... that we don't have any money. What did they hope to ... ?"

"Wait a minute," interrupted Janet. "Your father! He was involved with money. With a lot of money I guess."

"Well," allowed Barbara, "Joanie's right. Anyone who knows us, knows we don't have a great deal of money around here. Maybe your husband was ... "

"Well, he <u>was</u> responsible for some money. For a lot of money, as I understand it," mused Janet. "Your father! I guess he was stealing money from them. He <u>must've</u> been. That was why ... I think it was why ... why he was killed. I'm trying to remember back to that deputy sheriff, from Texas ... what he had to say. I don't think they were completely firm in their theory of why your father was killed. Maybe ... just maybe ... these people might think that he was sending the money up here. Giving it to us. That's the only thing I can think of."

"But, Mother," responded Barbara. "All anyone would have to do ... would be to see how hard you're working. How hard you've <u>worked</u>! Just look at the ... at the car, in the driveway, for God's sakes."

"I ... I don't know, Barb! I don't really know anything! It's just my mind ... what's left of it ... wandering."

"Well," allowed Barbara, "I guess it makes as much sense as anything. You're pretty sharp, Mother. I never would've thought of it. Yeah. The more I think of it, the more I can see that you're probably right."

"I don't know any more than you do, Barb."

"Yes ... but that was pretty smart. Like I said, it never would've occurred to me."

Both looked at Joan – who seemed on the precipice of some sort of breakdown.

Janet hugged her youngest daughter – then, eased her into one of the dining room chairs. She wandered to the window that faced out onto the street.

"Damn," she muttered. "If only I'd come home earlier. Come home sooner. If only I hadn't gotten hung up with your Aunt Anne ... and those two bloody lechers!"

"You have no reason to feel guilty, Mother," reassured Barbara. "You never get out. Never get away from the grind."

Janet turned to face her oldest daughter. "Neither do you, Baby" she responded. "Neither do you, Baby. You ... you work your fanny off! And when it came time for me to be here ... be here in an emergency ... I'm off with your aunt! Your aunt and a pair of world-class creeps! It's just not ... "

She was cut off – by the sudden headlights, accompanied by the flashing reds-and-blues! First, one police vehicle – and then a second black-and-white – roared into the driveway! Joan was on her feet in a second – rushing to the front door, to let them in! Four uniformed officers filed into the living room. They were joined – five minutes later – by Detective Oscar Goyette, of the Livonia Police, who took immediate charge of the investigation!

As the plainclothesman interviewed first Joan – and then Barbara – in the living room, the impact of Patti's danger was beginning to overwhelm Janet! Like a wave of freezing water that begins at the feet – and then works relentlessly all the way up, to engulf the head! The stark, unthinkable, realization that she may never see her daughter again, had snatched her up in its icy, bleak tentacles! She meandered, aimlessly, out into the dining room.

Why Patti? Why her? She's such a good girl. Such a dear, sweet girl. A beautiful girl. Would never hurt a fly! Dear Lord! Why her? Why? Why?

By the time Goyette began with Janet, she was sitting – statue-like – in one of the dining room chairs. She was totally unaware of the fact that she'd shredded three paper napkins, from the box on buffet.

Barbara had accompanied the detective into the dining room – then, seated herself across from her mother.

Janet began to tell the officer of Jim's connection in Fort Worth. Then, she filled him in more fully – with respect to her late husband's money-laundering career.

What little concentration she'd been able to develop, before facing the inspector, had been consumed in a frenzied-but-futile attempt to remember the names of the two men Deputy Claiborne had asked her about – that memorable day at the laundry. It seemed that one of them was from Inkster – and the other was located in Pontiac. She was spectacularly unsuccessful in her attempts to remember their names.

Her mention of the two men created an entirely different attitude in Goyette.

"I wish someone would've mentioned this before," he snarled – as he arose and hurried toward the living room.

"Well, pardon me," snapped an obviously exasperated Barbara.

Goyette snatched up the phone – and dialed a number! Then, another! Then, a third! Apparently, each had been a no-answer.

"What's Francis' number?" he bellowed – in the direction of the dining room.

Janet was totally unprepared to hear Steve's name brought up!

"I told him about Steve, Mother," advised Barbara.

The young woman reeled off Steve's number – from memory. Another surprise.

Goyette mashed the buttons – hurriedly – and listened, as the phone on the other end rang! And rang! And rang and rang and rang! He uttered an oath, under his breath, and returned to the dining room.

Plopping himself, once more, into a dining room chair, his eyes pleaded with Janet, as he asked, "Please, Mrs. Bolton. Please. Please try and remember those names. I'm somewhat familiar with the case … and I know Detective Francis a little bit. Well, I've never actually met him, but I know who he is. I've tried to call three other people. People who also have some working knowledge of the case … but, they don't answer either. Neither does Francis. I don't know where the hell everyone could be at this hour. Please concentrate, Mrs. Bolton. See if you can't come up with something! With some little something! In a case like this ... every minute counts! You never know what these bastards are going to ... "

He obviously wished that his frustration hadn't caused him to blurt out the last half-statement. Janet – already rattled – was turning more and more pale! By the second! He reached over and put his hand on her arm.

"I didn't mean that, Mrs. Bolton," he said, in his most placating tone. "Not like it sounded. I didn't mean for it to come out quite the way it did. It's just that ... well, the warmer the trail, the better the chance. I mean the faster we'll catch those schmucks ... and, of course, the faster we'll get your daughter back home to you."

At that point, the phone rang – shattering Janet even further! Despite the fact that it was in the other room.

Goyette jumped to his feet! "Probably for me," he announced. "I'll get it!'

Again, he hurried into the front room – and scooped up the phone. Janet strained to hear what the officer was saying. It was no use. Barbara and Joan got up – and made a beeline for the living room.

Sitting at the table alone – two of the uniformed officers had, by then, left, and the remaining pair had seated themselves in the living room – Janet was certain she would be, literally, sick at her stomach. Her head was spinning! How could the night – the entire night – have disintegrated so? Why had she gone out? Why had she allowed herself to be taken back to Anne's apartment? Why had she not called for a taxi – immediately? Especially, once the purpose of Mike's reprehensible open-the-window/close-the-window ploy had become so readily – so tastelessly – apparent?

She'd have been <u>home</u>! Where she <u>belonged</u>! Where she <u>should've</u> been! Her daughters would not have had to have taken the heat – the trauma – of Patti's abduction!

She thought of Anne! Another horrible hypothesis: With Janet having left in such a huff, would it have fallen to her sister to "service" Jeremy? With Mike there? Would "taking care" of Jeremy provide her sister with a quantum leap in her career?

What would Mike think? Would he be furious? Would he be passive? Janet had never met Mike before that evening. Anne had regaled her in story and song, as to how absolutely dynamic he was.

Yet, he'd seemed almost wimpy, around Jeremy. Assuming he had made some sort of commitment to Anne – and assuming that Jeremy had "put a move on" Anne to accompany him to the bedroom – would Mike have had enough principle, enough moral courage, enough backbone, to have stood up to Jeremy?

On the other hand, if your lover consents to go to bed with someone else – especially while you're present – would she be worth standing up for?

Oh! Dear Lord! Everything's such a mess! Such a damnable mess!

Goyette was still on the phone, in the other room! Snatches of his gruff conversation were bleeding through, interspersing his words into Janet's reverie.

Dear Lord! What am I doing? Sitting here ... thinking about Anne and her tawdry sex life! My own daughter is in mortal danger! And here I sit ... worrying about who the hell might be boffing my sister!

Making a determined effort to wipe Anne's exploits – the entire evening's adventure – from her consciousness, she found the image of Steve Frances replacing the twisted thoughts! Twisted was right!

Where is he? Where could Steve be? What business is it of mine? He certainly doesn't have to account to me! Or to anyone else! Well, presumably not anyone else!

Another distasteful hypothesis: Had Steve found another? Compared to the orgy-in-the-making at Anne's glorious apartment, the snapshots Janet had found in Steve's car now seemed almost out of some kindergarten, somewhere. Well, maybe not that innocent! Seriously, though, was what he'd done – was it actually that serious?

She jumped – to the point that she almost fell off her chair! It was the doorbell! Who could that be? At this hour? Could it be Steve? Dear Lord! What's happening? Before Janet could collect herself, Joan had answered the door – and ushered the caller inside. It was Fletcher Groome! He rushed into the dining room! Pulling Janet up from the chair, he took her in his arms!

"Fletch ... Fletcher," she stammered – avoiding his kiss. "What ... what're you doing here?"

"I came ... just as soon as I heard."

"Heard? Heard what? From whom? Who told you?"

"Oh, a friend of mine. He happened to see the police cruiser out here ... in your driveway ... with its emergency lights on. He knew that we were very close ... and so he gave me a call. Mere happenstance. Took me awhile to get dressed."

He pulled her more tightly to him!

"Fletcher," she replied. "I really wish you wouldn't ... wouldn't ... "

In her effort to disengage herself from Fletcher, Janet had not heard the knock on the front door. Joan had, however – and, once again, she'd answered and ushered the newcomer inside! It was Steve!

He entered the dining room and – seeing Janet apparently in the embrace of Fletcher, blurted, "I'm ... I'm sorry! I saw all the cars ... the black-and-whites out there ... and I thought that something might be wrong!" Directing his slate-cold stare at Fletcher, he continued: "But, I see that you're in good hands."

Janet tore herself from Fletcher's grasp!

"Steve! Wait!"

The detective had whirled – and was heading for the front door! Barbara stepped in his way!

"It's not what you think, Steve," the young woman advised – smiling warmly. "Old What's-his-face, there, just busted in here ... like always! And the embrace? It sure wasn't Mother's decision! Or choice! Believe me!"

At that point, Goyette extricated himself from the telephone!

"Hey!" he shouted. "Are you Francis?"

Turning from Barbara, Steve answered, "Yeah! What's this all about?"

Goyette introduced himself to the state policeman – and began to fill him in on the kidnapping. Janet – her back turned on Fletcher Groome – stood off to Steve's right. Barbara took the detective's left hand into both of her own. Joan joined her mother – draping an arm around Janet's shoulder.

"What the hell is this? *Grand Central Station?*" snarled Fletcher – obviously outraged.

He tramped, noisily, out the front door – slamming it, for bone-jarring effect!

As soon as the tense situation had sunk in – the fact that Patti had been abducted – Steve disengaged his hand from Barbara's, and reached out for Janet! He pulled her into his arms. She nestled her head on the right side of his chest – and rested her right hand on the left side.

Goyette inquired of Steve – relative to the two men about whom he and Claiborne had questioned Janet. Steve rattled off the names – and addresses – without hesitation! Another surprise. Janet gazed up at him – with a warmth that surprised her. Well, everything was surprising her on this night.

"You didn't even have to look in your notebook or something?" she asked.

"No," he answered, gently. Then, in a more abrasive tone, he informed her, "I'm damn familiar … with both those SOBs. Damn familiar!"

"I think there's a few things that you and I need to go over, Francis," grunted Goyette! Looking directly into Janet's troubled eyes, he softened his tone. "In private," he said.

"Why don't you and the girls go on out in the dining room?" suggested Steve. "And maybe one of you could whomp up a cup of coffee, for a poor old copper."

As Janet pulled away from him, and began to walk to the dining room, Steve patted her, softly, on the bottom! Yet another surprise! The night was filled with ever more surprises!

"Everything'll be fine," he assured her, as he patted her again. "I guarantee it."

Unable to truly decide whether she was happy – or outraged – at the gesture of affection, Janet ushered Barbara ahead of her, and into the dining room.

"I'll whomp you up a cup," volunteered Joan, over her shoulder – as she followed her mother and sister from the living room.

Steve nodded his thanks – and joined Goyette and the two uniformed officers in the far corner. It was impossible for Janet – or Barbara – to hear any of the hurried, almost-frenzied, half-whispered, conversation. When Joan delivered Steve's steaming cup of coffee, a few minutes later, the confab came to an abrupt halt – until the young woman had returned to the kitchen to pour cups for Goyette and one of the patrolmen. Then, once the young woman had repaired to the dining room, the conference resumed!

Fifteen minutes later, Steve stuck his head into the dining room. His expression didn't convey a great deal of confidence or encouragement.

"Look, fellas," he began. "Inspector Goyette and I have to leave. The other two officers ... they'll stay for awhile. They'll be here ... in case whoever-that-was calls back. You guys might as well hit the sack. Oh, Joanie ... I think the one officer might need a refill on the coffee. And I think the other one would welcome a cup of joe too. If you don't mind."

Silently, Joan arose – and headed toward the kitchen.

"Steve," implored Janet. "Can't you tell me ... us ... anything? Not a thing?"

He made a valiant attempt to cover an exceptionally pained expression.

Shaking his head, slowly, he rasped, "Not at this point, Janet. I wish to hell I could. We've got some leads to go on ... solid, iron-clad leads, I assure you ... so, it's <u>not</u> hopeless! <u>Anything</u> but hopeless! But, we've got to get moving! It's critical that we get moving!"

"What ... what about if they call back?"

"The officers are tapped into your phone. When you answer, look at them ... watch them. They'll guide you. Follow what they say. Follow it ... to the letter."

"But ... but ... but, Steve," Janet implored. "I don't know if I can ... "

"Just try and act as natural as possible," he advised. "Just remember that it's natural ... natural as it can be ... for you to <u>be</u> distraught. Don't try and be Bette Davis or someone. It would be a tip-off! You've got every right to be upset ... every right to be pee-oh'ed. But, you're also frantic at the thought of your daughter. Of her being in their crummy, crappy, hands."

She inhaled – then, exhaled! Loudly! "I'll be natural all right. Distraught as hell!"

<<>>

At 5:15 AM, Janet was still sitting in the dining room – her head resting in a hand, which was making a heroic attempt to hold it up. She stopped dabbing a spoon at a soggy teabag, in the saucer – and snapped erect, as a pair of headlights illuminated the driveway outside.

She'd succeeded in shooing Barbara to bed a little more than a half-hour before. Joan had succumbed an hour before her sister. The two officers lay sleeping in the living room – one on the couch and one on the floor. Both cops arose – as Janet hurried through the living room!

"Ma'am! I wouldn't ... "volunteered one of them, as she bolted out the front door – and off the porch!

Steve took her in his arms – and kissed her tenderly. Part of her responded to his kiss. The majority of her was frantic – for news of her daughter!

"Where's Patti?"

She could feel the hysteria begin to rear its ugly head once more!

He shook his head, slowly.

"No news right now." His voice was hoarse. "But, Goyette and the FBI ... even the State Police ... they're all doing everything they can. They ... the kidnappers ... they didn't call back, did they?"

"No." Her answer was practically inaudible.

"Don't despair, Janet. I'm not just blowing smoke ... when I tell you that we have leads. They're just ... sometimes ... just a little hard to hurry. Sometimes, you have to have a little patience ... in a situation like this."

"Steve! Steve ... they've had all this time. While we're standing here ... talking about not rushing ... they could be doing all kinds of things ... all kinds of horrible, God-awful, terrible, rotten things ... to her! They could be ... "

He covered her lips – with three of his fingers.

"Don't even <u>think</u> that," he admonished. "They're not interested in <u>her</u>. They're interested in <u>money</u>! It's <u>always</u> about money. Money they believe that Jim held out on them! Hell, he probably did. I'm <u>sure</u> he did. I'm sure that he held out a helluva lot of money. He just didn't send any of it up here. We've got to take a shot at convincing them that you never got any of the damn money."

She drew back from him!

"How can you <u>say</u> such a thing? That they're not interested in <u>Patti</u>? That all they want is <u>money</u>? How can you <u>say</u> that? What makes you even <u>think</u> that? You have no idea <u>where</u> she is! No <u>idea</u>! No idea <u>where</u> my beautiful ... my wonderful ... Patti <u>is</u>!"

"I know. But, there are ways. We have <u>contacts</u>! We <u>do</u>! The

State Police have a few. Goyette's a good man ... and <u>he's</u> got a couple. But, Janet, the FBI ... they're pros. <u>They're</u> not going to let anything happen to Patti! Your beautiful Patti! Your wonderful Patti! Neither is Goyette! Neither am I, dammit! Neither am I! We'll have her back here ... before you know it! I <u>guarantee</u> it!" He turned her toward the front door – and slapped her smartly on her bottom. This was an undeniable swat! Not merely a pat! "Look," he advised her, "we're going to throw those cops out on their butts. I'll take over for 'em. But, the main thing is ... priority number one ... is we've got to get that beautiful fanny of yours into bed!"

He literally marched her back inside. Janet stood to one side – as Steve dispatched the uniformed officers.

Once the pair had departed, Steve turned to her – and proclaimed, "Now, it's off to bed for you!"

He made as if to level another soft – but, firm – spank at her! She wheeled around, however, and nestled into his arms – kissing him! Kissing him – unleashing an incredible mixture of tenderness, fear for what the future would bring, and a bountiful amount of gratitude. It was all in there! All in the soul-stirring mix!

"Okay, Massa," she rasped – breaking the kiss, at long last. "I'll go quietly!"

FOURTEEN

Janet snapped awake – and sat bolt-upright in her bed! It was light outside! The sun had definitely come up! What time was it? She looked – frantically – at the aged clock/radio, beside the bed!

"Quarter-after-nine! Quarter-after-<u>nine</u>? Dear Lord! How could I have slept this long?"

When she'd crawled – reluctantly – into bed, almost four hours before, she was certain that she'd never get to sleep. Yet, she didn't remember her back hitting the sheet.

She threw back the covers and looked down at herself! And shuddered! She was naked! Bounding out of bed, she snagged her powder-blue, chenille, bathrobe from an "elephant hook", on the inside of her closet door! Wrapping the garment around her, she headed downstairs! She was giving a final tug to the lopsided bow, in the sash – as the lower part of Steve's body came in to view! He was obviously lying on the couch. She hurried into the dining room! It was empty! Entering the kitchen, she surprised Barbara! Both women jumped!

"OH! Oh, God! Mother! I didn't know you were up already."

"Already? I damn near slept the day away."

"Not so," laughed Barbara. "I'm the slothful one. Sit down. The coffee'll be ready in a couple minutes."

"Where's Joanie? Is she asleep? I don't hear the boys."

Barbara nudged her mother through the door – and into the dining room.

"Joanie's got the boys at the playground," explained the younger

- 225 -

woman, as they seated themselves. "Thought it'd be better if they weren't around. For a while, anyway. Don't know how long we can hold out … without having to tell them something about Patti, though."

Janet's smile was as wistful as it was sad. "My champion," she rasped. "When things get tough, I know I can always depend on you, Barb. I'm so proud of you. So lucky to have you as a daughter."

"You're not all that lucky. It was, actually, Joanie's idea. She's pretty good with a bat, y'know. Said she'd hit some balls to the boys … let 'em get some use out of their new gloves."

"That makes me even luckier."

"I gave her a few bucks. Told her to keep 'em occupied. Take 'em to lunch … or to a movie, or something."

Janet reached over and patted her daughter's hand, as Barbara rose to fetch the coffee pot. It had been percolating over the previous couple minutes – percolating violently – in the kitchen. The welcome aroma had wafted out into the dining room.

Once the coffee had been poured – and Barbara had seated herself once more – Steve staggered into the dining room. Janet had to smile at his craggy, unshaven, sleep-laden face – and the untamed thatch of hair, which looked as though it had been styled with an eggbeater. She had speculated, from time to time – as to what he would look like, of a given morning. The image had been something like the man who stood before her. Pretty close – well, very close.

"Morning," said Barbara, brightly. "Can I interest you in a cup of coffee? Before you disintegrate altogether?"

"Mmmmmm," he mumbled – as he raked his hair with his right hand. "I'll be eternally in your debt, My Good Lady." He sat down – and made a valiant attempt to focus his gaze upon Janet. "Not much to tell you," he answered the silent question. "But, don't worry. I'm supposed to meet Goyette … and a couple heavyweights from the FBI … at about ten-thirty."

She started to speak – but, he cut her off.

"Gonna have to get off my butt … and get out there," he continued, as he gratefully accepted a cup of coffee, from Barbara. "Would one of you ladies have a razor that is in a moderate state of repair? And can a fella take a shower here?"

"Our bathroom is your bathroom," answered Barbara.

"How romantic," responded Steve.

"Takes after her mother," muttered Janet. "I've got a brand spanking new razor ... untouched by human hands."

"How nice," he replied. "After I get through with it ... it <u>still</u> ain't been touched by human hands."

"Steve," implored Janet, "Look. I can't kid around! What am I going to <u>do</u>? What is <u>anyone</u> going to do? My dear, sweet, little, <u>Patti</u>! She's been out there, Steve! Out there the whole damn <u>night</u>! All night! Who knows ... dear Lord ... who <u>knows</u> what they've <u>done</u> to her? Steve? Steve ... you've <u>got</u> to find her!"

"We <u>will</u>, Janet. We will! I <u>promise</u> you! We <u>will</u>!"

"Shouldn't they have called us? Called us back?" asked Barbara. "Called us by now? Shouldn't they have called back ... and talked to Mother? I mean, they have no way of knowing what her response would be. What her response will be. They only spoke to Joanie ... and they know that she's just a kid. Just a young girl."

"Yes," agreed Janet. "Why wouldn't they have gotten in touch with me by now?"

"My guess," he responded, "is that they want to get you good and worried."

"Yes," she muttered. "Well, they've <u>succeeded</u>! Beyond their wildest ... most optimistic ... <u>expectations</u>! I'm <u>worried</u>! Worried as <u>hell</u>."

"My guess," expanded Steve, "is that ...when they do call you ... they don't want any fight left in you! They're going to want to have you give right in! Right away! Gonna want you to do whatever they say! All the money! Right now! Wherever they want you to drop it! That's why you haven't heard their saintly goddam voices!"

"What ... what am I going to do, Steve? I don't have any money. You know that."

"Yeah. We'll take care of that, though."

"Take <u>care</u> of it? <u>How</u>? How in heaven's <u>name</u> can you ... ?"

He put his hand on hers. "Hey!", he said. "Don't go through the roof on me now. We're going to need you at your best. Now, listen. Goyette has a couple of connections. For one thing, there's a ... what the hell do they call 'em? ... a philanthropist! That's what they call 'em. The Police Department has money at their disposal! Cash! This guy has ... years ago ... donated it. For cases just like this one! Plus, the

FBI has certain funds at their disposal! Lots more red tape, though ... than dealing with this guy that Goyette has up his sleeve. Now, don't worry. We've got it covered ... from that end, anyway."

"Don't worry," Janet repeated. She spat the words.

"There'll be a guy here ... from the FBI. Probably any minute. They've got more sophisticated phone stuff ... than the Livonia guys. But, the Livonia boys have the neighborhood staked out. Picking license numbers off any cars that might cruise by. That sort of thing."

"I ... I guess I didn't realize there were all those things they could do," responded Janet, softly.

"If the bad guys call you," advised Steve, "just follow the lead of the man from the FBI. These fellas deal with this stuff ... practically every day. It shouldn't be ... but, that's the way things are these days. Believe me ... everything's going to turn out fine!"

He gulped down the last half-cup of coffee and observed, "It's getting late. I've got to take a shower and shave."

As he got up, Janet arose with him. "Here," she offered. "I'll show you the way. Have to get you a couple towels ... and my as-yet-untouched razor."

He followed her up the stairs. She stopped at the linen closet – and whisked two fluffy, emerald-green, towels from the third shelf. Then, she closed the door – and hurried into the bathroom. Putting the toilet seat down, she set the towels on top.

Then, she whirled around and said, "I'll get you a razor. It's in my bedroom. I'm sure you'll be able to figure out the combination to the shower."

Caught up as she was – in her mission – she was unaware of the fact that Steve had followed her into the bedroom. She'd hurried directly to the chest of drawers, opened the top drawer – and snatched up a sealed-in-clear-plastic, disposable, razor. As she spun around – to return to the bathroom – she, literally, bumped into him!

"OH! Oh my God! You ... you scared me! I thought you were still in the john!"

He wrapped his arms around her – pulling her close!

"Steve! We can't ... "

The rest of the exclamation was lost – in his kiss! She responded immediately! Exactly what she wanted not to do! Melting against him, her lips desperately hungered for some footing – some foundation – in a world gone mad!

If he'd had any doubt that she was wearing nothing beneath her robe, Janet's yearning, clinging, embrace most certainly would've dissolved it! He ran his hands, frantically, up and down her body! His tongue entered the warmth of her eager mouth! Janet pressed herself even more tightly against him! She'd been aware – since the first magic second that he'd taken her into his arms – that his manhood had been summoned!

He caressed her – up and down her back! Then, he began to ruck her bathrobe upward! Higher and higher, he pulled the garment! Until his hands came to rest upon the tingling exposed flesh of her derriere!

There they remained! For fully 15 seconds! His tongue probed the depths of her mouth! His hands caressed the soft, milky, twin mounds of her behind!

Then – as though he and the woman in his arms had been hit simultaneously by some runaway bolt of lightning – he withdrew his tongue and removed his hands, letting the robe fall, once again, covering her! Her arms recoiled – from his neck! The indescribable, terribly-troubled-albeit-silent, expressions – on both faces – shouted: "What are we doing?" He took the razor from her trembling hand – and hurried out of the room!

Minutes later – as she sat shivering on her bed – Janet heard the shower spring to life! Steve was under that showerhead! Behind that closed door! Across that hall!

<<>>

It took twenty minutes for Steve to shave and shower. As soon as she heard him shut off the water, Janet – still badly shaken – made her way downstairs. She was totally unprepared to encounter the small, balding, slightly-built, man – seated primly on the living room sofa! Barbara arose, from the other side of the couch, and introduced the newcomer:

"This is Mister Cribbert ... from the FBI ... Mother."

Janet – extending her hand and offering as genuine a smile as possible – made her way toward the agent, as he arose and handed her his credentials.

"I'm sorry," Cribbert intoned, in a nasal voice, "for the circumstances which bring me here, Mrs. Bolton. We're certain that the kidnappers will attempt to contact you today. Probably within a few hours. We've installed a tracer device on your phone. It should give us the caller's number ... in a matter of fifteen or twenty seconds. Of course, if they're calling from a payphone ... which they usually do ... it's not nearly as helpful. However, it's still a help ... in most cases. The main thing is to follow my lead. I have an outlet ... this earphone here ... whereby I can listen in on the conversation. It's important ... it's vital, it's critical ... that you follow my lead. Completely. Follow it to the letter."

Janet was bowled over – by the agent's immediate thrust into the reason for his presence. She was certain that the FBI must have other people in Cribbert's position – people who are much more empathetic. People who are not so terribly – clinical.

"I'll ... I'll do my best," she said, weakly.

"Something you must remember ... remember right from the very start ... Mrs. Bolton! They're expecting you to be somewhat distraught. The one situation ... the one single thing which will make them suspicious ... is if you are too cooperative."

"What ... what do you mean 'too cooperative'?"

"Let's us sit down. Shall we?" Everyone seated themselves. "What I'm getting at," Cribbert began once more, "is that it's important for you to be ... be at all times ... be realistic. For example, this is Sunday."

"Yes. I'm aware of that."

"On Sunday, Mrs. Bolton, the banks are closed. Therefore, if you agree to give them money right away ... it may not strike them as you're being totally truthful."

"What ... what should I do, then? What should I say?"

"That you can't get the money before the banks open Monday morning. That's factual sounding. It'll buy the Bureau a little more time."

"Buy them ... buy the Bureau ... a little more time? Does that mean that I won't get my daughter ... my Patti ... back today? Back soon?"

"Well, Mrs. Bolton, we just never really know. As long as everything seems factual, your daughter will probably be safe."

"Prob ... probably?"

"Well, Mrs. Bolton ... quite frankly ... in these sorts of cases, we never <u>really</u> know. We <u>can't</u> know. Not for <u>sure</u>."

Janet was staggered by Cribbert's unfeeling onslaught.

"What ... what should I say?" Her voice was scarcely a whisper. "What should I tell them ... if they want the money <u>before</u> Monday? What if they tell me that they've got to have the money right now? Today! What if they tell me that they have to have the money today ... or they'll ... or they'll ... " Tears flooded her eyes – and began to trickle down her cheeks. "Mister Cribbert," she managed to say, "I don't know where I'd ever be able to lay my hands on a large sum of money! Even a small sum of money! Today ... or any other day! Even if my life depended on it! Steve talked about getting me some money ... from some connection that the Livonia police are supposed to have. But, I don't know when ... or how much! Or anything <u>else</u>, dammit! What would I <u>do</u>? What would I <u>say</u>?"

Cribbert affected a hung-dog look.

"Just follow my lead, Mrs. Bolton," he replied. "Just follow what I indicate. We have techniques. We have replies. It'll depend on what they're saying. What kind of questions they're asking. Inflections in their voices. Subtle nuances ... that we're specially trained to pick up on. Trained to pick up on that sort of thing."

"We're going to have to trust Mister Cribbert, Mother," advised Barbara.

The expression on the young woman's face fairly shouted, "He's all we've got!".

"What the hell's going on?" It was Steve – bounding down the stairs, three-at-a-time.

Cribbert launched himself from the couch – and met Steve at the foot of the staircase.

"You must be Detective Francis," he proclaimed. "I'm Ernest Cribbert." He produced his credentials. "I'm here," he continued, "to guide Mrs. Bolton ... when the kidnappers call."

"Yeah," Steve grumped. "So I heard. You're a real comfort for her, I'm sure."

"These are troubled times for us all, Mister Francis," snapped Cribbert. "I'm here to help as much as is humanly possible. I'm not a rookie at this sort of thing, I assure you. I've been through this area before. Many, many times. You may rest assured that Mrs. Bolton is in the very best of hands. The most capable of hands."

Steve flashed Janet the same expression that Barbara had shown moments before. He hurried across the room to Janet – and pulled her up from the couch. The move caused her to display much more leg than she'd preferred. Wrapping his arms around her, he gave her a quick kiss!

<u>Why do his lips always taste so good?</u>

"I've got to be off, my little chickadee," he said. "Do what Mister Cribbwell tells you to do, Honey."

"Cribbert," corrected the little man.

Janet – for some inexplicable reason – was offended by Steve's calling her "Honey". Especially in front of the prissy little agent. Everything was so mixed up! Even the brief brush of Steve's lips helped emphasize that fact! It brought to the foreground of her swirling, deeply-troubled, mind – that she was wearing nothing, beneath her robe. A fact, she was certain, of which Barbara was aware. Maybe the visitor from the FBI had determined that fact, as well. She <u>had</u> shown a lot of leg, when Steve had pulled her up from the couch. Had shown a lot of leg – and who knew what else? She shuddered!

<<>>

Forty minutes later, Janet had just finished drying herself – after an almost-scorching shower. She'd used almost a half-bar of soap – and virtually all the hot water in the tank in the basement. It was an insane effort, she knew – an intense attempt to scrub away the events of the past 12 or 15 hours. She donned her robe – and headed across the hall, to apply a little makeup and brush her hair.

The phone rang!

"Mother!" shouted Barbara – at the same exact moment Ernest Cribbert was calling, "Mrs. Bolton!".

Janet barreled downstairs – no longer concerned with modesty! Or lack thereof! She grabbed up the phone!

"Hell ... hello?"

"Mrs. Bolton?" It was a man's voice – one she'd never heard before. Of that she was certain.

"Yes?"

Cribbert had his tiny receiver pressed up against his ear. He rotated his forefinger – in a circular motion – and indicated, with his lips, a silent, overdone, "Go ahead"!

"Mrs. Bolton? I'm sure that you're aware of the purpose of this call." The voice was like a piece of chalk – being drawn across a slate!

"Yes?"

"We want money, Mrs. Bolton. We want <u>the</u> money! The whole damn lot of it. Every cent your husband sent you!"

Janet stared at Cribbert! The little agent signaled her! An overdone shrug!

"I ... I don't know ... what you're talking about," she said, into the receiver.

"Cut the crap, Mrs. Bolton." The kidnapper's tone sent a massive shudder through Janet's body! She almost dropped the phone! "Do you realize," the voice asked, "what we can do to your daughter? Now, are you gonna play games with us, Mrs. Bolton? Because ... if you are ..."

Cribbert shook his head.

"No! No. No, I ... don't want to play games. I ... I just want my daughter ... my ... my little girl ... I just want her back! Is she all right?"

"She's <u>fine</u>! For the time <u>being</u>! But ... and you <u>listen</u> to me, Mrs. Bolton ... she's not <u>going</u> to be! Not if you're going to try and jerk me <u>around</u>! I realize that the FBI are there! Probably all over the joint! I'm sure that ... even as we speak ... they're trying to trace this call! I'll call you back in a half-hour! Maybe forty-five minutes! At that time, we can talk turkey! I'm not going to jack with you, Mrs. Bolton! I want that money! Now, you'd better be ready to part with it ... or be ready to part with your <u>daughter</u>! You'd better be ready to <u>deal</u>, Mrs. Bolton ... when I call back! Otherwise, it's going to be awfully <u>serious</u>! <u>Awfully</u> serious ... for <u>Patti</u>!"

Hearing the kidnapper say the name of her daughter was too much! It was almost as though he'd <u>spat</u> the name. <u>Sacrilegious</u>! That such an animal should be permitted to even <u>speak</u> the girl's name! He was <u>blaspheming</u>! Janet burst into tears – sobbing wildly!

The caller broke the connection!

<<>>

Janet's legs had turned to two strands of overcooked spaghetti! Dizziness was overtaking her! She began to sink to the floor! Cribbert's surprisingly-strong arms broke the fall! The diminutive agent guided her, ever-so-gently, to the sofa – and eased her down into a sitting position! He seemed not to notice that her robe had fallen away – exposing her thighs. Her thighs – and, hopefully, nothing else, thought Janet – as she'd crumpled on to the couch.

"Mother," a frantic Barbara shouted. "Can I get you something? Anything? Coffee? I think there's a bit of blackberry brandy out there, in the dining ... "

"No." It took a mighty effort for Janet to speak. "No. No, I'll be all right. I'll be all right. Just ... just give me a ... a minute. I'll be ... I'll be fine."

"What did he say?" pressed her daughter – the only one who'd not heard both sides of the lethal conversation.

"They're ... they're not playing games," rasped Janet. Her throat seemed made of plastic tubing! "He ... he said he'd call back in a ... in a half-an-hour," she informed the younger woman. "Maybe forty-five minutes."

"He'll call back," advised Cribbert. "Trust me. He'll call back."

Barbara glared at the little man! "It seems to me," she groused, "that we trusted you with this call. Trusted you ... all the way ... on this call! And now ... look at my mother!"

Janet reached out and groped for her daughter's hand. Finally grasping it, she admonished the young woman:

"Mister ... Mister Cribbert was fine. I'd have had absolutely no idea what to do ... what to say ... to that horrible man! But, Mr. Cribbert coached me. Guided me ... all the way. All the way through." Looking up at the agent, she rasped, "Thank you."

A wee smile crossed his lips – for just the briefest of an instant. It was as though anything more would've broken his face.

"That's my job," he replied, impassively. "That's my job."

<<>>

Seventy-five minutes later – an anguish-filled hour-and-a-quarter – the phone, at long last, rang once more! Janet, clad in grey woolen pullover and blue jeans waited for Cribbert's nod – then, lifted the receiver!

"Yes?"

"Have you given any thought to our earlier conversation, Mrs. Bolton?" It was the same chilling voice! Dear Lord!

"Yes. Yes, I have."

"Good. Now, I want you to get the money together ... and follow my instructions. Follow my instructions ... to a tee! Follow them ... to the letter!"

Cribbert had hastily scribbled the word "bank" on a stenographer's notebook, from his attaché case.

"The ... the money," stammered Janet, "it's ... it's ... I'm not going to be able to get my hands on it. Not till Monday."

"Oh? And why is that, Mrs. Bolton?"

"The ... the banks. They ... they're not open. Not on the weekend."

"Don't give me that gas, Mrs. Bolton. Don't you think we know that you've never put that money in a bank account? In any account! Don't you think we know that? If you'd have banked that money ... let me assure you ... we'd have known about it! So, please! Save everybody ... including Patti ... a lot of trouble. Stop BS'ing me! You know perfectly well that you're holding onto that dough! Holding onto it ... so that no one would question you about it. Figuring it'd never have to be accounted for. Well, the time for accounting, Mrs. Bolton, is here! It's now! So I'm not going to hold still for you jerking me around ... about the stuff being in the bank. If you're listening ... if you're paying attention to ... to those sorry goofballs from the FBI, you're going to be sorry, Mrs. Bolton! Terribly sorry!"

Cribbert was shaking his head – frantically!

"I'm not ... I haven't," stammered Janet. "I don't care about the FBI! I want Patti back! I want my Patti ... want her back!"

"I don't know if that's really true, Mrs. Bolton. If you're going to follow what they advise you ... let me tell you, Mrs. Bolton ... you're going to wind up being dead sorry!" She wished he'd not used the word "dead".

"I'm not," she maintained – relieved, slightly, at Cribbert's nod of approval. "I don't care what they say. All I want is my Patti back."

"They've got all those fancy theories," the voice responded. "The FBI has all these fancy theories." The tone, of the caller, had moderated somewhat. "What the hell," the man continued. "It's not their kid that they've got to worry about."

"Please! Please listen to me! I haven't ... "

"No, Mrs. Bolton! You listen to me!" He was back to being combative. "I've only got a few seconds left ... before I have to hang up! Now, you get that money! All fifty-thousand of it! Do you understand that? You get that fifty big ones ... and you put it in a shoebox or something like that. And you take that money ... you take it with you! And you haul yourself to the *Seven-Eleven* store on Seven Mile and Inkster Road. There's a bank of phones there. Outside the store. You'll wait there! Wait for one of the phones to ring! When you answer, we'll give you further instructions! You have twenty-five minutes! I suggest you start now! Immediately!"

Again, the receiver went dead in Janet's hand! She dropped the phone onto the couch, beside her! Totally drained, she leaned back – practically collapsing on the cushions behind her!

"What ... what am I going to do now?" Her voice was practically unrecognizable even to her.

Barbara replaced the receiver into its cradle.

"Well," responded Cribbert, "at least we know how much money they're talking about. As it happens, I have that much here with me ... courtesy of one of Livonia's benefactors. A philanthropist that the Livonia police have on the string. Do you have a shoebox that we can use?"

Janet blanched at his matter-of-fact tone! She'd had no idea that this mousy, prissy, little man would have a mountain of money in his attaché case! He popped the valise-like thing open – and withdrew six or eight stacks of money!

"You ... you do have a shoebox?" he repeated.

"Yes. Yes, of course," replied the badly-rattled Janet.

"I'll get one, Mother," volunteered Barbara – bounding toward the stairs.

Cribbert counted out $50,000 – in $100 bills – and stacked the currency, fastidiously, inside the box that Barbara brought down. Handing the box of money to Janet, his expression softened – slightly.

"Will you be all right?" he asked. "Will you be able to drive? Drive over to the *Seven-Eleven*, Mrs. Bolton? You're going to have to be pretty much on your own, now. I'm sure they'll be watching you … to assure themselves that you <u>are</u> alone!"

Janet nodded, absently. "Yes. Yes, I'm … I'm fine. I'm all right."

"Do you have enough gas in your car? Do you need some money for gas?"

The little man reached into his pocket.

"No," she replied. "I've got a half … maybe three-quarters … of a tank, I think."

"You're going to have to get on your way, Mrs. Bolton. You'll have more than ample time to make it to the *Seven-Eleven*. And don't be upset … don't panic … if they're five or ten minutes late with the call. They're simply trying to unnerve you."

"Yes. Well, they've succeeded. Like I told Steve, they've been very successful. Beyond their wildest dreams."

"I can assure you that the next three or four or five calls … will simply direct you to another location and another location and another location! They'll be watching you … all the time. Maybe you'll be able to spot who it is … but, don't make a conscious effort to. Drive carefully. You won't be required to go at breakneck speed. They'll allow you plenty of time … even if they say they're not … to get to the next stop. Do you have any quarters?"

"I … I don't know."

He reached into his pocket – and pulled out a handful of change. Fumbling through the coins, he picked out eight 25-cent pieces – and handed them to the distraught woman.

"Now," he counseled, "go get 'em! It'll work out. We just have to play their little game … for the time being, anyway. But, soon, the shoe'll be on the other foot. You'll see."

Barbara hugged Janet tightly – and rasped, "You're a rock, Mother. An absolute rock. I'm so proud of you."

"If I'm such a rock … why, then, are my knees knocking against one another?"

"You're doing fine, Mrs. Bolton," added Cribbert. "Go get 'em!"

She looked at the agent. He seemed nothing like the prissy, fussy, little man she'd been introduced to. How can a person be so misjudged?

He was turning out to be a solid – a wonderful – man. A massive help. A tower of strength.

Janet stashed the box-full of money under her arm – and hurried out the side door, taking short, deliberate, strides. Her hand seemed to have absolutely no strength – zero dexterity – as she pulled open the door of her wounded Maverick. She eased the car out of the driveway – and drove, slowly, to the convenience store – as the horrifying voice on the phone had directed. Pulling into the parking slot – in front of three payphones – she rolled the driver's window down! And waited! And waited! And waited! Despite the fact that there was a definite damp chill in the air, Janet was perspiring! Profusely!

Twenty long, mind-warping, minutes later, the phone rang! The one in the middle! She'd only been waiting – and sweating – for an eternity! She almost tripped – as she hoisted herself out of the car! She ran to the ringing phone, and snatched it up!

"Yes?"

"Good ... very good, Mrs. Bolton. You're alone?"

"Yes." Her throat was made of concrete.

"And you have the money?" Janet hesitated – all of five seconds! "Well?" grated the voice. "Do you have the money ... or don't you?"

"I ... I've ... yes. I've got the money. Yes."

"Good. Now, you're not trying to jerk me around on this are you? I mean, you <u>do</u> have the money? No BS?"

"I've got the money! No BS!"

"You'd <u>better</u> have, Mrs. Bolton. You just <u>better</u> have! If you're playing a game ... well, it'll be the sorriest game <u>you've</u> ever played."

"Yes! Dear Lord! Yes ... I understand! I'm not playing games! I'm not! Now ... <u>please</u>! What do you want me to do?"

"That's better. Now, listen ... and listen carefully! There's another bank of phones ... in that big strip plaza on Seven Mile and Grand River. Where they come together. It's right in front of the grocery store ... the *Kroger's*. On the Seven Mile end. Go there ... and wait for one of the phones to ring! You have ten minutes!"

The connection was broken! Janet replaced the receiver – and noticed that she was shivering and perspiring at the same time! How was that possible?

Concentrating on each and every movement, she crawled back into

her Maverick – and swung out of the parking lot. She made a right turn
– heading toward the assigned strip plaza. Seven Mile Road and Grand
River come together at 45-degree angles to one another. Janet had to
devote her undivided attention – her unyielding focus – to holding to
the speed limit. She certainly didn't need to be pulled over. A speeding
ticket was the last thing she needed! Not with so much at stake!

Once she'd pulled in to the large plaza, she spotted the phones in
front of the *Kroger's* store – and pulled the battered car to the curb, in
front of the huge market. She rolled down her window, once more!
And waited, once more! She was sitting in a <u>No Parking</u> – <u>Fire Lane</u>
zone! And headed the "wrong way"!

<u>Dear Lord</u>! <u>Please Lord</u>! <u>Please don't let some cop come chase
me out</u>! <u>Chase me away</u>! <u>Please don't let them see me with a cop</u>!
<u>Anywhere near a cop</u>!

Again, an eternity dragged by! Almost a half-hour – before the
phone on the left end of the group rang! Janet answered the phone –
before the second ring!

"Yes?"

"Very good, Mrs. Bolton. My compliments. You're doing fine.
Now, I want you to drive out the Grand River exit. Turn left on Grand
River. You'll have to negotiate yourself around the median ... but,
you'll be heading toward Farmington. Got that?"

"Yes."

"Good. Once Grand River branches off to become Interstate
Ninety-six, I want you to stay on Grand River. Go on in to Farmington.
There's another strip plaza ... a good bit smaller than this one ... about
a half-a-mile in to Farmington. When you pass a *Citgo* station on your
left ... pull into the plaza, immediately on your right! Right across
Grand River from the gas station. The pay phones are in the middle,
there ... pretty close to the drug store. You have fifteen minutes to get
there!"

Once again, Janet was holding a suddenly-dead receiver in her cold,
trembling, hand!

Pulling away from the curb, Janet felt slightly more in command!
She didn't know why! But, she was gripping the steering wheel much
less firmly!

The perspiring had even abated! Had practically stopped altogether!

She'd had to turn right – heading away from Farmington – and, a half-block later, negotiate a "U" turn through the wide, grassy, median. In so doing, she'd not noticed a small, white, sports car, barreling along, in the inside lane – heading toward Farmington! Janet pulled into its path! It was a tribute to the driving skill of the young woman, in the tiny car, that a potentially-serious accident was averted – how-ever-narrowly! Janet was back to shaking and perspiring! And holding the steering wheel in her patented death grip!

Fifteen minutes later, she wheeled into the shopping plaza that the chilling voice had indicated! The phone was already ringing!

<u>Dear Lord</u>! <u>Don't let me</u> ... <u>please don't let me be late</u>!

She screeched to a halt – and jammed the gear selector into Park! Abandoning the car in the middle of the driving lane – and leaving the driver's door open – she dashed to the jangling phone! She grabbed at it – frantically! She managed to pluck it out of its holder – on the third attempt!

"Yes?"

"A little late there, Mrs. Bolton."

"Please! Please! I'm about to lose my mind! How many more of these damnable things have you ... do we ... are there going to be? No one is with me! I swear to you ... by all I hold holy! I have the money! Won't you ... please won't you ... won't you stop all this? Please! Won't you let me have my daughter back?"

"We're almost there, Mrs. Bolton. You have to understand that there are certain precautions that we ... "

"To <u>hell</u> with you! To hell with <u>all</u> of you! And your damn <u>precautions</u>! I've chased my rear end around half the country now! And I can't keep this <u>up</u>! You <u>must</u> have satisfied yourself, by now. You <u>must</u> know that I'm alone!"

"We'll do, maybe, one or two more," answered the voice – its tone substantially more plodding. "You never know! The next place ... well, that just might be <u>it</u>! Might be the <u>drop</u>! I want you to go to another shopping mall ... the big one on Seven Mile and Middlebelt! I'm sure you know where it is. Huge mall. Park your car in front of the *Crowley's* store! Do you understand that? In front of *Crowley's*!"

"Yes," responded Janet. She was in tears. "Yes, I understand. *Crowley's.*"

"Okay. Then I want you to take the shoebox with the money ... you <u>do</u> have the money? And it's in a shoebox, is it?"

"<u>Yes</u>! Yes, damn you! Yes!"

"Very good! Now, just stay calm, Mrs. Bolton. Just stay cool! This is not the time to panic ... and to do something stupid! Like getting into an accident! Like you almost did ... with that little sports car! Now, listen to me! You are to park ... in front of *Crowley's*! But, I want you to walk back ... to the other end of the mall. Walk ... with the shoebox under your arm ... and go all the way to the bank of phones by the *Sears* store, at the far end. We'll give you a little longer to get there ... you shouldn't have an accident. But, the time we're allowing you ... well, it is definitely not infinite! Patience is not our strong suit, you know."

Once again, the phone went dead! She walked away – leaving the phone dangling! As she approached her wounded Maverick, it occurred to her that she'd just abandoned the car – with the motor running and $50,000 lying on the front seat! It took a monumental effort for her to climb back into the automobile.

She drove back down Grand River – out of Farmington – headed for Middlebelt Road. She had to, she knew, concentrate on every movement – no matter how minor! She almost missed the right turn at Middlebelt Road. Every traffic light – between Grand River and Seven Mile Road turned up red! Not only red! But, a <u>long</u> red! One of the reasons that she felt that she was cutting it too close.

At long last, she pulled into a slot, in front of *Crowley's Department Store* – and killed the motor. Totally drained, she pulled herself out of the car, tucked the box of currency under her arm – and began what seemed to be the million-mile walk, clear to the other side of the huge, "L"-shaped, mall! Every phone, outside the *Sears & Roebuck* store, was in use!

<u>Dear Lord</u>! <u>What now</u>?

It took three gut-wrenching minutes for a heavy-set lady to finally hang up – and walk away! No one picked the phone up! Janet stood there – shivering mightily, once again! Nothing happened!

Oh, <u>please</u>! <u>Please</u>!

A woman approached – heading for the vacant phone! Before the stranger got to the phone, it rang! Janet sprinted in front of the lady!

"Please," she implored. "I'm sure that call's for me. It's an emergency! Please!"

The woman – a matronly, black, lady – smiled and, with an elaborate flourish, indicated that she would gladly yield.

"Yes?" Janet answered – before she'd gotten the mouthpiece into position.

"We're almost home, now, Mrs. Bolton. I want you to go back up Seven Mile … across Grand River. Retrace your steps. When you get to Telegraph Road, there'll be a *Marathon* gas station, on your right. Pull in there. There's a phone on the point … not by the station itself. But, right out … where the two sidewalks meet. We'll be watching!"

Janet ended the call, for a change! She slammed the receiver back onto the holder – then, nodded, gratefully, at the black woman. She hurried back to her car – at the other end of the mall! She was surprised that she'd still had the energy to sustain the half-walk/half-run!

Despite the fact that the trip was much further than the journey from Farmington to the mall, the trek seemed to go much more smoothly. Thank God! She would drive past the initial point of contact – the *Seven-Eleven* and past the strip plaza at Grand River!

Dear Lord! They sure have me chasing my tail!

As she approached Telegraph Road, Janet spotted the service station – and was gratified to see that no one was using the lone phone on the "point"! She wheeled in – and lurched to a halt, close by the payphone! And sat there! And sat! And sat!

Again, she was forced to knife her way through a beastly long wait! A half-hour turned into 45 minutes! By then, Janet was beside herself!

Dear Lord! What could've gone wrong? What could be wrong now? Oh, Patti! My poor, dear, sweet, little Patti!

Fifty-five minutes passed! An hour! Sixty-five minutes! Janet continued to sit in harried wait! Her white-knuckled grip was just as tightly clamped onto the steering wheel, as when she'd rolled to a stop at the gas station.

Then, the phone rang! Finally! She banged her head on the top of the doorway of the Maverick – as she burst out of the car! In three giant steps, she was at the phone!

"Yes!" she shouted into the receiver. "Yes, damn you! Yes? What do you want me to do now?"

"Janet? Janet ... are you all right?"

It was <u>Steve's</u> voice!

FIFTEEN

"Steve! **Dear Lord! Where are** you? Where's Patti? Is she ... is she ... ?"

"She's fine, Janet! Fine! She's fine! Safe and sound!"

"Did they ... did she ... get ... did she get ... get <u>hurt</u>?"

"No! She's fine! We've had her for awhile! We just weren't able to get our hands on her, before that SOB. sent you on that wild goose chase! Long story! Look! You're going to have to keep talking to me for a couple minutes anyway. You're being watched ... and it'll probably be another two or three minutes before we can get there to nab the guy! He's the only one left. So, gesticulate a lot ... and act like you're going out of your tree!"

"I don't have to act! Let me tell you ... ! Oh! There's ... it must be a police car! It's pulling up in the lot of the furniture store ... across the street!"

"Maroon Oldsmobile?"

"Yes! Well, a maroon <u>something</u>!"

"They heading for a cream-colored Mercury?"

"Yes! I guess it's a Mercury! My God! They ... they went and they ... they pulled the guy out of the car! He landed on his fanny! Right on the concrete!"

"Not too gentle, hah? Do you recognize anyone over there?"

"No! Well, wait a minute! It's too far to ... ! Just a minute! Isn't that the ... that deputy? The one from Texas?"

"None other!"

"He's being a little ... well, a little rougher ... than the other officers!"

Steve laughed. "I don't wonder. Mostly, it's because he hasn't slept in almost three days! He's worked harder on this thing ... not the kidnapping, necessarily, but on this whole thing ... worked harder on it than anyone else. Than any of the rest of us, let me tell you."

"Well, they've kind of thrown that guy into the police car ... that maroon one!

"Okay! Good! Now, can you drive home? Do you want me to come and get you? Pick you up?"

"No! No. No, the sooner I can get to see my Patti, the better I'll feel!"

<<>>

She hung up – and hurried to her car! As she backed up – to turn around – the Oldsmobile pulled into the station's driveway and stopped next to her battered Maverick. Deputy Claiborne rolled down the window in the rear door. Janet's window was already open.

"Howdy, Miz. Bolton," the man from Fort Worth greeted her. "Had a bit of excitement there for awhile. But, it's all right ... everything's all right ... now! Steve's been tellin' me just how well things been goin' for you. Glad to hear it. Couldn't happen to a nicer lady. No ways!"

"Why, thank you. It's ... it's nice to see you again. Especially under circumstances like these. Dear Lord, it certainly could've been far <u>worse</u>! I shudder when I think of how ... "

Claiborne grinned. "You remember my askin' you ... back at that wonderful laundry ... about two fellas? One of 'em's name was Pierce Hawkins? The other was a guy named Willard Culp? You remember that, don'tcha. Well, may I present Mister Hawkins! He and Culp ... and a couple or three other bad guys ... they were all behind this terrible thing with your little girl."

All of a sudden, Janet was overcome by a terrible, hollow, sinking, feeling!

"But ... but ... " Her voice seemed to have vacated her body. "But, Steve ... Steve said that ... he told me that ... he said that Patti was all <u>right</u>. Said that she was <u>fine</u>! That she hadn't been <u>hurt</u>! Or ... or ... or <u>assaulted</u>!"

"That's right, Miz Bolton! She's <u>fine</u>! But, for that south-end-of-a-horse-headin'-north to go ahead and pull such a thing ... to take that fine little girl ... it's a really terrible thing! Terrible, terrible, terrible thing! If I had my way, we'd head on out to the nearest meadow ... and throw the rope over a branch! Do 'er right now! Hang the whole lot of 'em! We're too easy on the bad guys, nowadays!"

It took a few seconds for Claiborne's "south-end-of-a-horse-headin'-north" remark to sink in. Janet smiled – broadly – at the deputy, as the Olds backed away and headed out onto the street. She pulled out behind the police vehicle – but, made no attempt to keep up with it.

<<>>

Fifteen minutes later, the Maverick peeled into the Bolton driveway! Janet was out of the car in a flash! Patti dashed out of the house – to greet her mother! They came together on the front lawn – in a monumental hug!

"Oh, Patti! Patti, Patti, Patti! My little Patti! My little baby! Are you all right, Baby?"

"Yeah. I'm ... I'm fine! A little rattled ... even yet! But, yeah! I'm fine!"

"They ... they didn't ... they didn't ... didn't do anything ... to you, did they?"

"No, Mother. Really. I'm fine. Well, maybe not fine, exactly. It was ... oh, God ... a terrible experience. But, no. They didn't hurt me. They didn't try any ... any ... any funny stuff! I was ... they took me out ... out to a lake somewhere. I had my own room, even ... and no one ever tried to come in! Nothing like that! That sort of told me that ... if I behaved myself ... I'd probably be all right. They kept telling me that. That I'd be all right. That all I had to do ... was to behave myself. They said that they ... that they ... they wouldn't hurt me. So ... I just behaved myself."

Janet pulled her daughter close again – and began to weep.

Barbara and Steve – inside the house – gave the two a few minutes of "privacy", then, both rushed out to greet Janet! The latter's knees were becoming more and more wobbly – as possible horrible scenario after possible horrible scenario continued to batter her all-too-vivid imagination!

Steve's steadying hand felt so welcome on her arm – as he led her inside.

Barbara had prepared a pot of coffee! Once they were all seated at the dining room table, Steve explained what had taken place:

"You remember," he began, "about the time you went to Chicago? I was involved in a super-secret caper?"

Janet nodded, absently – impatient for the detective to get to the "meat" of the kidnapping! And, more importantly, the rescue!

"Well," Steve explained, "there was a whole kaboodle of those guys around here. They were all involved in that same ring that Deputy Claiborne was investigating. The go-betweens were those guys ... Culp and Hawkins. We could never get anything on 'em. Nothing we could go to trial with. Not at that time, anyway. But, we shadowed 'em! Shadowed the hell out of 'em! For the better part of two weeks, they were under constant ... like, twenty-four hour ... surveillance! Got to where we couldn't continue to expend that much manpower on 'em. Not after a while, anyway. But, we did manage to snag eleven men ... eleven different men ... in that operation."

"The one that the deputy was working on?" asked Janet – suddenly less impatient.

"Yep. Got 'em all with the goods, too. But, Culp and Hawkins? They were just too damn smart! Well, at least, they were just too damn slippery!"

"You ... you <u>knew</u>?" gasped Janet. "You <u>knew</u> that those two were involved in Patti's being taken? Why ... why couldn't you go after them? Why <u>didn't</u> you go after them?"

"Well, knowing and proving ... they're two different things. As it happened, we did! We did go after those two! Went right after 'em!"

"How? Why did it take so long for me to get her back? Why did I wind up ... chasing my fanny ... chasing my fanny all over town ... this afternoon?"

"Culp ... the black guy ... he's got a cottage up at a little lake," replied Steve. "Up near Fenton ... about twenty-or-so miles from Flint. South of Flint. We knew that. We'd established that last week. Maybe the week before. I simply had a hunch that that'd be the place where they'd take Patti."

"You knew I'd be up there?" Patti was incredulous. "You <u>knew</u> that?"

"That's right, Darlin'," affirmed Steve. "Well, we didn't actually <u>know</u> it. Not for sure. But, we'd had that place staked out from … I don't know … from maybe two or two-thirty, last night. From then on! From just a few minutes after Goyette and I were able to compare notes … and get hold of a few people."

"Then, why … why didn't you go in and get her, for God's sakes?" fumed Janet.

"Well, like I said, we didn't know … <u>couldn't</u> know, not for sure … that that's where she was. Even if we woke some judge up … in the middle of the night … he'd never hold still for us breaking down the door. Not on just on some kind of a hunch, anyway. Besides, we didn't know how many bad guys were in there! We didn't know exactly where they'd have Patti. If the creeps had her tied up … to a chair in the middle of the room, or something … that'd be a whole lot different, than if she was asleep in some separate bedroom. In some room … where no one was keeping an eye on her."

Janet experienced a massive, head-to-toe, shudder – as Steve spoke of the possibility of her daughter being tied to a chair!

"The lights were all out, when we got there," Steve continued. "There wasn't any point in raising a ruckus! Not at that point! The 'Big O' snuck up to the cottage … and, using a glass cutter, he cut out a little corner of one of the windows on the back porch."

"'The Big O'?" asked Barbara.

"Goyette. Oscar Goyette. The Livonia inspector. That's what they call him. 'The Big O'."

"You were out there then?" asked Patti. "Right outside? Last night?"

"Yeah, pretty much. I'm the one who led everybody … led the good guys … out there. It was Goyette, though, who was in charge. He went and slid a tiny microphone in … where he'd cut out the piece of the window. All we could hear was a whole lot of snoring. This was at … like … three-fifteen or three-thirty. I decided to come back in here … look after your mother. I knew that you were in the best of hands out there. 'The Big O' was out there … for all that time. All night … and well into today."

"Why didn't you tell me ... when you got back in ... that Patti was all right," grumped Janet. "Tell me ... so that I wasn't crawling up the walls?"

"Couldn't! I didn't actually <u>know</u> that. Not for a fact. Couldn't <u>promise</u> you that she was there. Never heard her in there. Never heard her ... or any of the kidnappers ... say anything. Just a whole bunch of snoring! I couldn't tell you ... tell you for certain ... that she was there! Not if I didn't actually know it, f'heaven's sakes. I kept trying to reassure you ... as much as possible ... when I kept telling you that we had good leads. Iron-clad leads. I'm sorry, Janet ... but, that was the best I could do."

"Yes ... but, still ... "

"Janet, Listen. We couldn't play it any other way. I couldn't! They couldn't! I knew that it was going to be holy hell for you ... but, I also felt certain that, once you got your dear, sweet, wonderful, beautiful daughter back ... "

"C'mon, Steve," laughed Patti. "Even <u>I'm</u> not going to buy that."

"Well," responded Steve, "we didn't actually know <u>anything</u>! Not for sure! Not for certain. We couldn't even tell ... for sure ... how many guys were in there. There were three cars in the yard, behind the cottage. But, that could mean eighteen people ... though we doubted that. We had, like, six or eight cops out there ... at all times. Most of 'em came from the Michigan State Police command in Brighton. By the time the people in the cottage finally started to stir ... in the morning, this morning ... Goyette and the state cops had pretty well determined that Culp was the one who was going to have you chase your fanny ... as you so beautifully put it. We were going to try and follow him."

"Well, why didn't you?" asked Janet.

"Turned out that he wasn't at the cottage. I wasn't there, at the time.. Neither was Claiborne. And none of the guys out there knew his voice. We tried to follow ... they tried to follow ... everybody. Follow everyone. But, there were only two guys ... two bad guys ... that left early in the morning. They were in one car!"

"Well, what happened?" Janet was back to being impatient.

"Well, the cop who was following these guys ... he lost 'em! Somewhere around Milford! Bad break there! Turned out that they were the ones that wound up taking turns following you all over hell's half acre. They'd split up, after they'd gotten into town, obviously. One of 'em picked up another car. The other one was Hawkins. He was in that Mercury. The rest of 'em kept Patti out there … for a good while, after the first two took off. We decided not to go in after her. From what we were able to hear … over Goyette's handy-dandy little mike … we determined that she was safe. We were certain that … eventually … they'd have to move her from the cottage. That they'd have to move her somewhere else."

"Why didn't they just go ahead and arrest the first two?" demanded Janet. "The ones who chased me all over town? Arrest 'em right then and there? On the spot? That way, they wouldn't have lost the officer who was trying to … "

"For openers, nobody knew <u>what</u> they were up to. Didn't know … not at that point … that they were going to send you racing from pillar to post! For another thing, we didn't know where Culp was."

"How did you find Culp?" asked Barbara.

"Process of elimination, My Good Lady. I'd followed that creep … for weeks … to a whole lot of different places. Just got out the ol' notebook … and started hitting all those places. He used to hang out in a bar … on Michigan Avenue, right near Inkster Road. That's where the slimebucket hung out most of the time. So, I went there first thing. That's where I found him! In the office! He had dozens of phone numbers! Payphone numbers! The ones where they were going to be chasing and calling your dear old mudder. Fortunately, the schmuck had the locations written down! I just started calling 'em … until I got hold of your mother. Took three calls."

"Where … where was Patti, all this time," asked the still-shaken Janet.

"I was all right, Mom," advised Patti.

"There were," explained Steve, "two guys left out at the cottage, with Patti. We waited for 'em to come out. They had Patti between 'em. But, hell, we had 'em surrounded! They weren't going to do something stupid!"

"Were … were you there?" Janet's exuberance failed to hide the fatigue in her voice.

"He sure was, Mom," answered Patti. "Was I ever glad to see him!"

"Once I'd made sure that Patti was safe," continued Steve, "I set about tracking down Culp! Goyette was the one who brought her home." He gazed directly at Patti. "Unfortunately," he went on, "I wasn't able to lay my grimy little lunch hooks on him … on Culp … on our esteemed Mister Culp. Not until well after he'd put your mother through all kinds of hell!"

"I don't think I was ever so glad … in my life … to hear someone's voice," said Janet. "Not as happy as when I heard yours. Well, outside of maybe hearing Patti's. Why did it take so long for you to reach me? I was dying a thousand deaths … waiting for that damn phone to ring!"

"Well, we didn't have Hawkins in tow either. I'd gotten ahold of Deputy Claiborne … and he showed up at the Inkster Police station. About the time I got there with Culp. Culp wasn't talking to me. But, Claiborne has a … well, he has a way … with guys like that. Took him into one of the interrogation rooms … to … ah … reason with him!"

"He has a way? A way to reason with him?" Janet was totally confused. "What do you mean … he has a way? How was it that Deputy Claiborne was able to reason with him, when you … ?"

"You remember when you told me … over the phone … how he'd pulled that guy out of the Mercury? How he'd pulled Hawkins out of the Mercury? You remember telling me how the guy had landed on his butt? Well, ol' Claiborne was about as … as kind and gentle … with Culp as he was with Hawkins! Culp finally decided to cooperate. Told us where Hawkins was. Well, he told us what he was doing, anyway. At that point, it was just a matter of us getting to him … which we finally did. Across the street from that fabled, storied, *Marathon* station."

"Isn't there … I mean, couldn't he … Mister Claiborne … couldn't he get in trouble? Bad trouble? I mean … for the way he … he would've handled … Culp and Hawkins?"

"I didn't see a thing," replied Steve, with a big grin. "Neither did anyone at the Inkster station. Besides, he'll be out of here … in a matter of hours. I can't really see anyone bothering him … down in Fort Worth. The main thing is that we got Patti back … in reasonably good shape … and we managed to snarf up the sainted Mister Culp and the wondrous Mister Hawkins! Those two schmucks were driving all of us up the wall! Especially Claiborne. Listen, he was a man on a mission. He'd worked on this thing for months and months and months! So, he really didn't have a whole lot of charity in his heart. Not for any of those folks."

"Steve," said Janet. "I'll never be able to thank you enough ... never be able to repay you ... for bringing me back my little girl."

"Oh, <u>Mother</u>! Really!" exclaimed Patti. "Your little girl?"

SIXTEEN

At eleven-fifteen that night, Janet's eyes snapped open. It was unlike any other experience in her life. It took her fully fifteen or twenty seconds to figure out where she was! In her own bed!

Earlier, once she'd "come all the way down" – after having dealt with the fact of Patti's kidnapping and safe return, and after having done her best to cope with the many horrible possibilities which could have come from the terrifying sequence of events – she had invited Steve to stay for supper. He'd declined – citing her degree of exhaustion – suggesting that, instead, she grab some shut-eye. Janet hadn't argued with him. Six o'clock had found her crawling under the sheets – and drifting, immediately, into the arms of Morpheus.

She seemed not to have dreamed at all – at first. However, as the hours had ticked by, she'd found herself immersed in a montage of almost-hallucinations – running the gamut from the insipid to the frightening and back to the just plain stupid. Then, all at once, she was awake! Groping for her bearings, in the darkened room!

She was haunted by snatches of one especially-disconcerting dream, wherein she and Jeremy Bloodworth were attempting to close a huge window – one which was easily ten or twelve times the size of a normal sash. One which had no wall surrounding it. On the other side was Steve – striving mightily to get in! To crawl through the surreal opening! Janet and Jeremy were doing their best to close the detective out! Jeremy had seemed to be costumed in the striped sweater and ratty pants which the character "Billy Bigelow" had worn in *Carousel*. Steve appeared to be decked out as "Fred Graham" – the male lead in *Kiss Me Kate*. Why, in heaven's name, would Janet be siding with Jeremy? What did it mean? What <u>could</u> it mean?

She shuddered.

In an effort to put the troubling dream behind her, Janet's mind flashed back to Saturday night – at Anne's apartment. She found herself intrigued with what might have happened after she'd left the trio – in her sister's living room. What a positively stupid line of thought. Here she'd just finished groping with the most traumatic crisis in her entire life! And she was hung up on some stupid, fly-by-night, situation with three – yes, three – very shallow people! It sent a shiver down her spine to realize – and, ultimately, to acknowledge – Anne's complete lack of depth. Her almost-grifter-like mentality. She wondered, once more, whether Anne would've gone back to the bedroom with Jeremy. She'd like to think not. Still, after hearing how her sister had come upon her job, her apartment, and her car, Janet was reaching the sad realization that her sibling was capable of practically anything – to further her financial situation. <u>Practically</u> anything?

She scrunched her eyes shut – and clenched her fists – in a monumental attempt to force her thought processes onto a more intelligent – certainly a more worthy – level. Thinking about Anne and Jeremy and Mike was patently stupid! Especially in light of her traumatic experience with Patti's kidnapping!

Patti! Was Patti secure? Or had she simply dreamed of her daughter's safe return? Had she dreamed the entire sequence? Had it all been a total hallucination? Nothing – absolutely nothing – seemed to make sense any longer.

Janet bolted out of bed! It took fully three strides before she noted that she was naked! That was another thing: Why had she, all of a sudden, taken to sleeping in the nude lately? She hurried to her closet and grabbed her robe. Donning the wrap, she ran out into the hallway. Then, she brought herself to an abrupt halt – just outside her daughters' room! Slowly, carefully, she inched the door open! Her eyes searched – frantically – for Patti's bed! She practically filled the hallway with the gush! Her sigh of great relief! Safe and sound! As were her other two daughters!

Thank God!

<<>>

Janet returned to her room, shucked herself out of her robe – and crawled back into bed. Snuggling down into the soft mattress – and pulling the covers up over her shoulders – she looked forward to dropping back off into a nice, gentle, peaceful, sleep.

Good try! Just as she seemed to be crossing over the abyss – into the welcome chasm of darkness and peace, once more – the frightening image of that damn oversized window surged into view once again! Looking larger – and more foreboding – than before! This should not be! A dream, she could understand. But, she was still awake. Maybe not wide awake – but, awake nonetheless. And there was Steve – still in his "Fred Graham" mode! But, he was smaller! Much smaller! Then, he disappeared altogether!

Startled awake again, Janet began to toss and turn. Sleep became a taunting, elusive, now-you-see-it-now-you-don't, commodity! The more she tried to relax, of course, the more tense she became. Finally, she looked over at the big green digits on the clock/radio: Twelve-thirty!

She arose, once again and – clad, once more, in her robe – made her way downstairs. After brewing a cup of tea, she seated herself at the dining room table – and, as had happened so many times before, did her best to immerse herself in *The Detroit Free Press*. It was, of course, a losing proposition. She'd "read" three articles. Nothing, as usual, had sunk in.

Dear Lord! I'm really becoming a basket case! Damn! Now I'm even hearing people knocking!

Actually, she was not hallucinating – although it took three series of raps for her to realize that fact! Someone actually was knocking on her front door!

Oh, wonderful! Now who the hell can that be? At this hour?

She was unsure whether she should answer. On the other hand, if she didn't, and it was a "bad guy". he'd simply come in anyway. He'd get into the house one way or another – and "get" her! Arising, she walked slowly – almost stealthily – into the living room. Then, down into the vestibule. Looking through the peephole, she was unable to determine who was standing, so stoically, on the front porch. Now why was that not such a big surprise?

Then, all of a sudden, she <u>did</u> recognize her midnight visitor! Steve had illuminated his face – with his trusty flashlight! Janet threw open the door!

"Steve! What on earth are you … ?"

"Couldn't sleep. Can't sleep. Was hoping you couldn't either. May I come in?"

"Well, yes. Of course. But, it's …. "

He entered – and closed the door behind him. Then, he followed her into the dining room.

"About all I can offer is a cup of tea," she said, tentatively. "Maybe scramble you up an egg or two."

"No. Tea's fine. It'll just hit the spot."

He was right behind her – as she walked into the illuminated-by-her-"eternal-flame"-kitchen. She cranked some fire under the monster teakettle. Despite the fact that she had her back to him, Janet could feel his presence! Mere inches away! It was almost as though the scene was part of a cartoon. A whimsical drawing – wherein the figures were stationary! Stiff! Yet, imaginary, dot-connected, arms reached out for one another!

Janet turned to face him. Looking up into his eyes, she couldn't fail to see the longing – the hunger – in them. The eyes! Truly, they <u>were</u> the "windows of the soul"! She supposed that whoever had come up with that beautiful saying had positively known what he or she was talking about. She couldn't afford, though, to become entangled with this man. Not right at that moment. She was, after all, naked beneath her robe.

She ducked around him – to hurry to the cupboard, on the other side of the room.

Pulling out a mug, she placed it on the counter, close by the door to the dining room. Then, picking up the canister from the drain-board, she produced a tea bag. Placing the bag in the cup, she returned to the stove. Steve had not moved!

She placed the cup on the stove – just as the kettle began to spout forth a stream of steam! Shutting the burner off, she picked up the gurgling steel pot – and filled the cup.

"Well," she observed, returning the cumbersome kettle to the stove, "there it is. For better or for worse."

"Janet," he rasped, not moving. "Janet, I'm on the horns of a dilemma."

"Do people still say that?"

"The old bromides are the best," he replied, with a half-smile. "Let me ask you this: Do you still feel like you can't believe me? That I had nothing to do with those damn pictures? Do you still feel as though I'm the man in those crappy pictures?"

"Steve ... look. I ... I don't know what to think. I'd more or less forgotten about them. Well, not really ... but, after what happened with Patti, I guess that the stupid pictures kind of lost their ... their significance. Found out there ... for sure ... are more important things. Significantly more important things ... than some damn photographs."

"But, you do still think that I was the one involved in that little orgy?"

"It's ... it's not that important. Not right now. I ... look, you're a grown man. A free man. I have no hold on you. You've made no commitment to me. I have no right to expect you to live a ... well, a ... a virginal life. It was just that ... after hearing you tell me about how you'd been ... how you'd lived, since your wife and your daughter ... I was kind of ... well ... I was terribly upset. Now, though, let's just say that ... after the thing with Patti ... I've got a better ... a more even handle, I guess ... on what my priorities should be. I had no right to get so upset over ... "

"It may sound kind of perverted for me to tell you this ... but, I'm glad to hear you say these things. I'm glad that you'd seemed to forgive me. Kinda sorta forgive me, anyway. Forgive me, that is ... even if I'd been the clown in those ... "

"I didn't say I <u>forgave</u> you, Steve. For one thing, there's nothing to forgive. I have absolutely no hold on you. You're free to do whatever it is that ... "

"Well, I'd really like it ... if you <u>did</u> have a hold on me. But, that's a whole different conversation. Would it make you feel better ... if you could be <u>assured</u> that I'm not the dipstick in those photos? That it wasn't <u>me</u>? That the scumbag who you were seeing ... that you thought you were seeing ... was <u>not</u> me?"

"It's not that big a … well … yes. I guess maybe I would. But, listen. There's no need to … "

"I have a way of proving to you … proving to you that … that I'm not the guy."

"How is it that you now … all of a sudden … have proof?" she asked, stiffly. Her voice had taken on an icy – a terribly distant – quality.

"It's not all of a sudden, Janet," he assured. "I've always had the proof. For one thing, you never gave me the chance to show you the incontrovertible evidence. Number two, I'm not sure whether I've got the moxie to show it to you, anyway. Even now."

"Then … don't."

"You're not helping."

She was completely bemused. "Look, Steve," her voice still heavily stilted, "I have no idea what you're talking about. I haven't the foggiest inkling … of what you're leading up to. Can't imagine where this is all going. Not the faintest clue."

He placed his hands on her shoulders – holding her at arm's length. "Can you shut the door to the dining room?" he asked.

"Why … why, I guess so." Hesitantly, she closed the door. Then, she turned to face him. "There," she said. "Now, what's going on?"

He gazed at her "eternal flame". Gazed at it – intensely. "This," he assured her, "is going to be … well, it's going to be … awfully off the wall, Janet. Please … I beg you, please … bear with me. Please wait till I produce my … my proof. My evidence. Please don't do anything. Please don't say anything. If you never indulge me again … never indulge me in any fashion … please indulge me this one time. Just this one time. Please! This is … well, it's … it's very difficult for me."

"Steve … look, Steve. I'm at a total loss. Whatever are you talking about?"

"Just stand there," he rasped. "Don't move. Don't say anything. Please!" He hesitated – then, repeated, "Please!".

She nodded, absently. He turned his back to her – and began to unbuckle his belt. Hearing the unmistakable sound of the belt coming loose – then, the equally-obvious sound of a zipper being undone, she clenched her fists!

In a voice which had risen an octave, she asked, "Steve? Steve, what on earth are you doing?"

"Please! Please ... just ... just give me thirty seconds. Everything'll be fine! I assure you of that!"

What she feared was about to happen – happened! Steve pushed his trousers and undershorts down to mid-thigh! His shirt tail covered his derriere.

"Steve! I don't like this! I don't understand it ... and I certainly don't like it!"

"Please, Janet! If you'll just take a look ... just this once, take a look ... at my butt! If you'll take just one look ... you'll see why that idiot in the pictures ... you'll see that he <u>couldn't</u> have been me."

"Steve this is ... "

He raised his shirt tail! Janet's first impulse was to close her eyes! Slam them shut! Hold them scrunched closed – as tightly as possible. For as long as possible! She'd not seen a man unclothed! Not since Jim had left! She couldn't imagine what had possessed Steve! Still, she couldn't pry her eyes away from his uncovered, right buttock! He exhibited a God-awful mark! A shriveled, almost-round, scar! Slightly larger than a silver dollar! It had obviously decorated that cheek – for some years!

"You see, Janet," he said, peering over his right shoulder at her, "it couldn't have been me. Seven or eight years ago, I got into this knock-down, drag-out, fight! The bad guy ... well, he landed a haymaker! The lights went out! I fell back onto this metal casing! And ... as you can see ... it left me with this little decoration! Now, the guy in the picture ... he had a fanny that was smooth as a baby's kazockus! Couldn't possibly have been me!"

At that moment, Barbara walked into the kitchen – clad only in Baby Doll pajamas!

"Oh!" she gasped – and turned to leave!

Steve made himself presentable – with great haste! Janet, put her hand on her daughter's arm!

"Barb," she blurted. "It's not what it looks like."

Barbara smiled and – once assured that Steve had become a model of decorum, turned to face him.

"Look," she stated. "You guys don't have to explain anything. Not to me ... not to anybody. You're a grown man ... and my mother's an adult woman. I'm just sorry that I had to come barging in the way I did. I was just a little worried about my mother. Sorry 'bout that."

Then – suddenly becoming aware of her own immodest attire, the young woman beat a hasty retreat – hurrying back upstairs to her room! Steve looked at Janet – sheepishly.

"I'm sorry," he said. "It didn't occur to me that anyone would ... would ... "

Janet lowered her eyes.

"It's ... okay," she assured. "Poor Barb. She's been through the mill for years. She's had to grow up so fast ... from about ten minutes after her father left. I don't guess there's much could bowl her over." She sighed deeply. "I don't know," she said. "I really don't know. I guess that my major frustration ... my really big disappointment ... is that I couldn't have done better for her. Done better by her. Couldn't have done better ... for all of them. For each and every one of them."

Steve took her in his arms.

"Hush," he soothed. "Look all about you. Look at this house. This ain't no bad place to live. You haven't done badly. Not badly at all. There's zillions of kids who'd give four fingers and their left ear ... to live in a snazzy place like this."

"It's not snazzy ... and you know it. No, I wasn't talking about the house. Well, not necessarily, anyway. I was talking ... mostly, I guess ... about the lack of a father figure. Especially for the boys. But, you know, for the girls too, there being something special between daddies and daughters ... as you so accurately put it."

"Well, you know, there's one way of remedying that."

"Steve. This is no place to propose. Not the place ... or the time."

"Why not? Beats hell out of the *La Brae Tar Pits*, or someplace."

"You know what I mean. Steve ... look It's been a hellish day. A hellish couple of days. I don't think either one of us can really ... "

His lips silenced her! She clung to him! She didn't want to! Lord knew – she didn't want to! But, her mouth responded to his kiss – in almost-fevered desperation! His hands worked their way between their bodies – and, in an efficiency which surprised the both of them, he unfastened the knot in the sash, holding her robe closed! As he spread the chenille apart and slid his hands inside – caressing her bottom – she pressed her flesh up close against him! He melded their bodies even more closely together – by clamping a large hand onto each soft, milk-white, mound of her behind, and pulling her even more tightly to him! His obvious urgency was shooting super-charged bolts of electricity through her! Voltage – high voltage! Terribly high voltage! How could she cope with it? Then, he broke the kiss, and gently pushed her back! His eyes devoured her sumptuous breasts – jutting proudly, firmly, toward him!

"My God," he wheezed. "I'd almost forgotten how beautiful those are! How beautiful you are!"

Bending forward, he teased first one lush pink nipple – then the other – with his tongue! They'd long since become erect! He dropped, slowly, softly, to his knees – pressing his lips up against her abdomen! Then, snail-like, he began an esoteric trek with his tongue – from the clefts of her breasts downward over her navel. His hands kneaded the soft, pliable, surface of her bottom! She'd begun to writhe! She pressed his face tightly to her suddenly-chilled flesh! His tongue – having done its duty at her navel – resumed its path downward! It was too much!

"Steve! Steve," she rasped, "we can't do this! Not here! Come … up to the bedroom!"

He regained his feet! Then, he picked her up! Using her derriere to push open the door to the dining room, he carried her upstairs! Janet was semi-conscious of the fact that her robe was dangling – half off her body! Especially when Steve practically tripped over the wrap – on his way up the stairs! Fortunately, none of her children had witnessed her practically-nude trip to her bedroom! As had happened downstairs, he pressed her behind up against the bedroom door – and, once it had opened, he padded across to the bed! There, he gently laid her down!

Practically ripping his clothing from his frame, he hurried to the door – and closed it! Returning to the bed, he beheld the surprisingly-calm Janet – her robe spread wide open! Her demeanor was surprising to her, at any rate.

"You … you're so beautiful!" His voice sounded like a rusty file. "You're so beautiful … so very, very, very, beautiful! Oh, Janet! Janet, I love you! I love you … love you so much! So very much! Oh, just so, so, so, so, much!"

As they were joined in the frenzied act of love, Janet was overtaken by a run-away kaleidoscope of emotions! Of newly-discovered feelings! Of heretofore untapped depths of arousal – the likes of which she'd never known before! Had never really known existed!

<u>This must be real</u>! <u>This must be right</u>!

SEVENTEEN

The following day, Monday, the phone rang at the Bolton house. It was 6:15 PM – and Barbara, on her way though the living room, picked up the receiver.

"Hello?"

"Barbara. What're you doing home?"

"I live here, Aunt Anne."

"That's not what I mean ... and you know it. Don't you work tonight?"

"Well, if anyone's conducting a survey, I was just on my way out the door."

"Same old Barb. When are you going to show me some respect, Young Lady?"

"As soon as you ... " Barbara let her voice drift off.

"Look," an exasperated Anne demanded, finally, "I don't have time for this. Put your mother on."

"My mother isn't home, Aunt Anne."

"Where is she?"

"She's out. Steve took her out to eat."

"Are you sure she's not there? I wanted to talk to her about the thing with Patti. It was all over the eleven o'clock news last night. All over this morning's newscasts. Ye Gods! Why didn't someone tell me what was going on?"

"Things have been very ... very hectic around here, Aunt Anne. By the time we got Patti back, my mother was exhausted. Went to bed at something like six o'clock, last night. She must've needed the sleep. She was late getting up this morning. Really had to hustle to get to work on time. She's in kind of a new situation there, you know."

"Yes. Well, I tried to call her several times today and she couldn't … or wouldn't … come to the phone. You're sure, now, that she's not there? Are you sure that she's not avoiding me?"

"I'm not used to having people question what I'm saying, Aunt Anne. If she was here, and she was avoiding you … well, I don't really know what I'd do. But, she's not here. And she's not avoiding you. At least, to the best of my knowledge. She told me that her day was very, very hectic. I'm sure that she didn't want to be distracted, you know, by personal calls or anything. She told me that the kidnapping was simply all anyone wanted to talk about, at the office."

"You … you're sure, then, that she's not avoiding me?"

"Aunt Anne, why on earth would she want to avoid you?"

"She … she didn't tell you? About the other night?"

"What other night?"

"Saturday night. She and Jeremy … they double-dated with Mike and me."

"Oh. I'd really forgotten about that. Mother's never mentioned it. Of course, from the time she got home … well, things were in such a hellish frenzy around here. We really didn't have time to discuss much of anything! Except the thing with poor Patti, of course."

"How is she?"

"Who? Patti?"

"Yes. It must've been quite … quite … quite harrowing."

"You bet it was. But, she went through it like a trouper. And now? She's a celebrity. Took her almost two hours to get home from school. Everyone in the world wanted to know about it." Barbara laughed, quietly. "She's lapping it up," she continued. "But, what about the other night? Why should my mother want to avoid you? What happened? She didn't get … uh … get hurt, did she?"

Anne's laugh was totally devoid of mirth. "Same old Barb. Always protecting your mother. You're not going to be able to protect her all your life, y'know."

"You act as if my mother is some kind of a feeble-minded imbecile, Aunt Anne." Barbara's words were close-cropped – each one almost like a verbal stiletto. "I don't have to protect my mother from anyone," she said, crisply. "In my life, my mother has protected me. She's protected me from hunger. She's protected me from having to sleep in the gutter, or something. She's seen to it that I have clothing. She's guided me."

"That's not the way most people see it."

"Then, they've got their head up you-know-where! My mother has raised me. She's seen to it that I have a pretty fair sense of values. I'm not protecting her from anybody or anything. You've got it all wrong, Aunt Anne. You've got the protector and the protectee ... got 'em completely backwards. My mother has been my friend. You ask Patti or Joanie ... and they'll tell you the same thing. Ask Robbie and Rickie. Go ahead and ask 'em sometime. Ask 'em who their best buddy is. It's your sister. So, get off my back, Aunt Anne. Get off my back with this protecting thing. You don't know what you're talking about ... with all due respect."

"Barbara! I'm not going to listen to this! Not one second longer!"

"So hang up. Just come off all this stuff ... all this crap about my mother being childlike ... and naïve. And dependent on me. Or anyone else! She's accepted her responsibilities, through the years. God-awful responsibilities. She's done as well in meeting them as anyone else could have. And better than most. If ... by you ... that's being childish and unsophisticated, then so be it."

The phone went dead in Barbara's hand. The young woman smiled – then, laughed out loud. She replaced the receiver – and hurried toward the front door.

<<>>

Shortly after ten o'clock the following morning, Steve phoned – to advise Janet that he'd be unable to keep their luncheon date.

"Another super-secret operation," he told her. "Going to be out of town, actually. Way out of town. That's all I can tell you at this exact moment. Just keep the faith ... and I'll call you when I get back. Hopefully, this weekend. I'll try and call you from time to time. But, I think it's going to wind up being one of those things where I'm going to be incommunicado, for all practical purposes."

Janet could feel her knuckles whiten! Her hand melded itself into the receiver! A queasy feeling overtook her. A terrible sensation! A feeling of God-awful foreboding! And it held her – firmly – in its iron-like talons!

The last time Steve had been "incommunicado", she'd found a group of X-rated snapshots in the glove box of his car. True, he'd denied that he'd been a part of the orgy depicted in the photographs. Actually, he <u>had</u> proven that it could not have been him in those despicable pictures. Then, suddenly, a smile crossed her lips. That would probably be the one time when a scar on the fanny could be considered a blessing. Hopefully, to two different parties. The smile disappeared as quickly as it had come, though – and she felt, once again, as though she might be the slightest bit sick at her stomach.

In point of fact, the truth was that Steve had proven – to his own satisfaction – that he could not have been the man in those dirty, rotten, lousy, horrible snapshots.

But, Janet had never really taken a close – really incisive – look at the buttocks of the man in the photos. Her rage had gotten in the way of a totally clinical look, for one thing. For another, she didn't have to inspect the *Polaroids* inch-by-inch to determine what they'd depicted! Even had she examined the man's bottom closely, the photographs were not large enough, to her way of thinking, to have clearly shown the scar! At least, she didn't believe they were! She probably would've needed a magnifying glass.

She thought back to Sunday night – where Steve had bared his backside. The entire episode had been quite traumatic to Janet – at least in retrospect. First of all, Barbara had walked in on them. Her daughter had assured her that it was "no big deal". But, one had to wonder. Didn't one?

Also in retrospect, it had been rather disconcerting when Steve had renewed his denial of having participated in the orgy. It had been the reopening of a troublesome sore. After his heroics of the day – his role in the safe return of Patti – Janet had been totally prepared to overlook a sexual adventure. One which, by all indications, would've taken place well before she'd ever met him. She'd felt that she was being quite magnanimous – in overlooking such a peccadillo. His bringing up the situation – and denying participation in it – had only served to take some of the luster off her gesture. Well, for a moment or two, anyway. She really had to admit that the encounter had turned out well. Had turned out <u>extremely</u> well! They'd wound up in her bed – making love – afterward. That had been wonderful! Had been more than wonderful! Never had she been so fulfilled by a man! Any man! Ever! Under any circumstance!

To add to the thickening plot, they'd returned to her room on Monday night – after having dined out. The result was every bit as enriching as had been the case the night before. As glorious as it had been that magnificent first time! That remarkable fact was, to Janet, even more significant.

And now? Now, here he was! The very next day! Telling her that he would be out of pocket! For days! He would be "incommunicado"! Was it possible that he'd already grown tired of her? Of the intimacy? That quickly? Had she been "too easy"? Had the "thrill of the <u>chase</u> – the thrill of the actual <u>conquest</u>" – now been removed? Had that been the motivating factor, all along? For the whole, entire, sequence?

"Janet?" Steve must've called her name three or four times. She'd completely lost track of the fact that she was still on the phone with him. Still talking to him. "Janet? Are you there? Are you all right?"

"Yeah … uh … yes. Yes, I'm … here."

"Is something … is anything … is there something wrong?"

"No. No, I was just … just thinking that … uh … I was just thinking that I wish you all the best … in whatever operation you're … ah … involved in. Involved with."

"Well, thank you," came his uneasy reply. "Are you sure that nothing's wrong? I mean …" he broke off the sentence. "Look, Janet … I can't <u>help</u> this. I really <u>can't</u>. Just came up this morning, it did. And I have absolutely nothing to say about it. I've … look … I've really got to go. There's no other way. Oh, they've got an appeals thing … sort of an arbitration board … but, no one ever wins at that game."

"No. That's all right. Go and … and do whatever it is that you … that you have to do. I'll look forward to seeing you this … this weekend? That is, of course, if you … if you can get back by then."

Once the connection had been broken, Steve held the receiver in his hand – for fully a minute. Was it his imagination? Or did smoke seem to be billowing from it? During that same minute, Janet was brushing the tears from her eyes – and setting about immersing herself in her new duties.

<<>>

The following day – Wednesday – Gloria Tapp invited Janet to lunch. When Janet declined, Gloria became more and more insistent. "I've got something to tell you," she persisted. "Something of the utmost urgency. I simply need to discuss it with you, Janet. Need to discuss it with you … only not here. Not in the office."

Hoping that her sigh of resignation wasn't as obvious as she feared it was, Janet agreed to "do lunch" with her coworker.

<<>>

Later that afternoon, ensconced in one of the back booths at one of the area's sandwich shops, Gloria came right to the point. "Janet," she began, "I just want you to know that I've been such an old … such an old poop!"

"An old … ? Gloria? What're you talking about?"

"Well, I've seen how you've been working your rear end off up there."

Gloria's statement tripped an alarm bell in Janet! She'd recalled what Peggy had told her about Gloria's penchant for trying to shoot down anyone she perceives as getting ahead. The "brown-nosing" syndrome. Terri had also made a few – more veiled – comments, along those same lines.

"Oh," Janet replied, "I don't really work my rear end off up there. I'm just so happy to have the job, that … well, I don't want them to even think about letting me go."

"I don't think that's anything you have to worry about, Janet. Not to worry."

"Dear Lord! I don't know what I'd ever do … where I could ever make it … if they were to … "

"No! Believe me when I tell you, Janet. You're working your rear end off. And I can only imagine how difficult it must've been … for all those years … raising your kids. God! All those kids! So many kids!"

"I'll tell you what, Gloria. Each and every one of those kids has been such a … such a complete and utter blessing … to me. I'm the luckiest woman in the history of the world … just to have had them." Then, thinking of Patti's abduction, she added, "And to … with God's help … have been able to keep them."

"Yeah," persisted Gloria, "With that thing over the weekend! God! Your own daughter … being kidnapped! My God! I'd have been a damn basket case!"

"Who told you that I wasn't?"

"No. No, you came through it with flying colors. As with everything else. I want you to know, Janet, … I want you to know that I admire the hell out of you."

The totally-unexpected comment had come out of left field. Especially – coming as it did – from Gloria. It left Janet totally flustered. Additionally, she'd had no idea where the strange – almost disjointed – conversation was leading. And she'd had no clue as to how to respond to the many compliments raining down upon her! Especially from the woman seated across from her! Equally perplexing was the reason for "doing lunch" in the first place. She was certain that Gloria's plea of urgency in getting together, had gone much deeper than simply complimenting Janet for "working her rear end off".

"Just admire the hell out of you," continued Gloria – without missing a beat. "That's why … it's the reason why … why I've got to … well, to … to come clean with you."

"Come clean with me? Come clean? Gloria, whatever are you talking about?"

"You know those … those pictures? Those photos that you found in Steve's glove compartment? When you were driving to Chicago?"

Janet was the picture of total mortification! "How … how did you know … how could you know … about those pictures? How could you possibly know?"

"Because I set the whole thing up! I'm the one who caused you all the trouble! That's why I'm telling you … telling you that I've got to, finally, come clean."

"Gloria … you've got me … I'm really … really confused."

"It was mostly Fletcher's doing. But, it couldn't have happened … not without my fiendish little hand being in there. Without my getting involved in the damn pie."

"Fletcher? Do you mean Fletcher Groome? Oh, you can't be meaning … "

"The same! Oh, Janet! I'm so ashamed! I've been sleeping with him … on and off … for the past four or five years. Maybe a little bit longer. I guess that I'd probably have a better shot at keeping him interested … if I'd drop forty-five or fifty pounds. But, I keep throwing myself at him. He's got money up the you-know-what! And … "

"Surely, that's not why you … uh … sleep with him."

Gloria sighed deeply. Before she could reply, the waiter set two mugs in front of them – and filled the trendy, decaled, containers with steaming, hot coffee.

"I keep thinking," muttered Gloria, once the man had withdrawn, "that I have really lofty motives. But, I'm only kidding myself. I've spent all my life … my whole damn life … looking for the easy way. Maybe the moralists are right. Maybe there is no easy way. But, that's beside the point." She sighed once more. "I guess," she groused, "I guess that I've pretty well made a career of trying to cultivate Fletcher … for whatever reason. He knows that all he has to do is to squiggle up an eyebrow … and I'm falling all over him. He knows that I'll do whatever he wants … whatever he tells me to do… no matter how reprehensible it might be. If he feels like a roll in the ol' hay, these days … and, of course, if there's no one else available … just give ol' Gloria a call! What the hell. She's easy! Rounded heels … and all such crap as that."

"Gloria, don't … "

"Let me finish! Let me get this off my chest! You can't imagine how many battles I've had to fight. I went and told Fletcher … about how you were borrowing Steve's car. He did the rest. Well, with a little help … from an ass of a nephew of his. The nephew … that piece of shit … he's even more rotten than I am."

"I … I still don't understand, Gloria. How could you know about my trip? Why would you alert Fletcher to it? Especially if it might've resulted in Fletcher and me getting together? And maybe even shutting you out? Shutting you out of his life … maybe forever? In theory, anyway. How could … ?"

Once again, the waiter appeared – and set their food in front of them. After he'd disappeared, once more, Gloria delivered herself of a self-conscious laugh. "First of all," she answered, "it made me a good sport, in his eyes. Fletcher likes good sports. Besides, I knew that you could never fall for him. Not for a creep like him. I know that his money had never meant a hill of beans to you. If you'd have been dazzled by all his wealth, you'd have glommed onto him a long time ago. I figured that ... no matter what ... you'd give him his walking papers."

"I still don't understand. Why should that ... why would that ... concern you?"

Well, I was hoping that, maybe then, the light bulb would flash on ... and he'd see that dear, sweet, lovable, old Gloria was the one reliable one. The only one on whom he could always depend. That maybe ... just maybe ... the damn light would flicker on."

"How did you know I was going to Chicago?"

"Don't you remember? I was in Terri's office ... when you were asking for time off. I was standing right there ... when she offered you an advance. Hell, she never offers me an advance. Ever! You were telling her that Steve was going to switch cars with you. I sat in on the whole conversation. Don't you remember? Well, maybe you don't. I know you were quite distraught at the time."

"Well ... Gloria! Where did those God-awful ... those horrible ... those damnable pictures come from? How did they ever get into Steve's glove box?"

"Fletcher has a million of 'em. More pictures ... just like those ... than you can shake a stick at. I didn't really see these pictures. Well, maybe I have ... at one time or another. God knows, he's done his best to show me as many of them as he can."

"Fletcher? He has ... has ... has ... ?"

"A million of 'em," nodded Gloria. "I really don't know which ones ... which of those masterpieces ... he'd had his nephew plant in Steve's car. Presumably, they were pictures where the guy must've looked a lot like Steve. As much as possible, anyway. Especially the ... uh ... lower part of his body."

"I guess so," sighed Janet. "That's about all they showed ... was the lower part."

"Well, Mister Groome has a virtually inexhaustible supply of faceless porn pictures. Snapshots. Eight-by-ten glossies. Movies ... your choice of eight or sixteen millimeter. He's even got some of those new-fangled videotapes. And God only knows what else."

"I ... I can't tell you ... tell you what an ... what an education this is."

"Yeah. Well, he got this scumbelly nephew of his to plant the pictures in the glove box ... and then to do something to the mechanism that holds the thing closed. The gismo that holds the door ... to where it won't fly open. Except that our friend Fletcher most certainly <u>wanted</u> the thing to fly open ... sometime during your long drive to Chicago. Worked, I guess. <u>Must</u> have! Must've worked ... like a charm."

Janet sat her fork down – with more clatter than she'd intended – and studied her luncheon companion. "You're damn right it worked," she seethed.

"Janet, listen. I know how feeble it must sound to you ... me trying to tell you how sorry I am and all."

Janet's scowl softened. After a minute or so, she placed her hand atop Gloria's right hand – and sighed, once again. Mightily.

"Oh," she muttered, "that's all right, Gloria. I guess I can't really blame you. But, Fletcher, now ... that's a whole n'other story. That miserable, no good ... "

"Yes, you can! You certainly can blame me. If I hadn't gotten a bee in my bonnet ... about trying to brown up to Fletcher ... the whole damn thing would never have happened. He slipped, too ... Fletcher did. Told me that the sleazeball kid ... when he planted the pictures ... the little S.O.B. stole Steve's credit cards! And, I think he mentioned something ... about some sort of a cassette, which was in the tape player. The little bastard! He took everything, I guess, that wasn't nailed down."

"That's ... why that's ... that's horrible! What did Fletcher propose to do about it? About the credit cards? Why, he could ... "

"Well, our friend Fletcher told me that he told the little schmuck to cut 'em up ... and throw 'em away. To be sure not to use 'em ... but, who knows if the kid followed orders."

"That's ... that's ... I just can't believe that Fletcher ... that he would stoop so low! So low, as to ... "

"Believe it! He would, Kid. In a heartbeat. He has. He does."

"Gloria? Has Fletcher ever said anything about ... about driving past my house?"

"Oh sure. Of course. He drives past ... all the time. At all hours of the day ... or night. I thought that ... at one time or another ... you would've seen him. You're his big conquest, you know. And ... listen to me, Janet ... once he gets his eye on something, he'll stop at nothing! He'll do whatever it takes ... to get whatever it is that he wants! Trust me! Trust me? That sounds really presumptuous ... since I'm the one who betrayed you."

<<>>

On Saturday afternoon, Janet was putting the finishing touches on the weekly – "really thorough" – cleaning of the kitchen. She was clad in a blue-and-white checked cotton top and a pair of royal-blue shorts which were probably a little too short – and definitely a little too tight. More than a little too tight. She was stashing the dust mop and three containers of detergent – when she heard the knock! Someone was at the front door! Could it be? Slamming the door of the broom closet, she hurried to answer!

It was! It was! It was <u>him</u>! It was <u>Steve</u>! She threw open the door! Within seconds he was standing in the tiny vestibule – holding her in his arms!

"Oh, Steve," she managed to rasp – once they'd come up for air. "Steve! Oh, Steve, Steve, Steve! I'm so glad to see you! So very glad! Was your stakeout ... or whatever it was ... was it dangerous? Did you catch whoever it was? Are you back? Back for good, I mean!"

"Hold on! One at a time! Sheeee! It really wasn't a stakeout. Not as such, anyway. Wound up with most of us going through silly-assed garbage cans ... looking for sinister stuff. No action at all. Glamorous as hell. Thrill a minute. No, there was no danger. I think we were able, though, to build a pretty good case against the head gazinks of this really big ... this really bad ... dope ring. They worked out of this building in Lansing. It was a kind of a spin-off of the clods who stole Patti."

"Patti? Good Lord! What will they ... ? Well, I hope they stay in jail till ... till hell freezes over! Till hell freezes over ... and maybe a decade longer Hope they rot in jail!"

"Well, they're not there ... yet. But, soon."

"But, you're ... you're back? For good?"

"Yeah," he answered, with a broad grin. "As 'for good' as any state cop ever is." Janet had never noticed the fact that his grin was so – so beautifully crooked. "Hoo boy," he expounded. "Are you a sight for sore eyes. Especially in those shorts … the ones you're almost wearing. Looks like you threw 'em on … and almost missed."

She did her best to nip the inevitable blush, in the bud – and, surprisingly, was moderately successful. "Oh," she responded, mustering as much bravado as possible, "just something I sprayed on."

"Did I ever tell you, Mrs. Bolton, that you've got a great butt?"

"I think so. You probably did. In fact, I'm sure you did. But, that was a really long time ago. A <u>really</u> long time."

"Well I herewith renew the statement. You gots a great fanny, Kid. And I speak with absolute, unmistakable, authority. I've had a couple of situations, y'know, where I was able to take inventory."

Janet lost the battle of the blush! She led him into the living room. Once they were seated on the sofa, he declined the offer of a cup of coffee – and pulled her up onto his lap. He kissed – and nipped – at her neck, as she wound her arms around him.

"Steve!" Her husky voice surprised her. "Steve! Oh, I'm just so glad to see you!"

She planted a rather soggy kiss on his forehead.

"Hey," he gasped. "I'd have to believe that. What brought all this on? Such affection! Did you … ? Aw, no. You couldn't have missed me that much!" He looked around – quickly, furtively – to determine if anyone was within earshot. Satisfying himself that no one lurked nearby, he continued: "Did Sunday night … or Monday night, for that matter … get you all <u>this</u> worked up? Get you all this hot and bothered?"

"You don't have to be so surreptitious," she advised him. "We're alone. I usually am on Saturday … when the cleaning's to be done. I can't complain, though. The kids go above and beyond the call … on every other day. And it's not like I was still in the sweating-for-dollars industry, at the laundry. Had to devote Sundays to the clean-up, fix-up, paint-up thing, back then. Of course, I usually had help. Still do the laundry on Sunday, though." She kissed him on his nose. "But," she went on, "to answer your question? Yes! Yes, yes, yes! The thought of our making love has me all a-twitter! Has <u>had</u> me all a-twitter … for the last day or two. Or three. Or four."

"Oh, good! All compliments gratefully accepted. How about we do a repeat performance? Maybe a refresher course?"

She laughed heartily – and pulled his head into her bosom.

"I'd love to," she answered. "But, we're not <u>that</u> alone. They'll be traipsing in and out from time to time. All of 'em. All the kids. Schlepping in and out ... constantly. You can depend on it."

Once again, they kissed – lip-to-lip. An incredibly tender exchange. The only sound was a radio playing – upstairs. And the subdued sound of Steve patting Janet's derriere. When the kiss was broken, she pulled his head, once more, to her breasts.

"No," she rasped, after 30 or 40 seconds. "I think the main reason I'm so glad that you're back is ... well ... it gives me a chance to say I'm sorry."

"Sorry? Sorry for what? What do you mean you're sorry? It's supposed to be carved in stone, somewhere, that love means that you don't gotta say you're sorry. Besides, you don't got nothin' to be sorry for. You're a wonderful woman! A great lady! And a remarkable lover! Tremendous! Stupendous! All those hokey adjectives!"

"You've got a one-track mind," she admonished – fighting to keep a goodly amount of seriousness in her voice. "No, what I'm talking about is ... I'm talking about those ... those God-awful pictures. The ones in the glove compartment."

"Oh, them. I'd thought that we'd pretty well settled the pictures thing. I would hope that you wouldn't give 'em another thought, Me Fair Beauty."

"Yes. Well, you see? I really <u>shouldn't</u> have given them another thought ... a long time ago. From the very first ... I shouldn't have given them another <u>thought</u>."

"No biggie," he responded – burrowing his head even more deeply into her chest.

"Not to you, maybe," she persisted. "But, they were to me."

"Were is past tense."

"Right. But, not so past tense ... as you may think."

He pulled his head back – and looked up into her eyes. The blue/green had always seemed so vibrant. At that moment, though, her eyes seemed rather faded! Almost colorless!

"What ... what do you mean by that?" The tone in his voice bespoke the puzzled look on his face. "What do you mean ... not as past tense as I think?"

"Well, until … until Wednesday, I still thought it probably <u>was</u> you in those pictures. I was willing to chalk 'em up … to an unattached, virile, good-looking, handsome man … one that I'd had no claim over, when the pictures were taken. Otherwise, I don't think I'd have gone to bed with you. Not once … let alone twice."

"Dammit!" He almost spat the exclamation. "I thought we'd cleared that whole thing up! Especially after I showed you my rear end! I can't tell you how … well, not degrading, actually … but, how … !" He eased his head back, softly – to where his right ear was resting on her bosom. Then, suddenly, he pulled it back – away from what had been the comforting warmth of her breasts. "And," he continued, "of course Barb … she'd have to come walking in. Right at that precise, damn, moment."

She yanked him back – and snuggled his head into her chest, once more. Then, she kissed the top of his head. "I know," she replied. "It seems almost funny … now," she answered.

He pulled back – yet another time. "No," he groused. "No, it doesn't. It sure doesn't seem funny to me. I was really quite upset, y'know. Quite disappointed … that you hadn't believed me in the first damn place. That you'd doubted me … when I'd <u>sworn</u> to you that I was <u>not</u> involved! Sworn on the memory of my <u>daughter</u>, for God's sakes! I'm as certain as I can be … just as sure as I'm sitting here … that I'd have damn well believed <u>you</u>, if the damn shoe would've been on the other damn foot."

Clearly, he was upset!

"Yes," she agreed. Her voice was barely audible. "I guess … I'm sure … that you <u>would've</u>. I'm … I'm sorry, Steve. I'm really and truly as sorry as … as I can be."

"Then, once I'd shown you my scar, I was positive that the whole shebang had been cleared up. Past tense!" It was as though he'd not heard her apology.

"Oh, Steve," she said, her voice still a wisp of what it normally was. "I didn't look … not that closely … at that guys' fanny. The guy in the pictures. I was upset … when I saw them! Damn upset! I most certainly wasn't going to go looking! Go looking to see how many of … or what kind of … scars he might have had on his fanny!"

"Well then, how'd you find out? How'd you prove to yourself ... erase all those damn doubts ... that it really wasn't me?"

"Gloria."

"Who?"

"Gloria. Gloria Tapp. At work. She finally 'fessed up. Said it was Fletcher Groome. He had his noodnick nephew put 'em in your car. Put the pictures in there."

"Fletcher's nephew? How did he know that you were ... ?"

"Gloria <u>finked</u>! To Fletcher! Told him ... that I was borrowing your car to go to Chicago. His nephew's got your credit cards, by the bye. Or, at least, he <u>did</u> have 'em. And he's probably got the *Kiss Me Kate* cassette."

"Why that ... that little sonofa ... "

"I agree! And I'm sorry, Steve. Really sorry that I doubted you."

"Yeah," he grumped. Then, his manner changed – and so did his voice. It became mock-serious. "Listen ... do you know what I ought to do to you?" he asked.

Janet was ecstatic that the tension seemed to have been broken! Finally! "Whazzat?" she asked. "What ought you do to me? Or can we speak of those things ... in mixed company?

"Do you remember *Kiss Me Kate*? What 'Fred Graham' did to 'Lilly Vanessi'?"

"What he did to her?" she responded. "What'd he do to her?" At that point, the light suddenly flashed on! It finally hit home that Steve was referring to the famous spanking scene. "Ohhhhh," she gushed. "C'mon, Steve! You ... you wouldn't!"

In his most stage-villainous voice – the tenor of which would've made *Snidely Whiplash* proud – he replied, "Wrong, Me Fair Beauty!"

In one move, Janet found herself no longer seated upon his lap! She was lying across it – staring at the carpet!

"Steve! Stop it! What do you think you're doing?"

"Three guesses! And let me tell you! It's a tempting target that you got there!"

"I'm sure it is! I wish now that I'd worn different shorts! Jeans maybe! Two or three pairs of 'em! Half my fanny's probably hanging out!"

"You're telling me? You're advising me of that fact? It's more than

<u>probably</u> hanging out! And a delightful-looking fanny it is, Me Fair Beauty."

"Steve, look. Really, it's … "

"No! I'm not going to let you up! Not till I've done what I intend to do."

"I'm afraid to ask what <u>that</u> is! Well, I guess I <u>know</u> what that is."

"Will you marry me?"

"Will I <u>what</u>? This is a hell of a position for us to be in … when you propose. I never really thought that you'd actually get down on one knee, you know. Not like in those schmaltzy old melodramas. But, then, I never figured it'd be like <u>this</u> either."

He laughed. "A <u>perfect</u> position for a proposal," he decreed. "If I don't get the answer I want, I can make an appeal! Directly to your … uh … more sensitive side."

He swatted her – lightly!

"That? That's my more sensitive side?"

Playfully, he swatted her again – with a little more "mustard"!

"It can get awfully damn sensitive," he advised. "A <u>lot</u> more sensitive! If I don't get the answer I want."

"I suppose there's something to be said for that school of thought. I'll marry you … but, on one condition."

"That I let you up? Unspanked?"

"No. If you really want to spank me … go ahead. I probably deserve it. No, the condition is that you propose to me. Propose to me properly. What you say is: 'Will you marry me … Fathead?'."

"You drive a hard bargain, Me Fair Beauty. Especially considering the position you're in. But, you've convinced me … smooth talker that you are. Put me right to sleep. All right, I'll play your silly little game. Ahem! Will you marry me … <u>Fathead</u>?"

"That's better! NO! No, I won't marry you!" He brought his hand down – firmly – cracking it loudly on her bottom! "Ouch," she yelped. "I'm not the <u>only</u> smooth talker, here. Yes! Yes, I'll marry you! I just had a sudden change of heart! Suddenly," she assured, as she reached back and rubbed her derriere, "I've decided that I want nothing more than to spend my life with you. You done talked me into it."

"Excellent choice, Me Fair Beauty. My dear, you've made me the happiest of men." The last was an over-emoted line from *Kiss Me Kate* – and he "hammed" it up as much as "Fred Graham" had.

He continued to hold her securely across his thighs – resting his right hand on her tingling behind. It was at that moment, of course, that Barbara walked in. It was becoming a habit – possibly a tradition. If the young woman was upset at the vision of her mother draped across Steve's lap, she didn't let on.

"I'm going upstairs and change, Mother," she advised. "I dropped Patti off at the playground. She said she's going to watch a ballgame … one that Robbie and Rickie have gotten themselves into. A pick-up game, I guess they call it. They'll walk home. I've got to get changed. Jimmy's got tickets to the Pistons game this afternoon. He's going to be here in fifteen or twenty minutes. Hi, Steve."

"Hi, Barb. It's good to see you again."

"Nice to see you too, Steve."

With that, she made her way upstairs.

"Why the hell don't we just sell tickets?" muttered Janet.

"Who's Jimmy?" he asked.

"Fella she met. Works at the pizzeria." Then, she hollered toward upstairs. "Barb? This Jimmy? What's his last name? Roundtree?"

"Yes," came the answer from the top floor. "Roundtree."

"I thought you said that he had a lot of hang-ups," mused Janet, still positioned across Steve's lap. Then, looking up at her newly-minted intended, she elaborated: "I didn't want her to get into any kind of serious relationship with him."

"It's just a basketball game, Mother," came the voice from upstairs. "It's not as though we're going on some moonlight cruise or something."

"I know. I guess I just … "

"I think that he probably figures that, with sixteen- or eighteen-thousand people around … how-ever-many people go to Pistons games … that there's not much chance of a one-one-one deal with someone."

"I should've known better," said Janet with a sigh. "You're always in control."

"Not always," replied the voice from upstairs. "I'm proud that you care enough about me to question where I'm going. And who I'm going with."

"Our little girl," rasped Steve, "is growing up. God! They're <u>all</u> growing up!"

"That was a different little girl," whispered Janet. "Will you let me up now?"

"Maybe in a little while. I really like the view from here. Besides, I don't know if I'm going to let you off the hook. I probably ought to fix it to where you could sit on a dime ... and tell me whether it's heads or tails."

"Well, I'll tell you one thing. It's awfully hard ... awfully difficult ... to counsel my high school-age daughter. When I'm laying across some guy's lap! Wondering whether I'm going to be able to sit down for awhile or not."

"Oh, it's good for the soul ... among other things. Besides, we haven't talked about the wedding. I don't have a hell of a lot of people to invite. My three sisters ... and their husbands. Few nieces and nephews."

"I've just got the kids. Oh, and maybe Terri and Peggy. Maybe a few other girls from the office. Probably should invite my sister ... but, right now, I'm a little upset with her."

"So ... it won't be a really big shew?" he asked, in his best Ed Sullivan voice.

"Well, no. But, I would like for it to be a church wedding, though."

"Fine! It is done! When?"

"Two weeks ... if we can find a church."

"One! One week! We'll find a church! I'm sure that the pastor ... at the church we used to go to ... I'm sure he'd be glad to ... "

"Oh no, Steve. That's awfully soon." (SLAP!) "Ouch! Okay! One week is fine. You really <u>do</u> have a way with words."

"Honeymoon? What about a honeymoon?"

"Hadn't thought much about it. In fact, I hadn't thought anything about it. Until this ever-so-romantic interlude. I really ... I'm not sure that I can get away from the office."

"My brother-in-law owns the joint. Remember? I'll put the fix in. I don't think we should take more than a week, though. Don't really want to impose on ol' Rich. Not that much, anyway. Besides, I probably can't get much more than a week off, my-own-self. How 'bout a cruise? Like … to the Caribbean?"

"Can we … can we afford it?"

"Yeah. One thing about me, Fathead: I never undertake anything … not unless I can jolly well afford it. I'm sure the trusty ol' travel agent'll be able to come up with some sort of cruise, in our time range. And in our price range. I think we probably can do a little better than steerage … but, you never know."

She laughed! Her entire body erupted! Gale upon gale upon gale of laughter.

"I like to see you laugh," he said, patting her on her bottom. "So much of you has a good time. Now, Me Fair Beauty, where we gonna live?"

"I would hope you'd live here!" It was Barbara. She had just come downstairs – resplendent in a pair of beige cotton slacks and a brown pullover sweater.

"I'm game," replied Steve. "If your mother is."

"The position I'm in," muttered Janet, "I'm going to say no?"

"Good thinking," said Steve, with a grin.

Looking up at Barbara, he asked, "You're sure you don't mind? I mean … well … how about your sisters? What about your brothers?"

"Nah," responded the younger woman. "Don't give it another thought. We're all looking forward to it. Well … I've gotta go."

She bent down – and kissed her mother. She'd practically had to have been a contortionist – to plant the buss on Janet's lips. Then, she straightened back up.

"See you later," she said. "Should be home about seven-thirty or eight o'clock. Don't have to work tonight! Hallelujah! I would imagine we'll stop for something to eat, after the game. Bye, now. Steve, it's so good to see you."

"It's great to see you too, Barb."

"Bye, Darlin'," called Janet. "Have a good time."

Once Barbara had left, Steve sighed – and shook his head, slowly.

"Y'know?" he mused. "I was really afraid that <u>she</u> wouldn't take to me. I wasn't worried about the boys. Wasn't really worried about Patti or Joanie. But, Barb's a horse of a different color."

"You're calling my daughter a 'horse'?"

(SLAP!) "No," he said, expanding on his previous statement – as opposed to answering his fiancée's question. "Barb has been kind of the major domo around here … and I'd kind of worried that she'd resent me. Think I was trying to horn in on her act, don'tcha know."

Janet looked back over her left shoulder, and up at him – deeply moved by the inner glow that his face revealed.

"On the contrary," she observed. "She'll be glad … more than happy … to give up a goodly portion of her major domoship. Remember … just a few minutes ago? When I told you that you were hearing a different little girl? I meant it. She'd changed! Just like that!" Janet snapped her fingers. "I could tell," she continued. "Could really tell. She's never really had a father, y'know. None of 'em have. I think that she'll be … well … grateful to be relieved of some of the responsibility … the God-awful, awesome, responsibility … that's fallen on her. I think she'd look forward to just being a dopey high school kid. Just like any other dopey high school kid. Happy to have to start accounting for herself … like she did, just now. I've never heard her tell me when she'd be in. Well, not in a goodly number of years, anyway. She would always … well … just come in. Always on time. Always when she had to be home. Oh, Steve! This is going to be just simply the greatest thing! The greatest thing in the world for the kids! And, hopefully, for you."

A tear coursed down his craggy cheek! "Okay, Fathead," he intoned. "Up you go."

As he helped her to her feet, she smiled down at him. "I thought you were gonna spank me," she said.

"Naw," he replied, grinning broadly. "Left my hand on your butt … way too long. Forgot what I was upset about."

"That's what I was counting on," she replied, in her best Mae West voice. She drew him up from the sofa – and pressed herself, tightly, into his arms. "That's exactly what I was counting on!"

THE END